"Hav
complet

"Please say it isn't true. What a loss it will be to the world." He waited, eyebrows relentlessly arched.

"A *V*," she repeated faintly. "It's the shape of . . ."

His puzzled frown deepened.

"The shape of you," she admitted, resigned.

She sat up and released the blanket. It rolled to her lap, and his avid, unabashed eyes focused on the parts of her revealed instantly. The lamplight was likely making her nightdress nearly transparent, or casting her in tantalizing shadows.

She was wickedly, dangerously glad.

With one finger, with slow, exaggerated patience, she sketched a broad V in the air, beginning at the vast shelf of his shoulders—the left one—slanting slowly, slowly down to that hard narrow waist scored in muscle and golden skin and scar, drawing it upward to the hard round wonder that was his right shoulder.

Perhaps the world's most *glorious V.*

Romances by Julie Anne Long

I Kissed an Earl
Since the Surrender
Like No Other Lover
The Perils of Pleasure

I Kissed An Earl

Julie Anne Long

An Imprint of HarperCollins*Publishers*

This is a work of fiction. Names, characters, places, and incidents are products of the author's imagination or are used fictitiously and are not to be construed as real. Any resemblance to actual events, locales, organizations, or persons, living or dead, is entirely coincidental.

AVON BOOKS
An Imprint of HarperCollins*Publishers*
10 East 53rd Street
New York, New York 10022-5299

ISBN 978-0-06-188566-2
www.avonromance.com

First Avon Books paperback printing: July 2010

Printed in the U.S.A.

10 9 8 7 6 5 4 3 2 1

Acknowledgments

My gratitude to the people who make my dream job even more of a pleasure: my delightful, clever editor, May Chen, and wryly brilliant agent, Steven Axelrod; to all the talented, hardworking people at Avon who helped create the book in your hand; to Kim Castillo for priceless (and fun!) assistance; to all the warm and wonderful and passionately opinionated readers who spread the word about books they love; and deepest appreciation to romance booksellers the world over.

I Kissed An Earl

Chapter 1

"He looks like a bored lion lounging amidst a flock of geese. Tolerating the fuss long enough to decide which one of us he intends to snap up in his jaws."

Miss Violet Redmond peered over the top of her fan at the newly minted Earl of Ardmay and issued this verdict to three people: the lovely blonde Hart sisters, Millicent and Amy, who breathlessly hung on her every word, and to the married Lady Peregrine, who suffered torments when Violet was the center of attention. Which, as the beautiful, legendarily capricious daughter of the wealthy and powerful Mr. Isaiah Redmond, she invariably was.

Which is no doubt why the married Lady Peregrine said, "*Jaws*, Miss Redmond? La, I'd rather snap *him* up between my legs."

The Harts hid gasps and wicked giggles behind their fans.

Violet hid a yawn.

They had taken up a prime viewing position near the ratafia in Lord and Lady Throckmorton's ballroom. It was a crush, as usual. The Harts hovered near Violet because they wanted to *be* her. Lady Peregrine hovered near Violet because she wanted to be *seen* with her. As usual, even in the crush of bodies in the ballroom, Violet was profoundly aware of presences and absences. Her parents, Isaiah and Fanchette Redmond, were here, as was her brother Jonathan. Her best friend, Cynthia, and her brother Miles, who'd lately married, had remained in Pennyroyal Green, Sussex.

Of course, the biggest absence of all was her oldest brother Lyon, the ton's golden boy and the Redmond heir, who had disappeared a year ago, taking with him the clothes on his back and a little rosewood box he'd owned since he was a boy. A box he'd made himself.

And the reason behind his absence was all too present: Olivia Eversea, eldest daughter of the Everseas of Pennyroyal Green, ancient if civil enemies of the Redmonds, stood across the room, looking slim and pale and earnest in green. Olivia had *always* been earnest. Fiery, even. Given over to working passionately for causes. She'd even distributed anti-slavery pamphlets in the Pig & Thistle in Pennyroyal Green, to the tolerant bewilderment of the pub's proprietor, Ned Hawthorne.

Olivia was here, and Lyon was not. Because Olivia had broken Lyon's heart. And everyone said this fulfilled the curse: an Eversea and a Redmond were destined to fall in love once per generation, with disastrous results.

Violet decided she best stop looking at Olivia lest her gaze scorch a hole in the woman's gown.

"We mustn't look as though we are gossiping." Miss Amy Hart was new enough to the ton to think it ought to be said.

"Of *course* we must look as though we are gossiping. How else will we keep everyone frightened and intrigued?"

Everyone agreed with vigorous nods, and everyone missed Violet's irony.

"Why a lion?" Millicent wanted to know. "Why not a bear, or a wildebeest?"

"A wildebeest has *hooves*, you ninny," her sister, Amy, corrected wearily. "It's hardly a romantic creature. Though I'm not convinced *he's* a romantic creature, either. The scowl looks as though it might be permanent. They say he's a savage." She gave a delighted, theatrical shiver.

"I know why! It's his hair. It's . . . *tawny*." Millicent sighed the word.

"Tawny?" Lady Peregrine turned to her in feigned alarm. "Did you actually say *tawny*, Millicent? Well, I can't say I didn't warn you that poetry would make porridge of your brains, and now here you are using a word like *tawny* and I do believe I heard you use the word *gossamer* as well just the other night to describe the morning mist—is this not true?"

Millicent hung her head in shamed confirmation.

"My dear, his hair is *brown*, and he has too much of it. But—of course. I see the problem. You've *lines* here, Millicent"—Lady Peregrine pointed to the flawless corners of her own eyes—"from squinting, I daresay. Perhaps it's just that you've begun to need a quizzing glass to see him clearly?"

They all turned speculative gazes on poor Millicent, whose fingers flew up to pet at those imaginary lines.

"Honestly, do take another look at him—squint if you need to, we shall none of us mind if you do, isn't that so, ladies? You'll see that he's the veriest brute. So uncommonly *large*. He is American-bred they say. Surely his true parents were a bear and an Indian."

"Oh, now *who's* fanciful?" Millicent was indignant.

"The title is much wasted on him since rumor has it he doesn't plan to spend time on English soil, but the King does have his whims. What do you think, Violet?"

Violet, who knew the goal of all of this clever talk about the earl was to impress and shock her because everyone knew she was so very difficult to impress and shock, and who was in truth so bored, *so* bored, so tired of endless balls and parties and everything about them she thought perhaps her internal organs might grind to a halt from lack of stimulation, and the only thing keeping her awake was a keen yet quite impersonal hatred of the women who stood near her, was thinking:

Blue, possibly.

Everything in the ballroom gleamed aggressively. Light from legions of candles and lamps ricocheted off silks and taffeta and jewels and polished brass and marble, creating an obscuring glare. But when the new Earl of Ardmay had glanced toward them his eyes had caught and flicked light like faceted jewels. *They must be blue.*

"They say he did something heroic to earn the title," was all she said.

The rumor abided; the specifics, however, remained elusive. The extinct title His Majesty George IV had resurrected, dangled before the Everseas and Redmonds, and then in a stunning about-face, bestowed upon a mysterious and allegedly American-reared, English-born Captain Flint. Doubtless it amused the King to seize an opportunity to keep the powerful Eversea and Redmond families humbled and in check, for it seemed so little else could.

She moved her fan beneath her chin in languid, carefully neutral sweeps. Her sharp-eyed mother, presently engaged in conversation with a sturdy, be-turbaned Lady Windemere, would know instantly if she was fomenting mischief among the bloods who gazed with calf-eyed if wary admiration at her from all corners of the room, hoping for, dreading, an invitation signaled by her fan. The betting books at White's were filled with wildly hopeful conjectures about what Violet Redmond might do next, because it had been an intolerably long time since Violet had done something epically, deliciously rash, such as threaten to cast herself down a well during an argument with a suitor and then get a leg over before she was pulled back by the elbows, or challenge a man to a duel. Between times her manners were faultless, exquisite, innate, which made the swerving from them all the more invigoratingly shocking.

Only the foolhardy wagered who might finally be a match for her. Many had attempted suit. All had failed. Some had tried and failed *spectacularly*. To the bloods of the ton, Violet Redmond was El Dorado. And she was terrifying.

The new earl was in truth tall but not uncommonly so, she assessed. A few other men in the room would likely be able to look him evenly in the eye.

But he *was* large.

And whereas her brother Miles Redmond was large in the manner of, oh, a *cliff*—he had an indestructible quality yet somehow seemed an integral part of the landscape and could therefore occasionally be overlooked—there was nothing unobtrusive about the Earl of Ardmay. It was difficult to place a finger precisely why. His hands were folded behind his back; one knee was casually bent. Most of the other men in the room struck similar poses while they held conversations. His clothes were beautifully cut and unimaginative, fawn for the trousers, white for the cravat, black for the coat, subtle pewter stripes on the waistcoat.

But his palpable physical confidence, an animal comfort in his own skin, issued a subliminal challenge to all the men present.

Not to mention profoundly disturbed the accepted notion of attractiveness of the assembled ladies.

In short, he was as unsettling as a Trojan horse wheeled into the center of the ballroom. And he most certainly did not belong to the English landscape.

"That scowl . . . he does look like a savage," Violet mused. "He ought to try smiling. I wonder if he has all of his teeth. Have any of you been close enough to see?"

It was determined that no one among them had yet seen

the earl's teeth, and that perhaps one of them ought to be dispatched to take a look, or to even dance with him, if this could be arranged.

"I *like* the scowl. He looks as though he's squinting into the sun while standing on the prow of a deck with the sea breezes blowing his hair back." This was Amy Hart, dreamily.

"But bad-tempered men make terrible dancers." Millicent said this.

Violet couldn't allow this particular inanity to pass. She turned slowly to stare at Millicent. "For heaven's *sake*," she said, heavily pained.

Millicent looked suitably abashed.

"Oh! Do let me tell what I know about the size of men's thighs and what it means about their *prowess*," Lady Peregrine insisted, as three entire seconds had passed since she'd been the center of attention. And the Harts swiveled their heads toward her and leaned in, because Lady Peregrine, being young and married, knew things they did not.

And on they buzzed, like wasps about rotting fruit, until Violet felt just as somnolent as though a picnic sun truly was beating down on her, and wished herself far away. Not too long ago she'd gone with her brother Jonathan and two friends—Cynthia and Lord Argosy—to have their fortunes told by the Gypsies who camped on the outskirts of Pennyroyal Green. She'd of course been told she would be taking a long trip across the water. And then the Gypsy girl Martha Heron had shouted something nonsensical. A French word. Likely a name. At the time, Violet had greeted all of this with rolled eyes. Martha Heron the Gypsy, it was generally agreed, was both a looby and quite a bit too flirtatious for her own good.

But at the moment Violet conceded a long trip to *anywhere* away from this ballroom would have suited her.

"Now, for a truly attractive, very refined man, one must look to the earl's first mate. Have you seen him? Probably a

French aristocrat who lost everything in the revolution and forced to serve a savage now, for he's titled! His name is Lord Lavay." Lady Peregrine was eager to share superior knowledge of the ton's newcomers.

Violet jerked her head toward Lady Peregrine and fixed her with a stare so strange and brilliant the color drained from Lady Peregrine's cheeks.

They all watched Violet with breathless, anticipatory glee.

"S-something on your mind, my dear?" Lady Peregrine managed after a moment. Her breath seemed to be held.

"Will you please repeat his name?" Violet was all careful politeness.

Lady Peregrine gathered her composure and began to quiver with delicious anticipation of scandalous behavior.

"Oh, I can do better, Miss Redmond," she purred. "Would you care for an introduction?"

"They look like hyenas bent over a carcass," Flint said by way of greeting when Lord Lavay returned bearing a cup of ratafia.

Lavay followed the earl's gaze across the ballroom to the ring of young women. "*Your* figurative carcass, it so happens," Lord Lavay, his first mate, confirmed cheerily. "I overheard a good deal while I was fetching this swill. In fact, she said—"

"Which 'she'?"

"The pretty blonde." Lavay gestured vaguely with his chin.

"They're all *pretty*," Flint said irritably. And they were. All of them uniformly pale, clean, scented, groomed, genteel. Pretty, pretty, pretty. The *English* version of pretty. Every country had a version of pretty, and he'd partaken of perhaps more than his share of them.

"The one with very *pale* blonde hair—east of the entrance,

near that emasculated-looking statue of some . . . Roman, I think? She's wearing blue and has a feather poking up out of her headpiece? As I was helping myself to this . . . this . . ." Words failed him as he sorrowfully examined his fussy ratafia, but he rallied. ". . . I heard her say, and I fear I do quote, that she'd heard that the size of a man's thighs was directly related to the size of his—the word she used was 'blessing,' but the inflection made her meaning unmistakable—and if that were indeed true then the new Earl of Ardmay's *blessing* surely put Courtenay's to shame."

They immediately spent a moment in bemused silence in honor of the perilous little paradox that was the English female. They *seemed* as fluttery and brittle as their fans; their conversation—outwardly—was exquisitely polite and demure. And yet they used those very same fans to signal shockingly provocative invitations across ballrooms, and their stays lifted their bosoms up out of their bodices like pearls presented on pillows for a pasha to inspect. One gaze directed lingeringly at the wrong bosom and an inebriated, over-bred lordling would begin shouting about pistols at dawn. One right *word* and lingeringly directed gaze and one could be invited to hike up a handsome aristocratic widow's delicate dress in an alcove at a dinner party and partake of the pleasures that lay between *her* thighs.

Flint had been reminded of both of these things in his first few days on English soil. He'd apologized in the first instance and demurred with polite regret in the second.

"I don't know which one Courtenay is," Lavay added on a hush, since it was now impossible not to wonder who Courtenay was.

While Flint had met with the King regarding his mission and attended several tedious dinners in his honor attended by men who unsurprisingly begrudged him the resurrected title—born an English bastard, raised an American rogue—Lavay had spent considerably more of his time in the more hospitable environment of a brothel called The Velvet Glove.

Flint spared a moment of longing for his Moroccan mistress Fatima, who had eyes like melted chocolate and a nose that ended in a hook and straight black hair that went on for ells and ells. Fatima would crook the finger of one hand while parting curtains between her sitting room and incense-scented bedroom with the other—this was the extent of *her* symbolic communication. And then she would clamber atop him, or he atop her, and they would spend an unambiguously sweaty and delightful afternoon. It was Flint's firm opinion that societies lacking enough hard, honest work to do became needlessly intricate.

The truth was: At the age of thirty-two, after traveling the seas for nigh on two decades, after having dined and slept in ships and prisons and palaces, having bargained for his life with princes and rogues, having captured criminals for bounties and made and lost more than one fortune, Captain Flint, mixed-breed bastard, privateer and trader, newly styled Earl of Ardmay, belonged everywhere and nowhere. He danced to no man's tune but his own. The men in this ballroom could go to the devil for all he cared. He wanted what they had likely taken for granted their entire lives: an opportunity to build a dynasty. Something of his very own, something to belong to.

He'd need land, a fortune, and a wife. The land he coveted was in New Orleans, Fatima would do for the wife, as she was at least dedicated to his pleasure and comfort, but the necessary fortune remained elusive, and the seller of the New Orleans plantation was growing restive.

A fortnight ago, everything had changed.

He ironically cursed again his fatal flaw, which is how he'd come to be in this ballroom in the first place: He never could leave well enough alone when it came to *rescuing*. He'd been anchored in Le Havre, wondering how to restore his badly depleted fortunes after a storm damaged his cargo of silk, when he'd rescued a drunken fool of a young gentleman from footpads in Le Havre. As it turned out, the grateful man was a beloved cousin of Lady Conyngham, the King's mistress. Word of Flint's heroics—which amounted to nothing more than swift swordplay and some menacing growls, really, though there *were* two footpads and one of Flint—reached her ear through Flint's acquaintance, the Comte Hebert, in Le Havre.

Which is how the King of England had learned about Flint and his talent for bounty collecting, and he'd seen an opportunity to both ingratiate himself with his mistress and to solve a sticky little problem on the high seas. He proposed to resurrect a grand English earldom and bestow it upon Flint. All Flint had to do capture a pirate called Le Chat who'd been robbing and sinking merchant ships, a number of them English, up and down the coast of Europe. The *title* was his to keep, as were the rich farmlands attached to it, lands that would provide a steady income—as well as require an enormous income to maintain.

The bounty was entirely dependent upon delivering the pirate into justice.

It was a diabolical proposition. It was a thing of beauty, really: practical, capricious, and cruel.

Flint *greatly* admired it.

And Flint rejected it.

Not since he was a lad of ten years old, when Captain Moreheart of *The Steadfast* had given an abandoned boy a home, a purpose, and the knowledge he'd needed to become the man he was today, had he danced to anyone's tune but his own. He didn't intend to start now, even if the King of England was the one playing the hornpipe. Even if, in one fell swoop, it held the potential to give him everything he wanted.

Of course, if he *failed*, it could destroy him.

The King wheedled. Flint demurred. The King cajoled. Flint demurred.

The King, astonished, resorted to issuing subtle threats. Flint, amused and unafraid, demurred.

When he heard the King had actually thrown a wee tantrum, he began to thoroughly enjoy the game.

And then Le Chat sank *The Steadfast*.

The news reached Flint in evening while he sat with his crew in a pub in Le Havre. He'd gone still, his hand tightly curled around a pint of ale, roars of bawdy laughter eddying around him. He was stunned to realize the news felt like taking a shot to the gut.

Steel-spined Captain Moreheart, going gray and gouty but still shrewd, ferociously opinionated, dignified . . . forced at swordpoint into a launch by that damned pirate and floated with his men to an almost certain death on a rough sea.

While behind him the pirate blew *The Steadfast* to smithereens with cannon fire.

This was why he agreed to become the Earl of Ardmay.

And now those great tracts of English lands, a century-old estate included, dangled like both a carrot before a donkey and like a Sword of Damocles.

A half hour ago the press of the ballroom and his mission and the memory of Moreheart sent Flint strolling restlessly to the doors on the terrace to open them an inch. Outside the wind was howling like a cornered, wounded animal and smelled of coal-sullied London and sea. His schooner *The Fortuna* was anchored out there. Calmer winds would likely prevail tomorrow, and they would sail as early as possible with his small but loyal—and gleefully violent when necessary—crew.

Well, loyal save one. He might be an earl now, but the duties of a captain were myriad, mundane, and often maddening.

"Did you manage to find a replacement for Rathskill in between, shall we say, bouts of ecstasy at The Velvet Glove?"

Rathskill, the boob of a cook's mate needed to go before Hercules, the cook, finally lost all patience and sent him through the meat grinder. Rathskill was lazy, he was sloppy, and they'd all stared in morbid fascination at the biscuit crumbs clinging to his lips while he'd lied about stealing rations with his hand over his heart. He'd grossly exaggerated his experience in a ship's mess, making fools of both Flint and Lavay.

Neither of them countenanced being made to feel a fool. Ever.

Lavay sighed. "I spoke to a few men at the docks but naught were suitable. Perhaps we'll have better luck in Le Havre. We can sail at least that far without a cook's mate."

"Hercules will be . . . unhappy."

Unhappy seemed too pale a word for what Hercules would be. Their cook was Greek, diminutive, and he expressed displeasure . . . operatically. *All* of his emotions were operatic.

"*Speaking* of unhappy, Flint, your scowl could wilt flowers at fifty paces. This is a ballroom, and do recall it's a title you've been handed, for God's sake, not a Turkish prison sentence. God knows I have done my best to impart my gentlemanly ways to you—"

Flint snorted.

"—but you really ought to try smiling. One of those women in fact described you as a 'savage.' "

Savage. Flint went still. Even after all these years, the word still touched between his shoulder blades like the cold point of a rapier.

"Which one?" he said sharply.

"The brunette—the one in blue."

Flint found the brunette in question easily. She was part of that group but seemed separate somehow, limned in stillness. Her hair was dressed intricately up; a pair of calculated ringlets dangled to her chin; her features were fine apart from a decidedly lush mouth; her dress a singular shade of blue, cut low enough to reveal the tops of a more than acceptable bosom above which dangled a single bright jewel of some kind, strung on a chain. Her throat was long. Her fan flapped below her chin as disinterestedly as if the hand holding it belonged to someone else altogether.

But her eyes were brilliantly alive, and the corner of that lush mouth was dented with wry contempt.

For herself? For her companions? For everyone in the room?

Funny, but Flint was distantly reminded of himself.

"*That* one is bored, Lavay. And I'm willing to wager there's nothing more dangerous to a man's health than a bored, spoiled, wealthy young Englishwoman."

"I won't take that wager, Flint. I'd like to see the morrow."

The woman in question and the pretty be-plumed blonde detached themselves from the group and began to move rather purposefully in their direction, joined by another English gentleman en route.

"Well, bloody hell." Lavay was amused. "Try to look civil, for a change, you scoundrel, because I feel we're about to be compelled to dance with Englishwomen after all."

"My apologies, Lavay," Flint murmured. "I'm sure it has everything to do with my majestic thighs."

Chapter 2

Lady Peregrine, as promised, had contrived an introduction to Lord Lavay and Lord Flint through a cousin of her husband who had been introduced to the pair earlier, and who abandoned them rapidly once it was clear that the earl and Lord Lavay now felt obliged to ask the ladies to dance.

A waltz began, lilting and insistent, and all around them men and women swirled off in pairs.

Lord Lavay dutifully bowed in the direction of Violet and Lady Peregrine. "I would be so pleased if you would do me the honor of dancing with—"

"It would be my pleasure, Lord Lavay," Lady Peregrine said smoothly, and up went her hand to intercept his.

That hand hovered in midair, chandelier light winking on the blue stones in her bracelet. They all stared at it for a surprised—and in Violet's case, resentful—moment.

Lady Peregrine's eyebrow gave a smug, infinitesimal twitch.

Then Lavay, like the gentleman he was cursed to be, gracefully took it and led her away.

Violet watched, quietly seething.

"Miss Redmond?"

"Lavay" is what that Gypsy girl had shouted to her. And

surely it was significant that someone named Lavay should appear in a ballroom just as she was about to expire from boredom?

"Miss Redmond?" came the voice again.

She whirled, almost startled.

The large earl bowed dutifully to her, and when he was upright again, outstretched a hand, and raised his eyebrows expectantly.

She took swift note of him and immediately again thought of jewels. His face was faceted, too: high-planed cheeks, jaw hard and clean-edged as a diamond. Chin stubborn, brow high and broad, nose bold. A good mouth, drawn with elegant precision. An Indian, certainly. She could imagine Indian in his bloodline. His complexion was what marked him as decidedly un-English and as a man with no particular pedigree: more golden than fair and likely to darken and darken rather than burn in the sun.

But he knew how to waltz.

When he expertly, gently took her hand in his and placed his other hand against her waist, she knew a moment of peculiar breathlessness, as though she were being pulled inexorably into an orbit. His intangible power was such that she was tempted both to resist it and surrender to it, and being Violet, she preferred the former to the latter, and promptly set about doing it.

Dash it. It was *Lavay* she needed to see.

Grrrr.

She peered over the earl's shoulder in time to intercept Lady Peregrine's triumphant glance before she was twirled out of her view.

She stared darts at the back of Lady Peregrine's head.

"I don't bite."

The earl's voice was a low rumble near her ear.

Violet was startled. "I beg your pardon?"

"You were staring at me as if you wondered whether I might."

His accent was interesting: flat, commanding American crisped about the edges with something like aristocratic English. His *R*'s were softer, almost rolled. It was as though he'd absorbed a bit of the music in the language of every land he'd traveled.

"Oh. No, I was satisfying . . . another curiosity."

"As to the number of eyes I might possess?"

"I ascertained the number rather quickly, thank you."

"Ah. So you were staring *beyond* me. *I* see." He sounded distantly amused. "What does it say about an evening when *bad* manners seem refreshing?"

He'd all but murmured it to himself.

Violet was seldom dumbstruck, so this was novel. She stared up at him.

She'd been right about his eyes. They were a remarkable, cloudless sky blue ringed in darker blue. Thick lashes, golden tips where the sun had touched them again and again. Lines, three each, at the corners of his eyes, like the rays she used to draw about suns when she was small. Squinting into the sun from the deck, indeed.

"Have you considered it might be bad manners to insinuate that *my* manners are bad?" she said with some asperity.

This amused him. "You presume that I care whether you care."

She blinked. What manner of man *was* this?

His brows went up. *Well?* Inviting a volley. But his air was still somewhat resigned and detached. As though he entertained no real hope she could ever possibly divert him.

She in truth possessed exquisite manners and knew how to employ them, and she considered that she ought to exert a modicum of effort to charm him. He was an earl, after all, the captain of a ship . . . and he might be able to tell her something about Mr. *Lavay*.

"How do you find England, sir?"

He gave a short laugh.

She bristled. "I wasn't trying to be witty."

"Were you trying to be banal?" he asked politely.

"I've never been banal in my entire life," Violet objected, astonished.

He leaned forward as he swept her in a circle, graceful for a large man. As though he were a chariot and she were simply along for the giddy ride. He pulled her a trifle closer than was proper. She smelled starch and something sharp and clean; likely soap and perhaps a touch of scent. She was eye-level with the whitest cravat she'd seen outside of Lord Argosy, and suddenly she was overwhelmingly aware of his size and strength.

"Prove it," he murmured next to her ear.

And then he was upright again, all graceful propriety, and they were turning, turning, gliding in the familiar dance.

Which suddenly felt astoundingly unfamiliar thanks to her partner.

Well.

She was stunned.

Still . . . she had the peculiar sense that the earl was simply amusing *himself*. His eyes remained on her but still oddly . . . uncommitted . . . even as they moved gracefully together, even as his hand rested warmly, firmly at her waist. She suspected he had already taken her measure, categorized her, and neatly dismissed her, and was now simply prodding at her like a toy that he wished could do more than roll or squeak. To make the waltz more interesting for *him*. For as long as he needed to endure the tedium of it.

"Customarily," she said with gentle irony, "in England, it's the *gentleman's* duty to charm his dancing partner. Perhaps you've been at sea so long you've forgotten."

He was instantly all mock contrition. "You could very well be correct. It could be I've become a *savage* while I was away."

Her eyes narrowed.

He met her gaze evenly.

For a moment they swept along in time with the music.

"It's impolite to eavesdrop," she said finally.

"I wasn't eavesdropping," he said easily.

"Then it's impolite to send spies to do the eavesdropping *for* you. For clearly you did."

This pleased him. His eyes brightened; the hand at the small of her back pressed against her approvingly, and it was a new sensation, startling, almost intimate. "I'm not certain *impolite* is the word you're looking for. In all honesty the o*verhearing*, as it were, was happenstance. But as you are an expert in the matter of etiquette, please refresh my memory. How polite it is to gossip?"

The man was a devil. And yet she was awfully tempted to laugh.

"I was being gossiped *at*," she tried after a moment. And offered him a mischievous lowered-lashed smile that usually all but dropped grown men to their knees. Generally hothouse bouquets arrived at her door the day after she'd deployed one.

He wasn't entirely immune to it. She was rewarded with a pupil flare.

"Ah, but are you a *complete* innocent, Miss Redmond?" His voice had gone soft. His mouth tipped sardonically. Up twitched one of those brows again. This time it was almost a threat: *Don't bore me*.

If this was a flirting relay, he'd just handed her the baton.

Violet felt that familiar surge of exhilaration when tempted with a reckless inspiration. She'd seldom been able to resist that surge.

She briefly went on toe to murmur the words closer to his ear than was proper, so close she knew he could smell her, feel her breath in his ear when she spoke. Once again she was rewarded with the heady smell of the man himself: sharp, clean, heightened by his warmth and nearness.

"What do *you* think, sir?"

She instantly had his full attention for the first time since the waltz had begun.

And yet once she had it she wasn't certain she wanted it. It was like being passed something too hot to hold overlong. His gaze was potent; there was nothing in it of the entreaty she was accustomed to seeing in the face of men. He was weighing *her* with a specific intent in mind. His eyes touched on her eyes, lips, décolletage, taking a swift bold inventory of her as a woman that somehow both shortened her breath in a peculiarly delicious portentous way and made her fingers twitch to slap him.

And then he smiled a remote, almost dismissive smile and his gaze flicked up from her as they negotiated a turn in the dance.

And then froze.

He dropped the remnants of his flirtatious demeanor as abruptly as a boy drops a toy when called into dinner.

Before her eyes his jaw seemed to turn to granite; tension vibrated in the hand pressed against her waist. He gripped her fingers a trifle harder than he ought to.

What in God's name had he just *seen*?

She flexed her fingers. He absently eased his grip.

"Miss . . ." He glanced at her perfunctorily. And returned his gaze to whatever—or whomever—riveted him.

He'd forgotten her *name*? She clenched her teeth to keep her jaw from dropping.

"Redmond," she reminded him with exaggerated sweetness.

"Of course," he soothed. He gave her another cursory, dutiful glance, meant to placate. Then returned to the object of his focus. She'd seen a fox look at a vole that way before. Right before it pounced.

And shook it until its neck snapped.

"I believe I may be acquainted with the gentleman dancing with the young lady in yellow. If I'm correct, his name is Mr. Hardesty. Are you acquainted with him?"

With some perilous head craning, she managed to follow the direction of his gaze.

And her hands went peculiarly icy inside her gloves.

He was looking at her brother Jonathan.

"I believe the gentleman to whom you're referring is Mr. Jonathan Redmond. He's my brother."

The earl's attention sharply returned to her. But the expression on his face stopped her breath as surely as though he'd stabbed an accusing finger into her sternum.

She felt him *will* tension from his big body. Obediently tension went.

"Is your brother Mr. Jonathan Redmond a merchant, by any chance?" His tone was mild. "A sea captain?"

He somehow kept Jonathan in his line of sight even as he moved her by rote in the waltz. *ONE two three ONE two three . . .* She felt utterly superfluous. Suddenly she was the means by which the earl could stalk her brother about a ballroom.

But Jonathan, who like all men his age possessed of good looks and money and prospects was convinced he was fascinating, chattered gaily to the woman he danced with, and she glowed up at him.

"Good heavens, no, sir. Jonathan lives with our family in Pennyroyal Green and London. His amusements are in

London and Sussex, and if he's ever been on a ship, I assure you he wouldn't be able to stop bragging of it. Jonathan has never even expressed an interest in the high seas. Perhaps you will have an opportunity to meet him this evening. Upon closer inspection you may discover his resemblance to Mr. Hardesty is not so strong."

This was meant to reassure him—and protect Jonathan.

The earl remained coldly silent.

She was beginning to feel a bit like a ship steered on a voyage. And as much as Violet craved novelty, this was a sensation she could easily have done without.

"He doesn't 'resemble' Mr. Hardesty," he explained, as if to a slow child. "He could be Mr. Hardesty's twin."

The conversation was now making her uneasy. Her hand twitched restlessly in the earl's. He gripped it tightly, almost reflexively. As though he alone would dictate when or if she could leave.

"I can tell you Jonathan hasn't a twin, sir," she said tartly.

Violet peered over his shoulder for Lavay, who would have the pleasure of the next dance, and noted with relief that the waltz approached its closing notes and Lady Peregrine looked pleased with him, not troubled or irritated.

"Is Mr. Hardesty a fellow sailor?"

There was a hesitation.

And then his smile was a tight, remote thing. Oddly, it made all the hair on the back of her neck stand up.

"I suppose you could say that."

It really didn't invite additional questioning about Mr. Hardesty, which she supposed was the point of it.

He suddenly appeared disinterested in conversation.

"Are you staying in London long?" she asked.

"We'll return to the ship by dawn and sail shortly after sunup." A perfunctory response.

"You're bound for . . ."

"Le Havre." A curt two-word answer.

Moments later, mercifully, the waltz ended. He bowed beautifully to her, the epitome of graciousness, and she curtsied, and he handed her off to the approaching Lord Lavay with as much regret as if she were a tureen to be passed.

She peered over her shoulder as he bowed to Lady Peregrine and dutifully took up his position in the waltz.

Lady Peregrine turned quickly to Violet and surreptitiously tapped her teeth with one finger in a signal: *He has all of them!*

Violet doubted the earl would even remember her name.

Chapter 3

It quickly became clear that after the earl, Monsieur Lavay would be balm.

They began by admiring each other in silence. There was nothing ambiguous about *his* looks. Waving dark gold hair, narrow silver eyes, an aquiline nose, elegantly drawn mouth. Broad shoulders. Not lean at the hip like the earl, but not a barrel, either. Tall, but not oppressively so. *Politely* tall. Not a *loomer*, per se.

A splendid-looking man, and a bit like breathing the air of earth again after the peculiar heady, dangerous atmosphere one dance with the earl created. He had an air of slightly jaded reserve. Perhaps earned from watching the heads of various ancestors roll during the revolution.

"How are you finding London, Lord Lavay?" she tried. It was a perfectly acceptable nicety, she told herself. A nicety, not a *banality*. "Have you been here long?"

"We docked but a fortnight ago. But oddly, Miss Redmond, I now greatly regret that we must set sail tomorrow."

He said it lightly, but it was edged all around in flirtatious heat. The remark was entirely about her. His eyes glowed the subtext.

Violet nodded her recognition approval, gave a slight encouraging smile. *Very good beginning.*

Monsieur Lavay's eyes lit, amused, encouraged.

"And have you visited London before, Monsieur Lavay?"

"Under other circumstances, many years before the war. We are here on business for the King, and to deliver a diplomat from service in Spain. And of course, to be feted at parties and balls, for it is not every day one's captain is styled an earl."

Violet smiled. "And it is our family's pleasure, of course, to participate in the celebration of the new earl."

This wasn't entirely true. But Violet did know the appropriate things to say, the sort of things one laid out like paving stones at the outset of a friendship before one gets comfortable enough for frankness. She'd heard her father curse but twice in his life: once, when Colin Eversea didn't hang as scheduled, and next when word arrived that the new earl would be Captain Asher Flint.

Generally, she preferred to dodge *frankness* when it came to men, however.

And as she was a tester and risk-taker, she chose her next question deliberately.

"Are you acquainted with a Mr. Hardesty by any chance, Lord Lavay?"

The name brought a similarly intriguing reaction. Silence.

And then: "Are *you*, Miss Redmond?"

His manner was now a degree or two cooler.

"It's just that the earl thought my brother Jonathan resembled him, and described him as a fellow sailor."

She refrained from describing the earl's profoundly visceral reaction.

But Lavay's rueful smile told her he'd guessed at it anyway. "Ah. *Did* he. Interesting. Given that we've thought of almost nothing else recently, perhaps it is understandable the earl is seeing Hardesty everywhere. And I suppose it's not *entirely* an insult to your brother."

"I am eager to hear which part is an insult, then."

Monsieur Lavay smiled. "Well, to put your mind at ease, one hears that Mr. Hardesty is charm personified. And he *is* pleasant to have at one's elbow during a supper, as I have on one occasion. His manners and speech are exceedingly refined and he is clearly well educated, though how he came by all of this charm and wealth and excellent conversation remains a mystery. He was all that is correct and knowledgeable about trade. He has been seen in France and Belgium, in Portugal and Spain, in Morocco. Primarily he brings in goods from the West Indies and Cuba."

"He sounds delightful. And yet my impression is that your reunion with Mr. Hardesty would not be a joyous one."

Lavay enjoyed her circumspection; his brows went up. But there was another hesitation.

"I suppose there is no harm in telling you. We believe this Mr. Hardesty is in fact a man they call Le Chat. Who, as it so happens is a—well, *privateer* is the polite word—a more accurate word is *pirate*."

Good *heavens*. Violet was thrilled into silence. Which likely wasn't the reaction she ought to have.

She seldom had the sorts of reactions she ought to have, however.

"What on earth would a pirate be doing in a ballroom?"

"Miss Redmond, I'm certain Le Chat would brave the gallows if he knew he might have an opportunity to dance with you. Perhaps he prowls balls for just this reason."

Violet laughed and gave a surprised toss of her head. The compliment was cognac-smooth and unexpected enough to dissolve the fog of her ball ennui. The French accent that clung to the edges of his flawless English made listening to him a pleasure akin to hearing the strains of a minuet floating in from a distant room.

Lavay was encouraged to continue. "We've some intelligence

that suggests Mr. Hardesty and Le Chat may well be the same person. Mr. Hardesty certainly appears to be wealthy, for one. But one can hardly condemn a man for wealth. And many successful traders are wealthy."

"I would be the *last* person to condemn a man for wealth, Lord Lavay."

He smiled at this and wagged up a pair of golden brows. "We—that is, the Earl of Ardmay and the crew of *The Fortuna*—have been charged by your King with bringing Le Chat to justice."

"It sounds dangerous," she flattered.

Lavay somehow managed to shrug with one shoulder, even in the midst of the waltz. Too French, perhaps, to think communication complete without it.

"But why should a pirate be called 'the cat'?"

"It is said this is the name he uses when he takes over ships. Perhaps it is because he boards ships with a small crew and pounces, silently from out of the fog? From out of the night? Perhaps it is because he is said to have no allegiance to any crown or to any person? Or his charm when he wants something, perhaps—like a cat circling one's legs, purring? The ladies say this is so; Hardesty is said to have no heart, but happy enough to win and break them. Perhaps it is because he appeared from nowhere one day, like a stray cat, and began to take whatever he wanted. I cannot say, Miss Redmond. People do enjoy naming their pirates, for this is how myths are constructed. Pirates never seem to object."

At least *Mr. Lavay* had remembered her name.

And as she danced, she realized she saw the earl and Lady Peregrine nowhere in the room, and wondered whether she had managed to isolate him to test her theory regarding thighs.

Which was when she realized she'd actually been *looking* for the earl.

She ceased immediately.

Thankfully she did see Jonathan, dancing again, with a small be-muslined blonde. He looked bored. He looked like Jonathan. Not remotely piratical.

"What has this Le Chat done?"

"We believe Le Chat has boarded a number of merchant vessels and seized valuable cargo in just a year, And then he has sunk the ships. Four of the ships had English captains. The most recent ship is *The Steadfast*. He is a scourge, in other words," he said flatly.

"Is bringing pirates to justice a habit of the earl?"

"Achieving the impossible is a habit of the earl. It's how he became an earl," Lavay said shortly. "And what drew the attention of the King to him for this particular mission."

"I heard he did something heroic to earn his title."

"You heard correctly."

Mr. Lavay said nothing more. But he seemed privately amused about something. "But why, Lord Lavay, would a pirate attend balls by night and then creep out to sink ships?"

He managed a shrug again. "Power? Money? Notoriety? Vengeance? Who can say? Needless to say, he would never sink a ship if he knew you were aboard."

They smiled at each other, pleased with the progress of their flirtation; they understood each other almost too easily. His gray eyes smoldered with a comfortable heat, familiar but refined with a frisson of the exotic as he was French. His eyes and hands and very presence didn't . . . take her *captive*.

Unlike the earl's.

Oh! And there he was! The earl's expression fixedly polite, watching with sleepy fascination as Lady Peregrine's mouth moved and moved, as though she were a talking dog. A novelty. Doubtless not really listening.

She *almost* pitied him.

"We shall find Le Chat, however," Lavay told her. It was

a deliciously certain, arrogant statement, calculated to return her attention to him.

"How can you be so certain?"

He hesitated. And then he smiled. The smile was a beautiful thing, polished and shapely and easy, probably the same smile his ancestors had smiled through centuries. But it was cold. In a way that reminded Violet of her father, who, by dint of birth and influence, knew there was nothing he couldn't have, achieve, hide, if necessary.

"I have never known Captain Flint to pursue a goal in vain. The Earl of Ardmay wants Le Chat alive or dead for many reasons. And what he wants he is very certain to get."

Did she detect a hint of irony in his words? Or did French-accented English simply consign one forever to sounding ironic?

For many reasons.

She felt that same prickle at the back of her neck, some hybrid of unease and thrill. She wanted to peel back the layers of meaning shrouding the phrase, unwrap it like a gift, like the cure for her boredom.

And perhaps this was why the Gypsy girl had shouted "Lavay" to her. She found him appealing; she could not feel herself falling in love, however. Love seemed to come with extremes of behavior and loss of dignity, and in *her* family, disaster or grave compromises.

Still, she'd never before encountered men quite like these. And yet they would be gone tomorrow.

"Could Le Chat be in London this very minute?"

"Ah, you've naught to fear, Miss Redmond. *The Olivia* isn't docked here alongside our ship."

Forever after she understood what it meant when someone said "time stopped."

Because it did. Or at least stuttered.

His words seemed to echo peculiarly in her brain. And at first she thought she'd misheard him.

But then a cascade of facts and impressions came into speedy focus, as though she were falling toward them from a great height.

That's when shock blurred her vision. She stumbled; Lavay's arm stiffened, balancing her, the awkward half step she'd taken never interrupted the smooth flow of the waltz.

"Miss Redmond?" He was genuinely concerned. "Please forgive me. Perhaps we ought to speak of gentler things. One forgets, you know, when one is forever in the company of men, what a woman may prefer to discuss."

The poor man. He thought her constitution delicate.

She looked up at him. She couldn't feel her extremities. They'd gone numb.

She rallied. "Your conversation has been the pleasure of my evening. I merely trod clumsily in my new slippers. But I fear I missed the name of Le Chat's ship? It sounded intriguing."

A sick, thrilling portent flooded her as she awaited confirmation. The Gypsy girl shouting "Lavay!" echoed in her mind, and her ears rang from the beating of her heart, and considered the odd directions life could take, and what she ought to do next even before he spoke.

"Naturally, as it's the sort of thing that might interest a woman, for it is the name of a woman. It's *The Olivia*, Miss Redmond. Perhaps it's the name of the woman who did break his heart. Assuming he ever had one to break."

Already quivering with purpose, she exchanged bows and pleasantries with handsome Lord Lavay, who again expressed regret his stay should be so brief.

And then Violet ran.

Or *nearly* ran. She freed her ankles by tucking her dress

up with her fingers, weaving between dancers and clots of giddy gossipers. A smile pasted to her face. Her slippers nearly skidding over marble.

Oh, no. Oh, no, no, no. Lyon couldn't be that stupid, could he?

Or that . . . interesting?

Where the devil was Jonathan? If he wasn't dancing again—and a quick scan of the room told her he wasn't—he would be near the punch bowl, or close to the garden windows so he could sneak out for a cigar or a tryst or to hop over the fence to go on to his club without Father knowing, and—

She nearly crashed to a halt when she saw the back of him. So unmistakably a Redmond, long and lean, finally grown out of coltishness. He was indeed proximate to the punch bowl and the garden doors, but he was also strategically tucked behind a pillar, and one hand was outstretched and propped against the wall. He was obscuring someone or something.

She knew what it was when she heard the giggle.

She peered over his shoulder to get a look at the woman he was shielding: a delicate blonde in unimaginative white muslin: big-eyed, petite-nosed, a little overbite that gave her a not unappealing rabbity appearance peeled back in a smile. Lady Wareham? Wartsomething? Violet had been introduced earlier and had forgotten her name instantly.

Where had her brother learned to *do* that? To strike that indolent pose, to pour . . . silent, burning *attention* . . . upon a woman and to say things to cause her to picturesquely blush? Violet wasn't a blusher; growing up in a household of frank brothers rather inured one to that sort of thing. But her brother looked unnervingly like a . . . grown man. Which he of course he supposedly *was*.

It was just that she so seldom saw him behave like one.

"Jonathan," she said. Sotto voce. About two feet away from his ear.

He didn't turn.

"Jonathan!" she barked.

Her brother jumped and spun to face her, glowering. And in that instant he looked so remarkably like Lyon that Violet was intensely aware of the passage of time and the urgency of her mission. She saw instantly what the earl must have seen when he saw Jonathan, and wondered how she hadn't yet seen it.

"Viiiolet," her brother drawled warningly, by way of greeting. He cast a quick sidelong look at the blonde, and then a speaking one back at Violet. All of which was sibling for: *Go away.*

"Oh, please do excuse me for interrupting," Violet gushed insincerely. "But Jonathan—were you aware the gentleman accompanying the Earl of Ardmay is named *Lavay*?"

Her brother's frown shifted into irritated confusion. "Well . . . yes. I was introduced to him. Pleasant, if a tad oily, his manners so very, *very* exquisite you know. One gets the sense that he thinks he's better than you, but it's naught he does or says in particular, really. Not certain you can yet entirely trust anyone of French—"

"Do shut up, Jon. His name is *Lavay*. Don't you *recall* what happened when we visited the Gypsies?"

"I say, hardly cause to raise your voice, sister dear." The tone was condescending and came with an inclusive smile for Lady Wartle . . . Lady Wartham! That was it!

The *beast*. Jonathan was showing off. He really, really ought to know better by now.

"You *do* take telling a number of times, Jon. Don't you *remember*? The Gypsy girl shouted 'Lavay' " to me? The one who said you would have *ten children*?"

He went instantly rigid, alarmed as if she'd hexed him.

"That Gypsy girl is touched in the head, Violet," he said on a fervent hush. "That's pure *lunacy*, and you know it."

"You probably *will* have ten children."

"Bite. Your. Tongue."

"You *might* even have all ten of them with Lady Wartham here," Violet pressed wickedly.

Young Lady Wartham's eyes widened to saucers and began to sparkle with dreams.

Her brother was incensed. "Never! Never, I tell you! I'm nowhere near ready to be leg shackled and *she's* just a dallia . . ." He squeezed his eyes closed as he realized he'd neatly tumbled into his sister's trap. "Damn you, Violet," he croaked.

Violet shook her head to and fro, pityingly.

Jonathan opened his eyes in time to see Lady Wartham's dropped-open mouth clap tightly shut and her eyes narrow in an admirably poisonous way. She whipped around in an indignant blur of taffeta and clicked off without a word for either of the Redmonds.

Jonathan rounded on his sister. "See what you've done, you wretch!"

"Oh, stop. You just said yourself she was a dalliance. If you can tell me her first name now I shall profess abject chagrin and I will owe you a great favor of your choice."

He glared at her. Lips tightly clamped.

She smiled slowly at him.

As always, Jonathan struggled to maintain a snit and his mouth unsuccessfully fought a smile. "But one needs the *practice* with dallying, you see," he explained. "Or how will my reputation ever become the match of Argosy's?"

"Practice? For when you find the woman with whom you'll have ten children?"

"Enough!" he howled.

She put a conciliatory hand on his arm. "Jonathan, listen to me. This is important, I swear to you. The French gentleman accompanying the earl—his name is Lavay. Lord Lavay.

She—that Gypsy girl, Martha Heron—shouted 'Lavay' to me! Don't you recall? It was all very puzzling at the time. And Lavay is the mate of the Earl of Ardmay's ship. And she said I'd go on a long journey over water!"

He groaned. "Is *that* all? Oh, for God's sake, Violet, if that were true every time a Gypsy said it the entire country would be bobbing on boats in the Thames right now."

Losing interest, he intercepted the gaze of Lady Peregrine and began to produce what he believed was a sensual smile.

"Not her," Violet said. "She's awful. A terrible gossip. Stop *practicing* and listen to me."

Jonathan turned back to her irritably. "Listen, you're not usually so featherbrained. Why give this 'Lavay' nonsense any credence at all? Doubtless it's not the rarest of French surnames. There's something not quite right with that Gypsy girl, and you know it."

"I think you simply *hope* there's something not quite right with her," she said shrewdly.

He glared at her.

She mouthed *Ten children.*

She remained fixed in his glare.

She breathed in deeply, suddenly nervous. "It's not just that. When I was introduced to the Earl of Ardmay he saw you, and went . . . well, very like a pointer spotting a rabbit. I swear to you, Jon, he made the hair on the back of my neck stand on end. Quite chilling. He said you looked *exactly* like a trader who is also believed to be a South Seas privateer—a pirate—who goes by the name Le Chat."

"Me?" Jonathan's eyes went wide with shock, and then misty with the very notion. "Fanciful name, Le Chat. But I ain't a pirate, Vi."

"I know you aren't, Jon. And it means 'the cat.' "

"I know what it means," he said irritably. "I had a French tutor, too. "

His roving gaze intercepted the gaze of another woman, Millicent Hart.

"Not her, either. She has all the wits of a blown dandelion. And a *lion* is a big cat, Jonathan. Don't you see? The earl thought you looked exactly like this person named Le Chat. And a lion is a *big cat*."

Jonathan frowned, irritated now. "It's a damned silly name. Pirates do that, don't they? Adopt silly, dangerous-sounding—"

"His ship has a silly name, too, Jonathan. Apparently it's called *The Olivia*."

The effect of sudden comprehension on Jonathan was rewarding and extreme. She could have sworn his blood stopped moving beneath his skin, so taut, so pale, so still he went.

The mention of Everseas, and the disaster one particular female Eversea had wreaked upon their family, had that effect on the man.

Their eyes locked. His were darker and more inscrutable than she'd ever seen them, and she wondered again what kind of man her brother would make. Solid and formidable like Miles? An enigmatic emblem of power, like their father? Silently Violet willed him to believe what she believed. *Lyon is out there*. Lyon might very well be a trader known as Hardesty and a pirate named Le Chat sailing a ship called *The Olivia*. They needed to find him. To convince him to return home.

To save him from the Earl of Ardmay and certain justice at the end of a rope.

But surely it was all a mistake? Surely, if it was indeed Lyon, all wasn't quite what it seemed?

And then, spell broken, Jonathan scowled and shook his head violently.

"So your theory is that Lyon restyled himself as a *pirate* named Le Chat in the wake of his broken heart at the hands of that bloody Eversea woman and named his ship *The Olivia* to commemorate his misery or to take revenge upon her? It's—well, it's really the most ridiculous thing I've ever heard. *Think* about it."

"I grant you it *seems* unlikely. But *The Olivia*, Jon! It's—"

He held up a hand. "No. No, Vi, it's just . . . patently *absurd.* I mean—does this pirate board ships, rape and pillage, things of that sort?" Now he was struggling to keep his face straight.

"Why don't you ask the Earl of Ardmay? Until our king got hold of him he was known as Captain Flint and his mandate is to capture Le Chat for a bounty. He might tell *you* more than he'd tell a woman. He might speak more of raping and pillaging to a fellow member of his species. Then again, you apparently look *exactly like Le Chat.*"

The earl was easy to locate even in the crush, like a glacier in a sea. He was politely speaking to an older gentleman, Monsieur Lavay at his side, a coolly elegant foil to the earl's quiet smolder.

"I spoke to the earl," Jonathan said curtly. "Father introduced me to him and to Lord Lavay. He did ask whether I'd ever considered going to sea, said there was a fellow named Rathskill, a cook's mate whom he needed to replace. Incompetent and cheeky. I pity the sod. But I didn't care for the way he looked at me, Vi. Apparently the king decided to give the title to someone more given to heroics."

"A pity, then, that father isn't given over to heroics."

"I should think surviving *you* is an act of heroism," Jonathan said predictably enough. "Besides, why wouldn't Miles have heard of him, this Le Chat sailing on the *The Olivia*? Miles has been everywhere."

"But he hasn't been everywhere *recently.* And just because Miles has gone places on a ship doesn't mean he knows everyone *else* who has, Jonathan. For heaven's sake."

"Perhaps he has been too besotted with Cynthia to pay attention?"

"Miles notices everything. And he's still trying to find funding for his next expedition to Lacao. Perhaps he hasn't kept abreast of all the latest *pirates*."

They both dreaded Miles leaving again on a new expedition to the South American land that had made him famous by way of books and lectures, and taking his delightfully inappropriate new wife with him. Cynthia wasn't welcome in the Redmond home, an inflexible command of their father, Isaiah Redmond. But Miles, miraculously, hadn't been entirely disinherited.

It was Violet's fault, really, that Miles had fallen in love with the scandalous Miss Brightly at all. Her own misguided act of kindness—and mischief—she'd brought her into the Redmond household. Thus setting in motion yet another family uproar, another fissure.

Then again, uproar was generally Violet's bailiwick.

Lyon had, however, rather trumped her in that regard by disappearing altogether nearly two years ago now. Their father had abandoned hope of his return and made Miles his heir. Until the matter of Cynthia.

Violet couldn't bear how love in various forms was unraveling her family while everyone pretended all was well and tried to get on with things. She wanted to return it to the way it was.

"Jonathan, what did Olivia say to him to make him leave?"

His head swiveled toward her. "How did you know she said anything?"

"Ha! She did!"

He became closemouthed again. "He never said anything, Violet. He didn't tell me what she said."

She suspected Jonathan was lying, and wasn't very good at it. And this was interesting and new, too.

Silence, as Jonathan and Violet leaned against the wall

and perused the ballroom. Their father stood in conversation with a member of his investment group, the Mercury Club. Isaiah was difficult to miss. Tall, lean, distinguished, probably busily convincing a wealthy man to invest in the Mercury Club's fledgling railroad endeavor, or financing merchant ships to bring back goods from China, India, or America, much like the Earl of Ardmay was said to have done. Like this Mr. Hardesty had done. Amassing money and more money, influence and more influence through trade and other means. That was her father.

"Violet . . ." Jonathan began cautiously. Placating. *Damnation.* Her entire body tensed. "I know you miss Lyon. But I think this—"

"Don't," she hissed. "Do *not* use that tone with me, Jonathan Redmond, as though I'm some ridiculous child to be humored. He thought *you* looked like Le Chat, Jon. *You.* He thought you *were* Le Chat. And you look more like Lyon every day. *The Olivia!* At least please entertain the *possibility.*" She was very close to begging. She hadn't begged for a thing since she was a child.

Jonathan looked at his sister for a long while, his handsome face troubled. And then alarm leaped into his dark eyes.

"Leave it, Violet. Don't get any ideas!"

"Jonathan . . . What if he's in danger? The Earl of Ardmay wants to bring this Le Chat to *justice.* And you know what justice so often means, don't you? Don't you remember what almost happened to Colin Eversea? If that man, the Earl of Ardmay, has a go at Lyon, I'm not sure even *Father* can do a thing to help him. Don't you want him to come home?"

"Didn't say I didn't. But Violet . . . Lyon's not a . . ." He shook his head slowly. "I mean he just *can't* be a . . ." All at once his face blanked peculiarly. And slowly, slowly scrunched as suddenly the full portent of what he was about to say sank in. ". . . a *p-p-p-irate*!"

He could scarcely get the word out for throwing his head back laughing.

And apparently then the more he thought about it the harder he laughed. He gave his thigh a slap at intervals and coughed out gleeful things like "a *pirate*!" and "honestly!" and "Do you think he has a parrot now?" until Violet wanted to give him a good smack.

Lyon *himself*—the Lyon they knew and loved—would have thought it ridiculous.

Nevertheless.

Jonathan coughed and wiped his eyes, good humor thoroughly restored.

"More likely the only thing we should take from this is that you're meant to marry Lavay. I mean, we mustn't forget what that Gypsy girl said, isn't that so?" His dark eyes snapped wickedly. "What do you think, sister mine? Did he manage to keep any properties in the war? Was he one of the titled French who hid their goods and families away in some other country? Or is he impoverished, looking for a wife with a plump dowry? He's handsome, ain't he? The ladies seem to think so."

Jonathan knew best how to irritate *her*.

"I don't know the answers to any of those questions. I haven't yet met the man I can bear to marry," she said loftily.

But her eyes drifted once more to the Earl of Ardmay and Lord Lavay. It could not be helped, somehow; it was as though the earl exerted more gravity than anyone else in the room. He'd produced a smile for the man he was speaking with, an elderly gentleman, whose posture was stooped and hands animated with conversation. The earl's smile was surprisingly lovely; she could see this even from a distance. Genuine.

And yet there still remained that otherness about him, a remove. It occurred to her he wore his confidence and his difference a bit like a wound he favored: it served to keep everyone was at a precise distance, as if closeness was a danger. She looked at the lovely smile of the deadly earl and knew a fleeting, peculiar, aberrant sensation.

She felt . . . protective.

It was sharp and sudden and total and of course utterly absurd. And gone, mercifully, in an instant.

His head went up abruptly, as though he'd heard a silent call meant only for him. Even as the older gentleman continued speaking with him, he turned his head. Intercepted her gaze. His light eyes glinted cold in the chandelier light.

He was a dangerous man, the earl. And if Lyon was indeed a pirate, and it was the earl's mandate to bring him down, she had no doubt he would do it.

She turned her head away from him quickly.

But what if Lavay, that elegant Frenchman, were indeed the man meant for her? If this had naught to do with Lyon? What if this was what the Gypsy girl had meant? What ought she to feel in this moment? Did it happen quickly, or come on slowly, love? How had Miles and Cynthia known? How on earth did it feel to *not* feel bored and restless and trapped?

"Well, you better meet 'im soon, Vi, the man you'll marry, or you'll be on the shelf and our parents will be saddled with you and whatever will father do with your dowry?" Jonathan said this with apparent concern. Eyes dancing mischievously.

Violet cut a glance sideways at her brother. "Yes, I *best* hurry. Pity I'm an impoverished homely crone and no one shall want me a year from now, or two years from now, or ever."

Jonathan turned to his sister in abject admiration and exasperation. Gave his head a shake. Violet had more confidence than any man he'd ever met, far more than was healthy for a woman, and he knew enough of London gossip, and of the contents of the betting books at White's, to know the fascination she held for the bloods in the ton.

And yet he honestly couldn't picture her besotted with

any of the men he knew, or blushing helplessly like the poor woman he'd just been flirting with. When and if Violet ever fell in love, lightning would split the heavens, tectonic plates would shift, continents would reorder themselves.

Because she might be willful and spoiled and impetuous, but no one loved with the force of his sister. Her love story would be epic.

Which was why Lyon's disappearance had cut her deepest. Even he knew it.

And it could very well be the reason Violet never fell in love at all.

"Just . . . don't do it, Violet."

This had never been a successful admonition when it came to Violet.

"Do what?"

"Whatever it is you're contemplating."

She turned to Jonathan in surprise. "I seldom *contemplate*, Jonathan. Things just . . . happen."

And with that she blew him a kiss and sailed gracefully away across the ballroom, the eyes of yearning, if wary, bloods following her.

Chapter 4

Violet pushed back a heavy velvet curtain and peered out the Redmonds' London town house window and thought: *Rathskill*. The "incompetent and cheeky" cook's mate the earl needed to replace.

All was blackness below, as it was just past one o'clock in the morning. She had left the ball with her parents in the Redmond family coach; and her parents had gone up to bed . . . *together*. Simultaneously. This happened more and more frequently lately. Decidedly odd when their marriage had long seemed to be one of affectionate tolerance, where Isaiah invariably did as he pleased and Fanchette spent his money. In recent months some subtle shift of power had taken place, some fresh new fascination with each other had taken root, and Violet had begun to wonder whether she'd acquired her skills at managing men, such as they were, from her father, or from her mother.

She thought she could trace this back to one particular cozy family occasion, where all the Redmonds, including their young cousin Lisbeth, had gathered to watch Colin Eversea hang from a scaffold erected below the window. Naturally, since he was an Eversea, he'd instead disappeared from the scaffold amidst explosions and clouds of smoke.

It marked the first and only occasion she'd ever heard her

father lose his patience. Specifically, he'd shouted "son of a bitch!" The sound of his control snapping like a taxed gallows rope.

The crowd had rioted and all of London took to singing a particularly insidiously catchy song all about Colin Eversea, a song that lived on and on and on, in theaters and pubs, *everywhere.*

The Everseas had the luck of the devil, it was said.

Colin didn't hang. Colin had in fact *married* a mysterious dark-haired woman he brought to church every Sunday at Pennyroyal Green, and with whom it was said he was raising sheep and cows and the like. His brother Chase, who used to drink all night in the Pig & Thistle, occasionally even alone, was said to be marrying next. A very sudden thing, too, Chase Eversea's engagement. He'd sent to Pennyroyal Green from London a boy named Liam Plum and his sister, Meggie, who now worked in the Pig & Thistle.

But yet another Eversea, Olivia, had driven Lyon away. And of all the secrets and grudges that bound the Everseas and Redmonds throughout the ages, some of which Violet knew of, others which were only intimated, some of which she was certain she would only learn when her parents were on their deathbeds, this one was the newest cut and perhaps the deepest. Colin lived happily; the Redmonds lived on, dignity, fortune, influence intact, but their family had been torn asunder. Like a mouth with a critical tooth punched out of it, everyone had slowly begun to lean and move in cockeyed directions and Violet felt more and more unmoored.

And as for Olivia Eversea, *she* seemed in no danger of marrying soon. She could marry herself to her causes, Violet thought bitterly.

Well, the Everseas may have the luck of the devil; the Redmonds were left to make their own luck, Violet decided. Her *father*, she suspected, often bought luck.

She was about to make a little luck of her own. And as she had told Jonathan earlier, things just . . . happened. She couldn't leave it. She didn't know what would happen next, or precisely how she would go about achieving what she'd just decided to do. She only knew she had no choice.

There was a whisper behind her. "I've brought the trunk down you ordered packed and called a hack as you requested, Miss Violet."

She turned to the footman. "Thank you, Maurice."

"Do enjoy your stay with Lady Peregrine in Northumberland. A fortnight is it, miss? The house party?"

"Yes. A fortnight. Thank you, Maurice. I expect I *shall* enjoy it."

She pulled her cloak tightly about her and turned away from the window. She'd told Maurice she was leaving for Lady Peregrine's house party at dawn in order to meet up with another friend at a coaching inn en route.

She knew a twinge of regret at leaving Jonathan behind, and knew her family would suffer torments when—if—word reached them that she wasn't in Northumberland at all.

But she knew in her bones she would return triumphant.

One ship looked very like another to her, with their great masts and sails furled, massive chains tumbling down from the ships to anchor them in the water like restive beasts. Huge, hulking, intimidating when viewed from this distance. The water, black beneath the night sky and calm in the weather, lapped and slurped at the dock. It stank of sea and wood and tar; the air was cold, and she pulled her cloak more tightly around her as a fetid breeze tugged at her clothes.

"Are you *certain* this is where ye'd like to be put down, miss?" Uncharacteristic, if perhaps understandable, concern from the hack driver.

"Very *kind* of you to question my destination, sir, but yes."

It was her most glacially imperious tone. "But if you would kindly wait for a time? If I do return to the hack and ask you to take me back to St. James Square, I will double your fare. And if you agree to wait until I . . . depart . . . I'll pay you an extra pound now."

"*One pound*, miss?" It was a fortune for a hackney driver.

"Yes," she said. Her heart began to tick more rapidly. For luck, she crossed her fingers in the fold of her cloak she gripped.

He sighed happily, uncorked a flask, and slumped back in his seat to wait. Entirely blasé. Doubtless he saw all manner of behavior from the aristocracy at this time of the morning. The horses snorted and pawed the ground, then apparently resigned themselves to not moving.

She paid a dockworker to row a launch out to *The Fortuna* with her request.

And waited, head tipped back to watch clouds perform the Dance of the Seven Veils with a blue-white half-moon.

Within a few minutes the launch came rowing back, and a round, short-legged man in sturdy boots, a cap pulled down tight over his large head, a limp neck cloth tied about his neck in the manner of all sailors disembarked. His face was so pale it nearly glowed in the moonlight.

"Mr. Rathskill, I presume?"

"Aye," he said slowly, suspiciously.

"Five pounds if you take me aboard *The Fortuna*."

"Ye'd . . . like me to take ye aboard *The Fortuna*."

"Yes," she said impatiently.

He stared at Violet as if she were a ghost or a fairy. And then he apparently came to some sort of conclusion.

"Begging yer pardon, miss, but the crew they take their pleasure at The Velvet Glove. And t'aint a man among 'em who'll pay five pounds for a bit o' muslin, fine though she might be. And that include me, miss. Flattered ye thought to ask fer me, 'owever."

Good God. Violet's head swam. It was rather a lot of information to take in all at once, particularly picturing the crew cavorting at The Velvet Glove, whatever in God's name that might be, and she'd never before considered how much the company of such a woman might cost a man for the evening.

Interesting to know that a woman could be gotten for fewer than five pounds, however.

"I am not a prostitute, Mr. Rathskill." The word felt foreign and lumpen in her mouth; had *any* Redmond woman ever uttered it aloud over the centuries? "I mean to say that I will give you five pounds if you allow me to take your *place* on the ship, as I know you're unhappy aboard it."

This was sheer bloody bravado on her part and a very good guess. She crossed her fingers.

He gaped, eyes wide and white. And then gave a nervous little laugh. "'Ave yer been dared, then, madam? Did Greeber or Corcoran put ye up to it? The captain, e'll 'ave me run the gauntlet! Strip the flesh from me bones, they will."

"'E *will*? I mean, he will?" Barbaric!

"Aye. And worse," he said glumly.

What could be worse than having flesh stripped from one's bones? She didn't ask; she didn't have time to listen to a litany of gory nautical punishments.

"But if you *weren't* aboard, this couldn't happen, now could it? I heard a rumor you weren't entirely happy with your position here, Mr. Rathskill, and I had a conversation with the captain that leads me to believe that your fate will not be an entirely easy one, regardless. I am quite serious about my proposition." She crossed her fingers again against the lie. "You don't want to be aboard *The Fortuna*. I *do* want to be aboard."

He was instantly and rather touchingly alarmed. "Oh, I dinna think this is true, miss, whether or no the captain an' I are overfond o' each other, and I assure ye, we are not. 'Ave yer ever been aboard a ship?"

The never having been aboard a ship was rather the point of this adventure, so she ignored this. But the longer this conversation continued, the greater their risk of being interrupted or caught in conversation with Mr. Rathskill. The earl had said he'd return at dawn, but anything could result in his earlier return.

"He's not aboard now, is he?" she asked carefully. "The earl?"

"Nay. Hasna returned."

"Give your quarters to me. I shall *pay* you to abandon your post. Five pounds."

He stared at her. "But . . . yer a *woman*."

"You have eyes."

He sucked his bottom lip noisily in thought, studying her shrewdly. "Well, seeing as 'ow ye'd like this so much, I might ask for a bit more of what a woman can gives me, if ye take me meaning."

"I take your meaning, and you might ask for your throat to be slit by one of my brothers if you do trouble to ask for that sort of thing."

"Where's yer brothers now, miss?"

"Within earshot. In the hack."

The driver coughed messily.

"I dinna believe you."

"Test me. I *excel* at screaming. And kicking."

"Life is cheap, 'ere in London." He'd tried to sound menacing, but it emerged like something from a bad pantomime.

"Honestly, Mr. Rathskill," she admonished, embarrassed for him.

"Ye're an 'ard sort, ain't ye?" He sounded wounded.

"No!" Absurdly, this hurt Violet's feelings.

"You are," he insisted. "One of them Amazons, like.

Verra powerful." He said this with startling and unexpected relish.

"Perhaps you mean a *siren*?" she suggested desperately.

"Dinna ken what a siren may be. Amazons are them women in the jungle who conquer men, like." He looked hopeful. "The captain, 'e's been everywhere, seen every kind of woman, and 'twould swear 'es seen an Amazon or two, and I reckon ye're just like one of 'em."

The captain had seen all manner of women, had he? Somehow she didn't doubt it for an instant, thinking of the earl's near indifference to her. It still galled.

"*Sirens* lure sailors to their deaths on rocks by distracting them with their beauty and sweet songs. It's a myth." She was still hoping, absurdly, he'd choose this description instead.

"Oh, now. I may not be pleased wi' me captain, but dinna want to dash 'im to 'is death on rocks, necessarily. *The Fortuna*, she's a bonnie vessel."

"It's a *myth*," Violet repeated desperately. "A metaph—never mind."

They'd reached a stalemate.

"Ye're verra pretty, 'owever," he humored.

"Thank you."

"Mayhap ye'd care to pose as me wife in the pub as well as gi' me the ten pounds?" His mind was working out ways she could be of use.

"We haven't *time*." The strategic use of "we" turned him into a co-conspirator. "And I said *five* pounds. My offer stands at five pounds, and I will give you one minute to decide."

She was her father's daughter in her ability to drive a bargain.

"Miss," he said desperately, "I'm not 'eartless, ye sees. 'Tis just that I sleeps in an 'ammock wi' four crewmates. And Greeber, 'e shouts in 'is sleep, and Lumley, 'e farts summat terrible—"

"Perhaps you've a spare cabin," she interrupted desperately. "One with a lock on the door. Did you not leave a diplomat here in London, fresh from a trip to Spain? Surely he didn't sleep in the hammocks with the men."

He paused. "Aye, we've a cabin for guests of rank. The Distinguished Guest Cabin. And we carry none aboard this week. 'Tis empty now."

"I'll take *that* cabin. Take me there. Five pounds. One minute to decide."

The little man was silent, craning his head toward the city proper, perhaps imagining his life away from *The Fortuna* and the terribly unjust Captain Flint, his lips worrying against each other in thought.

"Which one is it ye're set yer cap fer, Lavay or the captain?"

She was startled. "Neither," she said vehemently.

He smiled, and when he did only a few teeth winked on his mouth, like scattered stars in a tiny black universe. He studied her a moment longer, and then shook his head peacefully.

"I dinna believe ye. But in speakin wi' ye, I think ye'll be the best revenge ever I could ere take upon the captain. And I'll take ye aboard and make meself scarce in the city. I'll be gone by daybreak, and mark me words, as 'e'll as soon feed me to the sharks as forgive me."

As much as she disliked this logic, Violet was certain he was correct.

"I'll deal with the captain," she said confidently. She was certain she could . . . eventually. Every man could be managed, even baffling ones like the earl.

She looked behind her at the hackney. The driver hoisted his flask in a mock toast to her, and took a long drink. All the time in the world to wait for his extra pound.

If this carried on for one minute longer her nerve would abandon her.

"You've to the count of ten to decide, Mr. Rathskill. My trunk is on the ground near the hack. One . . . two . . . three . . ."

And then, in a motion she was certain she would remember her entire life, because it seemed so decisive, seemed to divide sanity and insanity, safety and the unknown, he hoisted her trunk up onto his shoulder with the easy strength even small men seemed to possess.

She took what might be her last look at London. And London looked like inky water slapping at the dock, shadowy outlines of ships and buildings indistinguishable from each other in the dark, in the distance rolling carriages taking partygoers home, and she knew a certain delight that she might never have to listen to ball gossip again, and fought back the twinge she felt in leaving her family, a family that had already suffered its losses.

She would come home triumphant—*with* Lyon, or with news of him. How, she had no idea. She seldom considered the "how" of things.

Or she wouldn't come home at all.

And as Mr. Rathskill carried aboard her trunk, she handed up a one-pound note to the hack driver, who touched the brim of his hat, cracked the ribbons and drove off.

Violet followed Rathskill up the dock, which swayed and groaned in agonized protest, as though predicting a dire future for her. He held her hand while she stepped into the launch, and in the inky, chilled half-light, he rowed her out to the *The Fortuna.*

By half past eight, *The Fortuna* had lifted anchor and sailed from the London Harbor. Flint walked the deck, nursing a mug of delicious and poisonously black coffee and preparing to take the wheel from Mr. Lumley, just to feel his own ship beneath his hands again.

"Captain Flint?"

"Yes, Mr. Corcoran?"

"Mr. Rathskill, 'e brought 'isself a hoor aboard last night."

Flint's head shot up to stare at the man.

Then he dropped it again, perusing the charts. "Impossible," Flint said absently. "He knows he isn't allowed to bring women aboard."

Corcoran sounded wounded. "But I *seen* 'im bring 'er up, sir. Crept o'er the deck, locked 'er in the Fine Gent's quarters. They was in there fer a time, ye see, but I seems to 'ave fallen asleep, as 'e snores summat fierce and a body canna get shuteye unless 'e falls asleep first. I thought mayhap the rules 'ad changed and I jus' and't 'eard yet." He sounded hopeful.

Flint looked up again.

"The rules haven't changed. Whores are not allowed aboard *The Fortuna*. Mayhap you're simply trying to cause trouble for Rathskill."

Flint leveled his best honesty-extracting stare at the crewman, refraining from adding, as both he and Corcoran knew, that Rathskill rather did an excellent job of causing his own trouble.

"Wouldna dream o' it, sir." Corcoran whipped off his cap and slapped it over his heart to illustrate his sincerity. Though he didn't address the remark about the whores. "But 'e asna been seen a'tall this morning. Mayhap 'es tucked in wi' the hoor yet."

Flint sighed. "What makes you think this was a *woman* you saw on deck with im? You're certain you weren't dreaming?"

"Well, nay, sir. I was *trying* to dream, mind you. Verra nearly asleep, But I saw the shadows creepin', sir, along the foredeck, and at first thought naught of it. Thought 'twas men returning from shore, or the like. But then I *'eard* sir, a woman's voice, raised like."

"Did you hear what she said?"

Corcoran cleared his throat, and recited: " '*What manner of godforsaken vile stink is this?*' "

It was a startlingly creditable imitation of a refined woman's voice.

Corcoran blushed and cleared his throat again, and gave a short nod, like a soprano concluding a performance.

And it wasn't something Corcoran could have invented. He was a stalwart seaman and a creditably dirty fighter, but he had no hidden depths.

"She sounded *that* horrified?" Flint frowned.

"Aye, sir. And then I 'eard Rathskill shushing her, like. And the sound o' the door shutting. An' locking. Seems unlikely a hoor would object to stink, aye, sir? But I vow 'tis what I 'eard."

"It does seem unlikely." Flint was thinking rapidly now. What the devil was going on?

"And I reckon we've all manner of vile stinks aboard, but a man gets accustomed to 'em, aye, until dinna notice a'tall. But women, aye, they may get a bit of a shock? Eve if ye're *payin'* a woman, and she's accustomed to sailors, a stink may surprise 'er."

"Perhaps," Flint allowed slowly. Something was afoot; all of his instincts were on alert now. "And you haven't seen Rathskill at all this morning?"

"Havena seen 'im today, sir," Corcoran confirmed. "Wasna in 'is 'ammock this morning. Didna collect his breakfast in the galley. So I think to meself sir, mayhap 'es still in wi' the hoor. Or mayhap some 'arm 'as come to him."

"Thank you, Corcoran."

Flint was already striding past him. He all but threw his body down the foc'sle, wended his way to the Distinguished Guest Cabin door, and turned the knob.

It was locked.

And this, in and of itself, was indication that something was amiss.

Flint thumped a fist once on the door. "Rathskill!"

Picturing the crewman with a slit throat, murdered by a prostitute for his money. Picturing Rathskill and the prostitute inebriated, entwined, snoring. Imagining, with relish, running Rathskill through a gauntlet or tying him to the rigging, because he'd honestly had nearly all he could tolerate from the seaman.

He leaned forward and put an ear to the solid door.

Was that a shuffling footstep he heard?

Flint slipped his pistol from his belt and nodded at Corcoran to do the same, then tugged on the doorknob hard enough to rattle the door intimidatingly.

"Rathskill! If you're in there and sound, come out or I'll kick the door down and come in after you."

He put his ear against the door again.

Silence.

He stood back, raised his arm, and was about to bring it down for a good hard thump when they heard a click.

The doorknob slowly turned.

His fist arrested midair. Absurdly mesmerized, he and Corcoran watched the progress of the doorknob.

Creeeeeak. The door at last creaked open a slow and tentative two inches.

An instant later, the crack revealed a pair of long-lashed blue eyes, two slim winged dark brows and a sliver of pale refined nose.

The eyes blinked.

They were intelligent, bright, expressive, and admittedly guarded eyes. There was something uncomfortably, deucedly familiar about them.

"Hoor!" Corcoran announced, triumphant with vindication.

"I am nothing of the sort," came an indignant, elegant voice, muffled somewhat by the frame of the door.

Flint knew that voice. But the memory of it was less sound than sensation for some reason . . . a warm breath in his ear asking a provocative question . . . a creamy décolletage . . . the color blue? A woman in blue?

Why did he know that voice?

"Madam, I am the Earl of Ardmay and captain of *The Fortuna*." It was a voice calculated to quail even the most stalwart of men, and to establish his supremacy. "Are you in any way harmed or unwell? Have you been brought here against your will?"

A hesitation.

"No, sir," she said politely, tentatively. The door remained open just that one stingy inch. The eyes blinked again. It was very nearly an eyelash *bat*. A reflexively flirtatious gesture. Suspicion mounted.

"Very well. I must request then, madam, that you open the door and step out. We wish to ascertain that you are indeed sound. You have my word as a gentleman that you are safe in my custody. We're also interested in the whereabouts of a Mr. Rathskill, as it has come to my attention that he may have been the means by which you boarded our ship. If he is there with you, we need to know immediately."

"I am alone, sir."

"Forgot ye was an earl now, Captain," Corcoran murmured cheerfully.

"I occasionally do, too, Corcoran," Flint muttered irritably. "Fat lot of good the title's done me yet." He raised his voice. "Madam? I must ask that you open the door and exit the cabin now, or I shall forcibly open it. Please do don a cloak if you are in a state of undress."

Corcoran coughed in surprise, forgetting this was a tantalizing possibility. Flint scowled at him.

An indecisive silence crept by.

He heard the woman inhale at length. Likely gathering courage. But then she coughed out the breath again. Perhaps unable to tolerate the "vile stink" of the cabin entering her nostrils.

"Very well," she agreed at last with elegant dignity.

The door began to move. She pushed it slowly all the way open.

Creeeaak. Thunk.

A dumbstruck silence followed.

"Mother. Of. *GOD*," Corcoran said reverently. He plucked off his hat and placed it over his heart again.

For the doorway framed a tall, dark-haired, startlingly clean Englishwoman dressed in a gold-braided deep red walking gown and pelisse, which hung in the kind of effortless lines Flint recognized as both fashionable and bogglingly expensive. Her hair was dark, glossy. Blue eyes set deep beneath two fine very black brows. A ruler-straight nose. A pale, full mouth, fine, sharp jaw, a stubborn chin.

She was even wearing a bloody bonnet, albeit hanging on ribbons down her back.

They all stared at each other in a nonplussed silence.

Well, Flint thought. She was certainly different in this context.

She'd called him a savage. She'd been bored at the ball. She smelled of lavender, faintly, when she'd stood on toe and asked him to guess whether she was an innocent, and he'd known an instant of temptation, an infinitesimal sizzling sense promise, during which the veil of boredom and niceties had been dropped and they'd enjoyed an honest, if not entirely comfortable, exchange. But he'd known then she was merely testing herself. She was an innocent, indeed, one who could likely be urged to be wicked and reckless.

And there would also likely be a grave cost to any man who did urge her to do it.

Oh. And her brother resembled Le Chat. His nemesis. The reason he was on this voyage at all.

"Miss . . ." He could barely get the word out for incredulity. He could hardly believe he'd even *said* the word *miss*. On his *ship*.

There was a *miss* on his ship.

Oh, *God*. A very unwelcome turn of events.

"Redmond," she supplied with glacial dignity. As though she were accustomed to saying that name and then watching as everyone dislocated their spines in bows of obeisance.

Oh dear God.

Now he remembered. She was a Redmond. He'd been introduced to Isaiah Redmond last night; he'd learned all about the man's wealth and influence and reach. Isaiah Redmond would have an armada sent after *The Fortuna*.

If he knew where she'd gone.

Flint stole a desperate glance in the direction of London, as though wondering whether he could plop her into a long boat and have one of his men row her straightaway back to shore.

They were emphatically at sea, of course. And the nearest port was days away.

She curtsied. He bowed.

It all seemed *very* ridiculous.

"Name's Corcoran, madam," said the midshipman behind him reverently.

"Delighted to meet you Mr. Corcoran." Her voice was aristocratic and mellifluous.

She seemed sound enough, though she was definitely pale, and faint shadowed rings of sleeplessness curved beneath her eyes. He wondered if she'd been seasick in the chamber pot, but surprisingly she didn't seem to be suffering unduly—her skin would have been more green than white. In fact, one would have thought she'd simply enjoyed a standard night of dancing and debauchery, apart from shockingly crisp clothing. And the *bonnet*. A woman who had taken great care, even in the absence of a maid, to groom herself scrupulously.

He peered beyond her.

He saw a trunk, a cloak draped over a chair and that lumpy uninviting mattress that appeared undented by a sleeping body. It was one of only two traditional beds aboard. His was the other. The rest of the men slept in hammocks.

Behind her the cabin exhaled the singular aroma of a space in which legions of sailors had sweat, broken wind, drunk, and aimed for chamber pots with perhaps more urgency than accuracy. It had always been cleaned to the extent possible but always with the occupancy of men in mind. In other words, it smelled like every *other* cabin on the ship, apart, perhaps from his own, which was spotless, as he was the only person who'd ever slept in it.

His own aim was impeccable.

"Miss Redmond . . ." he said very mildly, very gently, in a voice that belied the momentum of his gathering outrage. "Why the devil are you on my ship?"

Corcoran cleared his throat. "Captain. Perhaps you oughtn't use the word *devil* in front of Miss Redmond, as she's a fine la . . ."

Flint whipped a scorchingly quelling look at Corcoran.

Who clapped his jaw shut audibly.

Then Flint returned a deceptively mild gaze to Miss Redmond.

He gave her a moment more to respond to his question. She didn't seem eager to do it.

"Very well. If you would just come with me, Miss Redmond, we shall speak in private quarters. Please return to your duties,

Corcoran. Thank you for calling my attention to these . . . circumstances."

"Aye, sir. Good day to you, Miss Redmond." He made a bow so extravagant the top of his balding head nearly touched his knees, and he backed away, soaking up the sight of Violet Redmond as long as possible, though she were a healing vision and the fetid little cabin a shrine.

He turned and scrambled back up onto the deck.

Flint was certain he'd spread word of her presence to the other men on board as quickly, and with as much exaggeration, as possible.

Unholy, bloody mess.

Trust an Englishwoman to complicate things.

"Miss Redmond," he repeated firmly. He gestured for her to precede him.

And after a hesitation, she tilted up her chin in a show of bravado—she'd certainly need that, he thought grimly—and obeyed.

Chapter 5

He opened the door to his cabin, his sanctuary: an elegantly simple, masculine room of the type he'd occupied since he'd captained his first ship at age eighteen. It was roomier than the typical captain's cabin, but not by much. His bed, his bureau, a mirror, his chessboard, a tiny painting, a dartboard, some books, a map-covered wall. Touchstones, these things. Everything in the room was either utilitarian or had been given to him by someone who mattered to him.

He ushered her inside and closed the door.

For sitting there were several chairs and a bed, but he didn't invite her to sit. He turned and fired questions like shots over a bow.

"How did you get aboard my ship, Miss Redmond?"

"I learned that your man Rathskill was discontented, and discovered he was easily enough bought, Captain Flint. He's not overly fond of you, you know."

Rathskill himself wasn't a terrible loss. He was mad to surrender to the urge to ask. Still, curiosity won.

"What was his price?"

"Five pounds." She sounded bemused that he could be got for such a bargain.

Flint was surprised, too. It demonstrated the man was

either a fool and he was better off without him, or far more diabolically brilliant than he'd originally credited him, because he'd certainly taken revenge upon the captain by leaving Miss Redmond as a parting gift.

"After the ball, I packed a trunk and paid a hack to take me to where *The Fortuna* was anchored. Rathskill rowed me aboard and installed me in the guest cabin, and then he departed to enjoy his five pounds and his freedom from you in London."

"And you're entirely unchaperoned on this misbegotten endeavor?"

A hesitation. "Yes." She didn't address his adjectives.

"Does your family have an inkling where you are?"

"My family believes I am at a house party in Northumberland and departed for it this morning by way of hired hack. At least, that's what I instructed our footman to tell them. He's a bit afraid of me, so no doubt it's what he did tell them."

Worse and worse and *worse.*

"*Why* in God's name are you here?"

Her silence seemed more reluctant than stubborn. She wasn't quite certain how to go about telling him. Very well. He would drill it out of her.

"Are you fleeing an arranged marriage?"

"No."

"Are you with child and intend to cast yourself off the side of my ship out of remorse and shame and a misplaced sense of drama?"

"No!" She didn't blush, though she sounded appropriately horrified.

"Excellent. So the option of throwing you overboard remains."

"I—"

"Has anyone in your family beaten or in any way mistreated you, such that you fled pell-mell to the docks to board my vessel, after calculatedly bribing my man in order to take his place?"

"N—"

"Have you fallen in love with Lavay and intend to follow him to the ends of the earth?

"No!"

Though her eyes darted interestingly here.

"Were you perhaps *dared* by one of your female friends to board this ship?"

"No."

He glared at her so fiercely, so pointedly, he was astonished a smoking hole didn't appear between her eyes.

"As much as I'm enjoying this guessing game, Miss Redmond, my time is valuable and I'm needed to command *this bloody SHIP*."

Well, then. His temper got hold of him on the last three words.

Her eyes widened. Her hands clenched reflexively, he noticed. More impressed with his temper than afraid of it.

Give her time.

Splendid color, he noticed. Those eyes. Crystalline blue, a bit like sunlight glancing off a foaming sea. In the grittier context of a ship, splendid things, grace notes, stood out in stark relief. And introducing feminine splendor and grace into a ship full of splendor-deprived men could spell chaos, if not disaster.

"Miss Redmond." Heavy as an anvil with irony, those two words. "Do you intend to tell me why you're on my ship?"

Again, her silence was more recalcitrant than considering. She was still working out her rationale. *Women.*

"Very well. While you contemplate how to begin telling me your story—for I assure you, you will, and you will tell me the truth—allow *me* to tell you a few things. Do you have any idea what the presence of a woman such as yourself can do to a crew of men deprived of female companionship for weeks and months at a time, and I do mean 'companionship' euphemistically? You're not precisely ugly."

Only a blink betrayed that she might be a trifle taken aback.

"Surely flattery is unnecessary, Captain," she said mildly.

"Oh, I wouldn't dream of flattering you. I've never seen the necessity of flattery and I'm not a frivolous man. *The Fortuna* is on an important mission, one that will likely be dangerous. I've a slim crew of hardworking, skilled men, each of whose full physical and intellectual capacities are needed each minute of each day. And each of them—as they are *men*—are disposed both to gallantry and, shall we say, animalistic behavior when confronted with a woman and the competition of other men for her attention and favor, regardless of this woman's family name or the status of her virginity."

He waited for her to go scarlet.

She did not. But her jaw tensed and there was a definite tightening of the skin about her eyes. Admirable fortitude, or more than her share of bloody cheek. He wasn't certain which it was.

"The wrong woman could tip the balance disastrously. You, I assure you, are *very* much the wrong woman. Your appearance could therefore jeopardize my mission and wreak havoc upon my crew, none of whom deserves havoc, or deserves the disturbance of his peace of mind. I thought I would share this on the off chance you possessed a conscience, if not a brain."

She listened to this, her face going tauter and paler. And she swallowed.

Good. Not entirely without a conscience, then.

But he was wrong about the source of the whiteness. He was indeed intimidating.

But Violet was angry now, too. And when she was angry, she was reckless.

"Have you so little control over your men, Captain Flint?" She said it softly.

He froze. And something so closed and hard and final passed over his face she felt her teeth jar. As though she'd run headlong into a wall.

His voice became low and even and much more frightening.

"You had better have an excellent reason for paying my man to board my ship. Because if you're here on a whim, I'll cast you overboard now with no regrets."

"Surely you'll know a twinge or two."

Why oh why did she say those sorts of things? What made her do it? Violet was even frightening *herself.* But flippancy was her only defense in the moment, and she supposed it was what cornered animals did: lash out with whatever defenses remained to them.

He sizzled incredulity at her.

"I cannot protect you every single hour of every day you're aboard my ship, Miss Redmond, and I cannot afford to charge one of my men with the duty. They are not *gentlemen*, Miss Redmond." Good heavens, how ironic he'd made *that* word sound. "Some of them, in other circumstances, might qualify as rogues and scalawags. In other words, they are sailors and fighters."

She knew she was the transgressor. Still, his arrogance made her feel rash.

"I wouldn't allow any of them to touch me, my lord. I am not so fragile as you may think. I managed to bribe Rathskill, did I not? And like as not they wouldn't dare succumb to *animal instincts*, as you say, if the know what the consequences would be? You'll simply make it known that you'll have the flesh stripped from their bones in a gauntlet. Since you are the captain and their loyalty is unquestioned."

Hoping she'd astonished him with her knowledge of nautical punishments, she angled her shoulders to leave, since she'd recalled her trunk was in the guest cabin and her twenty pounds were inside, and she could not recall whether it was properly locked.

As if in a dream, out of the corner of her eye, she watched as his arm stretched out and his hand closed over her upper arm—completely.

Shackling it.

She was just able to register the fact that his grip was impersonally ungentle, and that she'd never been touched like that in her entire life, and that she couldn't move at all despite a cursory attempt to do so, when he spun her around to face him.

Abruptly.

He held her motionless for a moment. As much with his hands as with the ferocity of his gaze. And then he slowly relinquished her, his fingers dragging along her arm, leaving behind an imprint of heat.

His point made: he could control her if he chose. And he could touch her if he chose.

She was thunderstruck.

She resisted the urge to rub at her arm. It didn't hurt, and yet she thought she could feel the brand of his five fingers on her arm. Heat started in her cheeks; she was uncertain whether it was fury or mortification or some combination thereof. Whatever it was robbed her entirely of speech.

She could only stare at him.

"Ah, that's better. I prefer to be *looked* at when I'm speaking, Miss Redmond, and as captain of this ship, I prefer to do the dismissing when I feel a conversation has run its course. This one has not. And, oh, look at that: I dared to touch you."

He waited for her to react.

She had enough sense this time not to say a single word.

"Here is what you fail to realize. *I* can take you whenever—and—however I *please*. *Should* I please to do so, and I can't imagine why I would, as I expect my women to do a little of the work, as it were. And I doubt you've done anything resembling making an effort in your entire life."

Absurdly, Violet was at first struck by his impeccable grammar. Little elegant hammer blows of words. She was reminded of her former French tutor; it was the same carefully flawless English spoken by those who didn't come native to it, but learned it as a foreign language.

The earl had *learned* gentility.

He balanced the trappings of it like a juggler with glittering clubs. Beneath it simmered whatever it was he showed her now, whatever it was everyone had sensed in him in that ballroom that night but would never have been able to identify.

Savage. Or so they'd said.

He was studying her face for the impact of his words. "I daresay you haven't the faintest idea to what I'm referring."

And that's when delayed shock settled fully in. A sweep of ice, then heat, washed her limbs and then settled into her stomach. For God's sake, of course she knew to what he was referring. *Take* her. *Animalistically*, he meant.

She'd never heard it referred to quite as "work" before, however. She imagined the "ladies" at The Velvet Glove viewed it as such.

"I do know 'of what you're speaking.'" She mimicked him icily. Or, rather, she'd tried for ice. Her voice emerged hoarse and shock-frayed.

What an absurd thing to say. It sent his eyebrows upward mockingly.

"Well, then. I do wonder what makes you think that I *won't* take you, on a whim. Brute that I am. And so forth," he said as though he were merely idly curious. His eyes belied the tone, however. Imperious, impersonal, cold anger.

They stared at each other.

"Savage," she corrected absently, "is what they say." She possessed enough wits at the moment to not address the rest of his sentence at all.

He gaze increased in incredulity.

She returned it warily, unblinkingly, with a penetrating interest that unbeknownst to her made her look remarkably like her brother Miles, the naturalist, when he peered at man-eating plants and crawling things in order to understand them. The Earl of Ardmay was showing no indication of being anything like any of the other men she'd ever known.

"Is it that you are accustomed, Miss Redmond, to treating men either as pets or servants? I'm curious—which one of those did you suppose *I'd* be?"

This gave her pause. She'd never thought about it quite in those terms.

And when she realized he was very close to correct, a fresh bolt of shock and anger shivered down her spine. As though she'd suddenly caught him peering at her through a keyhole. This was an entirely new angle from which she could be viewed, and it was hardly a flattering one.

Occasionally, she supposed, she treated the young men who naively hovered about her at balls rather the way she did *insects* at a picnic: their presence—in swarms—was integral to the festivities, though they honestly seemed to enjoy being figuratively swatted away, as long as *she* was the one doing the swatting.

"Definitely not a pet," she concluded tightly.

His expression went so odd then she thought maybe, just maybe, he was struggling not to laugh. Either that, or he was tolerating a gastric pain.

"Miss Redmond, it astounds me that I need to tell you this

at all, but on the slim chance you *might* have a conscience, in paying my erstwhile crew member to board my ship you've done something . . . *unconscionably* rash and selfish. Your reputation of course precedes you, but you've inconvenienced my crew and me, no doubt worried your family and created all manner of scandal, and all on what? A *lark*, a whim, a—"

Suddenly it was enough.

"Not a lark," she hissed.

He froze for a gratifying instant. The silence gathered an ominous density.

She stormed recklessly onward.

"Rash—very well, I'll grant you that. Impulsive? Oh, very good use of the word, Captain Flint. But *not* a lark. My brother Lyon, my father's heir, disappeared more than a year ago. You can't know what his loss has done to our family, but I will tell you: everyone pretends all is well, but it's a quiet sort of devastation. And I suspect . . . I suspect you're trying to find him, too. And it's the first I've heard anything of him in ages."

"What the devil does *that* mean?"

"It means I think my brother Mr. Lyon Redmond may be Mr. Hardesty. Or as you call him, Le Chat."

Chapter 6

A silence.

"You think . . ." His expression was indecipherable. "Go on."

"At the ball, your reaction to my brother Jonathan was rather striking. You said he could have been Mr. Hardesty's twin. Jonathan looks very much like *Lyon*. And Lyon disappeared at night a year ago. And the woman who allegedly broke his heart is Miss Olivia Eversea."

"*The Olivia*," the earl repeated darkly, after a tick of silence. She heartily approved of his tone, because she could never say Olivia Eversea's name in any other way.

"I tried, mind you, to tell my brother Jonathan what I learned from you about Le Chat. And his reaction told me I shouldn't attempt to tell my father. Because I can tell you this: *no one* in my family will believe me. No one *listens* to me. They're all very fond of me, of course, but I'm not certain they see me as *needed*. So why would they believe a woman? Why believe *me*, especially in light of my so-called rash behavior? Someone needs to find Lyon before you do, Captain, because I know how you intend to deal with him. And if I told *you* about my suspicions, Captain . . . would you allow me aboard your ship? Of course not. You are my best hope, Captain Flint, for finding Lyon and saving his life . . . from *you*. Furthermore—"

"There's a 'furthermore'?" His voice was utterly inflectionless.

"—I'm not a child. I'm a *lady* born of one of England's finest and oldest families, and I daresay even you know how to behave in the presence of a lady. Regardless of the inconvenience I've caused you, I'll thank you to remember whatever manners you've managed to feign to date, because the ones you're exhibiting do you no credit and merely reinforce the prevailing opinion, Captain Flint, that you are a savage." She delighted in giving the *S* a serpent-like sibilance. "The measure of a gentleman is how he behaves when he *hasn't* an audience to witness the beauty of his manners. And I wouldn't expect you to understand this, *my lord,* but centuries of fine breeding have ensured that I *need* not, as you say, exert myself if I choose not to. Only the likes of you equate the actual need to work with virtue. It is in fact due to the *work* of my ancestors that I no longer need to, and my family considers this a mark of honor."

During this, he moved only once: to blink. As though she'd flicked water into his eyes. After that, his eyes remained unnervingly vivid and disconcertingly, dispassionately *interested*.

She was done.

But he was quiet for such a long time after she stopped speaking that the fury animating her drained away for lack of a target. She felt hollow, spent, a cocoon abandoned by the caterpillar. A puff of air would carry her off.

He seemed thoughtful.

"And you honestly believe based on your younger brother's resemblance to Le Chat and the name of his ship that your brother—*Lyon*, is it?—is a notorious pirate?"

Well, anything he said in that particular tone of voice was bound to sound ridiculous. So she didn't reply.

"And you intend to do . . . what? *Stop* me from bringing your brother to justice?"

He was perilously close to mirth. Or hysteria. *Something* she wouldn't appreciate, she was certain. He issued his words with great care and control.

She simply straightened her spine. She would not confess to the fact that she hadn't thought quite so far as that. But she excelled at thinking on her feet. Or rather, she *preferred* to think on her feet, for it was the one way she could coax excitement from the routine of her life.

"Consider that you might be able to use me for bait on your stops in search of my brother, Captain Flint, if my brother is indeed Le Chat. You may be able to flush him out if you send word ahead that I am accompanying you. And yes, I fully intend to warn him of your presence . . . once you lead me to him. For if he is indeed Le Chat, I am certain all is not what it seems. Lyon is *not* a vicious pirate. So may the better player win."

Good heavens. *What* an array of expressions chased each other subtly over his face in the long silence that followed.

The earl stared at her a moment longer.

"Tell me, Miss Redmond . . ." he said thoughtfully. "Are you *often* bored?"

She could have sworn the ground beneath her feet swayed.

Her vertigo must have shown. She stared at him, feeling all but stripped bare. How did he *know*?

Because the corner of his mouth tipped up. *I thought so,* was what it meant. He was *amused.* The bloody clever man understood her too well, and too easily. But he was eons away from believing her.

This was when she had her epiphany: *She* was the one who had always been treated like a pet. Coddled, indulged, scolded, occasionally mildly punished, but kept always, always on a rarified, invisible silken tether, reeled in by her brothers or parents no matter what she did or where she went, no matter how absurd or reckless. No one particularly needed her. And she was of course so much more than equal to every single blood in London.

But this had left her entirely unprepared for the likes of the Earl of Ardmay.

His voice deepened, softened, lowered. The change was instantly disorienting, as she'd been using his asperity for a spine.

"And I would never, ever, Miss Redmond, equate the type of 'work' to which I was referring a moment ago with . . . virtue."

It was like incense drifting out from beneath the closed door of a bordello, his voice. She didn't so much hear as feel it; brushing up against her skin like rough silk.

It was also *utterly* calculated.

He was toying with her now. He found the whole circumstance so amusing he'd decided to *play* with her.

And it almost worked. She drew in a deep sustaining breath.

He'd cornered her into *reasoning* with him. Which for her felt like walking out on wobbly gangplank over uncertain waters. This was very much a last resort for Violet when it came to men. She'd heretofore always . . . well, *managed* them—which had staved off boredom nicely since strategy was invariably involved.

Pets or servants, *indeed.*

"Do you have brothers or sisters, Captain—Lord—"

"Captain will do. God knows. I might have dozens of them. I haven't the faintest idea who my father is."

Violet's mind went blank. Her mouth parted a little. Then closed again. *Nothing* in her experience had prepared her for a conversation with a man like this. Then again, it was difficult to imagine another man quite like this.

He had no one? No family at all? She was conscious suddenly of an aberrant sweep of pity and swatted it back. This was *not* a man who needed, or would graciously accept, pity.

"I appall you." He made it not a question but a statement.

She sighed. "Rather," she admitted. "Are you trying to?"

He blinked in surprise. And then, to her astonishment, he grinned, and three unforgettable things happened at once: A dimple, a devastating crescent moon, appeared at the corner of his mouth; his eyes lit, and it was like watching lightning crack over the surface of a dark sea . . .

. . . and Violet stopped breathing, as surely as that lightning had struck her square in the chest.

"I doubt I have to *try* to appall you, Miss Redmond. I suspect I need simply . . . be."

She breathed again, but she was still staring at the place the dimple had been. She dug her fingernails into her palm to punish herself for momentary witlessness.

Enormous, frightening men should not be allowed to possess anything quite so whimsical as dimples, she thought resentfully.

His face *was* softer now, but she wasn't so optimistic as to believe she'd actually charmed him.

"Nonsense. You underestimate me, Captain Flint," she said coolly.

This was pure bravado. He had in fact estimated her rather well up to this point.

Mostly you weary me, Captain Flint.

Well . . . and you frighten me. And no man had ever before frightened her.

Worst of all, you intrigue me.

This last was the most terrible realization of all, as it was the first time it was genuinely true for her of any man.

And it was the fault of a split-second smile and a dimple.

She *gravely* disliked the realization that she was human.

Her legs were trembling now from a toxic blend of fear and fatigue and bravado-maintenance when heretofore all that had been publicly required of her was pride and arrogance and elegance and wit. She wanted to sink into the oblivion of sleep, to forget him. But she thought of that dark, swaying, fetid little hole of a berth and the hard bunk stretched over with a lumpy bread-slice thin mattress likely teeming with the types of creatures her brother Miles would cheerfully write books about and manage to make sound *fascinating.*

She hadn't dared sit on it; she'd sat on a chair near it, and eyed it as though it was a predator for the remainder of the night. It had been a bad few hours, indeed. And then the feel of the ship lifting anchor and heading out to sea had nearly made her burst from her cabin in panic.

She thought of Lyon, and how it would be to have him home. And she glanced at the earl's chessboard and thought of her brother Miles longingly now. His head would likely be bent over chess across from old Mr. Culpepper's near the fire at the Pig & Thistle in Pennyroyal Green, engaged in chess warfare while his wife, Cynthia, adoringly and peacefully looked on.

How she wished she could have spoken with Miles about her suspicions. Would *he* have listened to her? Likely not, especially if she'd mentioned the bit about the Gypsy girl and Lavay. Even Miles would have given a tug on her invisible leash and a pat on the head.

Inspiration, albeit a desperate one, struck. So the earl could not be managed, per se. It didn't mean that games were *entirely* out of the question. That strategy could not be applied. She desperately wanted to win back a measure of pride. Not to mention credibility.

"You do play chess, my lord?"

He stared at her.

"Chess," the earl repeated. As if he'd never heard the word before in his life.

She gestured to the handsome chess set arranged on table in the far corner of his cabin.

"You see, I very much prefer not to sleep in that . . . that . . . *vole hole* . . . tonight—"

"I cannot tell you how it breaks my heart that you'll be missing your sleep, Miss Redmond. And voles always appear quite rested to me. Very vibrant creature, the vole."

She soldiered on. "I propose that we play a game of chess for the right to sleep in your much finer accommodations. If I win, *you* will sleep in the vole hole tonight."

As for chess, she'd had the very best teachers that Sussex could offer. And Miles, her brother, had honed his skills against her. She knew very well how clever she was. In spite of herself.

He almost winced at her temerity. "You'll . . . play chess for the right to sleep in my bed?"

But even he knew this was a too-easy innuendo. His mouth creased at the corner again. She watched it warily, less he launch another smile at her.

But he'd also once again managed to make her sound ridiculous.

"I shall, as you say, *exert a little effort*"—she was not unaware of a certain dark flare in his eyes just then, just as she was not unaware that she'd said it deliberately, for effect, as she was a quick learner indeed and not above bull-baiting—"and if I win the game, *I* will sleep in a more comfortable bed. You will sleep in the vole hole. Are you afraid I'll win?"

She knew the earl would be unimpressed with that particular gambit.

There was a silence, as he somberly assessed her.

And then he sighed, and there was so much genuine weariness in the sound she very nearly succumbed to sympathy before she recalled that the weary exasperation was all for her.

"Miss Redmond . . . for heaven's sake." *Such* dramatic, infinitely strained patience in his voice. "Good . . . *God.* I am *captain* of this ship. Why on earth you'd think I'd engage in a *game* of chess for . . . for . . ." He shook his head, as if he could hardly bear to finish the sentence. "I *excel* at chess," he said almost weakly. She had the sense he'd bury his face in his hands and rock it back and forth in a second.

"Then the game will be over quickly," she said briskly. But her hands were cold and clammy; she'd crossed her fingers for luck in the folds of her skirt.

The earl studied her. Looked at the door, as if contemplating the rewards of freedom versus the rewards of humoring his stowaway.

Then he sighed again and strolled to the chessboard. He reached out and pensively fingered the burnished ivory head of a knight.

"How much money did you bring with you on your voyage?" He looked sharply up at her. "I'm assuming you *did* bring money."

The question surprised her. "Twenty pounds."

"Twen—" He stopped. He shook his head again, with a cryptic, disbelieving half smile. "All right, then, Miss Redmond. We shall play one game of chess. If you win, you may sleep in my chambers instead of the accommodations assigned to you. I will sleep in the vole hole, as you so insultingly refer to the accommodations you've been assigned on *my* ship. And I will leave you at the next port, and arrange to hire someone to accompany you safely home. Using *your* money."

Oh. She did know a twinge of guilt when he put it that way: "vole hole" was indeed insulting. She supposed it had been impolite of her; then again, he hadn't yet drawn out her finer qualities.

Nevertheless, his proposition wasn't precisely what she had in mind.

"But—"

"Do not argue with me. I am not finished. And if you *lose*, you will give me five of your twenty pounds to cover the cost of your board and transport, and I will deposit you and your trunk on the dock at the next port. If the wind remains fair, we'll reach port Le Havre in two days. You can find your own inn, find your own way home, you can join a traveling menagerie, you can apply to a brothel, you can go to the very devil, for all I care. For you have taken for granted the protection of men your entire life, Miss Redmond. You have taken for granted your comfort and privilege and safety. Even now you think I'll see to your comfort, that some *man* will always look out for you even when you behave in unconscionably reckless ways. And I . . ." He paused, fished in his pocket, thumbed open his watch. Consulted the time. His mind, even as he delivered this speech, was elsewhere. ". . . don't like it."

He lifted his head when he said this. His eyes bored into her. He allowed these words to echo in the room for a second. His expression made it *profoundly* clear that he meant them.

She said nothing.

"Even now—even *now*—you probably don't believe I'll simply abandon you to your fate." He thumbed the watch closed, tucked it away again. "I invite you to test me."

He'd checkmated her before the game even began.

She stared up at him. After a moment, she swallowed.

He noticed; she watched the flick of his eyes. She saw satisfaction in those eyes. It struck her that he was the sort of man who forever assessed his surroundings, would miss nothing, as anything could become important at any time.

Her intestines were quivering like aspic, but:

"Challenge accepted," she said, her voice steady enough.

He nodded once, as if her acceptance was of supreme indifference to him, and with a shiny-booted toe, languidly pushed out a chair for her. Across from the white pieces, naturally. He gestured for her to sit.

Through some tacit agreement no attempt was made to converse throughout the game. They had no idea how to talk to each other pleasantly, anyway, the refined-savage captain with the unlikely title and the stowaway aristocratic virgin, and both were wary and already weary of each other.

And yet Flint couldn't say the game was objectionable. He enjoyed the silence, the necessary stillness, the feel of the elegant pieces in his fingers.

The set was a gift from his old friend Captain Moreheart, making their game more symbolic still.

He enjoyed it, that is, until it became clear he was losing.

Flint had played chess with rajas and rogues, with a range of obsessively skilled scholars of the game. He was clever, he was thoughtful, he was resourceful, he was ruthless and inventive, and he brought all of his best qualities to bear on the chessboard. It made him a very, very good player.

She was better.

When this dawned inexorably upon him, he suffered greatly . . . inwardly. Up welled a sense of outrage he tamped with some difficulty, but which stirred immediately with her very next clever, deliberate move. He suffered a veritable in-out tide of pride and outrage.

It was supplanted at last with dark amusement. A bead of sweat trickled down the back of his neck, traveling the road of his spine. *My pride dissolving,* he thought, sardonically.

She was steering him skillfully to the conclusion she wanted.

As she had, in a way, all evening, he realized suddenly.

I'll be damned.

She didn't gloat. She made her moves and then looked up at him with calm, if wary, expectance, signaling with those vivid, fatigue-ringed eyes that it was his turn.

And eventually something else stirred, something unwelcome and unexpected very begrudging: admiration.

Behind that smooth, pale forehead her mind clicked along with an easy and unexpected precision, a knack for strategy that might have been channeled into some masculine pursuit—perhaps battlefield maneuvers, or torturing prisoners—and might have served a *useful* purpose. Might not have tormented her the way he was certain it did, given her demonstrable predilection for rashness. Still, some women threw themselves into good works, he thought sourly. Perhaps he ought to suggest it to Miss Redmond.

Who taught you to play chess? With whom do you play? One of your brothers?

It seemed to him the sort of game she'd have no patience for. And yet . . . and yet . . . she was so *dogged* in pursuit of her brother. So very convinced of the truth of her quest, however absurd it seemed on the surface, however reckless.

What is it like? To love so fiercely, to feel so part of a family, of a place?

Soon enough he would have the luxury of building his own destiny—Le Chat was the means to his ends.

He refused to allow silence to draw curiosity out of him in the form of questions. He was certain Miss Redmond would know precisely how to exploit curiosity, interpret it as some kind of softening. But silence had a way of splintering things into details, for the mind disliked disengagement. He'd learned this in a Turkish prison. It could turn moments of nothingness into diversions. And he couldn't help but notice things in the silence. A tiny punctuation mark of a mole drew the eye to the elegant half-heart shape of the top lip, the soft full swoop of the lower. Her skin took the lamplight the way a good pearl would. Fine-grained and unlined thanks to the lifelong protection of bonnets and hats.

Odd. He rarely viewed women in terms of . . . *parts*. Primarily he simply heartily partook of women and they of him. And now he was thinking of Fatima and not of the game. He shifted restlessly.

You underestimate me, Captain Flint.

And yet he'd so seldom underestimated anyone. He was freshly reminded of how dangerous it was to do so.

He'd learned another humbling lesson in prison: how to accept one's fate like a man. He knew his chess doom was about two moves away. And so he manfully waited for Violet to make the first of those moves.

After a moment he noticed that she was taking inordinately long to do it.

She sighed, and her head tipped into her hand, which received it as though her palm had been carved specifically to fit her chin.

He waited.

And waited.

And wait—

He frowned. Leaned across the board slowly, tentatively . . . and peered. A strand of dark hair clung to her lips. It was slowly, rhythmically fluttering. Her eyelids, which he'd thought downcast in thought . . . were closed. Her lashes shivered on her cheeks.

She'd fallen *asleep*!

Well!

He leaned back in his chair, greatly amused. He crossed his arms over his chest.

Apart from that wayward strand of hair, she still looked as though she'd stepped out of a toilette presided over by French maids. Was this neatness a skill or an aberration? Somehow Violet Redmond didn't seem *mussable*, and mussability, in his opinion, was critical to the sensual appeal of any woman. And she wasn't one of those women who looked innocent in their sleep, despite that strand of soft hair fluttering over that decidedly lush mouth. He couldn't imagine her ever being *restful*, the sort of woman who could soothe as well as pleasure a man, and Fatima excelled at this. Even now, Violet Redmond's eyelashes shivered against the pale blue skin beneath her eyes as though they could barely contain the rush of foolish plans.

He could almost pity the Redmond men, for surely keeping her restrained was a battle they'd been destined to lose.

He was wickedly tempted to allow gravity to have its way with her. There would be some satisfaction in seeing her face drift inexorably down toward the chessboard, in imagining her awakening the next morning with an imprint of a rook on her cheek and the drool of sleep gluing her to the board.

Mussed, in other words.

She breathed in . . . breathed out.

Breathed in . . . breathed out.

Breathed in . . . breathed—

Bloody hell. He drew in a sharp breath. Puffed it out forcefully. And slid his chair quietly back and stood.

He didn't want her to wake up with a rook print on her check.

This realization irritated him. Could the Swedish fjords, for instance, claim any responsibility for their own majesty, for the respect they inspired? Or were they just made that way?

Violet Redmond was just made that way.

There was something about her inherent dignity he felt

compelled to honor, as though some atavistic servile quality in him responded to her centuries of breeding.

It didn't make him happy. But there it was.

He took another deep fortifying breath and bent low enough to scoop an arm behind her calves, and he got the other across her bent shoulders, and with some maneuvering he managed, awkwardly, to heave the sleeping woman up over one of his shoulders.

Oh God. The scent of her hair swamped his senses like sensual laudanum, induced a brief delicious paralysis. Her arms flopped down his back and her fingertips dangled tantalizingly across his arse, inconveniently reminding him of how long it had been since any woman's fingertips had dangled over any sensitive parts of his body and communicating vivid suggestions to his groin. She muttered something irritably then—it *sounded* like "Lavay." Surely not.

He forced himself to move. And his arm wrapped tightly around her deliciously female thighs, he hastened as quietly as he could across the room. For the duration of those three swift steps his deprived senses nearly shrieked "WOMAN! You're holding a *WOMAN!* For God's sake, you fool, a woman!" and lunged like chained dogs to savor how she felt, how she smelled, and it was everything he could do to keep his hands from wandering over his cargo.

But he'd known worse temptations. He wasn't a boy.

And he deposited her on the bed—*his* bed—quickly and gently, rather the way one would deposit a grenade. She sighed and murmured and frowned, but her eyelids never lifted and her head tipped to the right and her mouth dropped open slightly.

He'd seldom seen a sleep so abandoned.

Bloody foolish girl, he thought with an invigorating surge of fury. He ought to call all the Redmond men out. Who had been so misguided as to allow her to take protection for granted, given her wild spirit, to *trust* so? She was so exhausted she'd fallen asleep in front of a strange man who was hardly harmless. Who was perfectly capable of making love to a woman he disliked to satisfy a physical urge. Of skillfully persuading any reluctant woman that she *wanted* him to do precisely that.

He was a man, after all, and it was how *men* were made.

He backed away from her, eager for the door. His hand was on the knob when he paused, shoulders slumping. He sighed. He turned. And took himself back to the chessboard.

And with two fingers, flicked his queen over onto her back.

Miss Redmond would see it when she woke the next morning. She'd discover he'd known the outcome of the game. And if she were clever enough, she'd understand that no matter *what* she did, he would always know what her next move would be.

"Checkmate," he whispered dryly to himself.

And he took himself off to sleep in the vole hole.

Chapter 7

Violet awoke abruptly, but long moments passed before she understood she wasn't still dreaming. She recognized at once that she was fully clothed and swaying gently, as though a giant cradle held her. Startled, she fisted her hands in the counterpane to ascertain it was real, found it already warmed from sunlight pushing in through a blinded window. She saw strips of blue through the blinds. *Sky.* The rocking was caused by the *sea*. She was on . . . a ship.

Good God, she really *was* on a ship! Because of *Lyon*.

She took her first tentative breath, and the scent of the room was so overpoweringly, stimulatingly, foreign and masculine—smoke and cloves and starch and bay rum and sea and sweat—she sat bolt upright. Panicked. Which was when she discovered parts of her body were stiff from the unfamiliar mattress and that she'd kicked off one of her slippers during the night.

She peered beyond her feet, one slippered, one not, and saw in the room's filtered light a fine mirror reflecting a startled, sleep-flushed woman hanging above a fine low chest of drawers laid out with men's toiletries. In the corner was a washbasin perched on a washstand, with towels hung near. On one wall was a small fine painting of an exotic landscape—tawny beaches and fronded trees, mountains and small whitewashed houses; on another a great map was pinned; on another a dartboard. Two small, beautiful carpets, also exotic, in shades of ruby and cream covered the floors. Elegantly simple room, almost Spartan, and she suspected the things in it had been carefully chosen from his travels. She was suddenly reminded of Lyon taking only his rosewood box when he'd disappeared.

At the far end was a shelf of books she longed to inspect; near her were the two sturdy-backed chairs flanking a table upon which was . . .

Ah, yes. The *chessboard.*

Memory shifted into place in a backward rush when she saw the earl's black queen lying prone as surely as if she'd been shot down.

Well.

She smiled slowly, and a surge of triumph and pleasure flushed her cheeks with warmth. He'd known she was about to win. Ha! He possessed enough honor to both acknowledge it and maintain the spirit of their agreement, too.

This was something of a surprise.

The smile faded as something occurred to her:

How did she get to the bed?

She didn't recall a thing.

She frantically patted at herself and to reassure herself that her clothing was indeed on and fastened, then leaped to her feet to have a good poke around.

The ceiling was so low she felt both penned and securely enclosed. Her head didn't brush the ceiling, but the earl probably crouched a bit to move around this room.

She disentangled herself from her bonnet strings and tried to massage some shape back into her poor slept-upon bonnet. She unpinned her hair in the mirror the captain no doubt used every morning. She pulled the hairpins from her hair, where they poked up out of it at odd angles, raked her fingers through it, twisted it up, and re-pinned it with breathtaking speed and efficiency, which would have to do until she was able to return to her trunk in the vole hole for a good hundred strokes with her brush. She knuckled kernels of sleep from her eyes, shook out her dress and patted it down, and inserted her foot into her slipper.

Now she could prowl.

First she studied the landscape; it was likely meaningful to the earl, she suspected, as it was the only picture in the room. She wandered over to where the mysterious male toiletries were lined, and after only a moment's hesitation, lifted up his shaving soap for a sniff. She was just rediscovering the tantalizing whiff of the earl she'd had when he'd leaned in during the waltz when a knock at the door startled her, and her hands clamped suddenly. The soap shot from her hands and flew across the room, skidding to a halt under the bed.

Bloody hell.

"It's Lord Lavay, Miss Redmond, with a breakfast for you."

Lavay! The prospect of conversation with a handsome, easily charmed man cheered her, and the moment she heard the word *breakfast* her stomach whined like a punished mongrel. She dove for the soap and patted fruitlessly beneath the bed, but it remained out of reach. She gave up when he knocked again, and flew to the door and opened it.

Lavay took evident pleasure in just looking at her. Those gray eyes glowed in silent, subtle masculine approval. In other words, he didn't appear to be about to lose himself in a frenzy of animalistic behavior.

"Good morning, Lord Lavay." She curtsied. "I imagine the captain informed you I was aboard. Thank you so much for thinking of me. You are too kind."

Violet took the tray from him. A domed tureen perched on top of it. She looked around the cabin for a spot to place it, and decided to carefully settle it next to the chessboard.

When she did, the fallen queen rolled a bit, as though suffering a stomachache. Violet didn't yet want to right it; it reminded her of victory.

"Oh, yes. And Corcoran has been spreading your legend among the men on the ship. You'd think a mermaid had come up in one of the nets. We came to fisticuffs in the galley over who would have the honor of bringing breakfast to you, and I won."

"Fisticuffs?" This sounded ominous. It was precisely what the captain had predicted. Good God, she'd *already* laid his crew low. She surreptitiously inspected Lavay for bruising. "And yet . . . you won?"

Mr. Lavay laughed. "Your skepticism wounds me to the very soul, Miss Redmond! Very well. I'll confess the crew recalled my rank just as the discussion was growing heated. I apologize if I led you to believe you may have caused bloodshed."

Bloodshed! It was likely the one thing in her life she hadn't yet caused.

She supposed there was still time.

"Fear not, Mr. Lavay. I suspect I shall rapidly recover from my shock," she said gravely.

Which made him smile slowly. "You're not shocked at all."

She returned his smile. Freshly taking his measure. Approving his insight and his humor. *Oily*, Jonathan had called him. Jonathan was likely simply envious. She found him just as elegant and unforced as when she'd first danced with him. He showed no signs of influencing her breathing or her temper the way the earl did.

Still . . . she recalled her profoundly self-contained brother Miles throwing a fist into Argosy's face in the name of love. And of her brother Lyon vanishing and possibly taken to pirating. Reckless extremes and absurd behavior always seemed to accompany love.

Perhaps she was immune to love.

She wasn't certain whether or not she was relieved at this notion.

"I find it intriguing that we should meet again under these circumstances," he added. A leading statement to be sure. An invitation to expound. And how *different* this was from the captain's relentless interrogation.

As if the thought of him conjured him, they both whirled guiltily at the sound of booted feet rapidly heading their way.

Seconds later something like an eclipse fell across the doorway.

"Good morning. I trust you slept comfortably, Miss Redmond."

The earl's voice was formal, bass, and brisker than a carafe of coffee poured down one's gullet. It was the sort of voice that pulled spines straighter, would get a man's head swiveling guiltily in search of work to do. She could only imagine the effect it had on his crew, since her head swiveled, too, and she had no intention of doing any work. Lavay, spine immediately straight, bowed crisply.

She didn't think for an instant the earl cared very much how well she slept.

"I slept well, thank you for asking. Did . . . you?" she couldn't resist adding cheekily.

He frowned repressively. He looked none the worse for his night in the vole hole; he was flawlessly groomed, bright-eyed, tight-jawed. He needed a shave. The shadow of whiskers suited him. Made his eyes bluer, somehow. Like windows out onto the ocean.

He glanced a question at the domed platter of food.

"Lord Lavay was gentleman enough to bring a breakfast to me."

"He certainly is a gentleman," the earl agreed, in a tone that implied she'd instead called Lavay a "son of a bitch" and he quite concurred. "Lavay, you have duties to see to." His crisp captain's intonation made it clear that Miss Redmond fell distinctly into the category of "pleasures."

"Of course, sir. I simply thought to relieve you of the burden of feeding our guest."

An interesting, infinitesimal pause followed. The two men regarded each other evenly. Lavay was about the same height as the earl, but he hadn't the earl's air of arrogance and impatience, which was why in part he seemed to take up more than his fair share of air.

The ship gave a sway, sending the soap sliding gracefully out from under the bed. It came to rest at the earl's feet, as if eager to join the conversation.

He stared down at it. Clearly bemused. He bent to pick it up. Hefted it in his hand.

Then stared at Violet, eyebrows arched sardonically.

She gave him wide-eyed innocence.

"She's not a guest, Mr. Lavay. She's an invader as surely as a pirate or a termite, and we shall relieve ourselves of the burden, as you say, of her soon enough."

Good heavens. This sounded ominous. Perhaps he'd decided to cast her overboard, anyway, thanks to an unpleasant night's sleep.

Another silence, during which expressions remained impassive but she sensed Lavay was somewhat surprised. She waited breathlessly to see if he would step gallantly into the breach.

"A . . . termite?" The traitor was clearly *amused*.

Flint's mood, however, matched his name. "We shall of course extend to Miss Redmond all courtesy and respect due her station for the duration of her stay, which will be until we reach the next port. Which means two days, if the wind remains fair. I trust those are *your* rations, Mr. Lavay, you've donated to her breakfast?"

Said with almost no inflection. But the abrupt silence was

the sound of Lavay's surprise. She sensed Flint had meant a jab, though she didn't fully understand why.

"I took up a collection from among the crew," Mr. Lavay volunteered smoothly. "It's a combination, shall we say, of everyone's morning rations."

This was likely a lie, but Violet admired it immensely, and smiled at Lavay encouragingly.

"We do not issue rations in fractions. We'll deduct her breakfast from your rations," the earl said briskly. As if solving a problem of interest to everyone.

Violet had the curious sensation that entire portions of the conversation were somehow magically being held out of her earshot via steely male stares and shared personal history.

"Perhaps you need to take a double portion of rations this morning, Captain Flint, as your mood calls to mind a hibernating bear awakened well before spring."

Said with that smooth, exquisite politeness, but barbed all around as chestnut pods.

Surprisingly, only a short silence followed. The earl didn't immediately challenge Lavay to a duel.

"Thank you for your suggestion, Mr. Lavay. I shall take it under advisement," he said surprisingly easily. "Please meet me on the foredeck at half past the hour to discuss our supply circumstances and the charts. You will excuse me, as I now need a word with our . . . guest."

Captains, it was to be expected, always had the last word. Not to mention captains who also happened to be earls.

"Thank you again for seeing to my breakfast," Violet said hurriedly, before Lavay, her ally, departed.

"My sincere pleasure, Miss Redmond." He left behind his charm like a sparkly little gift, then Lord Lavay bowed with swift elegance, to both of them, and Violet curtsied.

She was alone with the earl.

"Why don't you eat your breakfast whilst I shave, Miss Redmond? It's porridge. "

It was really more of an order than a suggestion. Like as not he spoke to everyone in just that tone.

Violet lifted the dome and peered beneath.

It was indeed porridge. Accompanied by what appeared to be a pale rock. She poked the rock. It rolled on the tray. She sniffed the porridge. It had virtually no scent. Unless *beige* could be considered a scent.

A mug of tea alongside both smelled mercifully familiar. She sipped it first. It was bracingly black and bitter as a punishment. There was nothing with which to sweeten it. She didn't mind in the least. She sipped at it and shuddered as it surged its way through her veins. Very reviving.

"Haven't you a valet?" she said to the earl, surprised.

He threw a baleful sideways glance at her as he strode across the room with the soap in hand. " 'Haven't you a *valet*?' " he mimicked girlishly under his breath, shaking his head. He ducked slightly to avoid brushing his head on the ceiling, and peeled off his coat, folding it neatly and placing it over the back of a chair, and rolled up his sleeves, revealing hard brown forearms covered in coppery hair. He splashed his face with basin water. He twirled the brush into the soap vigorously then painted the bottom half of his face with soap. He whisked the razor up and tugged his cheek taut, and scraped the blade over it.

Violet spooned in porridge. She tried not to stare. Watching a man casually take off his coat and then whiskers seemed almost as intimate as watching him disrobe completely.

The porridge was nearly flavorless, though perhaps a bit of bacon fat had been stirred in. The rock, she finally concluded, was a sort of bread. It was about the size of her fist. She hefted it gingerly in one hand and tapped it with the finger of the other. It even sounded very like a rock.

He watched her experiment with the food in his mirror as he shaved.

"Likely the weevils were cooked from it before it was brought to you. They stalk off the bread when it's heated, you know. Disgruntled, I imagine, at the indignity of being so treated."

She froze. Her fingers loosened in horror on the bread, which suddenly seemed alive and pulsing. She would rather have died than drop it, however.

"Do you fire these from cannons at enemies?"

Insulting it would have to do.

"When we're out of shot," he said easily. "They taste a bit like mustard," he said cheerily. "Weevils do. Can't harm you if you bite into one. So tuck in."

Tuck in. How American he sounded.

She held the thing gingerly. She cleared her throat.

"How did I get to the bed?"

"Well, of a certainty you levitated, Miss Redmond. Angels such as yourself would surely never do anything so gauche as *walk* to the bed."

He turned as he said this, patting his face dry. His eyes glinted a wicked blue above the towel. He pulled the towel down, drying his hands, hiked one brow, unabashedly enjoying her discomfiture. Shrugged at her silence; conversation was of no consequence to him.

The hard angles of his face were even more pronounced now that they'd been polished clean of whiskers.

He'd carried her to the bed, and yet she couldn't remember it. She looked down, disoriented by a rush of blood to her head, imagining herself dead to the world, at his mercy in that moment, she who had truly never been at anyone's mercy. Had he slung her over his shoulder like a sack, or carried her in his arms, in the manner of fainting maidens hauled out to the garden during ton crushes?

The sharp, masculine scent of whisked shaving soap was now everywhere in the room, a sensual assault. But then, for some reason every one of her senses seemed heightened; every impression—sight, sound, smell—leaped out at her in stark relief now. She was strangely, startlingly conscious of her physical self and of his physical self.

He turned back to the mirror, deftly folded the towel, cleaned his brush and razor, set them aside. Somehow he imbued even these small acts with regimented authority and purpose, and yet they were so homely and intimate it was profoundly clear he didn't care in the least that she was watching.

She, in other words, didn't signify in his world. She would cease to be his problem soon enough, is how he viewed it.

She had other plans.

He rolled down the sleeves of his shirt and those hard brown forearms disappeared. He slid into his coat and buttoned it. Every inch the master and commander of this ship.

Wicked man. *Very* unlike Mr. Lavay.

He said, "Eat the rest of your bread, Miss Redmond. Lest you want Mr. Lavay's empty belly on your conscience. Rations are apportioned according to the number of crew members aboard, they are indeed finite, they cost money and weigh down the ship, and we all eat the same food. Nothing more will be forthcoming until lunch."

He watched her impatiently.

She resisted with difficulty the impelling force of his order. Something about his sense of command communicated somehow to one's reflexes more quickly than one's brain. She lifted the bread up. She imagined weevil corpses speckling it the way currents dotted a Christmas pudding. *Mustard,* she thought.

She stared at him defiantly. She opened her mouth.

And sank her teeth in.

Or tried. On first attempt, they merely skated across the surface.

She tried again.

In this manner she cracked the top of it in increments. Her molars finally got some purchase after she nearly unhinged her jaw.

She was finally forced to tear into it with a great undignified toss of her head. Like a dog with a chop.

She came away with a piece dangling from her lips. It flapped indecorously about her chin, until she darted out her tongue to fetch it in.

He watched all of this as avidly as though she were a pantomime he'd paid good money to see. His eyes glinted unholy hilarity.

"Are you going to chew?" he asked mildly.

She put up one finger: *momentarily.* She began the process of chewing. Her jaw clicked with the effort, like a wagon wheel struggling over rutted roads.

Mercifully flavorless, that lump. A bit like gnawing soggy paper. And not even a hint of mustard.

After three or four chews, she reached for her tea, and gulped it down. Where it sat in her stomach, solid as a fist.

"Don't forget to finish the rest. You can dip it in porridge or tea, you know, to soften it."

Now he decided to mention it.

"Thank you for the timely suggestion. But I might wish to . . ." *Hurl it at your smug face.* ". . . save it for later."

"Suit yourself. I'll have Corcoran bring a jug of heated water into your quarters so you can perform your own ablutions if you wish, Miss Redmond. I'll remind you once again that these are *my* quarters. You'll return to yours and stay there until I decide what to do with you. I'll escort you to them now, but you will not be up on deck without an escort, and I cannot spare a man to *mind* you at all times."

She placed her tray carefully aside, taking great care not to disturb the chessboard. And cleared her throat.

"I should like to discuss the continuation of my journey on *The Fortuna*."

"Under no circumstances will you stay beyond the next port," he said absently, shooting the cuffs on his coat.

"Captain Flint. I was quite serious when I said I believed you were in pursuit of my brother."

"If by 'serious' you mean 'delusional,' then I'm inclined to believe you, Miss Redmond." He was already at the door, hand on the knob.

"How long has Le Chat been capturing ships and stealing cargo?" she asked desperately.

He paused. "Over the span of a year."

"And why has no one definitively identified Hardesty as Le Chat?"

The earl was brisk and rote. "The evidence we have is circumstantial. A resemblance, a description of his ship, Mr. Hardesty's appearance in ports from where the pirated ships have sailed; he has the same knowledge of the cargo, and then the ships are attacked by night with a small crew when Hardesty is said to have sailed away. A woman said he muttered about *The Olivia* in his sleep. Someone reported that Hardesty sold silks allegedly stolen from one of the sunken ships."

She didn't like the idea of Lyon muttering in his sleep next to a strange woman. "And he looks like my brother Jonathan."

The earl waited impatiently.

"Here is my suggestion. I can assure you that my brother Lyon is fiercely protective. If he is indeed Le Chat, and word reaches him that you have his sister in custody and are considering . . ."

She seemed unable to choose the most appropriately appalling word.

"Defiling her?" he suggested brightly.

"If you wish."

"You're not a blusher, are you, Miss Redmond?"

She ignored this. "If you do suggest it, you may be able to flush him out. As Lyon would never tolerate it."

"At which point, when he is flushed out, you shout and wave, 'Run, Lyon! Run for your life!' "

She sighed impatiently. "He's much cleverer than that. He survived my father, you know."

"Not to mention *you*. Or is that why he fled?"

She ignored him. "If it is indeed Lyon, *I'll* find him and extract an explanation from him about why he's gone and if he is indeed doing what you allege, and at which point he'll explain to you that what he's about isn't what you think it is. The pirating. Because I know my brother, Captain Flint, and I know there's more to this than meets the eye. He hadn't gone mad and simply begun stealing and sinking ships."

Though a tiny part of her wasn't one hundred percent certain of this.

It changed nothing at all, however, such was the nature of her loyalty.

"I don't know how in God's name it could be anything other than what it appears to be. He boards ships, seizes cargo, and sinks them. Seems simple enough to me. The motive is generally greed and opportunity."

"But has anyone been killed in the process? Does he blow up the ships with men *aboard*?"

He hesitated. "He puts men in boats and sends them out to sea. As much as the cargo as possible is seized and transferred to his ship, *The Olivia*. Not all of the men have been rescued or reached shore before their supplies ran out, which means some here nearly perished. And not every man has been found, either."

"What manner of cargo has been seized?"

"Rice. Cotton. Silk several times. Tea twice."

"Captain Flint. Here is what we know. My brother Jonathan could be the twin of this Mr. Hardesty. And he resembles Lyon closely. The pirate's name is Le Chat. Is not a lion a big cat? Perhaps this is no coincidence. Perhaps it's a . . . message of some sort? And his ship is named *The Olivia*. I don't believe you can afford to ignore these clues, Captain, circumstantial or no, since your charge is to find him."

A great exasperated breath filled his lungs. She watched with fascination as his big chest swelled like sails, then sank again in a sigh.

"Miss Redmond, you simply . . . can't sail with us. I cannot allow it. For one, I would wager you know nothing of the world. I've been nearly everywhere on that map. You've *no* sense of the rigors of sea travel, you're bound to starve because the food is vile, you'll take ill because you'll never get a decent night's rest in the vole hole because I can assure you that's where you *will* be sleeping, one of the men is bound to offend you greatly, another is bound to at least attempt to *defile* you, and do tell me the farthest you've been away from home?"

She hesitated.

"Italy," she mumbled.

"Oh! *Italy. That* heathen land."

She glared at him.

"You will be a hindrance, Miss Redmond. Evidence or no, you are ballast now, and we must be shed of you posthaste."

Violet was not so easily deterred.

"Even *you* once had a first voyage. I have not yet been seasick, Captain."

"There is time," he said with grim cheer.

"I can choke dow—that is, happily eat whatever rations are made available. I shall pay for my accommodations on *The Fortuna* if you wish. I am made of sterner stuff than you think."

His slow, thorough look seemed to count her eyelashes and her hairpins, to take in the unscuffed toes of her slippers, her flawless, straight hem unsullied by dust or mud, every perfect, tidy stitch in her expensively tailored dress, every tender, creamy unblemished inch of exposed skin, which was indeed only her clavicle upward but which immediately heated as though he'd drawn his hand across the tops of her bosom.

It was a look both instructive and purely frivolous. He was making a point, and he was taking his inventory of her as a woman.

He, of a certainty, didn't find her wanting.

He did, however, find her superfluous and absurd.

"Nonsense," he concluded. His voice was strangely gentle. "You are not made of sterner stuff, Miss Redmond. But as you have pointed out to me, you do not need to be. I should not, if I were you, *wish* to be, because 'sterner stuff' is usually forged by hardship. Besides, every land has its own customs, Miss Redmond, and you are entirely accustomed to shaping the world to suit *you*. You would adapt poorly. And we don't know yet where our travels will take us, or how far. We might end up in darkest Africa."

He could very well be right about all of it. Odd to discover how desperately she hated losing, however.

She glanced at the little painting on the wall. "Isn't that Africa?"

A triumphant flare in his eyes. With a sinking feeling, she realized she'd just proved his point.

"Morocco. The home of my mistress, Fatima."

Fatima. His mistress. She was not so worldly she could hear this without blinking. Or without a rogue violent wave of curiosity that contained a bit of jealousy.

She was certain he knew, too. And yet he continued watching her with that maddening air of detached patience.

"I know more of geography than you think," she lied desperately.

"Oh, a scholar, are you?" He was distantly amused now. He

knew she was lying. His fingers dandled over the doorknob thoughtfully, longingly, she thought, as he studied her.

All of a sudden his eyes brightened with a speculative light that made her wary. He'd apparently had an inspiration, because he wandered over to the globe perched on its stand, ran his fingers over it.

And then he pulled open his bureau drawer and came out with a fistful of pointed feathered objects.

So *that* was where he kept his darts.

"Since you think you can travel the world, Miss Redmond, I have a proposition. Close your eyes and throw a dart at the map. I have been nearly everywhere a dart may possibly strike. If you can tell me two salient facts about the place your dart lands—be it land or sea—you can sleep in the captain's quarters again tonight, you may come ashore with us at the next port to meet with our contacts there, and I shall not leave you there ten pounds poorer than you were when you boarded."

"Ten pounds! It was five pounds yesterday!"

"We know at least your arithmetic isn't faulty. I've decided to up the ante, Miss Redmond—the ante is upped, for we will have *fed* you"—he spared an ironic glance for the lump of bread in her fist—"and housed you for additional days, as well as seen to your comfort, and I will have spent more patience upon you than I feel I can reasonably afford. And by 'salient' I mean some fact unique to the place. Not 'the inhabitants build their own dwellings' or 'the sun comes up in the morning.' Specifics, please. And if you fail, you will sleep in the vole hole and I will abandon you at the next port in the manner I have previously described, sans escort. I am busy. And I am weary of games."

She stared at the map stretched out across the wall, a big beige geometry of continents and islands speckling the vast open space of a sea.

In seconds she knew hope was lost.

Chapter 8

It wasn't that she wasn't intelligent. God only knew she could outthink most of the men and women of her acquaintance. It was just that the need to do so arose very, very seldom in the ton. She preferred to collect knowledge as needed rather than hoard it indiscriminately and spill it forth at the slightest provocation the way her brother Miles did. She liked to think that learning as she *went* added a frisson of excitement to daily life.

She still recalled her governess's undisguised eye-roll when she presented this as a defense against doing her lessons.

She stared hard at the map until it began to blur before her eyes, and understood all too well what he meant her to: he was master and commander of this ship, which meant the world she saw before her was *his* world, and he guessed—rightly, as it turned out, though she wasn't about to admit this to him—that she wouldn't be able to tell him the first thing about any of it apart from the insular, glittering world of the ton and everyone in Pennyroyal Green.

The Mediterranean Sea, Tunisia, Scotland, Morocco—where his *mistress* lived . . . oddly, she knew an errant impulse to hurl a dart *hard* into Morocco simply for the pleasure of it . . . a sea of words.

And then suddenly a word throbbed at her from the sea of all the other foreign words.

Lacao.

She froze. *That* bloody word was *seared* into her brain.

Her brother Miles, the explorer, had inadvertently become all the rage in ton circles after he'd returned from an expedition to Lacao, where butterflies as big as silk fans and snakes as thick around as . . . well, as the earl's biceps . . . dropped onto passersby unexpectedly from trees and affectionate women who apparently wore nothing at all above their waists greeted men with enthusi—

Well, well, well.

Hope yawned, stretched, and sprang from its coffin.

She stared at the word until it seemed to ripple in the parchment sea. So she possessed the facts. All she needed now was *aim*.

It was something the male Redmonds seemed to be born with. Jonathan had won the darts tournament at the Pig & Thistle, and he'd been as proud of that trophy as he would have if he'd brought down a three-pronged buck. Miles could blow a tiny apple to smithereens with a musket at fifty paces. Lyon excelled at swordsmanship and musketry, and had won competitions year after year. And her father had won Sussex shooting competitions, too . . . when some Eversea or another wasn't winning them.

No one was eager to hand *both* Jacob Eversea and Isaiah Redmond guns while they stood within twenty feet of each other.

The earl continued encouragingly as she stared at the map. "The wind is still fair and should be through the day. I expect we'll reach port by tomorrow morning."

He made a great show of thumbing his watch open, reviewing the time, tucking it back into his pocket. He threw a yearning glance at the door. A glance back at her. *I have vastly better things to do than converse with you, Miss Redmond.* Widened his eyes ironically.

Her eyes shot to the southern corner of the map, where she supposed England ought to be, and considered the long perilous journey homeward if she had to manage it herself. She was furious that the earl was correct. She would be disgraced and humiliated . . . if she made it home alive, that was. *Miles* could travel the world and become celebrated; she would become a pariah for her escapade, because surely her journey home would outlast her lie about the fortnight house party.

And then she thought of Lyon. Who might be on the high seas, and whom this large dangerous man avidly pursued.

It wasn't madness. She had to try.

She held out her hand for a dart. Winged her eyebrows up with a nonchalance she was far from feeling.

That mountain range of a shoulder lifted in a shrug and he handed it over. The pointed metal tip seemed to wink conspiratorially in the light. The other end featured what appeared to be a small fluff of split pheasant feathers.

God only knew how one hurled the little missile. She fingered it, as if its heft alone could reveal its secrets to her. She was a fair shot in archery; then again, firing arrows at large targets while one's eyes were closed was discouraged, lest one skewer wandering peacocks or footmen.

The earl gestured to the map with his chin. "Go on, then. And remember: you need to do it with your eyes closed."

The evil man sounded *so* pleased with himself.

She gripped her barbed missile with dampening palms. She silently made rash promises about future good behavior to every god she could remember, including the ones from her lessons in Latin and Greek, and apologized to the gods she may have forgotten, just to be safe.

Lacao. She stared at the name on the map.

She closed her eyes, inhaled extravagantly, drew her arm up. Exhaled. Took another breath for propulsion . . . jerked her hand . . .

. . . and shot the dart forward as if the word *Lacao* were prey about to bolt.

Thunk.

A ringing quiet followed. During which she knew a moment of fear that the *"thunk"* had been the sound of the dart striking the earl straight through the heart through that great wall of a chest.

Her eyelids furled up slowly. That whooshing sound in her ears was surely her heart hammering the blood violently on its journey through her body.

The dart was vibrating dead center in the *O* of Lacao.

Thank goodness for full skirts. Her knees had gone watery and began to bow. She locked them before they could betray her with a sway.

She stared at her triumphant throw, admiring it passionately. She tried to look deeply concerned rather than relieved to the threshold of losing consciousness.

"La . . . cayo?" She deliberately mangled the pronunciation and wrinkled her brow in feigned consternation. Then pressed her fingers against it to smooth it out. There were only so many sacrifices she was willing to make for this charade, and forehead wrinkles were not among them.

"La*cao*," he corrected somberly. "Rhymes with 'cow.' Tiny South American country."

"I can see it's in South America," she replied with convincing testiness. She drummed her fingers against her chin thoughtfully. "Have . . . have *you* visited it?"

"I have indeed. I was a boy on my first voyage on *The Steadfast*. I'll never, ever forget it. Please don't stall, Miss Redmond." He was impatient now. Impersonal.

But the word *boy—Thunk—*unexpectedly pierced her like a dart. Shocking and disorienting, as it didn't seem a word one would ever associate with him: surely he'd sprung from the sea, fully formed and immoveable as Gibraltar. And yet she suddenly saw him as he must have been: gangly, toffee-haired, tender-faced, those blue eyes saucer-sized with wonder at the sight of half-dressed women and the snakes and butterflies, ordered about by other men—imagining *him* following orders was a stretch, indeed—and thought: what a marvelous thing to be a boy and to have seen that.

Why had he been a boy on a voyage?

Had he ever been afraid? Worried about the food? Impossible to imagine.

"Miss Redmond. I can see you're enjoying a reverie of some sort, but would you kindly share what you know—or confess to what you don't know—about Lacao?"

"Ah. Mmm. Well . . . perhaps there are . . ." she allowed her eyes to wander across the ceiling, as if desperately searching for inspiration there ". . . *butterflies* . . . in Lacao?" She bit down on her bottom lip as though the guess worried her terribly.

Then she brought her gaze down again and looked up at him through her lashes.

There followed a silence. During which the very air in the room seemed to shift, like spectators at a boxing match realigning allegiances after recognizing the inevitable winner.

He narrowed his blue gaze. "Perhaps."

"*Blue* . . . butterflies?" She shyly nibbled the tip of her little finger for effect now.

His spine went mizzen mast stiff. His stare was decidedly competitive now.

"Yes," he admitted curtly, after a moment. "There are blue butterflies in Lacao. Tell me more."

"Mmm!" She nodded, demurely pleased and surprised.

His eyes narrowed even further and he beamed suspicion at her.

"Blue butterflies the size of . . . silk fans, or thereabouts?" She held her hands apart to illustrate. "Iridescent shades of blue and purple and green in the sun, but *primarily* blue?"

She looked up at him hopefully. Eyes as wide and innocent as a spring sky.

He looked at the space between her hands, and up into her wide hopeful eyes.

And there was another hesitation. "Yes."

The word was strangely muffled. Was he trying not to laugh? Or was he choking on his pride? His eyes glinted some complex emotion. *Some* of it was amusement.

"Would you like to know their Latin name?" she offered brightly. "It's *Morpho He—*"

"Oh no, that won't be necessary, Miss Redmond. But *thank* you for offering. Why don't you tell me the next thing you know about Lacao? The next salient thing. And quickly." He folded his arms across his chest.

They regarded each other across the chessboard the room had once again become.

When deciding upon the next fact she could bring forth of the many she possessed, Violet, naturally, considered strategy. She stared at that great arrogant insurmountable wall of a man, and that felt that familiar fizzing of recklessness, that childlike impulse to conquer what wasn't meant to be conquered. She wanted to jar loose that veneer of distance and arrogance.

She wanted him to see *her.*

"Well," she said, her eyes wide, her face the picture of innocence, but her voice soft, soft as dusk, which made his expression instantly and almost comically wary and reluctantly very interested, "I've heard that the women who live there walk about nude above the waist. Breasts ex*posed* to the world."

She actually *saw* his breath stop.

Heard the surprised catch of it, as though it was his turn to take a dart to the chest. Saw the quick flare in his pupils, like a nova bursting, dispersing.

And then his posture gradually eased, and something

dangerously speculative settled in his gaze. She remembered this look from the moment at the ball. She was certain he was imagining her in his bed doing some of the *work*, as it were. And wondered yet again why she'd wanted to court it. This wasn't the calf-eyed wonder in which she'd routinely basked in London. It was something much more sophisticated and perilous. It was carnal intent, stirred then tamped of necessity. But still simmering there beneath the surface.

The man was indeed a savage.

He did *not* enjoy being baited.

And yet he couldn't help but respond to her voice and to her words. Because he was a man, and she was a woman, and words like *naked* and *breasts* were conjuring words as surely as *abracadabra* and no doubt he was picturing her right now walking about wearing nothing above her waist.

I can take you whenever I please.

He took a step toward her. And stopped. Close enough for her to smell him again. Suddenly the image of him shaving with that sharp soap was poignant.

And as they regarded each other, the air changed again. Became dense as opium smoke, each breath Violet took now a pleasure and struggle, as anticipation of consequences, be they fatal or something more interesting, made her breathing shallow. Once again she was in far deeper than she knew how to navigate, and there was no escaping, only surviving, only negotiating, only maneuvering.

She was aware that she liked this feeling far more than she ought to.

Almost as much as she feared it.

"Why yes," he said evenly, softly. "It *is* true the women in Lacao wear nothing at all above their waists for clothes, Miss Redmond."

He smiled then. It was a slow, faint, knowing smile and she felt it peculiar places: at the back of her neck, as surely as though his finger had delicately drawn a curve in the same of that smile there. As one of those blue butterflies fluttering low in her belly. As a finger touched lightly to her nipples, which were markedly alert.

He was seeing her, all right.

Right *through* her.

Bloody hell.

This was maddening! Why, why, *why* did she want him to *admire* her? Perhaps because she'd never before needed to *earn* admiration. She'd never even craved it, as it had been in the very air she breathed since she was born, and likely only character-tempering sibling disdain and the occasional terrifyingly quelling looks from her father's cold emerald eyes saved her from becoming completely unbearable. And she suspected that despite what the invocation of half-naked women might do to any man's imagination, what the earl reluctantly admired was her *strategy*. Not her dusky lashes and sweet curves and all the other nonsense about which young men had yammered to her while feverishly gripping her fingers during a waltz. All the things the Earl of Ardmay could doubtless take or leave, as he'd seen it before, on dozens of continents, on dozens of women.

She sighed heavily in defeat, even though she'd won.

He grinned another of those beautifully lethal grins. Perversely, *now* the bloody man seemed charmed.

"Very well, I'll take the bait, Miss Redmond," he said, dismissing the topic of topless women, his mood almost sunny now; then again, envisioning topless women could be what cheered him. "How do you know so much about an obscure little South American country like Lacao?"

"My brother is Mr. Miles Redmond. He's—"

"—the explorer? Mr. Miles Redmond?" His head went back in surprise. And then he laughed. A *wonderful* sound, huge and so warm it could coax crops out of barren ground.

"Of course! Well *played.*" He shook his head. "Minx." And the word was almost affectionate.

He strolled over to the bookshelf and retrieved a red leather-bound book, words etched in gold on it, and handed it to her with a flourish.

My Journey to Lacao, Volume I, by Miles Redmond.

She smiled wonderingly at it. Miles's reach encompassed all the world. His words had even wound up in the hands of the savage earl!

She traced her brother's name with a finger, a soft smile on her face. Missing him suddenly unbearably. Regretting what her absence would do to all of them, once they learned—if they learned—she wasn't in Northumberland at a house party after all.

She stubbornly ignored her conscience.

"I should have guessed at the relation," he said, his voice even, soft. He was watching her closely. "Didn't he almost lose his life there?"

She flinched. She jerked her head up, startled. Only to meet his steady, probing gaze.

She'd never heard it put quite like that before. *Didn't he almost lose his life?*

She didn't like it.

She stared at him warily, hesitated before answering. As if a hesitation would make it less true.

"Yes. First he almost died of a fever. And then he was almost eaten by cannibals."

These were things Miles had been glib about and had written and lectured about and which had contributed to his notoriety, but which, yes, added up to the fact that he may never have come home again. Despite the fact that Violet had of course taken for granted that he would, since until Miles had rather lost his mind to love but gained a wife recently, he'd been as solid as the cliffs of Dover.

"Perhaps it's why you remember everything about Lacao in particular, though Miles has traveled all over the world."

Oh.

He'd ambushed her with truth again.

Her breath left her in a shocked gust.

She was suddenly sharply angry in an unspecific way. She bit down on her lip to chase the temper away.

"Perhaps." The hand gripping the book fell to her side; the fingers of her other hand twisted in her skirt. And she *never* fidgeted. Particularly with clothing, as wrinkles might encroach. She stopped, closed her fingers tightly to discipline them.

Saw his eyes fly to her fingers and back to her face. He missed nothing. Like someone who'd needed to vigilantly defend his perimeter his entire life. He noticed; he collected facts; he stored them up the way soldiers stacked cannonballs or bricks for the building of fortresses or launching of attacks.

"He matters very much to you." It was a statement, not a question. "Your brother. Your family."

She'd been too forthcoming. He knew her family was both her strength and her Achilles heel. She would need to learn to become more circumspect for Lyon's sake.

"Why were *you* in Lacao as a boy? Did you see the blue butterflies?"

He smiled faintly for some reason, and only then did she hear the yearning in her voice: She would have liked to see the blue butterflies, too.

"I did indeed see the butterflies. Splendid creatures. Otherworldly, like something from a dream. I was serving aboard a ship called *The Steadfast* when we docked there. Captain Moreheart's ship."

"Serving? But you were . . . weren't you just a small boy?"

He stared at her, clearly bemused. Thinking. Then pressed his lips together, considering which end of that vast question he should grasp to begin answering it.

"Yes," was all he said, finally. Sounding as though he was humoring her with even that. With a small, maddening smile meant to imply that bridging the distance between her life and his was too tedious a conversational journey to contemplate. And the longer the conversation went on, the wider the gulf would become, and they would become like two people forever throwing ropes to each other across a chasm. And missing.

This could become very embarrassing, in other words.

Violet had never feared embarrassment. And as far as she was concerned, a defended perimeter merely invited breech attempts.

"But your mother . . ." She left the question dangling open. A door he could walk through if he chose.

He must have seen something akin to distress in her face. Otherwise she was certain it wasn't a question he would answer.

"My mother became ill from drink and could no longer care for me. So I went to *work*." He pronounced the last word ironically, like a tutor reminding a student of a freshly learned concept. "And ships . . . how could anyone resist the lure of a job on a ship?" He said this in all seriousness. Reminding her of her brother Miles and his passion for all the exotic things that crawled and flew, and she was visited again by a wave of guilt and homesickness, and a peculiar affection for the idiosyncrasies and specific passions of men. It made the one who stood before her seem human and almost—almost—*endearing*.

"Unfathomable," she agreed soberly.

It was a nautical joke. He smiled again, pleased and surprised. One day she might grow accustomed to his smiles, but for now each new one was like stumbling across an undiscovered constellation. She felt unequal to them.

And with this latest smile, something startlingly like ease crept into the room. She smiled, too, and with two of them beaming at each other the atmosphere became rather heady.

"But you were raised in America?"

"I was born in England. And by the laws of England I am a citizen. But I survived the voyage across the sea with my mother, and we settled in New York State for a time, until she . . . was no longer able to care for me. I was fortunate to be mentored by Captain Jeremiah Moreheart, who gave me a position as a cabin boy, and made sure I learned everything there is to learn about sailing. *He* mattered very much to me."

He smiled a little. To her astonishment, she thought she heard a sort of gentle solicitousness: He was instinctively trying to soften his otherness, to ease that hint of distress she'd been unable to disguise. To reassure her that, at one time, there were people in his life he cared for and who cared for him.

The confidence felt like a gift, and she felt a little shy about it. Odd, because she would truly have to wrack her brain to recall the last time she felt *awkward*. Or at loss.

This man was truly the very frontier of "awkward" for her.

"But shouldn't you like to live in England, since you are now an earl? We do like our nobleman there."

To her wonderment, they were officially having a conversation, complete with rhythm and ease. *But don't think about it.* It was like playing the pianoforte: If you looked at your hands whilst you played a tune you would become too conscious and lose your place in the song rather rapidly.

But for the first time in her life she was greedy to know things, anything, about a man.

"Your mother was English?"

"My mother was Irish, Cherokee Indian, and perhaps a few other things as well, but those are the things I know about. My father was English. So I've heard." Very dry, that sentence.

She tried not to look too fascinated, but it was a struggle. *Indian* blood swam in his veins. He was so nonchalant about his parentage, when parentage was the source of everything that made her who she was: her privilege, her security, everything she'd known or enjoyed.

"And when did you go to sea?"

"I went to sea at about age ten, and after that I lived—"

He stopped abruptly. He went still, his eyebrows diving a little. His eyes flared wide in wary surprise, perhaps at the fact that he'd been *enjoying* their exchange. Had lost himself in it.

And as though his goodwill was contained in an hourglass and the sands had run out, he waved vaguely at the map. "Everywhere. But mostly in America or at sea. I took my first command at eighteen."

I took my first command. How easily he said it. As it "taking" was his birthright, even as a parentless child.

His cool faint smile was a polite punctuation mark to their conversation. A shutter came down over his eyes. Likely he'd said all of this purposefully, because it splendidly did the job of re-erecting a wall and emphasizing the differences between them. Putting her in his place.

"Captain Moreheart was captain of *The Steadfast*, Miss Redmond."

And Le Chat had sunk that ship and killed the captain.

He smiled with faint irony.

"And now I must see to my ship. You may stay through the next port, Miss Redmond. From there I'll decide what becomes of you. You will stay below decks in the *vole hole* until informed you may walk above. I'll send Lavay to escort you there. And your aim is impeccable. Really quite shocking, in fact."

At least something had shocked him.

He was gone, closing the door none too gently behind him.

Chapter 9

Flint found Lavay on the foredeck waiting for him as he'd been commanded. Lavay was too polite to look speakingly at his watch and back at his captain. He noted the tardiness with his eyebrows instead.

"I was detained. My apologies, Lavay. Come walk with me."

It was a mercifully sun-blasted day, with high, frisky, cold winds filling the sails and reddening faces. Flint's crew was going about the business of maintaining a ship, cleaning decks, inspecting rigging, stitching sails. He heard a distant lowing; a few cows were aboard below, destined for dinner. Hercules, the cook, was below, likely muttering darkly beneath his breath and doing the work of two men, slicing and chopping and grinding and boiling, since bloody Miss Redmond had paid the incompetent cook's mate to stay in London.

"In a hurry, Flint?" Lavay said mildly, which was when Flint realized he'd been striding as though he could walk across the water to Le Havre.

He paused at the bow. He craved a cheroot, perhaps a cigar, maybe even opium, for God's sake. He'd tried all of them but never thereafter partook in them, apart from the occasionally socially proffered cigar.

Something strange had happened a few moments ago.

Some strangely perilous door had opened during that conversation with Miss Redmond. He'd lost his equilibrium. He was uncertain how to regain it. He would take the wheel of the ship today, needing something to do with his hands. He said nothing. He put his hands in his pockets, but they didn't belong there, either. So he placed them flat on the rail, and touching his ship seemed to soothe him.

Still he said nothing.

So Lavay began, sounding amused. "She's only a woman, Captain."

Flint shot him a baleful look. "I don't believe I've ever before heard you use the words *only* and *woman* in the same sentence."

"A beautiful woman, then," Lavay corrected, a smile spreading all over his face. As if this explained everything one needed to know about an adversary.

"Is she? I suppose the nuisance factor rather obscured that for me."

He was lying. The first word—after *beautiful*, and then *nuisance*, that was—that sprang to mind when he thought about Miss Redmond was *determination*. He thought of the dark strand of hair fluttering as she breathed, asleep from exhaustion. Of a surprisingly lethal aim, and a seat-of-the-pants resourcefulness, and an arrogance that rivaled his own, and a sense of entitlement that made one want to either conquer or throttle her, and the feel of firm thighs beneath his arm as he carried her slumped over his shoulder to his bed.

Of the love and passion that had sent her after her brother.

And the bands of muscles across his stomach tightened.

He sucked in a deep lungful of cold sea air, as head-spinning as a good cigar. He willed the image of Fatima into his mind. Which was hardly more restful, because Fatima and the forgetfulness he would find in her soft, dusky, supple, demanding body was weeks away in Morocco.

"My point, I suppose, is that you've survived far more difficult circumstances than a *beautiful*, well-bred stowaway. Perhaps you'll recall your tenure in a certain Turkish prison?" Lavay excelled at irony, too. "Surely you'll survive this one without depriving me of *meals*."

"I needed to make a point, Lavay. The point being you shouldn't feed the animals, or they'll think they're welcome about the campfire," he said dryly. "And do you have to be so impossibly . . . *French* about everything?"

"One's charm needs to be *expressed* in the company of beautiful women," Lavay defended easily. "Or I may explode like a grain silo from the sheer effort of storing it."

"Grain silos explode as a result of trapped *gasses*," Flint pointed out dourly.

Lavay laughed at this.

"It's just that she was *particularly* unwelcome at this juncture." Flint felt grim. His funds were dwindling, his cook was unhappy, a pirate was elusive, his future was tentative, there was much that he wanted that remained out of reach, and there was a *woman* on board.

All in all, not one of his favorite weeks. Turkish prison notwithstanding.

"What does she want? Why is she here?"

"She believes her brother is Mr. Hardesty. In other words, the pirate Le Chat."

Even the urbane Mr. Lavay was made speechless by this.

Flint smiled. So Flint told him of Violet's theory and watched the usually unflappable first mate's brows rise and rise until they nearly vanished into his golden hairline.

"I'm not entirely convinced she's not a willful girl on a lark. Or grasping at straws because she misses her brother. Or that she's just bored and spoiled and reckless and enjoys causing uproars because she craves attention. Given that she's the one who threatened to cast herself down a well, and the like. Her legend precedes her. I was told of that after I danced with her at the ball."

"But if you're not entirely convinced, this must mean you're . . . partially convinced?"

Flint inhaled. Then puffed air out of his cheeks, capitulating.

"Very well. She's not unintelligent. She clings to her position like a barnacle, and shows a surprising—" *maddening, infuriating* "—singularity and clarity of purpose. She asked questions about Hardesty and Lavay, and they weren't entirely foolish questions. So, as much as I loathe saying it, I can identify a method to her madness. In short . . ." He sighed. "Bloody hell, but I find myself reluctant to discount her entirely."

"So she can stay." Lavay sounded a little too pleased.

"*One* port. We'll bring her ashore, introduce her at Comte Hebert's, where Hardesty is said to be dining. Hebert knows we're searching for Le Chat but he isn't aware that we believe Hardesty may be the culprit. And then we'll watch her closely while we're there. Because, Lavay." He turned his back on the sea, leaning against the rail. "Damnation, imagine the *pleasure* it will be to bring Le Chat to justice . . . with the help of his sister. I can't think of better revenge for Captain Moreheart. And quite honestly, the sooner we accomplish this the better, because God knows I need the money."

"She knows this is your goal?"

"She knows. She thinks that if her brother is indeed Le Chat then the blowing up of ships must simply be a *misunderstanding* of some kind."

Lavay laughed.

"And that she'll be able to protect him or prove his innocence or ward him off should we bring her near him."

Lavay musingly looked out over the water. "She *might* very well be a gift to us."

Flint snorted at the very idea. "I'm more inclined to think

she might be a curse. But we can manage either eventuality, and if she does indeed prove to be bait then I can't object to it. We'll see how well it works during one visit. Now to the supplies. My funds are low. Whatever else one might think of His Majesty George IV, he isn't stupid, and he certainly recognizes how to motivate a man. We'll need to negotiate for more supplies in Le Havre, if we can."

Lavay nodded, taking this in. "And you want *me* to handle supply negotiations, *oui*?"

"Oui."

"Hercules claims you give him nothing with which to work in the galley. He can only create bland mush."

"Bland mush is the traditional fare of sailors everywhere. If Hercules is bored with his job, tell him I'll happily find even more work for him to do."

Their irascible Greek cook worked like a donkey and fought, when necessary, like a wolverine, and when Flint noticed Lavay's amazed expression he realized his mood and not his sense, was speaking. He sighed. He was an excellent strategist when it came to managing his ship and crew.

"See what you can purchase in the way of spices in Le Havre with the minuscule budget I've given you and then tell him to become inventive with a slaughtered cow. But explain to him that if we do buy spices we may have to do without the cook's mate, and ask him to choose which he prefers. He'll understand this. And we'll have mutiny on our hands if the food momentarily improves vastly only to become porridge and durable biscuit rocks once more."

"Aye, sir. And Captain?" Too innocent, his tone.

Flint turned to look at Lavay suspiciously.

"Where will she be sleeping *tonight*?" A question directed out over the water rather than to Flint's face. But he could see a slyly suppressed smile at the corners of his friend's mouth.

Flint stiffened. "Miss Redmond and I have come to an agreement. She will be sleeping in my quarters again tonight. *I* will sleep in the vole—in our Distinguished Guest Cabin again."

Lavay turned abruptly, eyes wide. "How did this come about? Never say your heart has gone soft?"

"*God*, no."

"Something else gone hard?"

Flint scowled a threat at Lavay, who was struggling not to laugh, but also still clearly trying to puzzle out Flint's mood.

Good luck, Flint thought dourly. *I don't recognize it myself.*

He took another draught of sea breeze, felt the last of London's coal and soot and drink and smoke cleansed from his lungs. "Don't be tedious, Lavay. If it's so *necessary* for you to know," he said ungraciously. "She won a contest."

There was a short stunned silence.

"You . . . played a game?" Lavay said this slow, flat incredulity, hilarity suppressed, clearly trying to picture it. "And you lost to a . . . *girl*. What manner of contest was this? Ribbon-tying?"

Flint felt ridiculous now, in retrospect, which was doing nothing to settle his temper. "I challenged her to aim a dart . . . let's just say it landed rather serendipitously in the right spot," he finished curtly. "She was lucky."

"You speak metaphorically, Captain? She aimed a dart as in the vein of Cupid?" Lavay mimed taking a dart to the chest. He was laughing unabashedly now.

"Oh, for God's sake. Enough. If *you* would please escort Miss Redmond to her proper quarters to see to her trunk, and perhaps allow her to spend a half hour or so strolling on deck. She'll need to be escorted, and you're the only man who bears close enough of a resemblance to a gentleman to do it."

"You're certain you don't want that honor for yourself, Captain?"

"I believe I said *enough*, Lavay," Flint said. The tone was mild, but it was one that Lavay recognized as risky to countermand.

"Very well." He turned to go, then stopped and turned.

"She was *just* lucky?" Lavay asked shrewdly.

Flint surrendered to an impulse he'd been resisting for much of the day. He pushed his palms against his eyes and heaved a sigh—really more of a hybrid of moan and sigh, so gusty it could have filled a sail—and then dragged his hands up over his hair.

"Let me just say this, Lavay. If she is indeed Le Chat's sister, and if he's anywhere near as wily as she is, capturing him will prove more challenging than we dreamed."

About ten minutes after the earl's departure from his cabin—long enough to unpin, rake her fingers through her hair, re-pin it picturesquely, and tie on her bonnet, but not nearly long enough to do more of the poking around in his cabin that she would have preferred to do—she heard a genteel tap at the door.

"Miss Redmond?"

She opened the door to Lavay's golden handsomeness.

"I've been requested by Captain Flint to escort you up on deck should you wish to take the air. But first we shall first visit your quarters in the Distinguished Guest Cabin if you should like to address any personal needs."

"Taken for a walk," she mused. "Rather like a . . . pet."

Pets or servants. It still rankled.

"Would it offend you if I said that I wouldn't mind at all keeping you as a pet?"

He said this with all appearances of polite curiosity, but delightful wickedness lit his eyes.

She pretended to give this serious consideration. "I would say it's rather bold of you, but I should not take offense. But I should warn you I wouldn't suit as a pet, Lord Lavay. I am not in the least obedient."

She wondered into which category Lavay would fall. Lavay, she decided, would be a pet, not a servant, should she care to win him. He flirted with an expertise akin to dancing; it held as much pleasure and as few surprises, but it was soothingly sophisticated. He was a suitable whetstone for her own skills. She would be diverted, if not challenged.

"And yet here you are about to walk docilely alongside me to the deck," he reflected mischievously. "We shall see. Are you certain you needn't revisit your quarters before we take the air?"

"I should very much like to breathe the open air straight away, thank you."

She'd been lurking in the bowels of the ship long enough. She wanted to see what daylight and sea looked like from the deck, and she thought it was about time to learn whether her nerve would desert her when she was presented with the vastness of the ocean and no land in sight.

At the moment she felt nothing but excitement, however. So much so that she nearly skipped like a child.

He allowed her to precede him up the ladder to the foredeck. She was as certain he'd done this in order to enjoy the view of her climbing as she was that the view wouldn't disappoint him.

When she'd reached the top rung of the ladder the wind made a rude grab for her bonnet and then all but yanked her all of the way up on deck.

To her astonishment, she staggered left and then right like a drunk, pushed by the wind. She heard a scramble of boots, and then Corcoran was magically there, arm extended. She reached for it as she would a banister and he helped haul her up the stairs.

"Oh, hang on t'me now, mum, ye'll fly away like the wee bi' of kitten fluff ye are, ye will."

Violet was quite tall and fit and she'd never been accused of being anything so fey in her life. She didn't mind it at all. His arm felt like a hairy branch beneath her hand.

He took the opportunity to bow yet again. She heard a hearty cracking sound. Perhaps his knee. She hoped it wasn't his spine.

"Impressive bow, Mr. Corcoran," Lavay said smoothly. Corcoran was upright again. Not his spine, then. "And impressive timing. I'm certain Miss Redmond appreciates your limberness and convenient arm. But you've duties to see to. As do the *rest of you*." He raised his voice, and all around her Violet heard scattered hurried bootfalls as men lurking with feigned casualness scrambled off to see to their duties.

Violet took her hand away from Corcoran's arm lest he succumb to animalistic tendencies.

He didn't look so inclined. His face was radiant . . . with a faint cast of mulishness.

"Corcoran?" Lavay said a little more curtly.

Corcoran bowed again, crammed his cap back onto his head, and stalked off.

They watched him go, and Lavay offered her his arm. They'd promenaded not more than four feet when they heard an unmistakable voice and familiar impatient footfall behind them.

"Corcoran will now likely sell touches of his arm to the rest of the crew the way pilgrims sell relics."

The earl planted himself in front of them, looking rather like a fourth mast. *He* was in no danger of being toppled by the wind. He glanced at her hand resting lightly on Lavay's arm. Long enough for her to notice. She saw his brows twitch in a frown, which he immediately repressed. Smoothing his expression the way she often smoothed her own brow to ward away wrinkles.

For no reason she could identify, she slid her hand away from Lavay, as though her hand had developed its own allegiance. She was surprised.

He looked swiftly and penetratingly hard into her face before his own went inscrutable again.

"Ah, very good. I was looking for you, Lavay." He turned to look at Lavay a few seconds after he said this, a peculiar delay.

"Were you, sir?" Lavay said somewhat flatly, voice raised slightly to be heard above the wind and snap of sails. "And yet we just spoke a moment ago."

He looked a bit mulish, too, albeit in his refined French way.

Violet began to understand the earl's point of view about what the presence of a woman could do to a group of men. *Men.* No wonder every season the herd of fools was thinned out via duels and mad phaeton races.

Not that she wasn't enjoying it.

Particularly since she half suspected the earl had appeared to see *her.* Again.

The wind suddenly gave Violet another hearty push, and she clapped a hand to her frisking, bucking bonnet, which threatened to launch from her head and take her scalp with it. She planted her feet apart, getting purchase on the deck, learning how to stand upon it, and while the men stared at each other in another of those silent conversations, she stared about her, at sky and ship and sea.

And her heart slowly filled like the sails of the ship.

Everything was in elemental motion: the wind that made the huge sails snap and billow from three masts; the deck swelled and rocked beneath her feet as though she stood on the belly of a sleeping giant, as though the sway of its lungs beneath the sea sent the water heaving. Wind had scoured the sky to a blue so blinding looking upon it hurt and yet she did for as long as she could, then dropped them. The blue-green sea was silver-trimmed and diamond-shot in the sun. *The Fortuna* pared it into curls of creamy white foam and left a wake that closed behind it as though they'd never come that way at all. Violet tipped her head back as far as she could. Above the masts and rigging, in which a few men were perched, seagulls rode the air, their wings looking like sails against the blue. She wondered if these birds in flight were the inspiration for the first great sailing ships.

Something in Violet eased, stretched, breathed, at long last and the sensation was so utterly new she understood with finality how confined she'd truly felt her whole life.

Yet *surely* the opposite should have been true. Surely a sane and proper woman would have been frightened and humbled and nauseated by the pitch of the waves.

But it was like hearing for the first time a note that harmonized with whatever wild tone her soul sang. It was a foreign feeling for her. She suspected other people would have called it peace.

With a start, she finally remembered the men, who seemed to be honoring her wonder with silence. She whirled in time to see a startling expression fleeing the earl's face, and her breath caught.

He'd been looking at her, she thought, almost the way she'd been looking at the sea.

And then she realized she was squinting in the blinding light, and she reflexively reached up her hand to smooth her brow, and thought perhaps she'd been mistaken about his expression, because now the earl was officious and brisk. "You're fortunate. It's a fair day, yet, Miss Redmond. During storms, even grand sturdy ships like *The Fortuna* can be tossed like twigs in a river. "

"It's . . ." She couldn't finish.

"Don't try, Miss Redmond," he agreed, shading his eyes. "There are honestly no suitable words, so we shall not fault you for failing to find them. Nothing makes a man feel more like God than sailing a ship over the sea with no land in sight. And nothing makes a man feel less like a God than clinging to a shred of ship exploded by lightning in a storm."

It sounded uncomfortably as if he knew this from experience, and she hoped it wasn't one she would ever know.

"If you ever want to know your true place in the universe, Miss Redmond, the sea and a great empty night sky will put it all in very clear perspective for you."

She disliked the lecturing tone. Why did he feel it *necessary*? And yet she suspected he was right. He was the sort of man who would need to test himself again and again. Not against other men. By pitting himself against something he could never really conquer.

Perhaps this described her as well.

Oh God. She hoped not. She did want a peace not dependent upon *pitting* herself against things.

Then again, perhaps the earl had had enough of incessant challenge, and this was why he wanted to settle down on solid ground and have the sorts of things that everyone of her acquaintance took for granted.

He turned away from her. "I wanted a word with you, Lavay. I think we'll reach port sooner than expected, and I'd like to discuss our visit with Viscomte and Viscomtesse Hebert. Shall we say half past in the captain's quarters?"

"Of course. Yes, sir," Lavay said crisply.

The earl nodded crisply to both of them and strode off, on his way shouting something up at a man called Dewey, who appeared to be staring down at her through a spyglass. His words were lost to the wind, but Dewey heard them clearly enough. The spyglass swung instantly upward again.

"So it suits you," Lavay said, with a little smile. "The sea."

Her quick laugh sounded a bit too shrill and exhilarated in her own ears. "There are no words that don't sound woefully inadequate, but I should like to say it is beautiful. Is it always so windy? I might need to put a rock in my hat, if so." *Or a biscuit.*

The wind gave another hearty yank at her bonnet and her dress lashed her ankles, and she wished she were wearing half boots as she was sure sailors the deck over, as well as Lord Lavay, were taking the opportunity to feast their eyes on her stockinged calves and would later make wagers on the color of her garters.

"Winds and seas like these are our friends; easy enough to navigate in, filling our sails, speeding the ship along. Calmer days are pleasant but tedious, particularly if we've a destination we need to urgently reach. And too *much* calm can ultimately be deadly."

Too much calm can be deadly.

It was so utterly her life philosophy she considered she ought to stitch it into a sampler.

"Why are calm days deadly?"

"If we can't move, we may not be able to reach shore in time to replenish needed supplies. Though we've a stove with a still now. Fresh water lasts such a short time, and we need to share it with beasts when they're aboard. I do hope you enjoy small beer. Though the captain might be willing to share his wine." He grinned. As though the likelihood was hilarious.

She clapped a hand on her bonnet, which was flapping like a goose struggling to take flight. The decks of ships, Violet had learned today, were a challenge to one's dignity.

"Lord Lavay . . . I should like to ask you a question."

"I stand ready to answer it," he said solemnly, clasping his hands behind his back as they strolled, paces evenly matched as Violet adapted quickly to walking over a moving surface.

"I understand that you are indeed a lord, but I fear I am unaware of your title."

He answered easily. "I am a viscomte of the house of Bourbon, Miss Redmond."

Her jaw did not precisely drop. But her eyes widened, which allowed in such a painful amount of light she immediately restored them to normal gazing width.

"But why then . . ." She looked upon Lavay in an entirely different light now.

". . . do I serve Captain Flint?" He considered his answer. "Because he won me in a card game."

She halted.

He was pleased with her speechlessness.

"Oh! Did you want me to begin at the beginning, Miss Redmond?" he asked with feigned innocence, eyes dancing. "It's often easier to follow a story when it does begin there."

He strolled onward, and she followed, her hand now comfortably resting on her head like a supplementary hat.

"Well, you see, I sailed with him when we were boys. I was an officer, naturally. I am the older one. He was hired on. He took rather a lot of ribbing for his parentage."

She felt her rib cage tighten, as if she were the one taking the mockery. She was afraid to ask. "What . . . manner of ribbing?"

"They called him a 'savage,' among other things."

He wasn't accusing her of anything, precisely. But he might as well have shot her with a dart. She felt heat start up in her cheeks. She didn't meet his eyes.

She suspected Lavay knew precisely what she was feeling in that moment, as Lavay had likely been the earl's spy at the ratafia.

"Did *you* do any of the ribbing, Lord Lavay?"

"How did you know?" He sounded more amused than contrite or surprised.

"Because you were a boy and an aristocrat, and it's what boys and aristocrats do. I should know, having been raised among them."

"I did. It's how I know he doesn't suffer fools gladly," he said ruefully. "He pummeled me soundly. Outside the ship, of course, or we would have been soundly *punished*. The gauntlet or the lash. Moreheart wouldn't have stood for fighting."

Men were a mystery to Violet. How could they pummel each other or aim pistols at each other and remain friends? It almost seemed as though it was how they expressed affection.

"So our friend Flint rather earned a reputation. In fact, I would venture to say he owes his ability to fight—and fight *quite* impressively dirty, I might add—to that very thing. And I might owe my life to it, too. Here's to savages." He raised an invisible toast.

Splendid rationalization. But Violet still couldn't shake off a sort of residual anger on behalf of the earl. She could imagine that parentless boy layering on armor against words and taunts, becoming more and more formidable rather than bitter.

And now she remembered when he'd blinked. When she'd used the word *savage*.

So it was still a chink in his armor, then. She knew a quiet shame that had naught of mischief to it—in other words, not the sort of shame she felt when she'd disappointed her brother Miles by attempting to run off with Gypsies. This was a new sensation. It was perilously close to humbling.

She wondered, however, if his arrogance was native or something acquired.

Native, she decided, as she was rather an expert on arrogance. It seemed an inextricable part of him. Born of absolute confidence. It just needed the proper circumstances to be brought into full bloom.

"You said the earl was in the habit of doing impossible things. But how did the ribbing save *your* life?"

"Ah. I am glad our first conversation made such an impression upon you." It was impossible not to twinkle back at Lavay.

"I don't know if saving a life can be said to be *impossible*, though I certainly didn't make it easy for him. I played deeper than I should have with the wrong men in the wrong gaming hell, who then cornered me with knives when they wanted their winnings. Who could blame them?"

Another of those shrugs, which had begun to fascinate Violet, as did the content of the conversation. *Gaming hells? Knives? Mistresses?* The words that were tossed about so casually by these men made her light-headed, like hard drink. They sketched in a world of men she could scarcely imagine, and which she of course found fascinating.

"As destiny would have it, Captain Flint was in the same gaming hell and took note of the commotion. I shall endeavor not to horrify you with the details of the story, but in short, I've a grand scar and so does Flint, but we won and we're alive."

"Thank you for sparing me. The mention of the scars rather implied what transpired. Very good use of detail."

He laughed. "Thank you. And did I mention there were five of them? And two of us?"

Two sailors up high inspecting rigging saw her just then and dropped jaws, then whipped off their caps and went motionless.

"Have a care, Mcevoy, or a gull might fly in your mouth," Lavay shouted up to them. "This is Miss Redmond. Don't bow, for God's sake, Emerson. You'll crash to the deck. You've *seen* a woman before."

"Beggin' yer pardon, sir, but not one quite like that, sir." He beamed cheekily.

Violet curtsied for them, and they continued watching her as though she were indeed a siren.

Not an *Amazon*. A siren.

"Back to work!" Lavay half growled, half bellowed.

They scrambled back up the rigging, nimble as monkeys. Or some such animal. Likely Miles would have known what to compare them to.

"But . . . *five* men attacked you and the earl?"

She felt faint. And all too fascinated.

"Five men came at me, expecting me to surrender my purse. And the earl appeared just in time. They only *attacked*, as it were, when he appeared to object to their treatment of me."

She was speechless. She could imagine how the earl expressed *objection*.

Lavay smiled faintly at her expression. "Well, it's not as though he cannot help it, you see. The . . . *saving* of things. I suspect it's Captain Flint's way of telling the world, '*This* is how it's done.' "

She wondered if it was also Flint's way of showing the world, "This is how you could have saved *me* when I was a boy."

Breathing was strangely difficult as she thought about it. She did not particularly want to *like* the man whose raison d'être was capturing her brother Lyon, assuming Lyon was indeed Le Chat.

And yet he'd come to the rescue of a man who'd been born with every privilege, who'd once mocked him. Because he'd been needed.

Oh, Lyon, you fool. What a formidable enemy you have.

"And . . . you began to serve the earl as a result of this rescue, Lord Lavay?"

"Serve?" He quirked a brow, amused at the word. "Well, recall I'd been taken for all of my money. I do mean that

I was in rather straightened circumstances. Doubtless my rescue wasn't *entirely* altruistic on his part. He's cleverer than that, Miss Redmond. He knew I was an accomplished sailor, fluent in many languages, would not embarrass myself in grand company and would indeed smooth the way for him, and would be trustworthy as I not only owed him my life. He decided he could make use of me. And *of* my conscience," he added whimsically. "He gambled that I possessed one. And he was the only gambler who won that night in the gaming hell.

"He gave me a position as first mate on his ship. When he carried letters of marque during the war, he was allowed to sell any ships captured on behalf of the English king and to share the proceeds with the crew. As first mate, my percentage has been impressive. I have *earned* my share. And I taught him to behave as a gentleman in exchange, opening doors of trade to him in every country."

She noticed the distinction, and she didn't think it was an accident, for it was a snobbery she couldn't help but share: "*Behave* as a gentleman." For title or no, the Earl of Ardmay had been born a bastard. Not a true gentleman. He could never *be* one. He would always need to behave *like* one. His formal and flawless speech had hinted to her of this. It had nothing of, for example, Jonathan's indolence or offhand slang. Jonathan's birthright afforded him the luxury of carelessness. No one would mistake Jonathan, or any of her other brothers, for that matter, for anything other than the wealthy English gentlemen they were.

Violet wondered how Lyon, if he were indeed Le Chat, had acquired a ship. Had he bought one, or captured one, like the earl and Lavay? But one would need to be *aboard* a ship in order to capture a ship.

Where had Lyon *been*? Where had his journey taken him?

"The earl said he'd taken command of his first ship at eighteen."

"Oh, that he did. He served Captain Moreheart admirably, but in truth, by the time he was grown he chafed under command; Moreheart knew this. When Flint led his first raid of a pirate ship and captured it at the behest of Moreheart, Moreheart allowed him to keep it. He became its commander. He is best in the solitude of leadership, anyhow. It is where he is most comfortable."

The solitude of leadership? She'd never thought of it in quite that way. But it made sense. She imagined all leaders felt a singular loneliness. The earl had been *born* into loneliness.

But was it *comfortable*?

She pictured him standing in that ballroom, the picture of elegance, larger than life, and still so subtly removed from everyone there.

"But does it ever trouble *you* at all to serve below him in rank, given your title and ancestry?"

Lavay shrugged, that pleasing one-shouldered shrug. "I suppose I do not think of it as such much of the time. It is a grand adventure, you see. If I am to serve anyone, I cannot think of whom I would rather serve. I owe him a debt, and when it is discharged, I will return to my estates in France, which are beautiful, Miss Redmond, very grand, very profitable. I'm certain you would look as lovely strolling about the grounds as you do strolling about the deck here."

She tipped her head back, biting back a smile, despite it all enjoying the novelty of being shamelessly, insincerely wooed by this charming Frenchman who clearly needed more money to support his land and had such faith in his charm that he didn't care that she knew it.

"No doubt I would," she agreed placidly. Liking him anyway.

He smiled at this, too. "I understand you are to accompany the earl and me into Le Havre when we arrive. You should know the earl has secured an invitation to a soiree held by the Comte and Comtesse Hebert, who are also friends of my family's, and the comtesse is a particular old friend of the captain's."

He said in such a way that Violet was immediately certain the comtesse knew the meaning of "work."

She was immediately irritated by the notion of spending an evening under the jaundiced eye of a beautiful, bored married woman who doubtless could speak to the relationship between the earl's thighs and his *blessing.*

And in a perverse way, rather looked forward to it.

They paused, and she was conscious of a shift in Lavay's demeanor: he was a flirt and a charmer and a gentleman, but he took his duties seriously, and his primary duty was to his role as first mate.

She sensed he was about to bid her good day for now, with reluctance but with conviction.

Off in the distance, she saw the earl speaking to the sailor who had the wheel of the ship. The two of them peered up with grave fascination at the sails. He shouted some order lost to the wind, at least to her ears, and men on deck scrambled to tug them in a different direction. What a massive undertaking, the steering of a ship! The earl had dispensed with his coat, and the wind filled the back of his linen shirt, gluing the front of it to his vast chest, making him look, fittingly, like a galleon poised for sail. It seemed safer to study him from this distance. It was impossible not to admire him abstractly, as a—oh, thing of natural curiosity she might draw. He was curves and angles and distinct lines, the broad shelf of his shoulders narrowing to his waist made a perfect *V.*

His thighs were . . . oh, bloody hell, they could only be described as magnificent.

His hair whipped out behind him. She knew it was just shy of touching his collar when the wind wasn't having its way with it. *Too much of it,* Lady Peregrine had said. It wasn't true.

Any more or less would somehow seem all wrong.

It was a patently ridiculous thought, but a vehement one.

It was as though every part of him participated in sailing that ship. The magnitude of his responsibility and competence and the confidence with which he undertook all of this all at once struck her smack in the breastbone, as shocking and exhilarating as a gulp of sea air. *So that's what* breathtaking *means,* she thought.

Almost as though someone was steering *him* just like a sail, the earl turned toward her.

How did he *know* when she was looking at him?

She turned away, but not before she saw the sun strike a spark of light from those blue eyes. He shaded his gaze, perhaps settling in for a longer look at her, as if he, too, thought her safer to inspect from a distance. The way one might squint a far-off ship into focus, deciding whether it was friend or foe.

She looked up at Lord Lavay. "And Mr. Hardesty is invited to our dinner with the Viscomte and Viscomtesse Hebert?" she asked a trifle more tersely than necessary.

"*Oui.* As Mr. Hardesty believes the Comte is financing his next journey to the West Indies, you can be certain Mr. Hardesty is invited and will attend, which is, after all, why we are going. It should prove to be an interesting evening."

Chapter 10

Thanks to a fair wind, two nights—one of which Violet had been obliged to sleep in the vole hole, which meant fitfully turning and tossing in order prevent her body from touching overlong any part of that vile little mattress—and one day later they dropped anchor during clear benign weather in Le Havre, France, and were lowered over the side of the ship rather gracelessly into the launch by the means of pulleys. They got her into the boat without soaking her hem or peering up her dress, though the temptation must have been torturous, and a small crew, a staff really—Greeber, Lumley, Corcoran—rowed them into the busy harbor, where ships clearly from all over the world, judging from languages shouted by the sailors on their decks sailors and the words painted across hulls, were anchored.

"The Comte Hebert found himself in reduced circumstances since the war, which means he now holds only five properties, one palace, and two hundred or so servants among them."

The earl explained this to her. He'd scarcely spoken to her in the past two days, which made these words feel far more significant than they were. She had a peculiar hope he'd been ignoring her, because "ignoring" was more active than forgetting all about her.

"And the viscomtesse?" she asked the earl.

He looked at her at length then from his seat in the launch, and then frowned a little. As though he kept expecting to see something else when he looked at her, but simply saw her again and again.

"The viscomtesse is rather new to being a viscomtesse," the earl said shortly. Making it clear this was the *end* of any conversation about the countess.

Interesting, indeed.

Lavay seemed to find his amusing. "Ah, but she's *played* the part many a time on stage."

"Was she an actress?" she asked this a little too eagerly. *Actress.* Yet another word to add to her storehouse of knowledge of the darker side of men.

But Flint ignored this. Because he suddenly he had that fixity of expression again. Like a predator with prey in his sight. It never failed to make all the little hairs on the back of Violet's neck stand up.

"Lavay." He gestured with his chin.

Everyone in the launch turned and stared as they rowed nonchalantly past a handsome schooner. It had two masts to *The Fortuna*'s three; the hull was painted a dull, almost sea-foam green; the foredeck trimmed in yellow-gold.

From the deck, a sailor with a spyglass idly watched them pass, raised a hand.

The men raised hands in return. And continued rowing past.

Violet's heart leaped into her throat.

"It's . . . *The Olivia*, isn't it?" Her voice was hoarse.

"She's bonnie, aye?" Corcoran said this with ironic cheer. "Built for speed. Though I'd warrant she could carry a heavy cargo, too. Even human cargo."

Violet didn't quite understand the cold looks that ricocheted between the men.

"It's said Hardesty primarily makes runs to the Indies, or carries sugar cargo," Lavay mused.

"Fortunately we'll have an opportunity to speak with him about it tonight." The earl sounded grimly pleased.

And she knew he stared at her again, searching her the way he might search that ship for clues.

But she was staring greedily at *The Olivia*. She tried to *feel* Lyon, sense his mark upon it, but the launch was rowed quickly past, and she felt nothing at all.

The Palais of the Viscomte and Viscomtesse Hebert was a trifle less grand than the word might imply, but then again, Violet was accustomed to marble from Carrera, to gilt and ormolu, to fathoms-deep Savonnerie carpets. She felt at home, rather than boggled, though her father's tastes trended more modern than the Heberts' clearly did.

Reduced circumstances, indeed. And it was only one of their residences.

They were ushered through a grand, airy domed foyer into a sitting room furnished in a dozen shades of gray: fog, silver, and pussy willow, if she were forced to name them. A tall carved fireplace dominated one end, and over it was an enormous painting of a beautiful woman. Violet scarcely had time to inspect it when the rapid clicking of slippers over marble shot all of them to their feet.

The woman in the painting, human-sized, appeared.

"So. You have become an earl, Captain Flint, since last we met," the Viscomtesse Hebert said by way of greeting.

Her elocution was flawless, every syllable caressed, but the Comtesse Hebert still managed to make it sound like the earl had committed a crime against her by acquiring a title.

She extended her hand as though bestowing a blessing, and the earl dutifully bowed over it. She was tiny of waist, generous of bust and unburdened by modesty, as she appeared to have been all but sewn into her dress and her bosom appeared to be struggling to free itself from the low neckline. Her exquisite little feline face called to mind a cat bored of drinking naught but cream day after day but resigned to its fate.

"And you have become a wife and viscomtesse, Marie-Victoire," the earl replied. Please accept my belated congratulations on your splendid marriage. I have been remiss in not sending a gift."

Very good irony, indeed, Violet thought.

"Your presence is gift enough, my dear Asher."

Such exquisitely rolled *R*'s. She'd made it sound like both a promise and a threat, and Violet studied the earl for signs of impact. She found him, naturally, inscrutable. Which likely meant there had indeed been impact.

Asher. First names. Innuendo. It was a bit too reminiscent of London ballrooms. Violet was ready to smack someone with a fan already, and the dancing hadn't even begun. She never in her dreams thought she'd become nostalgic for the vole hole.

The viscomtesse next bestowed her hand upon Lavay.

"Lord Lavay. What a pleasure it is to see you again." Up went that hand to Lavay. Lace so gossamer it might have been spun from spring breezes and moth wings fluttered at the snug sleeves of her pale yellow dress. Violet surreptitiously fingered the sleeves of her own muslin day dress, reassuring herself of its quality.

Lavay bowed over that hand. "The pleasure is all mine, Viscomtesse. My felicitations on your marriage as well. It's remarkable; it seemed we were in Le Havre only recently and the next you are married! How time flies."

More innuendo. Lavay was very good at it. Violet was filled with admiration.

The viscomtesse's smile was decidedly tight. "It was a *coup de foudre*, of a certainty," the viscomtesse replied smoothly.

"My husband . . ." She stopped, and frowned faintly, looking surprised, searching for a word.

"Vicente?" the earl supplied. Darkly amused.

"Yes! Vicente," she recovered, flustered, "sends his regrets, as he is not at present in, but he shall join us for dinner and dancing."

"And isn't it amusing, Marie-Victoire?" Lavay pressed, as though she hadn't heard him at all the first time. "One never would have suspected Captain Flint would one day outrank your husband."

He beamed disingenuously.

The comtesse's smile officially congealed. Tiny fangs, thought Violet critically, would not look out of place in it.

"Or outrank *you*, my dear Comte Lavay. In every way." She purred it. She was very good at the innuendo, too.

The viscomtesse turned to Violet, while behind her Lavay mimed taking a knife to the heart and twisting it and the earl shot him a repressive look.

The viscomtesse laughed, a sound like cascading fairy bells. "Though I confess I have seldom seen a less likely earl," she added.

"From a vertical position, anyhow," Lavay murmured.

"And who is this darling creature?" She turned her back abruptly on Lavay and the earl to examine Violet. She tipped her head, and her wide eyes flicked over her speculatively.

Violet gravely disliked being called both "darling" and "creature," particularly in an overly precious French accent, as she was decidedly neither. She felt an invigorating surge of antipathy.

Related in part to the fact that the earl's blue eyes were glinting insufferably.

No petal ever floated toward the earth more gracefully than Violet curtsied to the viscomtesse. "Such a pleasure to meet you, Lady Hebert. I must say, it's exceedingly generous of you to extend your hospitality to me, as I'm the earl's lov—"

"May I introduce Miss Violet Redmond, Madam le Viscomtesse," the earl interrupted smoothly.

The rigidity of his spine, however, told her he wasn't the least amused.

It was pleasant to surprise him yet again. This man who likely had seen so much of the world and the people in it.

Nor was the viscomtesse. Her enormous sherry-colored eyes fixed upon Violet's face, and whatever she concluded during that silent inspection made her beautiful face go hard. She gave her head the minutest little toss.

Violet gave her a sympathetic smile. *So terribly sorry you can find no gruesome flaw in me.* Lady Peregrine represented the breed in London: dissatisfied married women who deployed their limited intellectual capacities into inventorying their appearances against other women. And losing sleep over it. And plotting petty, infinite games to prove superiority in matters great and small.

Violet was torn between two equally unacceptable impulses: yawning or taking off her shoe and giving the *dear creature* a little whap with it.

"Miss Redmond is Lord Lavay's cousin," the earl continued smoothly, "and we have lately been charged with escorting her home from Spain to her family. Knowing you as I do, I was certain you would hasten to make her feel welcome and comfortable and include her in the festivities."

It was the first Violet had heard of this story, and she admired its credibility, as well as the earl's pretty speech. She was also certain none of what he said about the viscomtesse was true, but that the viscomtesse would be unable to resist viewing herself as the gracious lady. Ah, he was a clever one.

Vanity the magnitude of the Viscomtesse Hebert's must be a terribly inconvenient affliction, Violet thought. It would make one so easy to *manage*.

Lavay, for his part, was still staring at Violet with something akin to awe. Clearly impressed with the sheer bald cheek of what she'd been about to say.

Up went her eyebrows in his direction. She gave him the slightest shrug, one that rivaled his own for insouciance. *You've seen nothing yet.*

"Of course, of course, my dear, Miss Redmond," the viscomtesse soothed unconvincingly. "You will be a welcome addition to our little party, though your stay will be so lamentably short."

Violet ducked her head demurely to hide her smile, because the words sounded very like a threat. As though the viscomtesse was telling her in a coded way that she would be dispatching her with the tines of a fork over dinner.

Then again, everything sounded ironic when uttered in French-accented English.

There was to be dancing, then dinner, then games and more dancing, the trio was informed before they were ushered up a flight of curving marble stairs. One of the footmen bore Violet's portmanteau up with him. Her hand trailed the carved gilt banister and balustrade, savoring the beauty and ostentation even though it was the sort that comprised her gilded Redmond cage. She didn't object to comfort and luxury. At the top of the stairs, when Lavay and the earl were led in an opposite direction, Violet looked down to see the viscomtesse standing perfectly still, looking up at her from the center of the foyer, beneath an enormous branched chandelier dangling on a chain that could have supported a ship's anchor.

Even from this dizzying distance, she saw the flare of triumph in the woman's eyes—she would not be sleeping in any proximity to the earl—before she clicked off in her satin slippers.

Oh, what *care I.* Because everywhere was blue in her

chamber, and it was clean, carpeted in plush, fringed, Savonnerie, hung with periwinkle velvet curtains and scented by an explosive profusion of hothouse blossoms stuffed into a tall Chinese vase. It was such an onslaught of comfort her senses hardly knew which pleasure to hoard first. Part of the advantage of sailing on a schooner, she decided, was how temporarily novel it made the luxuries she took for granted.

She unlaced her walking shoes to sink her bare toes into the fathoms deep carpet, and settled her body on the bed, and next she sprang up to order a bath. She intended to make the most of the amenities while she was here. For if she had her way—and she saw no reason why she should not—she would be continuing her voyage on *The Fortuna*.

She wondered if the earl would smell of his own soap or of borrowed Hebert soap when he came down for dinner.

The thought astounded her so thoroughly she froze for a moment dead center in the room, like a wild creature cornered by an unfamiliar beast. Uncertain whether it would tear her to pieces or curl up at her feet and purr.

A few hours after a bath, dressed in the fine gown she'd packed in her trunk for her journey primarily out of habit, Violet descended the winding miles of marble steps to join the guests milling about what the viscomtesse apparently called The Silver Salon, and the closer to the foot of the stairs she reached the harder her heart thumped.

What if she entered the room and Lyon—Mr. Hardesty—stood there, plain as day? She'd *never* before fainted. But she did pause with her hand on the banister then to accommodate the sudden anticipatory rush of blood to her head. She took each step with care to avoid treading her hem.

The gown was a glossy midnight purple lutestring gathered and draped at the bodice to show as much white shoulder and bosom as possible, and against the color her skin glowed like ivory satin. The skirt was overlaid with tulle in a mistier shade of the same purple, and a narrow silver ribbon wrapped beneath the bosom. She was a veritable Circe in it. Or so she'd once been told by a lordling who claimed he'd been literally brought to his knees by her sorcery, rather than brandy, though his breath made a liar of him.

Her own breath came in short gusts now as she clicked alone across the foyer in her dancing slippers, following the buzz of voices and the pleasant anticipator cacophony of stringed instruments being tuned.

She sidled into the silver room, hovering at first on its periphery. Tension stretched her skin drum-tight over the bones of her face. She took in a deep, long breath, and found herself looking for two men at once: Mr. Hardesty, also known as Le Chat, and the Earl of Ardmay. She would recognize a Redmond anywhere, instantly—that indolent grace and impressive height, the dark hair, her own *blood*—and just as quickly knew Lyon was nowhere among the score or more men and women in the room.

Disappointment and a peculiar relief were twin waves through her, and her knees weakened again. Because what precisely would she say if she saw him? And what would *he* do? Bolt?

Drag her out of the room by the ear and give her a scolding?

She naturally hadn't considered what might happen, as responding to the moment generally proved so much more interesting.

She felt lost.

The other man made her feel peculiarly *found*. Near the towering, intricately carved mantelpiece, clutching glasses of sherry, the Earl of Ardmay and Lavay stood in conversation with the viscomtesse and a saturnine fellow in black who looked permanently bored in the way those possessed of ancient titles often do. She imagined this was the viscomte.

The earl seemed like a landmark. Like something she'd always known. She tried for detachment again, wondering whether she thought him handsome.

His head turned slightly. Enough for his gaze to snag upon her.

He slowly straightened to his full height and went utterly still. A fleeting brigade of emotions chased each other across his face—she saw wonder, and something so nearly like pain her breath caught in surprise. Cold intensity settled in again at last. But still he didn't blink. As though he wouldn't dream of wasting a second on blinking when he could be looking at her instead.

Something as taken for granted as admiration had never before left her so breathless and unsteady.

She straightened her own spine, squaring her own shoulders, unconsciously mimicking him. It was as though she were finding her balance on the swaying deck of a ship. She gave him a short regal nod and a little smile and arched a brow. Pretending to accept his rapt attention as only her due.

He nodded once, smiling faintly, and turned away.

And thus she was reminded rather powerfully that he was nothing like the London bloods, refined dinner party notwithstanding, and that he was not a man to be trifled with under any circumstances.

Peals of adorable laughter sent the viscomtesse's froth of blond ringlets bobbing, and she rested her hand, gloved in copper satin, on the earl's arm. Violet stared at that hand as though it were a venomous spider. Naturally the earl turned to her, leaned his tall self solicitously down to her petite height.

And then the countess lifted her hand up again, and Lavay apparently said something equally mirth-inducing, and down came that hand again on the earl's arm—not Lavay's—as though laughter wracked her petite frame so violently she required the extra support.

Violet fought the urge to roll her eyes, and took a step into the room from her place at the periphery.

"Oi, *Mum*!"

What on *earth*? Something was *tugging* at her from below.

Down around her hip Violet found a boy of about five or eight years old or thereabouts—Violet was never certain about ages when it came to young children—gripping her skirt. Reflexively, she gently extricated his hand. Children were invariably sticky, particularly boys, and this one didn't look at all clean. His hair stood out in greasy spikes and there was *dirt* on his *knees*.

Where on earth had he come from?

"Ought you to be downstairs among the adults, young man? Does your nurse know you're not in bed?"

Interesting how easily lecturing came to her. Then, goodness knows she'd heard enough lectures in her day.

He held in his hand a sheet of foolscap. "Mum! I *waited* fer ye. I've *pictures* for you, Mum."

"Er . . . Pictures?" He'd waited for *her*?

Baffled, Violet looked about for rescue; saw no one who appeared to be a parent or a nurse. And the boy stared up at her so pleadingly, with such huge eyes, from such a seeming distance, that she found herself kneeling awkwardly to make herself closer to his size. Should she hold out her hand for him to sniff? What did one *do* with children?

He somberly pushed a sheet of foolscap at her.

She dutifully took it and looked at it, feeling foolish. At first glance, it appeared as though he'd been practicing his alphabet and drawing barnyard animals. He'd scrawled a few letters on it along with a picture of . . . was that a cow?

He twisted a finger in one nostril.

She looked up from the foolscap and frowned at him. The twisting stopped.

What did one *say* to children? She'd cousins all over England, and a number of them were filling up their homes with broods, but their visits to the Redmond household were rare. Something praiseful would do, no doubt.

"Did you . . . draw these for me? Oh look! That's a lovely cow! And is that a—"

"Ack!" the boy cried suddenly and darted off like a rabbit.

Well, then. Apparently she was a frightener of children.

She stood, feeling a bit abashed. Perhaps it *wasn't* a cow, and she'd insulted him inadvertently. Children were fickle creatures.

She glanced again at the souvenir sheet foolscap he'd left her with, holding it gingerly with two fingers, considering what he'd been doing with his own fingers.

But then her glance became a stare.

The random letters on the page were . . . astonishingly confidently formed. Eerily so. There was an *R* and *U*. Was the boy's name Rupert? Perhaps he'd lost interest in spelling his name in favor of an overwhelming urge to draw the cow? For in front of the *R* and *U* was . . .

Wait. *Was* that a cow?

She frowned as she stared at it, then absently rubbed the frown lines smooth from her forehead.

And then the hair prickled at the back of her neck.

It wasn't a cow. Or a bull.

It was . . . the *devil*.

As a matter of fact, a very good rendering of Beelzebub's *head*. He sported a sneer and two grand horns.

Unsettling, to say the least. She looked about nervously for the child and was relieved to see it had all but disappeared. She glanced up; the earl and Comte Hebert were deep in conversation.

She wondered if the rest of the drawings would prove similarly sinister.

But a collection of barnyard animals did feature. The thing she'd thought was a cloud was in fact a sheep, looking like a fluffy cumulus with legs; a great fan of eyelashes decorating its dreamy eyes. Clearly meant to be a *girl* sheep, then. Below the sheep was an excellent pig, very fat with a tail like a spring and perched on hooves as sharp and neat as *W*'s. Next to the pig was a long narrow stem or stalk of some manner of plant . . .

Realization slammed her breathless.

That pig . . . was standing next to a thistle.

It was a *Pig & Thistle.*

Goose flesh raced over her limbs. Her hands turned icy, then hot, then icy. She carefully raised her head, as though balancing one of the viscomte's precious urns upon it, then with what she hoped would pass for nonchalance scanned the room. Nobody new had entered it. Nobody had departed it. Viscomtesse Hebert placed her hand on the earl's arm and laughed her cascading bell-like actressy laugh yet *again.* For the first time this evening she didn't mind. Everyone was still chatting. She heard no distinct words; the guests might well have been a hive of bees buzzing.

Her hand was shaking now. She supported it with her other hand to stop the sheet from rattling. Then she gulped in the images with disbelieving eyes, willed her wits to realign, and rapidly . . . began to decode.

The first drawing was what looked like a teardrop or perhaps a water droplet, followed by a line—the symbol for subtraction, perhaps?—and the letters *E* and *R*. Then came the leering little devil face, then the *R* and the *U*. They were followed by the letter *D*, which was joined to that picture of a sheep—a *ewe*—by a plus symbol, and another plus symbol joined them with and the letters *ING*. Then there was an *H*, a plus sign, and . . . for heaven's sake, was that a seashell? A slice of potato?

And then she had it: It was an *ear*.

What the devil are you doing here? she finally deciphered.

A rush of pleasure, brilliant as a gulp of sunlight suffused her.

Oh, *very* affectionate, Lyon.

Another *R* and a *U* were followed by a drawing of a little well. Very like the one she'd threatened to cast herself down when she'd argued with a suitor.

Are you well?

And below this was the little Pig & Thistle.

But why? Was mentioning the beloved ancient Pennyroyal Green pub just his way of ensuring the message would make its sender unmistakable?

She exhaled, which is when she realized she'd been holding her breath, and when she'd discovered that the invisible anvil she hadn't known was riding on her chest since Lyon's disappearance was gone. The next breath she took left her nearly airborne with an untenable, sun-bright happiness. Her eyes burned with a veritable conflagration of emotions.

The world still contained Lyon. Ha! She'd been *right*!

It still didn't *prove* that he was either Mr. Hardesty or Le Chat.

That surge of sun-bright happiness was followed by an equally powerful surge of fury. Bloody man! What was he *about*? What the devil was *she* doing here? What the devil was *he* doing here? He was in danger, from the man who'd undressed her with his eyes moments before and whose arm was being felt again and again by a viscomtesse.

And clever, wasn't Lyon, to send a childish code in the *hands* of a child. Brilliant, really.

Where *was* he?

She peered anxiously in the direction the child had dashed. Down a hall, vanishing deeper into the house, perhaps into the kitchen? He wasn't a clean child. Perhaps he'd been recruited from the street and somehow found his way into the house proper. Cheeky and bold.

What *now* was she supposed to do?

She nervously glanced down again. At the very bottom of the note were two more letters: *Y* and *N*. Then a drawing of a leaf—it appeared to be an oak leaf, but she wasn't certain whether that mattered—then a tiny drawing of a bed with an arrow pointing beneath it, and a flower—a *violet*—drawn on top of it.

Violet—that would be *her*, she guessed. So she was to choose an answer regarding whether or not she was well—a *Y* or *N*—and *leaf* it under her bed.

She was tempted to laugh, if it wasn't all so deadly serious.

Lyon was certainly putting a lot of stock in her intelligence and forgiveness at the moment, given that she wasn't known for her scholarly impulses or selflessness, particularly.

She wasn't certain whether to destroy the foolscap immediately, but impulse made her speedily fold it in as many neat squares as the sheet would allow and tuck it deep into her bodice.

And the earl, with his knack for knowing precisely when she was looking at him, glanced at her just as she was sliding her fingers out from between her breasts.

She froze in that unfortunate position.

And because he was a man, his gaze froze right where her fingers were; his pupils flared interestedly. But it only took a moment for his gaze to fly from her bosom to her face, because he was also hopelessly clever.

And he clearly saw something interesting in her expression.

He went very still again. He contemplated her thoughtfully.

The longer she held his gaze the more suspicious she would seem. Bloody hell. She couldn't very well turn her bosom finger-dive into a full-on scratch. Her gloved fingers remained in that absurdly provocative position.

She finally pretended to adjust a necklace that wasn't there, while silently screaming *Touch his arm again!* at the petulant viscomtesse.

Destiny favored her.

That small hand came up again, tapped the earl flirtatiously on his forearm, and for the first time this evening Violet wasn't peculiarly tempted to bite off the woman's fingers when the earl was forced to turn his attention to her once again.

Violet turned, hoping to find the stairs and dart after the mysterious child through the kitchen just as the strains of an orchestra started up.

Out of the corner of her eye she saw elbows lift bows to cellos and violins; the first bars of the waltz lilted forth. She committed to taking one step out of the room. Oh God. The stairs seemed acres away. Across a noisy expanse of slippery marble. From where she stood they seemed endless, insurmountable, like something out of a feverish nightmare. Her heart pounded with pugilistic ferocity.

She turned around to glance back into the room. Blocking her vision of everything else was a startlingly white cravat and crisp linen shirt.

Inside them, of course, was the earl.

How had he moved so quickly? She supposed it was helpful to possess seven-league legs.

And then she realized she was in essence under surveillance for as long as she was here. He'd appeared to be talking to the viscomtesse, absorbed in the group.

Likely he hadn't missed a thing.

She wondered just what he'd actually seen and how much.

So much for destiny.

She looked slowly up. His eyes bored into hers, and his hand was outstretched, and he was prepared to escort her—like a prisoner?—into the dancing. His expression brooked no argument.

"I do enjoy the waltz, Miss Redmond. It affords one the opportunity for private conversation in the midst of company. I would be honored if you would join me in this one."

She knew it wasn't a suggestion. It was an order.

In mocking contrast to his uncompromising expression, the music loped sweetly along. She recognized Mozart. The "*Sussex* Waltz." Somehow this seemed significant.

What could she do but take his hand? And hope he didn't feel that rapid tick of her pulse in her wrist.

Chapter 11

It was difficult, however, and she certainly tried, to continue to feel like a resentful prisoner, when dancing with him felt like soaring. She recalled this now: he seemed to bear the weight for both of them. Again she was torn between surrendering and resisting, and because her nature was simply to rebel, she did try. But exchanging glances from across the room was one thing. She'd forgotten how potent it was to have the entirety of his attention in such close proximity while he was in fact touching her, and how much nerve it took simply to withstand it without incinerating.

And then she sniffed surreptitiously to answer her question. *His own soap.*

"Your dress is beautiful, Miss Redmond."

It was such an ambush of a compliment she nearly stumbled.

"Thank you," was the clever response she finally managed.

"But it seems to itch."

The devil!

"It's silk. It doesn't itch," she said shortly.

He was smiling slightly at her, but his smile wasn't entirely pleasant. He was enjoying her discomfiture, and was clearly simply getting warmed up when it came to cornering her into some kind of confession.

"My mistake. Perhaps you simply have caught a good case of insects on the ship and that's why your fingers were in your bodice. Crawling things abound on ships."

"So I've been instructed. But I am not infested with crawling things, thank you. However attractive crawling things might find the vole hole," she said stiffly.

But she felt that folded square of foolscap as surely as if it were a second heart beating right over her own.

Damn. His eyes lit upon on her bosom and lingered for a speculative, caressing second. It was like a match touched to her skin.

Two hot spots kindled high on her cheekbones.

He brought his eyes slowly up again, with obvious reluctance. Something about his speculative expression unnerved her. He was picturing things, carnal things beyond her experience, and they involved her.

I can take you whenever I please, Miss Redmond.

It was a moment before he spoke again. His own composure, then, was not made of steel.

"How do you know for certain you're not infested, Miss Redmond? Are you certain you don't need to be scratched anywhere in particular?"

His mouth was somber, the tone solicitous. His eyes were glinting now.

"Thank you for your consideration, but no."

Though now she was picturing it, and it had the bizarre effect of making her itch in earnest and making her a little breathless from picturing his fingers rummaging about in her bodice, and an errant sizzle of longing radiated out from the base of her spine to decidedly more feminine places.

This was new. *Dear God.* She glanced at the stairs.

But he noticed.

"Forgive me for coming to that conclusion. It's not every

day I see someone with her fingers between her breasts at a dinner party."

Oh, *enough.* It was time to produce an excellent lie.

"If you must know, I was attempting to retrieve a necklace I believed dropped into my bodice."

"You weren't wearing a necklace when I first saw you this evening," he said easily. As if he had all the time in the world to watch her lay her own trap and then walk into it.

"It's a fortunate thing you're so observant," she said smoothly. "Because this means it must have fallen during my descent of the stairs, or perhaps even in my room, and I failed to take note. I should go up and take a look before dinner is served. Or perhaps it lurks in my bodice still. Have a care when you steer me beneath the chandelier. It might strike a beam from the stone hidden in my bosom and blind you."

He laughed, surprised. She basked hopelessly in the sound; she couldn't help it. Why was it such a pleasure to please him? This man who was happy to use her to trap her brother?

Her brother, who might very well be somewhere near. She felt as though she were being pulled to pieces, like a wishbone, by two desires that were growing dangerously equal and entirely opposite.

"You were speaking with a child." Casually, he said this.

Oh God. He'd seen after all.

"So were you," she rejoined.

He smiled slowly, comprehending. "Now, is that any way to speak of your hostess?"

"I notice you haven't *disagreed* with me."

"Marie-Victoire is an old acquaintance."

Violet snorted. "Please. Even *I* know she was more than an acquaintance."

It was then she felt something in him relax infinitesimally, the way he had for a moment in his cabin a few days ago. He was enjoying himself, easing into the rhythm of conversation, and she understood what his ease meant: tentative trust.

And despite everything, that peculiar sensation reared again: she felt protective of that trust. She sensed it was rare and worth having.

"Very well," he allowed. "Marie-Victoire was indeed an actress. Much sought after and fought over in France. She professed herself madly in love with me, promised she'd wait for me to make my fortune, and then married the viscomte, it would seem, the moment *The Fortuna* sailed from port."

"A girl must have a contingency, I suppose. Were you hurt?"

It was a bold and quick question, designed to throw him off balance and divert his attention from her.

He hesitated. "The viscomtesse is an opportunist who did very well for herself in the world, often serendipitously, but then I suppose that rather describes me, too. And she certainly had more than one *contingency*, as it were. I do believe Mr. Hardesty was reputed to be among them."

An answer and not an answer.

Though Violet disliked picturing Lyon consorting with that nasty, beautiful, vapid little creature.

"It isn't necessary for you to like the viscomtesse, Miss Redmond. But do enjoy her hospitality. Insects are not on the menu tonight nor in the beds, and I cannot guarantee this will be true for the remainder of our voyage."

"Are you trying to discourage me from *continuing* this voyage, Captain?"

"Have you seen anything that might encourage you to continue?"

And there they had the crux of their dance.

"So far we have both failed to draw Mr. Hardesty's interest. Unless you have been introduced to him," she lied.

"I have not, as it so happens. Because Mr. Hardesty has

sent his regrets by way of the viscomte. Isn't that a coincidence? And the viscomte and viscomtesse do *not* have small children," he pressed. "So who was the child? He dashed off when I looked at him."

Ah. So *that* was why the child had fled. Anyone unused to that blue stare would be tempted to flee. At least she hadn't frightened the little boy.

Violet was strangely gratified and relieved.

She would need to tread lightly. She forced herself to keep her gaze level with his. She breathed in, breathed out, to steady her nerves. And when her chest rose, the corner folded sheet of foolscap scraped at her skin.

"I don't know. He may have come from the kitchens. I believe he thought I was his mother. He called me mum. Suppose he meant madam."

"He called *you* mum?"

He sounded a little too surprised. And amused.

"Why should that be amusing?"

"Well, you're certainly old enough to be a mum."

"Thank you for noticing," she said tersely.

"Do you like children?"

"I don't *dislike* them."

He studied her again, puzzling out her tone. His face somber and gentle and assessing, and for some reason this gentleness made her very conscious of all the parts of his body that touched her, that warm hand pressed against her waist, the hand gripping hers, when all the dances of her life until him had been rote. And the places he touched felt suddenly new, as though they'd never before been touched. For a disorienting moment she couldn't feel where she ended and he began and didn't mind. So unlike her, for there had never been a moment in Violet's adult life when she willingly surrendered control.

Suddenly she recognized this sensation: It was rather the way she'd felt when she'd first seen the sea. It was that sense of peace, of wild beauty that contained nothing of passivity in it. Just infinite possibility.

She reared back from it, as furious and frightened as a confused child.

"Do you have any children?" she asked abruptly.

A blunt and unkind question to ask a man who wasn't married and who was a bastard. She'd meant it to be unkind. She wanted to jar the both of them back to earth.

His features went utterly immobile. Very like when she'd called him a savage.

She disliked herself for doing it. And this made her irritable, for she'd known contrition before, but never before had she genuinely *disliked* herself.

How about *that*? Yet another new sensation she could attribute to the earl. She was a veritable Pandora's box of qualities, and he'd opened it up.

"I don't know," he said quietly after a moment.

Such a simple answer. And such an *appalling* one. Doubtless most men in all honesty would answer in precisely the same way.

She was sorry she'd asked. And as usual with him, she didn't know quite what to say.

"I haven't been reckless," he added.

Oh God. She didn't need him to *explain* himself. She very much didn't want to think of him in circumstances with women during which he was *careful*.

"Of course not. You've simply been male. Don't smile."

It was too late, and the smile was slow. But it wasn't wicked. It was almost gentle. Something in him seemed effortlessly able to anticipate and parry, with a word, a smile, a silence, her every attempt to get the better of him, and this should have maddened her. It didn't.

It panicked her, but it didn't *madden* her.

She looked down for a moment, seeking escape from the

array of emotions buffeting her. She encountered only his snowy cravat. When she inhaled to clear her head, Eau de Earl of Ardmay came in with the breath. Better than wine, than cognac, than sea air. Momentarily she was speechless.

"Do you want a family?" she asked his cravat.

"Yes," he said immediately.

This made her look up at him in surprise.

"Why should this surprise you? Shouldn't I have what so many others have?"

"Of course," she said quickly. And too gently, because his face instantly hardened. He would not tolerate being patronized.

"With Fatima?" She was surprised to hear the word emerge faintly snide.

His lips curved. He enjoyed her tone. "Perhaps. Probably. It should be a simple enough thing. I'll need a wife, land, a fortune, and then I'll start my own dynasty."

Simple enough! She recalled the legend of the Redmond origins. And the feud with the Everseas that dated back to 1066, allegedly. Families were many things, but "simple" wasn't one of them.

"But you're an earl. Shouldn't you make a grand match?"

"Shouldn't the fact that I'm an earl mean I should do as I please?"

"Probably," she allowed gloomily, after a moment.

He was smiling again, as though he couldn't help himself. Those lines about his eyes deepened in a fascinating way when he did. "Don't you look forward to having a family one day, Miss Redmond? A brood to call you 'mama'?"

She thought for a moment. The answer took a moment to take shape in her mind, for a family would require a husband, and she'd never been able to imagine the man who would fill that role. The man who wouldn't make her father disown her, that was.

"I suppose I do." She hesitated. And suddenly she knew it was true. She simply didn't know why it was true, or how she knew it.

"A family like your own?"

She thought of her father and mother and their complex and mysterious marriage, and Miles the explorer and Cynthia, his charming wife, and how they'd upset the Redmond family order, and Jonathan the arrogant rascal and closest in age to her, and the missing Lyon, damned Lyon, whose note scratched away at her skin inside her bodice, and she needed now to get upstairs, to try to find him.

How very much she loved them all, and how she desperately wanted things the way they were when Lyon was home.

"No," she said, surprised but certain. "Nothing like my own."

The earl seemed surprised, too.

He was about to say something when the music ended and as gracefully as they had begun he brought her to a halt.

Too quickly she tried to tug her fingers from him.

This, naturally, made him reflexively grip her fingers harder. Suspicion, and something that may even have been entreaty, darkened his eyes for an instant. He searched her face.

Search away, Lord Flint. She stared back at him. Hiked her chin for measure. For Lyon's sake, she would at least try to cultivate inscrutability.

"I need go avail myself of the . . ." She trailed delicately. She wasn't going to say "water closet" to the earl. She needn't explain herself. For God's sake, she *wasn't* a prisoner.

She gave another subtle, insistent tug on her fingers, brows raised to imply impropriety now.

That did it. Finally, reluctantly, he released her hand, as slowly as if he thought he'd never see her again.

And she knew he watched her as she turned and tried not to headlong dash for those endless stairs.

* * *

She flung open the door to bedchamber, and with one hand rummaged in her bodice for Lyon's note while lunging at the writing desk for quill and ink with the other.

She circled the *Y*. Sprinkled sand over it. Then began to scrawl a note of her own. She added the word *but* and a frowning face with slanting eyebrows—she was angry with him—and a heart—she loved him. And then, because time was short, she wrote a *W* and a plus sign and drew an eye. "WHY?"

She sprinkled sand on this, too. Though she had no hope of his being able to answer that particular question by means of pictures.

And then she heard a faint scuffling sound. From somewhere in the room.

She froze. The hackles rose on the back of her neck.

There it was again. A rustle, very like the sound of clothing rubbing against clothing.

Could it simply be a rodent? Or . . .

No. Dear God. She thought she heard breathing. She held perfectly still. She held her own breath, and heard the faintest, shallowest sighing in and out of a human breathing.

And realized it was coming from beneath the bed. *Lyon?*

Just in case, she seized the letter opener in one hand, and tiptoed over to it.

The thick carpeting silencing her footsteps. Gingerly, slowly, quietly, she knelt . . .

. . . and yanked up the counterpane.

Revealing a face and two huge frightened eyes.

"AHHHHHH!" she and that dirty little child screamed into each other's faces.

She stumbled backward and the child slithered out from under the bed on his elbows and got upright and ready to bolt.

"CHRIST!" she said, and slapped her hand over her

heart, which had nearly failed altogether. "Who are you?" she demanded, stalking toward him, reaching out to seize his arm.

He backed away. "Look under the bed."

She actually made a lunge to grab him. Then scurried to attempt to head him off at the doorway.

He dodged easily. She wasn't amused.

"Who *are* you? Who sent you?"

"Mr. 'ardesty, Mum. But you're not to tell! Not to tell *anyone*!" He looked frantic. "He said I could trust ye."

Violet was desperate. "Where is Mr. Hardesty now? I'll give you *one pound* if you tell me. Please tell me!"

A rash promise. His eyes bulged from his little skull. "Nay, he'll kill me, Mum, 'e will. And I'm to sail wi' 'im," he said proudly. "Work in the kitchens 'ere now, but he'll gi' me SIX shillin's to work in the kitchens on a ship!"

Of course the child wasn't old enough to know the value of money. To him, six was of course bigger than one. She didn't have time to play schoolmarm.

"Look under the bed!" he said stubbornly, backing away from her. And he turned and darted out the door. She heard little footsteps in the marbled hallway.

She took three running steps after him. And two toward the bed. Then three more back toward the door.

But she knew if she tarried the earl would come looking for her, and after a few seconds of feinting between the door and the bed, she dove to scrabble beneath the bed.

She found another sheet of foolscap. She grasped it, dragged it out, her heart hammering sickeningly.

One eye on the half-open door, she quickly scanned it.

More coded drawings. A scrawl of a man's head in profile, and inside the head was something that looked like a wad of wool. Not wool—a brain! Then the word *like*, and a winged foot, like the messenger God Mercury possessed—she *knew* that symbol, thanks to her father's investment group—followed by what looked like a cudgel.

Think . . . like . . . Mercury . . . Club

Her father's investment group was called the Mercury Club.

But not precisely *it. Like* it.

She was to think of Le Chat and a group of investors?

And then, astonishingly, really quite embarrassingly, he'd signed with a florid drawing of breasts.

The bodice they wore he'd clearly scribbled as an afterthought, possibly remembering too late who his audience was, because she could see he'd actually drawn nipples on them.

An arrow was pointing at the left breast.

Good God. *Men.* She felt her cheeks heating.

These were followed by words she didn't understand: *Only 5. 2 to go.* And the last symbol was a large heart, followed by a large *U.*

Love U.

Finally, two words spelled out completely. *Forgive me.*

Forgive him? She wanted to kill him at the moment.

She also wanted to hug him and to shake him, and dear God, what would she do? Her *brain* throbbed, feeling as huge and cottony and useless as the one he'd drawn inside that head on the foolscap. She didn't know what to make of the rest of the note, and she hadn't time to decipher it.

If she didn't go down soon, of a certainty the earl would come looking for her.

She hesitated a moment longer. Then shoved her note with her inadequate scrawled message of anger and love under the bed, doubtless to be collected by that child, and patted at her hair in the mirror, then went down to dinner.

Chapter 12

Think like Mercury Club.

What the devil did that mean?

About a dozen guests were collected at a long, glittering table. Course after rich delectable course was born in by silent footmen and she watched it, soothed by the familiar rhythm of the serving of a spectacular meal, because her brain was a whirlpool.

And despite it all, Violet *was* hungry.

She was seated next to the Viscomte Hebert and across from the earl, who was directly opposite the viscomtesse.

As dinner progressed, it was clear the viscomtesse had taken to pouting a little, though pouting suited her, and doubtless she knew it. She'd lips like perfect little pillows, one curving neatly to sit atop the other with no dip at all in the top lip, and this fascinated Violet. Candlelight suited her, too. It was difficult not to admire her in aesthetic way—her dress was a shade of sherry satin that could have been dyed expressly to match her eyes, and her graceful little hands flashed in those shiny gloves as she lifted and drained glass after glass of wine.

Violet disliked her more and more the longer she stared.

The viscomtesse gazed across the table at the earl with a scarcely disguised combination of resentment and wistfulness, while Lavay whispered compliments and witticisms to her at intervals, which thawed her in an almost seasonal way. Smiles, pouts, smiles, pouts. She suspected Lavay was managing her the way he might manage the sails on a ship, catching the wind of her moods with his charm.

Until, that was, the viscomtesse caught a glimpse once again of the earl across from her, and was reminded of her tremendously bad timing at marrying a French viscomte when she could have had an English earl and sank into brooding.

Had the viscomtesse actually *loved* him? But how well had she *known* him? What could a woman like that understand of love?

Was it necessary to love or only to *believe* one is in love?

Who possessed these answers? she wanted to demand, and bang her fork on the table. *I want to know!* She had been denied so little in her life, and suddenly the questions tormented her like gnats.

The oblivious or indifferent Comte Hebert, having gotten his triumphant marriage to this vision out of the way, applied himself to his very good food and serious conversation with his guests and ignored his wife in the manner of husbands everywhere. He addressed his lovely English guest instead.

"Miss Redmond, how do you enjoy your voyage so far?"

His jaded dark eyes all but hugged the bridge of a nose that arced out like a perfect letter *D*. She'd seldom seen a haughtier face. She liked it.

"I think sea voyages suit me. I'm told you're interested in shipping enterprises, Monsieur Viscomte. Have you been plagued by Le Chat?"

She congratulated herself on the smooth introduction of the pirate into conversation, and was conscious of a pair of blue eyes fixed instantly upon her, she imagined—she hoped—in approval.

The words *Le Chat* sent up an excited murmur at the table.

"*Mais, non.* Not me. But the *The Maria Louisa* was robbed and sunk. My friend Monsieur Fontaine lost all of his money in the endeavor. And another ship, *The Gorgon*, she was boarded and sunk."

"How terrible! Was Monsieur Fontaine one of many investors in the *Maria Lousia*?" *Think Mercury Club.*

"I believe so," he said. "She was carrying silk. It is gone. Poof! Stolen."

"Silk. A great pity, indeed." She smiled at the viscomte, who, in a way inimitably French, admired her dress and décolletage with a swift sweep of his birdlike eyes. "Do you know who the other investors might be?"

"I do not. But a Mr. Musgrove in Brest is one, and I believe another of his ships is sailing from Le Havre for Brest soon. *The Caridad.*"

Brest! Ah. *Now* she understood the Breasts! And the arrow, for *singular. Brest, not breasts.* Or perhaps . . . it was a directional. Perhaps it meant Lyon was *going* to Brest, which was another port along the coast of France.

Dear God! If Lyon was headed to Brest, was *The Caridad* in danger?

"Perhaps it's enough for Le Chat to know that you are in pursuit of him, that there is a large bounty on his head. Perhaps he'll cease his scoundrel ways."

Don't count on it, Violet thought, her appetite suddenly diminishing.

"I heard he has sunk ten ships!" One the female guests volunteered breathlessly. "Boom! Down they go."

Mutters, both excited and censorious, ensued.

Violet thought of what Lyon had written on her message. *Only five. Two to go.*

Could this refer to ships?

She glanced at the earl, who had lost someone he cared about in one of those ships. His plate was nearly polished clean.

Her hands were suddenly chilled, even inside her gloves. She laid the silver fork alongside her plate and folded her hands in her lap to warm them.

And yet the food *was* good, as the earl had promised. None of it taxed her chewing capabilities. In a mere few days Violet had missed food that could lay claim to *flavor.* And she didn't at all miss the suspense regarding whether she'd bite into a baked weevil.

She looked at the earl. His features had gone hard and remote; his posture was of that unnervingly about-to-pounce-to-kill variety. She pitied her brother the enemy he had in the earl, she truly did.

He looked at her. The candle flames were reflected in his blue eyes, which seemed absurdly symbolic.

She was worried everything was going to seem symbolic from now on, thanks to that damn message from her brother.

"I hear he is truly ugly, with long shaggy hair and no teeth and terrible, terrible breath," one shuddered deliciously. "And an earring!"

"*Au contraire.* I hear he is handsome as Adonis, and his voice will melt all will from women, and that he is a valiant fighter."

"There is nothing gallant about piracy, madame," the earl said gently. "And nothing valiant."

"Oh, allow us a little romance, Lord Flint!" And all the guests giggled. "Perhaps you are jealous?" She fluttered her lashes.

He smiled politely, and Violet thought perhaps she was the only one who noticed the strained patience and the boredom and the hint of contempt behind that smile. He behaved beautifully; he was uncomfortable here. He knew so much more than they did about piracy. He likely knew so much more about most things than they did.

"*You* are a trader, Lord Flint." The viscomte addressed this to the earl. "Are you acquainted with Mr. Musgrove, another trader who makes his home in Le Havre?"

"I am. And a pity Mr. Hardesty could not join us this evening, too," the earl added.

"Because we could have long and dull and very pleasant conversation about trade over cigars, *non*?" The viscomte winked at Violet.

The viscomtesse muttered something in French here, most of which was unintelligible, but one was "Hardesty" and the other *cochon*.

A different view of her brother was coming into focus. And yet Lyon had once been so devoted to Olivia Eversea. Then again, she supposed he *was* a man, and the viscomtesse here was an opportunist, and not ugly.

"He was told of our gathering and our guests earlier today, but he needed to depart," the viscomtesse confirmed.

So that's how Lyon had guessed she was present and had found himself a clever messenger.

"Our earl here is from America, *n'est-ce pas*?" The comte showed no resentment of his guest's grand title. "I know of an American captain of a large cargo schooner. He was arrested for slaving."

"Despicable," the earl agreed emphatically. "But despite the laws, an illegal slave trade still thrives in Britain. I have alerted the navy to such ships on more than one occasion. Unfortunately, if the British navy catches them the scoundrels have been known to throw their cargo—*human beings*—overboard. I do not condone slavery, sir. I lament that states in the American South do. I never shall. And I shall do my part to end it in my own country, when it comes to that."

Violet stared at the earl, her fork poised midair. Horrified at the picture he'd painted, of people stolen from their land, chained, and then thrown overboard.

"Very good, sir," the viscomte said mildly. "I am careful about whom I choose to partner in trade with, you see. I needed to ask."

"I understand completely, sir." Flint was in agreement.

"Have *you* been to America, Miss Redmond?" The viscomte turned to her, his demeanor instantly different, warm, inclusive, charming, his dark eyes appreciating her thoroughly.

"Why would one want to go to America, Vicente? *I've* heard most Americans are savages, regardless." The viscomtesse said this sweetly to her husband before Violet could reply.

Peas fled from the viscomtesse's fork as she poked at them like an incompetent billiard player and stared at Violet. The wine had clearly played havoc with her reflexes.

Was Violet the only one who saw the earl's spine stiffen as though someone had shoved the barrel of a pistol into it?

Violet felt the hairs stir unpleasantly on the back of her neck. Like snipers rising from a crouched position, ready to attack.

Lavay shifted in his seat.

"You've an excellent cook, madam," the earl said almost too gently. "The lamb is particularly fine."

"Thank you," the comtesse purred, then skewered a piece of meat, licked it clean of sauce with her pink tongue, just like a cat, and pulled it into her mouth.

A prurient little show. She narrowed her eyes sleepily at the earl.

He watched, looking interested in a sort of abstract way. Violet was reminded of his expression when he danced with Lady Peregrine. Her appetite further fled when she pictured him *partaking* of this creature. His big nude body covering hers—

She clenched her hand tightly around her fork. Resentful that the conversation was robbing her of the desire to eat the excellent food.

"And they say, you cannot make a silk purse from a sow's ear, that is true, *n'est-ce pas*? Once a savage, *always* a savage. Particularly with those of shall we say, mixed parentage." The viscomtesse volunteered this with wide-eyed innocence.

And wrapped her tongue about her spoon to polish it, then held it up before her as if to admire her handiwork.

Violet could see her own reflection in it, upside down, from across the table.

Her jaw was clenched. Her eyes were narrowed to slits. She was a furious white. She in fact looked downright dangerous.

The comte stared at his wife with something akin to astonishment.

The earl remained politely quiet. *Excruciatingly* quiet. Enduring for the sake of manners and the company he was in, for the sake of the viscomte who'd married a beautiful actress/whore because he could, and would likely live to regret it.

And something *savage* spilled over in Violet.

And yet she took pains to sound somewhat timid when she spoke.

"Allow me to say I'm not so certain, Lady Hebert. I imagine many would say your own transformation from sow's ear into silk purse is *very* convincing."

Her tone was so credibly humble it took the viscomtesse a moment to realize she'd been gravely insulted.

She froze. Instantly calling to mind an arching cat, fur all on end. Her big eyes glared, as if deciding which part of Violet she would like to stab with her fork first. Clearly she was speechless.

"Oh, Lady Hebert," Violet said shyly, conciliatorily. She leaned forward and touched her hand to her hostess's, and the viscomtesse, anticipating an apology or explanation, began to thaw. Violet waited a strategic moment.

"I should very much like to tell you how *much* I admire your wig. It almost looks like real hair."

The viscomtesse snatched her hand back. "*Vous êtes une putain grossière*!" she hissed.

"*Je crois que le pot appelle le noir de bouilloire*," Violet replied sweetly.

Thereby officially launching an uproar at the table.

The viscomtesse tossed her napkin down and began protesting with sharp little hand gestures and rapid petulant French to her husband, and Violet took the opportunity to slide her chair back and exit, very gracefully, to the terrace, out of range of the viscomtesse's fork and knife.

The terrace was so lovely it ought not belong to that *woman*, Violet thought.

The moon was a window of light in the midnight blue sky; a cobweb of cloud clung to it; a breeze shook it off gradually. Stars, near ones, far ones, shone in their ancient patterns, performing their myriad doing duties: a map for sailors, inspiration for poets, oracles for astrologers, excuses for lovers to behave rashly.

A fountain surrounded by little white stone benches sat in the middle of it, and it was enclosed by vine-trailed walls. She settled onto one of the benches. It still held the warmth of the day.

She was alone only for a minute or two. She knew precisely who had followed her out by the size of the shadow and because she thought, really, she would know him anywhere, and then he came into the moonlight immediately so she wouldn't be afraid.

He stood before her for a silent moment.

"Why did you do it?" He sounded genuinely curious.

She inhaled, exhaled at length.

"I suppose it's that I have a lower tolerance for bullies than I ever dreamed. My brother's wife Cynthia once told me I had a good heart. Don't." She held up her hand to ward off witty remarks. "I was as surprised to hear it then as you are now."

He was laughing softly now.

"*Do* you know what she said to me?" she asked after a moment. Curious about his facility with languages.

"Oh yes. My French is fortunately quite good. She called you a rude whore. And you riposted by saying that you believed the pot was calling the kettle black."

Violet sighed. Really, when she heard him repeat what she'd said, even she was appalled. And yet in that moment it seemed she'd simply had no choice. She'd been peculiarly unable to bear it. *He'd* born it often enough. It seemed he was forever defending someone. Someone needed to defend *him*.

She was still rather surprised it had been her, however, and not eager to look at the reasons she'd done it.

They were quiet for a moment.

"Thank you?" he offered dubiously.

"I suppose you're welcome. I hope I haven't caused any lasting . . . riffs."

"Fear not. The viscomte knows what he married and he . . . enjoys her . . . nightly. He's a practical man when it comes to business."

A silence, more easy than awkward, but a little of both. And they were both amused. It seemed easier to speak on the shadowed terrace, when one seemed little more than a shadow one's self. Words were safer here; it was like speaking in a dream.

He leaned back against the vine-trailed wall and took a look around, at the fountain, the sky, the bench where Violet sat. He breathed in the heady, heavy scents of jasmine and honeysuckle. Like a great powerful animal, she thought, taking in his surroundings, deciding upon a defensible position.

"I like it better out here than in there," she volunteered tentatively.

"So do I. But then I generally do like it better outside than inside. Particularly if there's a ball or a social occasion demanding social graces on the inside. Though I'm *capable* of graces. They do not come naturally," he confessed. "I have to *try*."

She liked him for the confession.

"*I've* never really been given a choice in the matter of balls. Then, I can't say I entirely dislike balls. It's just that there's all there ever is."

"You poor, poor dear."

"I defy even you to endure a London season without developing elaborate defenses. My brother would make comparisons to how animals adapt. Growing fur coats or sharp spines that make them untouchable and the like. Irony is my defense, I believe."

"That, and threatening to cast yourself down wells?"

She sighed. Did everyone in the world know about the well? And yet her company and approval was still endlessly sought by society. Such was the perversity of the ton.

"I imagine you're right," he conceded. "Regarding the fortitude attending endless balls and parties requires. Then again, as captain of a ship and as an earl and a man, I seldom need do what I don't wish to do."

He'd trumped her, naturally, with arrogance and station and gender, so she decided to punish him briefly with silence. But only briefly, because he'd said it good-humoredly and deliberately to tease her. And because she knew he'd *earned* every single one of those things, apart, perhaps, for the gender.

"Have you ever been in love, Miss Redmond?"

Well. That was one way to startle her into speaking. What on earth had prompted the question?

"I've *heard* of love," she said gingerly, the way one might say, "I've *heard* of the Griffin." Acknowledging its possibility and its rarity while implying truly *sane* people would treat it as a myth.

He laughed softly again. The sound was so companionable, so intimate, so strangely *earned.* So part of the night.

And the entire night was a caress. The air so thick with soft warmth she thought she might simply stand and lean back and be cradled by it, and like an opium addict happily just breathe in the perfume given off by flowers heated mercilessly all day long.

"How did you know about . . . 'savage'?" he asked softly. Genuinely curious.

"Lavay."

"Mmm." The earl took this in noncommittally. And was silent again.

"Did you know a Gypsy girl shouted his name to me only a few months ago? We'd gone to have our fortunes told in Pennyroyal Green, and out she pops with the word *Lavay.* Just *shouted* it. A non sequitur. I think she even frightened herself. But my brother Jonathan thinks she's a lunatic."

"*Did* a Gypsy say that?" he said mildly. It sounded as though nothing Gypsies did surprised him. "*Never* say it's why you boarded that ship. Or that she told you you'd be taking a long journey over water."

"Very well, then. I won't *say* it."

He smiled. Teeth a white flash in the dark. He turned toward the house. She took the opportunity to study his profile. It was a strange, painful pleasure to run her eyes over the strong, singular lines of his face.

What is happening to me? She felt as though she'd been given wings but denied flying lessons.

"He's a good man, Lavay," the earl allowed after a moment.

"He told me you won him in a card game."

"Did he tell you why he was playing too deep?" As if he'd heard the story before.

"He said you heroically rescued him."

"His family lost his money and much of his lands in the war. They weren't overfond of aristocrats during the revolution, as you may know. He was a bit desperate, and he played too deep, because he needed to take care of his mother and sister, ensure his sister had a dowry. She married well, thanks to him. A good man, Lavay. A very good man. Looks after his own."

She reflected, but didn't say, that the pot again was calling the kettle black.

It surprised her to realize it.

Was the earl fishing to discover what she thought of Lavay? Was he pressing Lavay's suit for him?

She said nothing. She'd said for now all she'd meant to say about Lavay.

Flint reached up a hand and idly snapped off a single white jasmine blossom from the vine, then held it up absently before him, as if to ascertain that it did indeed match the moon in color, or deciding whether he wished to install it in the sky along with all the stars.

"Why aren't people like flowers?" she wondered. "If you heat flowers long enough, they smell wonderful. People simply smell if you heat them overlong."

"Profundity from Miss Redmond. Is that a slur against my hardworking crew? I won't have it!" he teased. "Men invariably smell. Perhaps you should ask your brother Miles, the explorer. He'd likely shed light on his phenomenon."

"Likely," she agreed. But then, Miles would likely tell her she was mad and fetch her home. Like the recalcitrant pet her family believed her to be.

"Do you think your brother Lyon genuinely *loves* this Miss

Olivia Eversea? Or loved her? That he's out for revenge of some sort?"

Interesting question from the earl. *That's* why he'd wanted to know about love. She felt a little deflated.

She hesitated, dragging her fingers over the smooth warm stone of the bench, enjoying the sensation. "I will confess to something I have never said aloud to anyone."

"You *have* killed a man!"

"Don't tempt me, Captain. I will say that . . . Olivia Eversea is . . . tremendously *passionate* about things. For instance, she is involved with the anti-slavery society. You spoke of slavery this evening . . . she would have known more about it than any of you. She's very pretty, mind you . . . for an Eversea," she sniffed. "But I've truly no doubt she broke Lyon's heart. She *said* something to send him off. I just know she did. It's just this . . . sometimes I feel so angry with Lyon for leaving that I believe Olivia is just an excuse we all use . . . just something we prefer to believe, rather than think he left because he couldn't bear the weight of being the family heir. Very uncharitable, but there it lies."

"Do you suppose there's any truth to it?"

"I don't know. Who wouldn't want to be Father's heir?"

This for some reason made him smile, too. "A pity you were not a son, and the like?"

She nodded, as if this went without saying.

"Well, you see, in my family, Miles, he has always taken care of everyone, and Jonathan, he will go into Father's business, and I'm simply there, it seems. But Lyon was *heir*. Granted, a good deal was expected of him. But he was everything a father hopes for in a son. He seemed to revel in it, too—the attention, being the best at everything. So handsome, so charming, such fun, so bloody arrogant, too. We were all quite proud of him. And then love destroyed him," she said darkly.

" 'Destroyed,' " he mimicked with dark humor. "How *very*

melodramatic. How do you know he was destroyed? Perhaps Lyon is quite content. Perhaps he's found his calling, with the so-called piracy, and it's all because of love."

She snorted inelegantly.

"Perhaps you believe this about Lyon simply because you've never been in love, Miss Redmond."

She looked up sharply. "How do you know I haven't?"

"*Have* you?"

He sounded so unflatteringly skeptical it grated. She would have preferred him to sound possessive; she would have preferred him to be wrong.

She would have preferred not to discuss it, in truth, unless he could provide her with some answers about love, because she was genuinely suffering over the question.

"No," she said, managing with some effort not to sound defensive. "I do unquestionably love my family. I suppose I am very particular. An argument can be made for my own singular character and the challenge in finding a suitable match for me."

"What a very lengthy and elegant way to call yourself a piece of work, Miss Redmond." He was insufferably amused.

She shrugged. "People *do* marry without love. Out of affection or duty or convenience or mishap. Perhaps it's wiser to have the decision taken out of the hands of people irrational enough to fall in love. Perhaps love is an affliction or aberration, and all the sane people avoid it."

He sighed almost contentedly, leaning back against the garden wall, and twiddled the flower's stem slowly between his fingers. Back and forth. Back and forth. Looking very much like a man enjoying himself, enjoying a rare peace, rather than a man hunting a criminal. His peace became her own for a moment.

"Some might say that treating men as pets or servants," he mused, "is a *marvelous* way to keep them at a distance."

She went motionless. Stunned as he'd stepped toward her and knocked her flat.

She stared at him almost helplessly.

She'd no map for the truth. Just a knack for dodging round it.

Only with this man was she ever at a loss for words.

"It . . . *frightens* you," he guessed his voice low and slow and odd. Sounding like he was having an epiphany.

"Said the pot to the kettle," she answered, her own voice low and taut.

The flower froze in its revolutions.

She regretted saying it instantly. Because she sensed, somehow, she'd torn a strip from him and hadn't meant to.

She wanted desperately to unhurt him.

How tremendously odd that it should hurt her to hurt him.

"Oh, what nonsense," she revised with a quick, feigned nonchalance, and a little laugh, to save both of them from anything so uncomfortable as truth. "You love Fatima, don't you, after a fashion?"

It took him a moment to recover from their collision with honesty. He studied her, head tilted slightly, for a moment of silence.

"She'd think *your* name exotic, too, you know." Sounding amused.

"Why did you just say that?" She was irritated.

"It's the way you say her name. You make it sound as though your lips can scarcely form it for the sheer *exoticism* of it. And I know of a certainty it's *not* a struggle for you. It's very common name in her land, you know. Like *Anne* in yours."

She fidgeted. It was an uncomfortable observation.

"Oh. Are you in love with her?"

Out that question had come. She didn't want to know. Oh, that was a bloody lie. She wanted to know desperately. No she didn't. What manner of woman would a man like this choose to love? Was Fatima his choice simply because he wasn't a gentleman born, because he felt more comfortable with someone as exotic seeming as he was?

Or *was* he afraid? This man with no family, no ties. Why wouldn't he be afraid to love when he'd been abandoned?

"I think loyalty far more important than love," he said very formally. "I've never known a woman more steadfast."

"Steadfast. How very romantic."

"Said the pot to the kettle," he said.

She acknowledged she deserved this with a tip back of her head, then brought it down in a sage nod and a slight smile, as though they were two barristers exchanging arguments.

"*And* she has other talents," he added, predictably.

"Oh yes. I'm certain *Fatima* knows the meaning of 'work.' "

His grin was a quick, wicked, crooked crescent in the dark. He was pleased with *her*.

She said nothing. She watched the flower twist in his fingers, lulled by his seeming ease, by the whimsy of a big man who seemed, for the moment anyhow, happy to be precisely where he stood.

"But is not one a result of the other?" she asked. "Love and loyalty? I cannot see how could you *prefer* one to the other."

"No. My crew is loyal to me, but I shouldn't think but two or three of them actually *love* me."

She laughed at that, and she saw him smile, and wished he stood closer so she could see the dimple.

"Rathskill certainly didn't."

"Of a certainty that's true. He's responsible for your presence, after all."

"And I am a trial."

"Your words, Miss Redmond."

"Whereas *you* are a stroll in Hyde Park."

" 'Definitely not a pet,' " he quoted somberly.

She was smiling a little too often in his presence, and he in hers, and suddenly she felt as aloft, as softly glowing, as that moon. Dangerously, deliciously unmoored.

She waved her fan beneath her chin, simply because her hands wanted something to do, and a bead of perspiration was working its way between her breasts and her dress was silk and she'd no abigail to see to getting spots out.

"Very well," she said after a moment. "Here is how I see that loyalty and love are the same: You would lay down your life for someone for reasons of both love and loyalty. But loyalty implies dependence, doesn't it? For instance, dogs are loyal. It also implies indebtedness. For instance, *servants* are loyal."

"It also implies integrity. And honor. And—"

"Steadfastness," she completed, with only a hint of irony.

"So you see them as absolutes then, Miss Redmond? Love means to be willing to die for someone, and loyalty perhaps the same?"

"How can they be otherwise?"

She couldn't interpret his silence.

She did know he was studying her, and she suspected it was rather the way Miles studied things. Searching for a conclusion. Perhaps in it was some form of admiration.

"Captain Flint . . ." she began. "Know this. There is nothing I wouldn't do for my family. I will never allow you to take Lyon if I can possibly help it. And I can never forgive anyone who harms someone I love."

"Then the people you love are fortunate," he said softly, surprising her. "And I suppose it's a very good thing you aren't armed."

She waited a strategic moment.

"With traditional weapons, anyhow," she said languidly. She leaned back against the bench indolently as a cat, let her head tip slowly back, allowed the soft air to move beneath her chin; it was delicious. And she knew as she stretched back that the pale, smooth tops of the breasts he'd gazed upon earlier likely arced invitingly up out her gown, that her shoulders were temptingly creamy and smooth even for a man accustomed to the more exotic charms of a steadfast dusky-skinned mistress, and that no man with blood in his veins would be able to resist feasting his eyes on her, given an unguarded opportunity.

He had blood in his veins. She knew his eyes were feasting.

"Do take care with the preening, Miss Redmond. You might muss a hair." His voice was a little husky.

Her hand went up to cheek instantly, and he gave a soft laugh.

She found a wayward lock and tucked it back into place behind her ear, and she straightened on the bench almost instinctively. Like a soldier, like life itself was her drillmaster.

He smiled at that. And then detached himself from the shadowed wall and strode over slowly, and settled down on the bench next to her.

Her breath caught. She'd likely been unwise to tempt him.

She didn't think he did anything casually. He knew full well his own power and size and how it could be used. He settled himself down at a carefully polite distance, but still, only inches kept their thighs from touching, and the sheer size of him somehow reminded her that he was not entirely civilized, and she wondered just how much temptation he would tolerate before he simply *took*.

It took some courage to maintain her languid pose.

Then she abandoned the effort, and brought her hands into her lap to rest.

But he just bent forward, elbows on his knees, hands loosely clasped, jasmine blossom still dangling between his fingers.

"You do understand those are the reasons I will stop at nothing to bring Le Chat to justice. Loyalty. Honor. Indebtedness. Gratitude. To Captain Moreheart. I simply cannot forgive his death, either."

Not a shred of threat or melodrama in that. Just a calm, quiet conviction that might have seemed thrilling had he not been speaking about Lyon. And yes, the faintest hint of an apology.

For *he* had no doubts he eventually would bring Le Chat to justice.

Or of how she would feel about it when he did.

Such a quiet moment. And yet fear chilled the backs of her arms. And a terrible, bittersweet regret.

She breathed in the flower-scented night. Fear for Lyon, fear for her own inadequacy in the all-too-real danger of these circumstances, fear of the conflicting and utterly new things she felt in the presence of this man.

She couldn't allow fear to take root. She hiked her chin just a little.

"I understand," she said softly.

He looked toward the rectangle of light where the guests were, one of them very chastened. Lavay inside, making apologies and smoothing relations, charming people within an inch of their lives, as he did so skillfully.

"What did that child say to you?"

She jerked her head toward him. Her heart instantly took up a sickening pounding. "I told you. He called me mum and so forth."

He watched her quietly. "But you're not telling me everything, Miss Redmond." Also apologetic.

Apologizing that he was about to be *relentless* again.

Breathing was suddenly difficult.

"What makes you say that?" She tried for lightness.

"Because you looked so . . ." He inhaled deeply, exhaled at length, searching for the word. ". . . so *happy*."

She looked up at him, surprised.

Because he'd made it sound as though he'd witnessed a startling and glorious natural phenomenon, like a shooting star. "You should have seen your face." He gestured up at the radiant moon. "Like that. Aglow. Miss Redmond, anyone could have seen it."

She looked away from him, down at her knees. She finally drew in a long shuddering breath. Her eyes burned with unshed tears. She wasn't entirely certain why. But she knew he could likely see her eyes shining.

"I've never seen anything quite like it." His voice was so soft. Wistful. But infused with a peculiar passion, too.

He was still watching her closely, and yet she couldn't look at him. "He sent a message to you, didn't he? Via that child?"

She still didn't dare respond. And she knew her silence was tantamount to an answer, but she didn't trust her voice to be steady yet.

"*Is* he your brother?" he asked softly. Not looking at her. Looking toward the house. Hands gently clasped. The blossom still between his fingers.

If she said no, he might leave her here to find her way home. She wanted to find her brother. And yet for some reason she felt traitorous both to the earl as well as to Lyon.

She suddenly longed to tell this man everything that had happened this evening. She wondered if he knew this, was cultivating this impulse in her, as a means to his own ends.

The irony was cruel: Of all the people she knew, here was finally the one person she could have entrusted to find her brother. He seemed capable of anything.

So in the end she said what she knew to be true.

"I think so." She half whispered it.

He was thoughtful for a moment. He pressed his lips together. He breathed in deeply, and exhaled on a short nod.

"Do you know where he's going next?"

She knew if she ever wanted to see Lyon she needed to tell him.

"I think he's going to Brest." Her voice broke a little.

"Is he targeting *The Caridad*?" More quickly, intensely now.

"I don't know." She whispered it. "I honestly don't. I swear to you. And don't ask me how I know this, for I won't tell you."

He nodded shortly again. For a moment they simply sat quietly alongside each other. And he turned to look at her, and she at him.

And then Flint leaned forward. She thought at first he meant to stand. Instead, he hesitated. Her heart almost literally stopped.

Was he going to—did he intend to—

And then his hand rose slowly, tentatively. And lightly, slowly, he dragged that jasmine blossom along the line of her jaw.

Stunned, she stared up at him. She somehow felt that blossom everywhere, on her skin, as surely as he'd scattered cinders over it. Her eyes began to languorously close against the weighty rise of a physical longing so fierce, so new, it was nearly impossible to breathe through it.

I can take you whenever I please, Miss Redmond.

His face was mostly shadowed now, but she could see the

slight uptilt of his lips. And then his hands were in his lap again, the blossom dangling between his fingers.

"Couldn't resist," he said softly. "Your chin was just jutting up there, clean and proud, like the corner of a topsail."

She could not have spoken if Lyon had dropped from a tree in front of her and shouted "Ahoy!"

They watched each other in utter stillness.

She wanted desperately to retrace the path he'd drawn on her jaw with her own fingertips. To feel what he'd felt. She wanted to drag her own fingers along the diamond-angled line of his jaw.

When she saw that her hand had actually risen, was actually hovering an inch or so from her lap, she dropped it to her knee.

She stared at it, and suddenly her five gloved fingers looked like the petals on that jasmine blossom.

"Which reminds me, we should go say farewell to our hosts and return to the ship if we want to catch up to Mr. Hardesty in Brest. It'll be interesting to see if *The Olivia* has lifted anchor while we were dining."

He stood gracefully and turned to extend his hand to help her up.

She took it. His enveloped hers almost absurdly. She was suddenly abashed. Almost . . . shy.

She had never felt shy in her entire life.

He held her hand a moment longer, as though puzzled by this thing she'd given him. He frowned slightly down at it. Then released it almost comically quickly.

His eyes flared wide; she saw this in the dark. He turned away from her and straightened his spine.

He turned and strode back to the house.

She followed him, and glanced back over her shoulder at the fountain one more time.

Chapter 13

Violet was awakened at an ungodly hour by the next morning by vigorous knocking at her cabin door.

She rolled gracelessly out of her bunk, feeling as though she'd slept in a clothing press, worked her arms through her nightrobe, and staggered to the door, opening it just a crack.

"Good morning, Miss Redmond." It was Mr. Greeber's untenably sunny voice. "You've been given a job to do! You're to be cook's mate!"

He made it sound as if she were to be knighted.

Cook's mate? The position lately belonging to Mr. Rathskill?

"I'm to be . . . I *beg* your pardon?" She rubbed at her eyes. She peered beyond him, hoping he'd brought coffee or tea. She sniffed hopefully.

"When Rathskill left we were without a cook's mate, and well, mum, seeing as 'ow ye're a woman—"

She was instantly awake. "For heaven's sake, that doesn't mean I know how to *cook*."

"Well, the captain thought ye'd be perfect, mum."

The *captain* thought! Her reward for coming to his defense last night was to be set to *work*?

She didn't care who *he* was. *She* was a *Redmond*.

He read her expression. "Oh, scarce any *cooking* is involved," he reassured her. " 'Tis really more about preparation. And boiling. Though Hercules would prefer it fancier, like, but 'tis a ship, after all. Mostly mixing, boiling, shaking off the weevils and maggots, things o' that nature. Determinin' wot can be eaten and wot must be tossed o'er the side because the bugs 'ave got at 'em. Though we took on some fresh goods in London, so we mayn't have trouble with weevils fer a time."

"W-weevils?" She did *not* want to be the ship's weevil shaker.

"And we've vegetables as the trip is short," he said brightly. "We'll need to peel 'em. The captain may even give word to slaughter a cow, as they drink so much water, you know. Fresh beef!" he celebrated happily.

Cows? That would explain the lowing she heard on board.

"B-but I—"

"And I'm to ask, do you sew?"

"Of course I can sew!" She didn't know why she was defending *this* particular skill. She didn't want to *sew*, either, necessarily. She pictured sitting amidst a heap of filthy, rent sailor trousers and shirts and undergarments.

Given a choice between weevils and trousers, she would likely choose the trousers, however.

He brightened. "Aye, then, mayhap you can stitch sails, too. We all *sew*, Miss Redmond. Always need to see to those! They're verra important, the sails."

She was beginning to feel a little desperate.

"But I . . . generally only sew initials into handkerchiefs, flowers, things of that sort."

"Well, I will ask the captain if he'll allow you to sew a flower or two onto the sail, or mayhap his initials. So as you might enjoy yerself. I canna see 'ow 'ed mind. Flowers might be right nice on a sail," he mused cheerily. "Loverly to 'ave a woman's touch aboard."

Violet stared helplessly at him.

He stared worshipfully back at her.

She batted her eyes in preparation for talking him out of all of this.

He looked alarmed. Really, staring at her was all he had the courage for. He would quail before actual flirting.

"I'll wait right outside, like, whilst ye put on a gown ye willna mind mussing a bit, and take you in to see Hercules."

"I mind mussing all my gowns," she said tightly.

"Ah, nivver fear. Hercules will find an apron fer ye. Ye wouldna want a beef stain on yer gown! They're all so pretty!" he reassured her.

"Mr. Greeber, where are we currently heading?"

"Well, *The Fortuna*, she's sailing for Brest, ain't she?" He blushed over the word and sent his eyes toward the ceiling, as far away from her breasts as he could think of sending his gaze. "And then you and I are going to the galley."

She shut the door, cursed the earl, and wondered which gown would suffer least from a beef stain.

"*Ziss*? You bring me *ziss*?" Hercules's eyes bulged with disbelief.

He raked her a look from head to toe, his face wrinkled in panic at what he saw—a slim, pale, well-groomed, surly aristocratic woman—and then he whirled on Greeber. "What am I to *do* wis *ziss*?"

He clapped two despairing hands to either sides of his skull and shook his head to and fro as though he were trying to twist it off and hurl it overboard from sheer despair. He was a small sturdy man, with a broad torso and huge hands and short legs and a handsome, profoundly Greek face.

"Captain's horders, Hercules. Miss Redmond is to be cook's mate."

Hercules released a string of dark Greek utterances, and then sighed theatrically.

Granted, it was undeniably interesting to see how willingly these men followed captain's orders, no matter how distasteful they found them.

"Geev me your hands, Miss Redmond."

She slowly extended her hands, suspiciously eyeing the cleavers lined on the long, thick-topped tables forming an *L* for a workspace.

He took them in his, surprisingly gently given all the shouting he was doing.

He examined their fronts. Then turned them over and examined their backs. As though they were chops he contemplated purchasing. He lifted each up and squinted at her fingertips.

Greeber squirmed enviously. "Perhaps ye'd like my opinion o' them, too?" he suggested. He bent to peer at Violet's hands.

Hercules scowled at him and swatted him away with one hand.

Then he all but tossed Violet's hands back to her. "Useless! Soft, like butter, like kid, like supple, supple kid! Zeez hands are *useless*."

"Supple, sup . . ." Greeber trailed, sounding light-headed. "Mayhap ye'd like me to take a look, too, Miss Redmond?" He held out his hands hopefully for hers.

Violet discreetly put her hands behind her back and eyed both men warily.

"They are the hands of a lady, Mr. Hercules," she informed him icily.

Her eyebrows went up, and so did his. He had the blackest,

thickest eyebrows she'd ever seen, and his nose was a stately potato, and his long arrogant mouth was turned down in a marvelously malevolent frown.

They disdainfully took each other's measure.

"Oh? What can zey do, zeez hands of yours? Flutter fans?" He locked his thumbs and fluttered his fingers beneath his chin in imitation. "Pull bells to summon ze servants?" He imitated this, too, giving a great yank to the air.

"Yes," she agreed calmly. "That's all they can do."

He paused. Then narrowed his eyes at her.

Damn. He was smarter than she'd hoped.

"Everyone works on a ship, or you are extra ballast and we throw you over the side," he lied shrewdly.

They stared at each other icily again. He needed to crane his head up to see her, his cap sliding back over his bald head, as it could get no purchase on the slippery, perspiring surface.

Greeber looked worried, his gaze bouncing from one to the other and back again.

"Aye! Very well, then! I am rude! Rude!" Hercules conceded unapologetically, finally. "I am a busy man and I need to feed the crew and I do not wish to pamper a princess of no experience. Rathskill, he was clumsy, he nearly take off his limbs, he spill the soup, and now you! You will take off your soft white fingers with a cleaver for certain, and the men will find them in the soup and they will *complain*!" He whirled on Greeber. "You!" he wheedled hopefully. "*You* can peel a potato! *You* will help?"

He sounded so desperate Violet almost pitied him.

"I'm quartermaster's mate, Herc. Sorry. Go on, gi' the lass a chance. Captain's orders, Hercules, and 'es no fool, our Captain Flint."

A tricky *bastard*, surely, but no fool, Violet thought sourly, all of her formerly conflicting, scattered emotions regarding the man momentarily congregating in unity into a single one: resentment.

"Honestly, If 'twere up to me, Miss Redmond, I'd carry you about in a litter all day and feed sweetmeats to yer," Greeber said sincerely. Every one of his freckles glowed earnestly.

Good God. She wondered what on earth Greeber was reading in his spare time, or to whom he'd been speaking.

"Er . . . thank you, Mr. Greeber."

"But captain's orders."

"And if the captain ordered you to dive over the prow?" she asked acidly.

"Well, I'd get wet then, wouldn't I?" he said cheerily. "Off I go now fer he burns me ears fer skippin me duties! Good luck! Hope I dinna see ye in the surgeon's, Miss Redmond."

And off he did go.

Leaving Violet and Hercules to stare at each other in peevish silence.

Her hands still clasped behind her back as though Hercules might seize them and begin using them to do things without her permission, Violet looked about. The galley featured a long stove, a great thick-topped, iron-legged table, hacked and stained where doubtless potatoes and vegetables and the body parts of animals had been prepared for consumption, along with rock biscuits. The galley was hot and close and reeked of years of sailors' meals. Not a terrible smell. Just an emphatic, omnipotent one.

Sacks of grain leaned drunkenly against each in the back; bins, likely barrels hacked in two, held potatoes and onions. There were a number of other barrels. One was called "beef" and the other "cabbage" according to big black letters stamped upon them. Huge pots for boiling things sat on the stove. She suspected every meal was boiled, given that every meal arrived in a bowl.

She did know more than a bit about running a large property, given that her mother had tutored her in the ordering about of servants and the purchasing of supplies. The food, however, generally appeared magically, prepared by their temperamental cook—were they all temperamental? Perhaps their tempers were forged as a result of all the time spent over a stove—or cookfire?—and born in by footmen.

She wouldn't know where to begin.

"That's a very fine stove," she ventured.

She knew absolutely nothing of stoves. She did know about men, machines, and idiosyncrasies, however. And this, of a certainty, was an idiosyncratic man.

He eyed her warily. "It *is* a very fine stove. Lamb & Nicholson. Three burners! Can boil the meat and potatoes separately."

"Well, thank goodness for that!"

She hadn't the faintest idea why this was an advantage.

He approved of her enthusiasm. His complexion faded to a degree paler than choleric. "And it can distill water. Four gallons at time!"

"Better still!" she encouraged.

He stared at her a moment longer, his frown fading.

He reached into a barrel, pulled something out that made a hideously damp squishing noise, gave a mighty whack to hew it into smaller pieces. Meat for stew.

She winced as it spattered.

"Is your name truly Hercules?" she asked tentatively.

"Nay, they call me Hercules because they are witty and I am small," he said matter-of-factly. "Small and terrifying." He grinned at her. He had all of his teeth save one in the top row, unusual for sailors, it would seem. "My wife in Cyprus, she has no complaints," he said with an utter absence of humility. "Why are you called Violet? You are not small like the flower."

Clearly Hercules had no vested interest in charming her.

"Because I smell wonderful."

His cleaver hovered mid-whack. And he stared at her. Then he laughed boomingly. "Peel then, my blossom!" He gestured at the bins of potatoes and onion with a meat-dampened hand. "Peel!"

Hercules had whacked a few more sections out of the beef before he realized she hadn't yet moved.

The cleaver hovered again, mid-chop.

"Do you . . . *know* how to peel a potato?" *Oh* so hesitantly he said it. Weakly. As though he dreaded the answer, would simply be unable to bear it.

"No," she admitted.

He unleashed a muttered string of Greek prayers for strength or epithets or slurs against her parentage, and then sighed dramatically.

"It is like this."

He scooped a potato out of a bin, slapped it into one of her hands, inserted a small sharp knife into her other hand, then positioned himself for all the world behind her like a stallion preparing to mount a mare, and unselfconsciously covered her hands with his own.

And this is what the earl saw when he appeared in the galley seconds later.

Violet and Hercules froze. His Greek groin remained pressed against her rump and his hot fingers remained over hers.

The three stared at each other for a shocked moment.

"It's nothing animalistic," Violet hastened to reassure the earl, her voice faint.

"You sent me a maiden who cannot peel a potato," came a voice from behind her.

Oh, for heaven's sake. Hercules certainly knew how to nurse a grievance.

"And so you . . . decided to attack her from behind out

of pique, but you armed her first so the fight would be fair?" the earl guessed.

She'd known him but a few days but she recognized that cold, steady voice and straight spine as displeasure.

So did Hercules.

"I show her how to peel," he said defensively. "My hands on hers. Like so."

Not just your hands, Violet would have said, and knew this was what the earl was thinking.

"It's a very viable method," Violet defended. Realizing Hercules was still pressed up against her rump. Between the earl and Hercules, she'd decided to side with Hercules, as he possessed the knife currently and the earl, after all, was responsible for sending her to Hercules in the first place. To *work*. Bloody man.

"Viable?" He made the word sound like *scorpion*.

The earl held out his hand. "Give me the potato. And the knife."

"You should not trouble yourself, Captain." Hercules handed over the knife, looking troubled himself; Violet relinquished the potato.

He hefted the knife and potato in his hands.

"I certainly shouldn't," he agreed in an indecipherable tone.

The cook and Violet eyed him warily.

"Now . . . how were we going about showing her again? I'm to stand like . . . so?"

Hercules stepped aside, and the earl took his place behind her.

He hovered a silent moment.

A peculiar silence followed.

"She says she smells wonderful," Hercules volunteered. "But I did not sniff her." He said it as if encouraging the earl to do so.

She wished she could see the earl's face. Because she could feel him breathing. She could feel the in-out sway of his chest against her back, lulling as the sea. And she wanted to close her eyes.

As if in a dream, she watched his arms slowly, irrevocably come around her from behind. His arms were stunningly hard, their strength was unnervingly apparent. She remembered how his fingers closed around her arm had seemed like a shackle only days earlier.

But he was so *careful*. So gentle. It was ridiculous, and it was devastating. She felt fragile—she was decidedly *not*—and protected. Not the way her family protected her, by reigning her in, but the way sturdy buildings sheltered. His fingers were long, surprisingly elegant. The heat of his body made her want to sink into him the way water sinks into earth, and she fought the sensation as though she'd been unwillingly drugged.

It was quiet for a bit longer than was comfortable for anyone.

When he spoke, five soft words fluttered her hair.

"*Take* the potato, Miss Redmond."

She could feel the words vibrating in his chest.

"Oh." She took it slowly out of his fingers. It was already warm from his hand.

An absolutely motionless Hercules watched all of this with huge, fascinated eyes.

"Now take the knife," the earl suggested lightly. Very softly.

A moment's hesitation later, she slipped the short sharp knife from between his fingers.

"Carefully, now." The warning seemed less about the knife and more of a note to himself, as that's when his bare hand slowly wrapped hers, enclosing it completely.

She stared at it, as amazed as if she'd never seen a hand

before. Rivers of heat shivered through her limbs, fanning from where he touched her. Enclosed by his arms, and then by his hands, it was now impossible not to imagine what it would be like to be enclosed, taken by his entire body.

She understood at last what was happening between them:

More chess.

In place of queens and knights the two of them had, from the first moment, deployed jasmine blossoms and potatoes and preening in low-necked gowns in midnight-shrouded terrace gardens.

How did one win at this?

"Push the knife away from you, like so." More breath than words when he said them. His words so close to her ear sent gooseflesh over her as though he'd issued another instruction entirely.

Slowly he guided her hand with his, and together they stripped off a precise, curling, tissue-thin strip of peel.

Violet felt as if she were being shown the slow, inexorable precision with which he would strip her naked at the earliest opportunity.

I *can take you whenever I please.*

But then why hadn't he *kissed* her in the garden?

Everyone, absurdly, admired that peel for a long, silent time. Hercules stood on his toes to see it.

Flint cleared his throat. He straightened abruptly. He stepped out from behind her blinking, as though waking after sleepwalking, surprised to find himself among potatoes.

When he looked at her, it was oddly, faintly accusatory. Warily assessing.

"Everyone should feel *necessary,* Miss Redmond," he said finally. Softly. He nodded abruptly, and then turned left the galley.

Hercules turned and stared at Violet. He pressed his lips

together speculatively; his formidable brow beetled. Then he shrugged.

"Now you do and *I* watch," he ordered.

Her hands shook—the earl's presence was wearing off only like laudanum—but she managed to pare a strip away all on her own under Hercules's beetling, watchful eye.

He sighed and turned away. "Try to do the whole thing. If you cut yourself, do not bleed in the food."

He set to work hacking at things again and measuring out grain to grind while Violet laboriously peeled one potato, then announced that she was finished. Hercules insisted upon inspecting it. He was gravely disappointed.

"See, you take more potato than peel! *Look* at this sad narrow little thing!" He held up a sad narrow potato. "Do *not* be afraid of the knife!"

"I shouldn't encourage me to be unafraid of the knife if I were you," she said darkly. She was unaccustomed to being critiqued, let alone for potatoes.

He merely raised those furry brows. "Try again."

He returned to his work and began singing. God help her, it was a tune she recognized, perhaps the most ubiquitous song in the world. The song about Colin Eversea escaping from the gallows.

Oh, if you thought you'd never see the last of Colin Eversea . . .

In the end, Violet was a Redmond, and like her brother Miles, had a respect for precision and detail that rarely found its way into anything other than her embroidery or her grooming, and God help her, she did want to be the best at everything. Her second potato was cleanly, ruthlessly skinned.

Hercules turned it over and over in his hands critically, as though searching for a way in.

"It is a beautiful thing," he pronounced happily. "You must go faster now. We need to feed a score of men with stew."

Gradually the shock at being impressed to peel potatoes gave way to a peculiar, reluctant satisfaction in the rhythm of the endeavor. Naked potatoes piled up, Hercules whacked them into cookable, edible portions, and she felt so ridiculously pleased with her contribution to the proceedings that she was emboldened to hold a conversation.

Naturally she had a specific topic in mind. "How did you come to work for the earl?"

"Oh, he take me from prison." *Whack!*

"Prison! What did you do?" *Please don't say you killed someone with a meat cleaver.*

"We *both* were in prison. In Turkey. And then we"—he waved his cleaver about, illustrating a sort of fight, presumably involving swords or knives or cleavers—"escaped. I had a bad leg, aye?"

Good God. The earl's life story clearly rivaled that of Ulysses.

She could hardly get the words out when she asked them. "Very well. A bad leg. But what were the both of you doing in prison?"

"We serve on a ship captured by pirates. They took all the cargo, aye, and threw the men into prison. They hope for a ransom, but we are both poor bastards, Flint and I, and so the rest of the crew they leave; we rot there. Me, I cannot walk so well. Shot in the leg. Captain? He wounded, but he not so bad. He could escape any time. The guards, they are stupid, they are lazy, they are violent. Pah! No match for Flint. But he would not leave me. For a year, almost?"

"Behind *bars*? You were in prison for a *year*? And he wouldn't leave you."

She couldn't picture that larger-than-life man who freely roamed the seas trapped in a cell made of stone.

"Very few bars. Mostly walls. A window this size." He

paused to shape something like a two-foot square with his arms, cheerily. "But they allow us to walk in the courtyard. We see the sun once a day. We made our own weapons, aye, from bits of stone that fall from the wall? Each night we sharpen them." He gestured again with the cleaver to illustrate. "Against the wall. Until they are good for killing. And then we finally go over the wall one night. Attack with hands and feet and our weapons. Kill only two guards."

She felt woozy again. "Only two?" she repeated ironically. *Men.*

And this was the man who was in pursuit of her brother. Where other men saw walls he clearly saw opportunity.

Hercules missed the irony. "Captain Flint, he knew I could fight and he knew I could cook and he knew I would follow him anywhere. And so I am here."

He cannot help the saving of things. Because no one had ever saved him? Then again, *she'd* leaped to his defense.

She'd do it again.

But what if Lyon was the one attacking him?

Oh God. She squeezed her eyes closed momentarily, appalled by the vise of her circumstances. How had it come to this?

"What did you *do* in prison?" She wondered if it was anything like being imprisoned in Sussex.

"Oh, *he* read books. And read them and read them. The prisoners, they come and go, aye? Some are gentleman captured, then ransomed and freed. They leave books behind. Flint, he read them to me. He gulps them down like meals, the words. Becomes a learned man. *I* learn English. He learn many languages, our captain. In many countries. Mostly very naughty words." He winked exaggeratedly. "They are the most useful to sailors."

Violet didn't doubt it in the least.

"Peel, Miss Redmond, if you want to eat tonight," he said suddenly, sternly. "And I thank you," he added rather stiffly.

She knew this must constituted a concession for Hercules. "You're welcome," she said coolly.

Hercules abruptly gathered up cuts of meat and splashed them into a pot for boiling.

Everyone should feel necessary.

And as she worked—worked!—alongside the sort of man her mother would cross the street to avoid she was absurdly moved and utterly piqued that Flint understood what she needed better than she did . . . and had found a way to give it to her that, of course, benefited him, too. In just this way he'd rescued Lavay and won a first mate and saved Hercules and now had a cook, albeit a temperamental one, for life.

She began to understand why anyone would want to follow him anywhere.

The man was hopelessly, dangerously, bloody clever.

And he looked after his own in a way he'd never been looked after.

And the warmth in her body became a warmth in her chest.

Chapter 14

Flint had decided to take his meal in the mess with the men that night—Miss Redmond took hers in her quarters, as she had from the moment she'd stolen aboard—and when he emerged, leaving the crew behind deep in a card game, stars had begun to wink on, and mauve clouds were scudding over the surface of a rising moon like a crew of polishers.

He saw her leaning against the rail of the ship. Almost as though she was waiting for him.

A strand of hair whipped gaily about her lips in the wind, an escapee from her coiffure the way she was an escapee from her family. He found himself rooting for the rest of her hair to escape.

He was before her in two strides. Almost out of pique, he caught the strand between his fingers. Stilled it. It slid like silk in his grasp. He held on to it longer than he should, helpless not to. Captivated by the small, intense pleasure of it.

"One got away, Miss Redmond," he teased softly.

Her eyes were in shadow. But he could see her mouth curve a little. And even over the rush of the sea, he could hear her breathing.

Which mean her heart was beating faster now.

He liked being the reason for this.

Slowly her hand went up to take the strand from him. He

knew the backs of her hands were untenably soft, because he'd covered them today with his own rough ones during the Potato Incident. He sensed *everywhere* she was achingly soft, her smooth pale skin emblematic of her sheltered, privileged life. Such a contrast to his own.

He wanted to touch her again.

Likely he could.

Likely he *shouldn't.*

He was surprised that sparks didn't fly from that heating hairsbreadth gap between their hovering fingers.

And at last she took the strand of hair from him without brushing his skin at all.

The disappointment was so ridiculously acute it briefly knocked all thought from his mind.

She ducked her head and smoothed it slowly back behind her ear, a gesture that struck him as almost excruciatingly sensual. He told himself it was simply because it was a quintessentially female motion, that it had been too long since he'd abandoned himself to the pleasures of a woman's body. He wondered if her neatness was vanity, or her way of imposing order on a chaotic world. Perhaps neatness was her only real control Miss Redmond could lay claim to in her family. Perhaps that's why she occasionally flung herself about like a firefly trapped in a jar, and had ended up on the high seas with a savage earl as a result.

He had never *wondered* so much about any woman in his life.

Surely it wasn't healthy.

"Thank you," she said finally, once she'd got the hair back in place. She'd tried for coolly amused. But he cherished the tremble in her voice.

He thought enough time on the sea might unravel her in interesting ways. Beginning with that strand of hair and on down.

He contemplated the wisdom of fomenting this.

Wisdom had nothing to do with it, of course.

"I enjoyed my potatoes more than usual this evening," he volunteered devilishly.

"I cannot begin to tell you how very much this gratifies me, Captain."

He smiled. She smiled back at him. He wondered if the two of them held conversation in the dark because they both found it safer. It was difficult to see expression clearly in the dark, and so they could interpret them however they pleased.

"Did you think I ought to learn the meaning of work, Captain? Hence the potatoes."

Good volley!

"I would very much enjoy teaching you the meaning of work." His voice was quick and low and the meaning unmistakable.

Her breath audibly caught. He'd unnerved her.

She'd unnerved herself.

Irritated, restless, confused, he turned away then, looking out to sea. He placed his hands on the rail, soothed as usual by touching his ship. He began absently tracing a finger in the moisture collecting there.

"Miss Redmond, captaining a ship is nothing if not a constant exercise of strategy. You should know that I excel at it."

He felt rather than saw her faint smile. She understood both the innuendo and the warning.

"The potatoes were strategy?"

"An intricate one, in fact. Hercules wanted more spices and more assistance in the galley. I simply cannot afford to give him both at the moment. By now you likely realize how unwise it would be to make Hercules unhappy. I thought *you* might welcome the . . . variation in routine. It is my understanding that a bored Violet Redmond is capable of wreaking havoc, and I thought it rather poetic that you should replace the cook's mate you bribed to bring you aboard this ship. And I know, Miss Redmond, what it's like to be among so many others . . . but to never feel like you belong. Hence my solution."

"Clever," she acknowledged softly after a moment. Not disputing any of it. She sounded absolutely sincere. And rather surprised.

Why on earth he should feel unduly flattered was beyond him.

"Thank you," she said gently. She sounded surprised. And so uncharacteristically humble he was disconcerted.

But then she said quickly, as if belatedly hearing it: "'Cannot afford'?"

He gave a short laugh. Which contained very little humor. "Not everyone is a Redmond. My fortune has always depended either upon trade or upon bounty. The king discovered me, shall we say, *between* fortunes. The title is mine; my future, my income, everything I want, depends entirely upon capturing Le Chat."

Another warning, of sorts. He let her absorb this for a moment.

She turned abruptly to face the sea then, too.

Her elbow nearly touched his. He had never been so powerfully aware of a woman's elbow, not to mention his own elbow, in his life. It was beginning to make more sense to touch her than not to touch her. A dangerous rationalization, to be sure.

She was pensive for a moment. He had the unpleasant suspicion that she was *thinking.*

"While we're on the topic of strategy, Captain Flint . . . I'm curious about something. Were these ships robbed and sunk by Le Chat owned and financed by the merchants sailing them? Or were their voyages financed by another person or persons? A group perhaps?"

"Why do yo—"

And then he noticed that her hands were gripping the rail just a little too tightly.

"You know something I do not," he said sharply.

A hesitation. "I might."

"And *I* might hurl you overboard if you don't tell me what you know."

"If you intended to ever throw me overboard you would have done it long before now." Admirable imitation of bored insouciance.

"I will do whatever is strategically necessary, Miss Redmond. Try me."

She turned to him, trying to decide whether this was true.

"Very well. I will tell you, Captain, if you . . . trade your quarters with me for the rest of the week. While you sleep in the Distinguished Guest Cabin."

She was *bargaining*?

"If you peel potatoes without complaining, losing a limb to your knife or your temper around Hercules, I will allow you to sleep in my quarters on the third evening. I will sleep in the Vole—Distinguished Guest Cabin. *One* evening," he immediately countered. He was a trader, after all.

"Done," she said simply.

"Then tell me what you know."

"It's less what I know than what I *suspect*. My father is head of the Mercury Club, a very exclusive investment group. They are quite selective about their membership—only very wealthy, very clever men are ever invited to join, and they need to be approved by the entire club to gain membership. And since you've been a trader, too, surely you know entire groups finance ships and then take a share of the profits, to reinvest or disburse however they please."

He nodded shortly. "So what are you suggesting?"

"Mr. Hardesty is allegedly a legitimate merchant. The Comte Hebert fully intended to do business with him, having done business with him in the past. So what could be his motive as Le Chat? And what becomes of the goods he steals?"

"The motive in piracy is invariably greed and opportunity. And no matter the motive, Miss Redmond, what Le Chat—your brother—is doing is wrong."

A beat of silence. "Unless it isn't."

He was speechless.

"*How* could . . ." He stopped. He could *hear* his patience groaning like frayed rigging toward the snapping point. "How could that possibly be true?"

"Lyon is not *simply* a . . . a criminal. I *know* my brother."

"Or knew him. After all, he left the family fold, didn't he, and you didn't know he'd do *that*."

She went still.

He'd meant to be unkind. He wasn't sorry.

Well, he wasn't *very* sorry.

He was driven to try to explain. "Picture, if you will, an aging sea captain driven at the point of a sword into a launch and sent out to sea to an almost certain death. And then tell me how *right* that could be."

She shifted restlessly.

"Perhaps Le Chat robs from the rich to give to the poor?" she suggested desperately.

"You're suggesting Le Chat is *Robin Hood?* Good God in heaven, Miss Redmond."

"And how do we know how many of these piracies can be attributed solely to Le Chat?"

"We *don't* know," he said impatiently. "The *robbing* and *sinking* of ships is what seems to matter to everyone. But I do know Captain Moreheart owned *The Steadfast*. Whether or not he was but one of a group of investors I cannot say. And I cannot speak for the other ships."

"How can we learn about the other ships that sank?" she pressed stubbornly. "What they were carrying, how their journeys were financed? Aren't you *curious*, Captain Flint?"

She had the tenacity of a *weed*.

They stared at each other in silence. He sighed the sigh of the long suffering, and absently rubbed a finger into the moisture collecting at the rail of the foredeck, tracing and tracing a shape. He tipped his head back, seeking guidance. Saw Orion. Saw Sirius. Old friends and collaborators, he and the stars and his sextant and charts. But the stars offered up nothing but their beauty and their unflagging assistance with mapping his course across the earth.

Not one of them hinted at what he should to do about this bloody woman.

His mission had been so *simple* just days ago. And now, though he suspected he was indulging a fantasy, and that she was bound to be gravely disillusioned about her brother . . . he found he simply didn't want to disappoint her yet. He didn't want to be the one who darkened her hope. He admired it. He envied it.

For an instant he desperately wanted to be the one who made her face glow with happiness.

"We'll speak to Mr. Musgrove in Brest and inquire at the docks to see what we can discover about the ships."

"And I can accompany you to question him?"

"Yes." He said it curtly, after a moment. Not looking at her.

But he could feel the pleasure and triumph radiating from her. *I made her happy.*

Oddly, the realization that this made him untenably happy also made him irritable.

That strand of hair had gotten loose again. It whipped gaily around her head, giddy to be free.

"You won't forget our bargain?" She meant two nights

from now she'd be sleeping in his much more comfortable bed if she was a compliant cook's mate.

He pictured her in his bed, every one of those strands loose over his pillows.

"How could I forget?" He said it shortly.

He glanced down then. And suddenly realized what he'd been tracing in the moisture on the rail: Violet Redmond's clean, lyrical profile.

He stared, alarmed. Then wiped it almost frantically clean immediately.

"Good night, Miss Redmond. You'd best go below now."

She was clearly startled to be so abruptly dismissed.

"Good night, Captain."

He watched her go, spine straight as a soldier's, inevitably tucking her hair behind her ear as she went.

Chapter 15

It was the oddest bargain she'd ever struck, but she'd survived three days of potato peeling without losing her limbs or her temper, and two more nights of tossing and turning on the lumpy little mattress in the vole hole.

Two days during which the earl had made himself surprisingly scarce. At least when *she* was about.

He'd left her the other night with his patience nearly in tatters, she knew. But embedded like a thorn in her pleasure at winning a concession about Lyon was the worry she'd driven the earl away. Bored him, perhaps.

Feeling unaccountably deflated, she was nevertheless ready for a comfortable bed and a room that smelled like a clean earl and not like dozens of indifferently clean Distinguished Guests. So when the third evening arrived, she'd tentatively knocked on the captain's cabin door. And waited.

Then turned the knob when there was no answer.

She slinked in and closed the door. She slipped into her night rail, and unpinned her hair, and gave her head a vigorous shake to encourage it to plummet Rapunzel-like down her back. She divided it into two plaits, and watching herself in the earl's mirror, brushed it for fifty strokes on either side, until it gleamed and poured through her hands like water.

She lit the lamp perched on the little table next to the bed, which pulsed into life and illuminated about as effectively as a firefly. She thought she might read a bit before she doused it for sleep.

Miles's book generally did the trick for her when it came to inducing sleep.

She made her way to his bookshelf. And here were the books on English grammar the earl had studied. She furtively pulled one down and thumbed through it with a peculiar, furtive, tenderness, as though she were peeking into his heart. In the margins were notes to himself, in a hand at first very careful, clumsy, which she found unaccountably moving. Then bolder, freer, more certain as it went on.

And here was proof that he hadn't sprung fully arrogant from the sea, like Poseidon. He had transformed himself through sheer will.

She drew her finger across the spines of books in Spanish, which she could read a little. *Don Quixote* she recognized. Its presence was ironic: the earl wasn't one to tilt at windmills, while he thought her belief in Lyon's virtue and innocence clearly qualified as such. There were a few books in French, which she could read fluently: *Le Roman de la Rose*. Really, Flint? This amused her, as he'd steadfastly maintained he was not romantic. Though certainly it was a book of action. Embossed in the spines of other books was language that was Arabic or Greek and she'd no hope of ever understanding, the letters looking more like hieroglyphics to her.

He'd been everywhere, indeed. No wonder he wanted to *belong* to something, to someplace.

At last she took down her brother Miles's book on Lacao, and took it to bed with her. She pulled up the blanket that smelled so like the earl she might have been draped in him. Soap and man. And for a dizzied instant she rested her cheek upon her knees, and wondered, breathlessly, precisely what that would be like.

The book tipped from her knees, and pages gapped a very little in one spot, as though Flint had marked a place where he was reading. Perhaps at the anecdotes of the women who wore naught above their waists for clothes?

Curious, she slipped her fingers into the gap.

And a jasmine blossom tumbled into her lap.

She stared at it, as dumbstruck as though a star had fallen clean out of the sky.

Its bruised cream petals seemed to glow against the stark white of her night rail.

Gently, gently, she settled the book down on the bed. She took up the bruised cream blossom between two trembling fingers, as though she'd captured a fairy.

Succumbing to impulse, she closed her eyes and drew it softly along the line of her jaw. He'd done it as though he were trying to memorize her.

The realization was a sweet kick in her chest, like a blossom too tightly furled bursting opening.

Oh God. This was a man who only kept things that meant a good deal to him.

And that moment, again, was like her first glimpse out onto the sea. Infinite, terrifying, glorious, very uncertain.

And then she heard the unmistakable footsteps pounding toward the cabin.

She sat bolt upright. *Bloody hell!*

She snatched up the book, clapped the blossom back between the pages, frantically gauged the distance between the bed and the bookshelf, and finally decided to shove both beneath the bed and snatched the blankets up to her chin.

She froze in the semi-dark when the door opened and Captain Flint strolled in, already undoing the buttons on his shirt with one hand while depositing a lit lantern on a small table. He tugged the shirt up out of his pants and flung it off over his head and onto the back of his chair, then and paused in front of the mirror.

Good God.

The bands of muscle across her stomach tightened involuntarily, bracing to withstand his raw male beauty. Those vast shoulders she'd admired before did indeed taper down to a narrow, hard waist. He turned slightly, deciding to shake out and smooth his shirt more carefully onto the chair, and a mesmerizing series of muscles slid elegantly beneath the skin on his back, which was achingly tawny and smooth and gleaming in places and mapped in scars in others—here was a narrow white flat slash—from the time he'd won Lavay at cards?—and another, a round one, white and raised, low on his back near his waist; one that had clearly been stitched closed; it was uneven, puckered at the edges. From the prison escape? She thought of the woman at the viscomte's party giggling over the romance of piracy.

There was no romance in violence.

What to her was unselfconscious brute beauty was for him simply armor, a utilitarian suit he possessed and used to go about the daily business of being Captain Flint. He flung it into danger; he waltzed with it, he steered the ship with it, he saved lives with it.

He made love to his mistress with it.

She shied violently away from *that* thought.

He'd pressed a jasmine blossom into a book.

A vulnerable man might have done that. But it was a half-naked warrior who stood before her now.

She put her hands up to her face, found her cheeks hot,

brought them down again. Her entire body sang with a ferocious awareness, with longing. She felt, yet again, unequal to him. Which didn't mean she wouldn't love to try to feel equal.

"He's a *V.*"

She'd meant to think it. Too late she realized she'd murmured it rather than thought it.

Chapter 16

Flint went comically still. The words echoed in the semi-dark, an absurd non sequitur demanding acknowledgment as surely as if she'd wantonly broken wind.

Please ignore it, please ignore it, please ignore it.

He turned very, very slowly. He stared at her, the blankets clutched up to her bosom in one fist, her white nightdress slipping from one shoulder. The air chilled her skin where it was bare. The rest of her was certainly unusually warm.

"A *V*?" He studied her gravely.

He didn't seem surprised at all.

And suddenly she wondered if his appearance had been planned.

His chest was magnificent. Scored in neat divisions of precise muscle, begging for a finger to trace them the way one might use a compass to chart courses. Lightly furred, a dark trail forming a seam to vanish into his trousers.

She couldn't think or speak when her eyes were so very occupied.

"Have you given up speaking in complete sentences, Miss Redmond? Please say it isn't true. What a loss it will be to the world." He waited, eyebrows relentlessly arched.

"A *V*," she repeated faintly, a little irritably now. "It's the shape of . . ."

She couldn't finish this sentence. It could lead nowhere good. Or certainly nowhere *comfortable.*

"The shape of you," she admitted, resigned.

His puzzled frown deepened.

So she sat up and released the blanket. It rolled to her lap, and his avid, unabashed eyes focused on the parts of her revealed instantly. The lamplight was likely making her nightdress nearly transparent, or casting her in tantalizing shadows.

She was wickedly, dangerously glad.

With one finger, with slow, exaggerated patience, she sketched a broad *V* in the air, beginning at the vast shelf of his shoulders—the left one—slanting slowly, slowly down to that hard narrow waste scored in muscle and golden skin and scar, drawing it upward to the hard round wonder that was his right shoulder.

Perhaps the world's most *glorious V.*

Flint stood transfixed. As though he could see himself shimmering in the air between them.

And then he jerked his head away and sat down hard on the bed, his back to her. Surely his face was warm simply because the night was sultry. It seemed instantly important to work his boots off, to set to work on *something.* His deft hands suddenly felt huge and clumsy; he tugged; it clung. He abandoned the effort and put his hands on his thighs.

Why was he undressing? He ought to leave.

He'd forgotten it was her turn to sleep in his cabin.

Or had he?

Silence landed, butterfly soft, strangely fraught.

He turned to look at her. In the lamplight her skin was half golden, and this was disorienting: she seemed soft and exotic and . . . *eminently* mussable. *Made* for mussing.

"How on earth did you arrive at that conclusion?" he managed to ask casually.

"All English young ladies are taught to draw, and to view the world in terms of shapes when we do. I noticed that y-your torso is shaped rather like a *V*." She shrugged with one shoulder.

For some reason the one-shouldered shrug irritated him.

"Are you trying to tell me that I'm a work of art, Miss Redmond?"

He returned his attention to his boots. They were beautifully made and he cared for them meticulously, because he valued and respected all things beautifully made and useful. And yet the toes were still creased from uncountable steps across the deck of ships, across foreign lands, across ballrooms. If he could count those creases, perhaps he could measure the distance he'd come, the way one could measure the age of a tree by counting rings.

But this . . . why did this moment feel like terrain he'd never before crossed?

She's just a woman, Lavay had said.

When no retort ever came, he looked up sharply. He was certain nothing short of fatal apoplexy could rob her of a clever rejoinder.

He stared. Violet was . . . Good God, was she *blushing*?

If she was, this was clearly the very first time, as surely she would have contrived to do it prettily if she'd had any experience with it. As it was, she was blotchy to the brow and frowning so powerfully two distinct furrows cut across her forehead. She didn't even put her fingers up to her brow to smooth it into perfection again.

And *this* was so disconcerting he nearly reached over to do it for her.

No, not pretty. But definitely fascinating.

He finally got his damned boot off to the sound of silence. When it *thunked* to the cabin floor they both started absurdly. He set to work on the other one, and still it was a struggle, too. He stopped. He was an *earl*, for God's sake. Perhaps he *ought* to get a valet to help him do things he'd done for himself his entire life.

He looked up at her. "You're blushing," he said rudely, finally.

"Nonsense," she declared. The blush retreated almost instantly, as if by command. The forehead magically smoothed.

And thus aplomb was restored to both of them, and when she spoke, and it was in her cool Violet voice.

"It's just that a girl will instinctively seek diversions when her usual diversions are denied her, details can become more pronounced. More noticeable." She lifted one shoulder again, a Gallic gesture, an attempt at nonchalance. Again. And so reminiscent of Lavay Asher felt himself stiffen absurdly. Irrationally, he disliked seeing his first mate's influence stamped upon her. It was like watching the other man's hands on her.

"I see," he said thoughtfully. "Are you a very good artist then, Miss Redmond?"

"No," she said instantly.

He wanted to bedevil her. "Perhaps I'll inspire you to heights of artistry. My *V* might . . . as it were."

"I shouldn't nurture that particular hope if I were you," she said quickly.

He smiled, enjoying himself, more comfortable in the territory of volleys.

And then without warning he levered himself back on the bed, his bare back pressed against the satisfying scratch of the blanket, the mattress singing a siren song to his body. It fit him the way his boots did, the way no human did: with intimate knowledge of his weight and weariness, taking it upon itself willingly. *Close your eyes*, it sang. *Surrender to me.*

It was provocative, and it was a provocation. He heard the faint rustle of this girl who'd been teasing for days tensed with awareness.

But his body was strangely alert; he felt its contours and needs and temperature somehow more acutely now that he knew a girl was studying him . . . all of him . . . in terms of . . . shapes.

And the girl was but a few inches away from him.

He could think of a few *diversions.*

He ought to leave.

"When I was in a Turkish prison, my cellmate didn't speak a word of English, so I taught him words of English to pass the time. I pointed to things—my nose, my eyes—and the like. I'd say the English words for them. He did the same with his own nose and eyes. Told me what his nose was in Turkish." He pointed to his nose.

He sensed rather than saw her quick smile. He was pleased beyond all reasonable proportion.

"You're the only person I've ever met who casually begins sentences with things like 'When I was in a Turkish prison.' "

He smiled to himself again. "*Senin güzel bir burnun var,*" he murmured.

"What manner of Turkish insult was that?"

"Not an insult. It means you have a lovely nose."

He glanced up as her hand flew to her nose as if discovering it for the first time, then dropped it almost immediately. He could almost hear her thoughts: Of *course* she had a lovely nose. All of Violet's parts were lovely, both considered together and separately, and she knew it.

The two of them surely possessed far more than their respective fair quotient of confidence. Which made him smile again.

He inched backward until his head met his pillow. Lifted it up, and settled it down gently as porcelain teacup.

Breathed out a sigh with every appearance of nonchalance.

He thought perhaps two tenser people had never lain alongside each other.

He wondered just how far he intended to go, and how it would transpire.

"Where did you get the round scar?" she asked suddenly.

Not precisely what he'd expected her to say next.

"I was shot," he said simply.

She sucked in her breath sharply as though *she'd* just been shot.

He knew remorse. It had been a terrible thing to say so glibly. "An ambush on a trading mission in India."

She was quiet. "Did it hurt terribly?" Her voice was odd. As though she were steadying it through some force of will.

Funny to have a vertical conversation in which neither party looked at one another.

"It went through the muscle and bled quite a bit but I dodged quickly enough. So no vital organs were ruined. It *did* hurt. But it's a funny thing. The force of it knocks you to the ground. But there's this moment of numbness, of surprise, really, before the *real* pain sets in."

That seemed to be the end of her questions.

But not of his.

He propped himself up on his elbow to look down. "Only angles?" he whispered.

A hesitation. His bare chest was mere inches from her. She wasn't looking at him; her eyes were on the ceiling. Mesmerized, he watched the rise and fall, rise and fall, of her breasts as her breathing quickened. He could see the shadows of her nipples through her night rail.

Then a rustle on the pillow by way of reply: she shook her head back and forth. *No.* She understood what he was asking.

It amused him how well she could follow a thread. But then, perhaps, this evening had a theme.

The shape of things.

"What else, then?" he urged softly.

A swell lifted and swayed the ship almost tenderly, rocking them the way a mollifying hand rocks a cradle, and timbers sighed.

"Curves." A curt confession.

"Curves?" He feigned bafflement, in almost a whisper. "I'm not sure I understand."

She froze, eyes aimed ceiling-ward, decisively *away* from him, breath seemingly held. Thinking.

Always dangerous when Violet Redmond *thought.*

At last she sighed out a long breath, capitulating, and slowly she rolled her body toward him. And as her dark hair waterfalled forward with her, there was a peculiar sweet pain smack in center of his chest. Perhaps the most simple and profound jolt of sensual pleasure he'd known.

It was glorious to at last see all of that hair unleashed. He wanted to wind his hands in it.

"For instance . . ." Her hand came up slowly, and she pointed to the dark and woolly hollow of his armpit. ". . . here."

Her finger a mere half inch away from his flesh, she began, slowly, slowly to outline its contours: tendon and muscle, illustrating the depth of the hollow. Watching him with intent blue eyes, her lips parted ever so slightly, a half-drawn curtain of hair across her face, the ends of it brushing the tops of her breasts.

He froze.

His skin heated along the path she traced in the air as surely as if the tip of her finger was lit like a candle. Gooseflesh lifted the hairs at the back of his neck; the bands of muscle across his stomach were taut in sensual anticipation, and his groin tightened portentously.

She wasn't even *touching* him.

She knew precisely what was happening to him. Her own

breath came shallowly now. She was so entirely new to this but she was no coward; she was testing the boundaries of her own power by testing his control.

And venturing a little deeper, deeper into the waters of seduction. Where would she stop? Everything was a test of power with Miss Redmond. It would likely be her downfall.

She would stop when he stopped her. He ought to stop her.

"Where else?" he whispered. Urging her on.

". . . and . . . here . . ." Her voice was so soft. He watched her lips, fascinated all out of proportion by her words.

She pointed to the hard gold-brown curve of his shoulder.

And in the air, her finger just shy of touching his skin, she followed the terrain of his shoulder, his biceps. Slowly, slowly. And God help him, all the hair on his arms tingled to a standing position.

He shifted to accommodate the growing swell of his cock.

A word came to him now, unbidden, as natural as a breath, and it frightened him.

Breathtaking.

That was the word, the only word, for watching Violet Redmond discover her sensuality.

". . . and here . . ." Her hand hovered with torturous uncertainty, then drifted down, down, down to his waist, hovering above that straining cock.

And she knew.

God help him, he was nearly quivering now. Sweat beaded his back, where part of that round white scar was visible. And that lit match of a finger hovered above the scar, and circled it slowly.

Then stopped.

They stared at each other. His breath was hoarse now.

And then her hand fell next to her, and she pressed it against her hip, as though tucking a weapon back into its scabbard.

He instantly regretted the distance between it and his body.

He pretended to think a moment.

"I think I see now," he said conversationally, musingly. Very softly. "Curves. Well then, by your definition . . . would . . . *this* . . . be a curve?"

He brought a fingertip to her lips, slowly enough to allow her to turn her head if she so chose. She watched it, riveted, her eyes nearly crossing at the bridge of her nose.

He wasn't coy. He wasn't a green lad.

He intended to touch her.

Don't toy with me, Miss Redmond.

His finger landed on her lips. And as though it had found the road home, reverently, trembling a little, followed the line of them, and he was surprised to realize that he felt he already knew them. The bottom a full swooping curve, elegant and sensual, unimaginably pillowy, so delicate one would think a passionate kiss would tear it like a petal from a flower. The top lip as lyrically arced as a heart.

He hadn't expected to mesmerize himself. To feel an ache where his heart beat, an unnerving yearning, as well as that all-too-familiar throb in his groin. To want to whisper her name like the chorus of a song.

And yet she'd been entering his bloodstream like slow opium smoke for days.

He rested his fingertip at the center of her lips. And cocked a brow, reminding her he'd asked a question.

"Yeth," she whispered, finally.

He could feel her quickening breath against his fingertip. He took it away so she could speak clearly.

"What was that again?"

She cleared her throat. "Y-yes," she clarified. Her voice husky. "A curve."

"Ah, very good," he said softly now. "Very good. I might be a simple man, Miss Redmond, but I believe I grasp the concept now. But just to be certain . . . would this be a . . . curve . . . ?"

He drew the finger down that unthinkably satiny throat, lightly, lightly, slowly, slowly, watching with an achingly deep pleasure the gooseflesh rose in its wake.

". . . here?"

Beneath her nightdress, as soft and fine as her skin, was the dark shadow of her nipple at the tip of the upthrust curve of her breast. Without slowing the progress of his finger, he snagged the lace edge and dragged it down, down, down, until her breast, one beautiful, full breast was bare to his eyes.

Her breath shuddered. And she was trying to maintain aplomb, but he felt her rib cage leap up, then rise and fall swiftly.

Her eyes widened. She was afraid now.

And as mesmerized as he was.

And very, very aroused, he knew.

He drew his finger slowly, slowly along the unthinkably soft, vulnerable, arc of her breast, stifling a groan, the blood beating in his head, in his groin, the extraordinary, painful tumult in his body at complete odds with the precise goal of his finger.

Knowing he was the first man to ever touch her here was unbearably erotic.

He brought the tip of it to a stop on the ruched tip of her aroused nipple . . . and drew a slow, lazy circle.

Her head tipped back sharply; her teeth sank into her lip on a gasp of pleasure.

And the sight of her *experiencing* this for the first time was so erotic he bit the inside of his lip to stop his own moan. He took his finger away as casually as he'd begun, but now his hands were shaking.

She stared at him, eyes huge and dark, lips parted softly.

He wanted her with an ache that frightened him. He was suddenly furious in an unspecific way again.

Enough. It was time to call a halt to the games. He'd felt off balance since she'd stowed away, and hadn't yet found a way to regain his equilibrium. He knew the surest, swiftest way to regain his power. To prove to himself that she was just a woman like any other.

All he had to do was kiss her.

Slowly, gracefully, he leaned over her; he'd done this dozens of times before in his life. And as his lips came down he caught a glimpse of her sensually darkened eyes widening, her lips parting in surprise.

His lips touched hers. Sank against them. Her lips were a miracle of heat and silk and give.

Oh God. It was a mistake.

The kiss raced like a lightning strike along his spine and seized his lungs with a simultaneous rush of panic and joy. As though he'd willingly flung himself backward from the mast to the deck and not only enjoyed the flight but survived the fall unscathed.

He inhaled sharply and tipped back into the space shaped like him and folded his hands beneath his head, hoping to appear insouciant but in reality trapping them. He was suddenly afraid of what they might do: Plunder. Caress. Explore. Dear God, *take, take, take.*

He held his body motionless. His heart took painful jabs at his breastbone. His blood was a thick, hot liqueur. His mind a useless scramble.

He could hear her breathing hard next to him. Was aware her fingers were at her lips. Touching them, as if to prove to herself she'd been kissed.

He listened to her breath, the ragged rhythm of it a counterpoint to the incessant sigh of the sea, but for some reason he didn't want to look at her. He closed his eyes instead and saw her hair, shadow-dark, pooled on the pillow, the shudder of her lashes against her cheeks; he conjured the shape and texture of her lips sinking, opening against his, her breath mingling with his.

He tried and failed to detect the difference between this and every other kiss he'd ever taken.

He was *rattled.*

It would be a simple enough thing to restore his sense of control: all he needed to do was roll over onto her, peel up her nightdress, fill his hands and mouth with her breasts, slip his hands under that doubtlessly silky arse before she had time even to gasp, get a determined knee between hers to pry them apart, and press his hard *V* of a torso over hers and give her no choice but to wrap her legs around his waist and sink her nails into his shoulders because damned if she wouldn't need to hold on for dear life when plunged into her *Oh God* snug, wet . . .

He flung himself off the bed as though dodging cannon fire and stood stiff and motionless, looking down at her. His face must have been ferocious, because hers went uncertain, and then inscrutable. Suddenly she was painfully human and young, and *new.*

No less desirable, but much more frightening.

Her eyes slid down to the majestic bulge in his groin, magnetized there.

And then they bounced back again to the other side of the room as though she'd inadvertently gazed upon an eclipse.

He ought to laugh.

He thrust an arm blindly behind him, found and snatched up the shirt he'd abandoned on the chair and shoved his arms in, buttoned it haphazardly, stuffed half of into his trousers.

Bent over and seized his boots by their tops as though apprehending fleeing criminals.

And took himself off to sleep in the vole hole, shutting the door harder than necessary, as if trapping all unwelcome feelings in the room behind him.

Violet lay absolutely motionless. Apart, that was, from her breathing, which wouldn't settle any time soon. Her night rail remained in disarray, but she let the blankets lay where they were. She wanted nothing else to touch her while his touch lingered on her skin. She seemed to glow everywhere, like a just-lit coal.

She brought her hand up to her breast and touched it, to feel what he'd felt. And then she remembered how he *felt*. His firm lips, his breath, the heat of his body hovering near hers. She was weak with yearning that bordered on *angry*: it wanted satisfaction. A fire had been lit. She, who'd never been denied a thing in her life, wanted more.

I kissed an earl. Emotions and sensations kaleidoscoped; she couldn't seem to grasp onto only one. Joy and fear and ferocious desire and amazement took their turns with her. Pragmatism rallied for attention. She suspected pragmatism was masquerading as cowardice, because it said: *Nothing more ought to happen. Keep your distance.*

He'd fled as though he'd come to his senses, too. Perhaps now the game would be called. Perhaps the earl had bolted out of the room with his magnificent erection—Lady Peregrine had been correct about the thighs—because he couldn't bear the notion of touching her again now that he had.

She didn't believe it.

And she didn't sleep.

Chapter 17

Violet was driven out of bed before dawn, as sleep, naturally, proved elusive.

She *ought* to dutifully set to work. Hercules might be missing, but the potatoes were present. Instead, she ventured out onto the deck, finding the day blindingly clear and windwhipped. When she heard the bass of the earl's voice rumbling beneath the rush of wind, the creak of the deck, the flap of sails and wings, she migrated toward it out of instinct before she realized what she was doing.

Then stopped to watch him from a distance.

His head was bent to listen to Hercules, who was windmilling his arms, gesticulating wildly. It was rather like watching a hummingbird buzz about a great tree. Complaining about her? Or complimenting her? With Hercules, it was difficult to know.

She knew the instant the earl became aware of her presence. He didn't turn. He never took his eyes away from Hercules.

But his body tensed almost imperceptibly, as if his every cell was attuned to her.

Hercules finally stalked off, muttering in Greek, but he looked cheerful for a change. Perhaps he was thanking the captain for his new assistant. She could only hope. He didn't see her; doubtless he would come hunting for her when he didn't find her in the galley, either.

Flint turned and studied her for a moment from an assessing distance.

Said nothing. Just watched. A strand of her hair lashed at her mouth from the wind and clung. Bloody wind forever mussing a girl.

If she'd thought to feel a latent fit of virginal moral turpitude, it was entirely swept away by that first glimpse of him.

She watched him, wondering how well *he'd* slept. The wind caught and tossed his hair, turning him briefly into a maypole. Nothing else about him was the least whimsical. Shirt open at the throat, sleeves rolled up to expose those hard forearms, hard thighs and long legs poured into those shiny boots. She willed him to come to her, and was afraid that he would, and she'd never felt such simultaneous terror and excitement.

He strode purposefully toward her and stopped, looking down.

She snatched at her hair to clear her vision.

Wordlessly, almost casually, he cupped her elbow, turned her and promenaded her across the deck. As though he had every confidence she would come peacefully wherever he chose to lead her. He steered her around the corner to the launches and longboats, a nook he'd clearly known would be visible neither from the deck nor from on high in the rigging.

Impressively purposeful.

And he stood—or rather, *loomed* over her, she revised, as her view of sky, the sea, the sun, the deck—leaving her with two choices: to stare at the *V* of gold skin and curling copper hair exposed by two undone buttons on his shirt. Or to look up into his face.

It took her perhaps two seconds longer than it ought to have to look up into his face.

His blue eyes seemed startlingly vivid, perhaps because they were suddenly her only source of light. His body radiated heat like a blacksmith's forge.

In moments she felt it—felt *him*—like a low fever everywhere on her skin.

She drew in a long shuddering breath.

Behind them sails snapped, a gull screeched, some member of the crew shouted a filthy word from on high to someone below. She could not say for how long they stood transfixed; seconds only, likely. Forever, possibly.

But she gave a start when his hands rose. She eyed them warily, her hammering heart sending the blood ringing in her ears. His fingers seemed to tremble a little in the shimmering heat of the day.

But they were steady when he rested the backs of them against the base of her throat. And something like wonder, and confusingly like supplication, flickered across his face. As though he was testing his welcome, or his own feelings. Surprised by them each time. He exhaled.

It was only then she realized he'd been holding his breath.

And only then she realized hers was held, too.

His hands traveled slowly, slowly upward, his touch so incongruously delicate it was almost indistinguishable from a breath blown against her skin. And just like that, as surely as a swami sings a cobra out of its basket, something languidly uncoiled in her veins. He'd awakened it last night.

It was called to life again by his hands.

If she had to give the thing a name she would have called it *hunger.*

It seemed everything on her body stood on end—the fine hairs at her nape, gooseflesh on her arms, her nipples. Breathing became a delicious struggle. Her eyelids were suddenly too heavy to remain aloft. When he encountered the leaping pulse in her throat he slowed his fingers there to savor it, and then his fingers threaded up through her hair, sending sparks of sensation scattershot over her skin and lighting tiny bonfires in surprising places in her body, and with one languid, fluid motion he eased her head back and brought his lips down to hers.

The kiss was exploratory. His mouth brushed hers, nudging gently, coaxing her lips apart, until they slipped open and clung to his. Lovely. Lovely. A series of exquisite contrasts dizzied her: his breath, and his firm lips, and the warm damp velvet of his mouth.

And when his tongue delicately touched hers a bolt of *want* cleaved clean through her. A force as consuming as pain, but quite its opposite.

She actually moaned.

Which is when he broke the kiss abruptly.

His hands remained threaded tightly through her hair. He looked down into her no doubt kiss-clouded eyes. She considered, absently, once again, that his hands were trembling, but surely this was because the world itself had begun to spiral.

"Violet." He murmured it as though trying out a new, possibly Turkish, word. She detected in it a peculiar hint of regret. A hint of warning.

And then he sighed, and gave a short dark laugh. "Oh, Violet."

He tugged back on her hair and his mouth came down hard.

It landed on hers, hot and open. She felt her own shameless low moan of relief vibrate in his mouth. *God.* For balance she curled her fingers into the rough linen of his shirt, found it hot from his skin and damp from perspiration and sea spray. Drugging and complex, so new, so male, the textures of his mouth infinite, she found herself taking of his lips, his tongue, his mouth, the way any proper Redmond would—as though she was purely entitled to the pleasure—taking the way only she could: recklessly. Their lips feinted, clung, slid, nipped; their tongues lashed and tangled, teeth clashed. The kisses never seemed deep enough.

He groaned what sounded like a filthy foreign word and scooped his hands under her arse and lifted her hard up against the hard cock straining through his trousers, and *oh God* that was exquisite. He ground his body rhythmically against her as he dragged his lips from ear to her throat, his hands running hard and hot over her back. She threaded her hands through his hair, found it damp and warm as incongruously silky as a boy's. His hot mouth, lips, tongue, teeth, branded her throat mercilessly where her heart threatened to hammer its way clean out of her body; she arched, abetting this. He crouched to slide his lips down, down, to dip his tongue into the shadow between her breasts, where he stopped a bead of her sweat with his tongue. And then his hand tugged down her bodice and he took her nipple in his mouth and sucked.

She gasped, clutching his head hard to her. He swiveled swiftly then and backed her hard against the wall, into the corner. It was all a blur now, a languid grappling tangle of bodies. She may have kissed his eyelid. She did kiss his temple. She licked his collarbone, tasted salt and skin before his lips reclaimed hers. She wanted to bite him. She didn't. She moaned again quietly, a desperate sound, because she wanted and didn't know what she wanted, and shivered from the onslaught of sensation as surely as if she'd caught a killing fever, loving and fearing it. Her knees would have buckled, but his hands held her hard, and his erection was so hard against her it hurt even as she ground her body against it, wanting, wanting.

He began to drag up her skirt, and God help her, somehow

he'd unbuttoned two of his trouser buttons. "I want you." His voice was hoarse in her ear.

"I don't . . ." Her voice shocked her; a raw, shaking husk against his lips. His mouth took another devouring kiss, stopping her sentence, which was fine, as she couldn't recall how she'd intended to complete it. He slid a hand beneath her thigh, lifted it to fit his hips against her. "I just . . ."

Nor that one.

I want was the only thing true.

But *what* did she want?

And suddenly she found the strength or the fear to push him away, but her fingers remained curled into his shirt as though he was shipwreck flotsam and she was in danger of drowning if she released him. Her body swayed with ragged breaths.

She looked down and saw her own blurred reflection in the polished toes of his boots.

She looked up, and found him staring down at her. And then he seized her hands from their grip and dragged them down, down, down, over the sweat-dampened linen of his shirt, her hands scraping the bumpy row of his shirt buttons, over the steel-banded muscles of his narrow waist.

To the hard bulge of his cock. And pressed her palms there.

Her head shot back, shocked. Her hand jerked reflexively, struggling to free itself.

He held her fast. Watched her carefully, eyes narrowed, jaw taut, harsh breaths wracking him.

He felt . . . merciless. And so alien and male and enormous she realized just how dangerously deep in she was. It was as sobering as a cold wave thrown against the face.

She tugged her hands again frantically.

He refused to relinquish her.

"Look at me," he ordered tersely.

She did. Her face was flaming now. The consequences of that kiss, of the feel of him, of what he wanted to do to her, the overpowering maleness of him, nearly burned through her trousers through to her hand. His chest swayed with short, nearly angry sounding breaths. Behind them the sea ceaselessly heaved, mocking them.

He leaned forward; his forehead touched hers. His skin was startlingly hot. And then his mouth, his breath, was in her ear, stirring again the fine hairs on her neck again, washing gooseflesh along her throat, lulling her eyes into sagging closed. *Help*, she thought futilely, addressing no one and everyone. She heard her own breath gusting against his chest.

He spoke, his voice husky, so gentle it was nearly a caress. But he measured the words out as evenly as a threat.

"You can't *toy* with me, Miss Redmond."

Her head snapped backward.

Blue glare met blue glare.

She knew it for what it was: a warning. He was not a pet. He was not a servant. He was not patient. He was making it very clear that the societal rules that had so entrapped her—and protected her, she understood now, and allowed her to behave as capriciously as she wished with so few real consequences, and to engage in this coy virginal dance—did not apply to him.

Despite the grand title foisted upon him, he had his own rules and cared nothing for hers.

What makes you think I won't take you? he'd said.

Dear God. He'd been about to. She'd been about to let him.

Her brother's wife, Cynthia, had once pretended to be an expert markswoman in order to impress a suitor. As a result, she'd ludicrously maimed a replica of the statue of David with a musket and nearly killed a man with the resulting hurtling marble penis.

Violet had just been handed her own metaphorical musket: her own passionate nature, unleashed. She now knew her desire was as reckless as her spirit and the full equal to the Earl of Ardmay's, and if she wasn't careful, of a certainty someone would be hurt, if not by a marble penis, then in some grave equivalent and metaphorical fashion.

She could never succumb. Even she knew that way lay ruin. But the fact that she now knew what she was missing and could never know it seemed the height of cruelty. She'd been denied so little in her life.

She was learning so much on this little voyage.

He slowly lifted his hands, releasing hers. Her palms were hot now from pressing against him; he seemed to burn through to her hands. He was no less hard or formidable than he'd been a moment ago.

He was no less the man that meant to send her brother to the gallows so he could realize his own dreams.

She took her hands away with feigned casualness. But as her hands slid back over his cock, he hissed in a breath, an involuntary sound of pleasure. And despite everything her body leaped ferociously in response, meeting desire with desire.

She was tempted to study her relinquished hands to see if they looked different, because, for heaven's sake, she'd just touched an erect penis, albeit through clothing, and a tiny childish part of her was thrilled and wished she could brag to someone.

Instead she dropped them to her sides and turned her head starboard, seeking composure out on that endless, impersonal, overwhelming blue ocean. She felt lost. For the first time in her life, she was utterly alone. No one, not Miles, not the perfidious Lyon, no one, could help her now. She had only her own counsel to rely upon, and she knew precisely what that was worth.

Flint hooked a finger beneath her chin and brought her face back sharply toward him.

She met his penetrating gaze with a cool pride that would have made any of her haughty ancestors applaud.

"Enough. Here are the rules to *this* particular game, Miss Redmond. My plans remain entirely the same. Nothing changes about my mission. You will not dissuade me from it. Either we do this or we do not. Decide."

Do this. Her face was scorching.

His plans.

Capture her brother and bring him to justice—and an almost certain hanging. Marry steadfast Fatima. Live in America.

And sanity returned with the force of a slap. She stared at him, numb with shock. For an instant she simply couldn't speak. Her body was still in tumult.

The rest of her was gravely wounded. She wasn't sure why.

And out the words came. "I've decided that *you* can go to the devil, Lord Flint."

His face blanked peculiarly for an instant. One would have thought she'd hurt him.

Then the corner of his mouth twitched into a regretful, half smile. He clucked with mock sympathy and shook his head slowly to and fro.

She jerked her chin away from him.

He studied her a moment longer. Then gave a short, cold nod, turned on his heel and strode across the deck.

She watched him go. And even as he was fortunate there was nothing within arm's reach she could hurl between those retreating shoulder blades, she felt bereft, tugged after him as surely as if he'd wound her round with a web.

She realized then she was shaking.

Blast. Bloody tears. She dashed at them furiously with her knuckles. But even as she watched him walk away, she knew several things for certain:

No one who trembled was unmoved.

And Captain Flint had indeed trembled when he'd touched her.

And Captain Flint had pressed a jasmine blossom into a copy of her brother's book.

And she knew that flicker across his face for what it was: awe.

Oh, Captain. My dear earl. I suspect I can *toy with you.*

She realized fully then that he *was* just as afraid as she was. But somehow knowing she had this sort of power over a man who seemed invincible frightened her even more than if she'd none at all.

Chapter 18

Three days later the ship's bell rang, announcing their arrival in the benign, spectacularly blue bay that eased them into Brest.

The Olivia was anchored among a number of other trading vessels. Looking gay and enigmatic and sleek . . . apart from her four guns, of course.

The Caridad, due in Brest after sailing from Le Havre, they saw nowhere.

For the three prior days, Violet had astounded Hercules by spending almost the entirety of her time in the galley. He watched, gaping, as she scrubbed it spotless. She ground grain. She peeled and chopped whatever was placed before her to peel and chop. She stitched sails. She'd hoped to exhaust herself from her soul outward so thoroughly that sleep would be a black, dreamless escape.

As it turned out, her body wanted sleep less than it wanted the Earl of Ardmay.

It chose to toss and turn in a fever of resentment and desire, rather than oblige her with soothing dreams.

She wasn't *hiding* in the galley, she told herself.

She'd never hidden from anything in her life.

Of course, the moment she saw the Earl of Ardmay she realized this wasn't true.

The sight of him clubbed her breathless.

But she had to admit, within the past few days he'd begun to look a trifle . . . *disreputable*, she decided with critical surprise. He'd missed a minuscule row of whiskers beneath his chin, when usually his face was scraped scrupulously smooth. Blue smudges of fatigue arced beneath his eyes. Perhaps he'd taken to drinking the nights away.

He took a long, long expressionless look at her. She bravely, coolly met this stare, while her knees struggled to hold her up.

He'd clearly decided he needn't waste words on someone who had told him, quite clearly, to go to the devil. Because he said nothing at all. As they were lowered into the launches, he spoke only to the crew, and only to issue orders: Lavay would row out to *The Olivia* with Greeber and Cocoran to see if Hardesty were aboard, or whether they could discover anything else of interest about *The Olivia* or her crew; and then, if possible, they would query sailors on the docks to see if they could learn anything about the owners or crews of the ships that Le Chat had thus far plundered.

He and Miss Redmond would visit Mr. Musgrove, as promised.

From the rowdy dockside inn they sent word via messenger to the merchant of their arrival and the purpose of their visit. Within the hour he'd sent his own landau to take them through Brest's handsome, crowded streets to a villa of pink stone twice the size of the usual London town house. The least he could do for an earl, and so forth, according to his reply.

And what a cold, silent, albeit mercifully short journey that was. Violet and the earl sat opposite each other and watched a portion of town roll by out of the windows adjacent to their seats, like polite, mute tourists.

Mr. Musgrove himself greeted them at the door, beckoning them in.

"My apologies for the poor quality of the wine I'm about to serve you, Captain Flint. Sent Fenton running off to fetch it. Le Chat sank *The Caridad* in the Bay of Biscay and stole the beautiful sherry I was expecting just two days ago. You are lately styled an earl, I am to understand? Forgive me. Allow me to congratulate you and make my bow before I complain to you of my own tragedies. I have it all backward, the social niceties, but I have had a traumatic, traumatic time of it indeed."

They'd been too late to save *The Caridad.*

The shock of the news landed in her gut.

Followed by an odd thrill, odd because her feelings about it were decidedly mixed: she'd had indeed been right about Brest and about *The Caridad.*

She glanced sidelong at the earl. His fingers twitched, then flattened hard against his thighs. His profile was granite hard.

Angry likely didn't go far enough to describe how he felt at arriving too late.

Musgrove didn't notice. "And who is this young lady?" He belatedly turned to her. She was destined to be an afterthought for everyone today, she thought irritably.

"My ward, Miss Violet Redmond." Five curt, inflectionless words from the earl.

Ward? Very well. She was his ward, then. She curtsied.

"Ah, your ward?" Mr. Musgrove was clearly too distracted to feel any curiosity about her, and the Redmond name didn't ring any particular bells for him. "Pleasure, my dear."

The buttons of Mr. Musgrove's exquisitely tailored coat strained to hold it closed. Violet stood back warily when he bowed, lest one fly from it like a pistol shot and take out her eye. But he carried his belly before him like a trophy of his success; he strutted.

They followed him.

For quite a long way, as it turned out. The house was large.

From the looks of things, he'd acquired or copied taste, as his home was furnished with pieces doubtlessly purchased from French aristocrats fleeing the guillotine. Everywhere her gaze snagged on gilt and the fancifully turned legs of table and chairs too spindly to hold him. *They* were trophies, too.

But Mr. Musgrove's complexion was an unhealthy cherry color and he was sweating like a blacksmith in Hades. He dabbed at the rivulets racing down his forehead with a delicate handkerchief at rhythmic intervals.

It wasn't very hot in Brest. He was clearly suffering from nerves.

"Your loss is devastating, Mr. Musgrove," the earl agreed coldly.

"I should say so, Lord Flint! I should say so! Five thousand pounds worth of cargo, easily! I would love to guillotine that bastard Le Chat. It's the second of my ships he's captured and sunk. I feel persecuted," he moaned. "Persecuted! Do you mind if I sit?"

He dropped into a high-backed chair that gave an alarmed squeak and hoisted his feet up onto a plush red stool. Violet noticed his little feet bulged over the tops of his finely stitched shoes.

"Thank you, Fenton," he said to the be-wigged, dazzlingly liveried footman, silent as a cat, who brought in a bottle and two more glasses and then crept out again.

The earl and Violet settled into their seats slightly more gingerly than their host, because Mr. Musgrove had taken the sturdiest chair, leaving them to the spindly satin-covered ones.

He gazed at them, his thunderous expression and internal

chaos distinctly at odds with the need to provide promised hospitality.

Understandably, the smile he finally produced was sickly.

"How do you know for certain it was Le Chat who sank *The Caridad*?" The earl's voice was astonishingly calm.

"From what I hear, he lowered the crew of *The Caridad* into boats after he and his crew soundly trounced mine. Swords and pistols, they used. He wears a bloody mask, did you know?" He made circles of this thumbs and forefingers and held them up to his eyes.

"By way of disguise? Silly, ain't it? Pirates!" He shook his head in violent disbelief, which sent his hair and jowls swaying spellbindingly. "But my men made it to shore in the launch, parched, starving and their trousers all but pissed in fear. But lived to tell the tale. I want Le Chat's *head*! You've had a loss recently, too, eh, Lord Flint? Thanks to Le Chat? You were associated with Captain Moreheart?"

Associated with. The earl seemed to consider this as he took a sip of his port.

Violet watched his hands. *They shook when he touched me*, she thought. Those powerful hands of this powerful man.

She imagined his fingertips skimming her throat.

Her eyes half closed against the shocking onslaught of sensation.

His hands were steady now.

Hers no longer were. She carefully set her glass down.

"Yes. *The Steadfast* went down. Attributed to Le Chat. The crew hasn't been found."

Musgrove clucked, shook his head. "Moreheart was a damn good man, too. Begging your pardon, Miss Redmond. For the 'damn.' Oh dear, I beg your pardon once more. I did business with Moreheart, so I know. So we are united, then, in our determination to end this scoundrel's scourge, and I wish you the best, Lord Flint, for from what I understand, you are certainly the man for the job. Here's to retrieving Le Chat's head."

He raised his glass, and the earl raised his, but Violet sipped at her wine noncommittally, unwilling to toast to the decapitation of her brother, even in pretense.

"Would it be possible to speak to one of your crew about the incident, Mr. Musgrove? Do you know if they're still in port or whether they've hired on to other ships? Do you recall who captained her?"

"The earl could use a cook's mate," Violet tried sweetly. "If one is available."

"But the one I have now works so cheaply even if new to the concept of *work*, and is so devoted to work they scarcely see the deck anymore," the earl replied smoothly. Still not looking at her.

He was at least very aware she hadn't been on deck.

A pathetic thing to cherish. Nevertheless.

Mr. Musgrove was too immersed in his own woes to care about theirs, or notice any byplay.

"I don't know what became of the crew, sir. Likely they've scattered to the four winds and could be on their way to Ecuador by now. Cannot even recall their names. Good luck and God-speed to you. Wish you'd been earlier." There wasn't a shred of accusation in this sentiment. It was bitterly wistful.

"As do I, Mr. Musgrove."

The earl pulled out his watch and reviewed the time, then slid it back into his coat pocket. "I'm curious—did any of your men get a look at the pirate's ship? So much of what we know about Le Chat is hearsay."

Musgrove shook his head and winced at the flavor of the wine. Violet thought it was perfectly acceptable, though she wasn't tempted to drink it down. Now, if it had been champagne . . . or sherry . . .

"'Twas night, of course; there was fog, as this was on the Bay of Biscay. No one could say for certain. It happened very quickly. *Very* professional," he said snidely. And gulped down the remainder of his wine, made a face, and slapped the glass down rather too hard on a table that was likely a hundred years older than him.

Then gave them another weak smile. And sighed.

"Mr. Musgrove . . ." Violet began hesitantly. "You said you did business with Captain Moreheart of *The Steadfast*."

The earl tensed almost imperceptibly.

"Yes, Miss Redmond." Musgrove inspected her closely for the first time, his sharp brown eyes clearly approving everything from her coiffure to her slippers. No doubt tallying up the value of all of it with his mercantile heart, rather than lusting after her other feminine assets.

"Were you part of an investment group? My father is, and often likes to finance ventures such as these," she said brightly.

"Does he? I'm down two ships now, but not entirely shed of capital. We may wish to have a conversation, your father and I, my dear." He clearly found it endearing that she should bother her feminine head over business.

She leaned forward like an eager pupil. "Where do you invest your profits?" she asked almost breathlessly. Enjoying her own performance.

Mr. Musgrove poured more wine. Behind him, a clock pendulum swung. Once, twice.

Only three times, but it was enough to convince her he was officially delaying his response.

"Into more cargo, of course, Miss Redmond." He smiled again. "More wine?"

"No, thank you."

She glanced at the earl to see if he'd noticed Mr. Musgrove's hesitance.

He had. And was clever enough to follow it with one of his own questions.

"Where was *The Caridad* bound after she delivered her goods here in Brest?" he tried.

"I'd planned to send her on to Cádiz on a mission to purchase sherry, you know. Amontillado. Marvelous stuff. Another of our investors will send a ship from La Rochelle instead. *The Prosperar*."

"What kinds of cargo do you usually invest in?" she asked. It was an excellent question.

"It varies, my dear." He leveled upon Violet a look reminiscent of Isaiah Redmond. Disciplinary and indulgent. She hadn't missed those looks in the *least* for the past week or so, she realized. "I imagine you're interested in the latest silks, and that's why you ask?"

"Of course," she decided to say. She gave a little laugh and lowered her eyes, pretending to be abashed.

Charmed, he smiled benevolently.

At least the earl was looking at her at last. The look was decidedly bemused, but he was looking at her, nevertheless.

He spoke. "I'm curious, Mr. Musgrove. Have you spoken with Mr. Hardesty whilst he's in port? We were to dine with him in Le Havre but we unfortunately missed each other, and we've business to discuss."

"Ah, Hardesty." Musgrove leaned back in his chair. "Apparently if you want to see Hardesty all you have to do is look for your best friend's wife, and he'll be alongside her in bed." He chuckled richly, then gave a start when he remembered Violet. "Good heavens, begging your pardon, Miss Redmond. A man has difficulty minding what he says, you know, when he's lost five thousand pounds and a ship!

It's a shock," he murmured. "A shock." He dabbed at his forehead, as more sweat beads popped. "It's all hearsay regarding Hardesty, too, and his, shall we say, amorous conquests. Begging your pardon, Miss Redmond. But I've heard of women weeping and rending their garments over him. *Friend* of Hardesty's, are you, Captain Flint?" He said his as though it were unlikely indeed.

"Acquaintance. I dined with Comte Hebert in Le Havre and we'd hope to discuss a particular matter of trade with Mr. Hardesty, but he sent his regrets. Was otherwise detained. I'd hoped to pass on a message from the viscomte to him in port."

"Try the pubs. Or row on out to *The Olivia*. Someone's bound to know where he's got to. You now, I've met him but the once. No devil should be allowed to possess looks like his. What *choice* does he have but to break hearts? What man's wife or daughter is safe? Women are only women after all. Begging your pardon, Miss Redmond. Again. Though he certainly is a worthy competitor when it comes to trade. Has four guns aboard *The Olivia*. Fast ship, that one. He'll outrace Le Chat for certain."

"She is quick, indeed," the earl said ironically.

And Violet knew the "she" encompassed her, too, and was unsure whether to be flattered or uneasy.

The earl slammed his beaver hat down on his head as they departed in Musgrove's landau.

That was her first clue that he was angrier than she'd originally thought.

The next came immediately thereafter.

"What aren't you telling me, Miss Redmond? What else do you know? I do not appreciate being made a *fool*."

She was speechless in the face of his anger.

Ah, so it hadn't been silence so much as it had been a

gathering storm that had now broken. He was so coldly furious that he seemed to increase to twice his size.

"Speak, or I will leave you here in the port if you don't tell me *now*."

"Come now, Lord Flint. Are you angry at me, or are you angry at your failure to get here in time?"

Oh God. Why, why, *why* did she taunt him? She never, never could help herself.

He didn't like this at *all*. His eyes narrowed. He issued what sounded like a feral growl.

"If you've withheld *anything* from me that might have helped in any way . . ." He let the threat dangle.

Enough. Temper was an indulgence. *No one* spoke to a Redmond that way.

"I'm telling you *all I know*, you bloody arrogant man, and you should be *grateful* that I have. I swear to you on my family that I have—will that suit you? I'm not happy that *The Caridad* was sunk. Or to think my brother may have been involved. But I was *right* about Brest. Shouldn't that alone tell you something of my honesty? And furthermore, Lord Flint, as I said before, I know my brother. And it's *not* as simple as you would like it to be. You *heard* that hesitation in Musgrove's voice, didn't you, when I asked him about cargo? He's hiding something!"

She realized then that at some point he'd stopped truly listening to her words and had simply begun watching her. His thoughts clearly divided.

"*Didn't* you?" she demanded, a little more weakly. *Damn blue eyes*.

He was still studying her. "Miss Redmond?"

"What is it?" she snapped.

"You look horrible." His voice was brutally cold and censorious.

She recoiled as though he'd struck her.

Her first thought was, "That's *impossible*." She *was* Violet Redmond, after all.

He began to enumerate her flaws on his fingers. "You've dark shadows beneath your eyes. Which are red, by the way. You look pale. Nearly haggard. Almost as if you *haven't slept for days*. I wonder why that is? Could it be that something is preying upon your mind?"

She stared at him through eyes slit with fury.

"But your hair is *perfect*," he concluded snidely.

Scoundrel!

"My conscience is not tormenting me over something I'm not telling you regarding Le Chat, if *that's* what you're implying." Her words were taut.

"I know it isn't. It's not what I'm implying."

This brought her up short. She began to frown. Then stopped immediately, smoothing fingers across her forehead.

"*You* are not precisely the picture of radiant health, Captain. Speaking of sallow complexions and dark shadows and the like. You look quite . . . quite . . . *disreputable*, in fact."

He dropped his mouth open in mock horror. "*Surely* not disreputable!"

"*Worse* than that." Still, she could not bring herself to say *savage*.

His voice went frighteningly gentle.

"Ah, but do you know what *my* trouble is, Violet?" Very ironic. "Because *I* do. Here it is: I am the captain of *The Fortuna*. I have a great responsibility to my men and now to the bloody King of *England*. My fortunes are dwindling. My reputation and my entire future rest upon my success in capturing this pirate for bounty. And yet . . ."

And he leaned toward her slowly, slowly, confidingly, hands folded casually folded on his knees, his hat dangling from one of them. The more forward he leaned the more backward *she* leaned, until she was pressed back against the admittedly very comfortable seat of the landau.

He dropped each syllable heavily, wearily, ironically.

". . . and yet *I* cannot sleep at night for wanting you."

No lawyer had ever made an accusation sound quite so egregious. And yet it was infused with a sort of desperate wryness.

Her breath left her in a tiny shocked gust.

She stared at him. And then pressed her hands involuntarily against her eyes, like a child, wanting to hide from her own frustration and from the weary yet ferocious, wry and very determined desire she saw in his face.

And because she feared his will was more powerful than her own, and acknowledging this was a concession on her part indeed.

And then she pulled her hands away from her eyes so she could glare her feigned indifference properly.

"Tell me you don't want me," he said the moment she did. A quick low demand.

Her hands sought and found each other, folded tightly together in disciplinary solidarity in her lap. *No: you will not touch him.*

He shifted farther forward and spoke in a low, hard, persuasive rush. "Tell me you haven't lain awake each night imagining nothing else but my hands on your body. And my mouth on your breasts. And my cock inside you, Violet."

Her lips parted on a shocked *oh.* Heat roared over her body.

He knew precisely what he was doing to her. She'd been nearly *savage* in his arms, after all. He knew what she wanted, and how wildly she responded.

"I don't think of your *cock* in precisely those terms," she said tightly.

She'd never said such a word aloud in her life. It was desperately coarse and erotic and as thrilling as brandishing a loaded weapon. Then again, he'd handed the weapon to her.

So to speak.

It had the desired effect of shocking *him*. His eyes flared wide. She'd momentarily thrown him. He was not so impervious, then, as he seemed. He was not invulnerable. She was reminded again of her power over him. It was a power that baffled and tormented him, and perversely made her want to protect him. As she'd always wanted to protect him.

I don't want you like this, she thought desperately.

But she didn't know how she wanted him.

"Well, then," he drawled softly, pensively. "Why don't you share with me which of my *parts* you do think about when you're alone? I might find it instructive. I might even put them to use for your pleasure. I know so very, very much about pleasure, Violet. And I know you enjoy an adventure."

You would think by now you would have learned not to toy with him, her conscience told her, shaking its head wearily.

She could hear her own breath now, shallow and ragged with fury. And frankly, feral *want*.

He was enjoying this. He was also clearly in hell. Then again, he was eminently adaptable, and had managed to make a sort of heaven from hell many times in his life.

She was new at this.

He gave her a small, tight smile.

"Go on, Violet. Say you don't want me. Make me believe it."

"Unfair," she muttered.

"Unfair?" He sounded genuinely astonished, almost disappointed that she could only come up with that pallid word. "*Fair*? What the bloody *hell* does 'fair' have to do with . . . any of this?" His knuckles were white, so hard were his hands clenching the brim of his hat.

Any of this. Meaning desire. Pirates. His diminishing fortune. The fact that they could not be more at cross-purposes regarding Lyon Redmond's fate.

"It isn't my fault," she tried desperately. *I'm suffering, too.*

"Like. Hell," he disagreed evenly.

Well. So *American* he sounded then. And hardly gallant. He did have a point, however. It was *somewhat* her fault. She'd rather courted it all from the beginning.

"All I ask is that you look in my eyes and say it, Violet. And make me believe it."

Bastard.

She bravely looked into his eyes. Felt her heart constrict when she saw again those shadows ringing them, fatigue deepening the lines about them. His face was taut with emotion that she knew was equal parts frustration and something he would never admit to, something that was frightening and startlingly new to both of them, and had a good deal to do with why he'd saved that jasmine blossom in the book.

But desire was so much simpler to understand, and so desire is what they called it.

She leaned forward a little, matching his posture.

"I. Don't. Want. You."

Rivers had flowed uphill with more ease than she'd uttered that sentence.

Once she'd done it, she felt utterly spent. In saying it, she'd won. *I have no more lies in me*, she thought. *If he asked me to say it again, I simply couldn't. He could take me now.* Her limbs were weak.

He blinked.

And before her eyes the ferocity slowly went out of him. Blood returned to the knuckles. His hand loosened on his hat. He laid it delicately on the seat next to him. And studied her quietly.

Too drained to do anything else, she looked helplessly, wordlessly back at him.

Then he sat back and transferred a brooding stare out the carriage window.

And was silent the rest of the way to the inn.

She couldn't help but note that brooding suited him every bit as much as . . .

Every single other thing he did.

Lavay was the jarringly sunny opposite of the earl. They found him easily, as his hair shone like a polished doubloon in the raucous smoke-filled murk of the inn. He was lounging with long legs outstretched, managing to make the scarred table and sturdy battered chair he occupied look like a throne. In his hand was a tankard of ale and over him bent the barmaid who'd brought it to him, as though she was about to ease herself into his lap. From the surly, resentful faces of the men at the tables surrounding him and the condition of their pint glasses—nearly empty—she'd been lingering with Lavay for longer than was practical.

"Ah! Sit, my friends, sit," he greeted them cheerily. "Polly will bring each of you an ale, won't you dear?"

Polly straightened with apparent reluctance to take a look at Lavay's friends. Her bosom shifted tectonically in her bodice and continued quivering for some time after she stopped moving. Corkscrews of red hair sprung from beneath the edges of her white cap and she'd a veritable galaxy of freckles over skin fairer even than Violet's, and her brows and lashes were nearly invisibly fair.

She took the swift measure of the large thunderous earl. Her round face became comically fulsome with appreciation.

"I will bring *you* anything you want, monsieur," she vowed on a purr. "*Ma grandpére* Ned, 'e brew the finest in all of Brest."

Her hand went up over her own breast as if by way of illustration, and the earl followed it there with his eyes.

"I'll have a whiskey," Violet told Polly coolly. "And seven pints of ale."

Three pairs of eyes turned on her in astonishment.

Because that's *what it will take to even begin to take the edge off my nerves and temper.*

But something wriggled into her awareness beneath the nerves and temper. She began to frown. The barmaid's name was *Polly.* And her grandfather *Ned*? Polly was the name of Ned Hawthorne's daughter. She served the patrons at the Pig & Thistle and had had been moony every since Colin Eversea's marriage.

Ned Hawthorne owned the Pig & Thistle pub in Pennyroyal Green!

Polly and *Ned* were hardly French names.

"Bring a pint of dark, Polly, *merci*," the earl said, unabashedly, overtly enjoying the view of the barmaid's bosom the way one might admire any natural wonder. She was clearly accustomed to it. "And our friend here was jesting about whiskey. She will have one light ale."

He yanked out a chair for Violet with the other, and motioned for her to sit without looking at her.

Lavay deigned to reel in his legs so the earl could sit in the chair next to him.

Polly and Ned. Her spine was almost stinging with portent. Breathless now, Violet ducked her head and surreptitiously scanned the room. All around her were drinking sailors: it was evident from the weathered bristly faces, knotted neck cloths, dirty, turned-up sleeves on striped or dingy linen shirts. A scattering of men dressed very like the earl in casually elegant clothes seemed to be biding their time over ale while waiting to board ships leaving port. Myriad languages and accents rose and fell.

And, of course, she saw Lyon nowhere.

She closed her eyes in weary frustration. Thanks to Lyon's cryptic note she was clearly now doomed to see portent everywhere. She was generally accustomed to *causing* surprises, but her nerves hadn't yet become inured to enduring them again and again and again.

Getting her eyes open again proved to be surprisingly difficult. Exhaustion was wrestling with her will. *You wanted variety*, she thought wryly.

She got them open again. And saw the earl's eyes darting from her face. He'd been watching her.

His knee shifted, brushing hers beneath the table as he turned to look about the room, perhaps wondering what she was looking for.

He might as well have drawn a finger up her bare thigh, such was the jolt of sensation. Violet felt her knees begin to yearningly drift apart beneath the table.

She clapped them shut with considerable effort.

He was all too willing to fight dirty. Lavay had said this about the earl. She really doubted the knee brush had been an accident, as much as she doubted he was innocent of the effect it had on her.

One of the earl's eyebrows twitched in feigned puzzlement when he noticed himself framed in her fixed, accusatory gaze. He casually craned his head again, and looked visibly relieved to see Polly wending through the crowd with his ale.

Lavay, for his part, seemed entirely unaffected by the moods of his companions, but then he'd had a head start on the ale. "Well, I should tell you that I rowed out to *The Olivia* with Corcoran and Greeber. We were greeted by a few polite and quite closemouthed crew members, all of whom, I should say, were *enormous*, well-spoken and positively bristling with weapons. Would do our own crew proud, Captain. No, Mr. Hardesty wasn't aboard. He was ashore. No, they didn't know where he'd got to. He was likely in a meeting in Le Havre, as he was a Very Important Trader, and so forth. And as we could hardly demand to search the ship on circumstantial evidence . . . well, naturally we rowed back out again. *BUT* . . ."

He leaned back, and drummed his fingers, and looked decidedly pleased with himself.

"What?" Flint was in no mood for suspense.

". . . not before I issued an invitation for Mr. Hardesty to dine with me, Captain Flint, and Captain Flint's doxie, Violet Redmond, aboard *The Fortuna* tonight."

"Doxie?" Violet choked.

The earl pointedly did not look at her.

Lavay seemed mildly puzzled. "Well, but of course, Miss Redmond. Didn't you agree to be the earl's—"

"It's perfect," the earl interjected smoothly. "Lavay knows that we agreed early on, Miss Redmond, that your brother would, shall we say, *object* to the thought of you being defiled by the likes of me, which would make you very effective bait. Hence his stratagem. I commend it."

He took a little too much wicked, dark relish in the word *defiled.* With his eyes he warned her, and not kindly, to compose herself. Lavay was not stupid, and he was studying her with those cool gray eyes, and would draw conclusions about her and the earl she disliked.

They *were* going to lure Lyon into a trap, using her as bait.

Her hands turned to ice.

"It's the point of you continuing with us, isn't it? You agreed to be bait?" the earl said with intolerable calm.

Lavay had more to say. "I might have also put it about that the doxie Violet Redmond had been *very* reluctant to submit to the earl's attentions at first, but that the earl actually preferred a bit of a battle every time, so he considered this an asset. And that he would be happy to share her with Mr. Hardesty if he was in need of a little fiery feminine *companionship.*" Lavay was proud of himself.

"Good God. *Very* good work, Lavay," the earl approved admiringly.

Violet was horrified by the plan's brilliance. "But . . . It will *kill* Lyon to hear it. He won't be able to *bear* hearing it. He'll be determined to . . . kill *you*."

"That is the point," Lavay said a little too happily and bloodthirstily. "But no killing will take place if we can help it. We'll simply apprehend him then."

The earl's knee shifted ever so slightly again against hers as he turned to greet the barmaid like a long lost friend.

This time Violet had no trouble jerking it away from him. Appalled, in that instant to be touching him.

With what in God's name had she been *thinking*?

She hadn't been thinking with her brain.

Of course these men were deadly serious in their intent to capture Lyon. As the earl had said earlier in the landau, his entire future depended upon bringing him to justice. "Justice" in England was entirely too often synonymous with "hanging by the neck until dead."

Violet went silent. There was nothing like envisioning her brother dancing at the end of a rope or helpless at the point of a pistol to kill desire.

Polly the barmaid seemed to have suddenly sprouted eight arms and each one was carrying a foaming pint of ale. She crouched to begin plunking theirs down on the table.

"'ere you are, monsieur, the fine dark ye asked for and I hope you enjoy it, and for mademois—*OH*!"

She dumped the entirety of a light ale down Violet's bodice.

Violet gasped and shot backward, toppling her chair, scrambling to her feet, sending the now empty tankard rolling the length of her shins to land on the floor with a clank.

She flung out her arms, staring down at the sodden bodice. Ale had all but glued it to her.

Violet stared pure evil at the barmaid.

The men began to stand warily.

Polly began babbling inconsolably. "*Mon dieu*, mademoiselle, I am so, so clumsy! I am *horrified*! You must—"

Without preamble she seized Violet's arm with shockingly strong hands and dragged her through the chuckling, ogling crowd to the bar. She seized a rag and began scrubbing at her bodice and rattling rapid-fire unaccented, hushed and very aristocratic English at her.

"Quiet. Quickly. Short answers. Are you or are you not the earl's doxie?"

Violet's heart stopped.

"*Quickly!* Yes or no?"

"No. You work for—"

"Yes. For God's sake, don't say his name," she hissed.

"Is your name really Polly?" Clever Lyon!

"*I'm* asking the questions. Are you with the earl voluntarily?"

"This is silk. Have a care. Yes."

Polly became a bit less vigorous with the scrubbing. "Why?"

"To try to find Lyon. The earl wants to capture him. I want to find him. I am to be bait."

Dab dab dab Polly went at her bodice. "Are you truly well and safe?"

The questions and answers were swift, under-breath, staccato.

"The earl will not harm me. He is a good man. He has been charged by the king with capturing Le Chat."

He will test my will, he will haunt my dreams, he'll make me peel potatoes, he'll make me crave his touch with a mere glance, but no. He will not harm me.

And why do I feel like a traitor to that bastard even now?

Polly dabbed once more, giving up, and flung the rag over the bar.

"Another two pint of ze dark and light," she bellowed.

Violet put her hand on Polly's arm. "What the *hell* is Lyon doing? Why is he doing it? *Please* tell him to come home. *Why* can't I see him? Please. *Please* tell me."

"He has more work to do," Polly said shortly. "Hush now. Hush."

"Where is he going next? What does 'two more' mean? Tell me that at *least*! Is it ships?"

"Enough." Polly's lips clamped closed. "We are finished. Go sit down. I'll bring you another ale. Say nothing of this."

Violet drifted back to the table, damp, stunned, happy, furious, and utterly unmindful of the drinkers leering at her bodice, which was still clinging to her absurdly provocatively.

Her chair had been righted; she sat, still dazed. She felt the earl's eyes bore into her. She didn't meet them.

Lavay and the earl had been joined by a raw-boned, florid man who wore his shaggy blond hair pushed behind his ears. His black coat was well tailored, apart from the slash in the sleeve. As though he'd recently been in a knife or sword battle. A battered beaver hat sat in his lap.

"Miss Redmond, this is Captain William Gullickson, lately of *The Caridad*. Lavay met him this afternoon and invited him to join us here."

Ah. The captain of the ship they'd been too late to save.

Gullickson half stood and performed an awkward nodded to her. "A pleasure, Miss Redmond."

The voice was drink-and-smoke-roughened but the accent hinted at a formal English education somewhere in his distant past. He slicked a hand through his hair self-consciously. The hair was dirty. His nails were dirty. She was careful not to take too deep of a breath, because she was certain he bathed indifferently.

"I'm not certain whether this is a conversation a . . . *lady* . . .

should hear." He glanced up at Violet, then almost shyly glanced away. Too long at sea, too roughened to feel comfortable in a presence as refined as hers.

Polly appeared and plopped two ales onto the tabletop. "No charge, monsieur, due to my mishap."

She winked at the earl and ignored Violet utterly.

"Miss Redmond has a sturdy constitution," the earl assured Captain Gullickson. "You may speak before her."

She realized her bodice was still damp, and she shivered with it. She glanced down, and saw that her nipples were alert and staring directly at the earl.

He followed her gaze. His knuckles immediately went white around the tankard of ale he was gripping. He stared. He toasted her ironically, shook his head slightly, lifted the tankard and drank most of it down in one long anaesthetizing gulp.

She watched his throat move. And then she forced her eyes to her lap. Breathed in, breathed out. Lyon would be safe from the earl and Lavay for now.

He has more work to do. But *what* work was Lyon doing?

She was heartily sick of all the men in her life at the moment.

"You want to know how it happened?" Gullickson began. "With Le Chat. They came on in the fog, so we couldn't see his ship. Surprised us, they did. Came over the sides, quiet as cats. Le Chat, indeed." He shook his head bitterly. "Came in launches, from what we saw later. Had us surrounded almost before we could draw swords or pistols, and then they fought like devils. Swords. The pistols were for later, when they forced us into the boats. *Honorable.*" He laughed shortly and spat abruptly on the ground, and Violet jumped.

"The whole lot of them in masks. Like something out of a nightmare it was." He looked up for sympathy and got it in the form of nods from Lavay and Flint. "But he was a *gentleman*. No disguising that, is there?" Another of those ugly laughs. "I'll never forget it. He said, 'It's for the good of all, Captain Gullickson.' " Gullickson mimicked an absurdly refined drawl. "How the bloody hell could *that* be true, I ask you? Robbing and sinking ships? How did he know it was *my* ship? And then I hear the guns, and *The Caridad* . . . well, I watched her sink with my own eyes. I've been drinking ever since."

He drained his pint and banged it on the table for another, craning his head in vain for the barmaid. Flint didn't look eager to buy him another one. Violet suspected the captain had been drinking long before *The Caridad* sank and rather enjoyed the excuse to continue drinking.

"Did you see what Le Chat looked like?" Flint asked with cool detachment. "Any details would be helpful."

"Nay. Was dark. Foggy. He was tall, near tall as you, Lord Flint. Lean. Hair was dark. Saw that. Not long. Clean-shaven. Quite the *dandy*. Apart from the ridiculous mask."

She still had trouble picturing Lyon wearing a mask. How Jonathan would laugh.

"Earrings? Tattoos? Scars?"

Parrots? Violet wanted to ask, remembering Jonathan's fit of mirth.

He shrugged. "Saw none of those things. But 'twas dark, as I said. Lit only by ship's lamps."

"How did he get you into the launches?" Lavay prompted.

"He had a crew relieve us of our cargo right quick. And then they got us over the side at sword and pistol point. I'd no doubt he would have shot us if any of us had said *boo*. We bobbed out there like a load of bloody apples, set loose without a compass. Was picked up by *The Lilibeth* sailing into Brest, else we would have all perished."

The earl's long fingers tapped against the side of his now empty tankard. "It fits with all the other accounts we've heard so far of Le Chat. He isn't unnecessarily brutal, he isn't ugly, he's polite, and the blighter steals everything and then sinks the ships. So we can likely trust the accounts we've heard."

"You can trust mine. Good luck catching the bastard. He has nine lives. Like a cat."

"For whom do you sail, Captain Gullickson?" Violet asked this suddenly. "Who is your employer?"

She saw all the heads turning toward her, surprised.

He was still diffident. He turned part of the way; he didn't meet her eyes when he answered. It struck her that he behaved like a man who'd done things he wasn't entirely proud of, or perhaps he was being careful of her modesty, as her bodice was still damp.

"When I return from a voyage, I'm paid by draft drawn on an account held by an English firm in La Rochelle. Up the coast a ways, as you'll know. The Drejeck Company, they're called. A group of investors, I'm to understand. Dined with one of them here in Brest last night—Mr. Musgrove. Perhaps you know him? Right upset, he is. He lost thousands of pounds. *I* nearly didn't get paid. But I would have made the man walk the plank if I hadn't been." He smiled nastily.

Violet began to frown. Then stopped instantly as a flash from the earl's eyes warned her not to react.

Because Musgrove had told them earlier he couldn't remember the name of the captain or any of the crew.

And yet Gullickson and Musgrove had dined together *just last night*.

And Musgrove had said they'd be sending a ship, *The Prosperar*, from La Rochelle, to take up the task of purchasing sherry now that *The Caridad* had been sunk.

"Are you acquainted with a Mr. Hardesty, Mr. Gullickson?

Another very successful trader? Captains *The Olivia*." Lavay asked this.

"Met him a year or so ago in this very pub. I was just back from America then. So was Mr. Hardesty. We shared a tale or two."

So Lyon had been in *America*? Good God. Where *else* had he been?

Gullickson banged his empty pint again, making her jump.

Violet suddenly looked about for Polly. She was gone as if she'd never been in the pub at all.

"What ship did you captain then?" The earl's question. Mild, almost abstracted. He asked it as he peered out the window toward the harbor, as if thinking of his own ship.

A hesitation from Gullickson.

"Large cargo, sir." And he smiled. He refrained from answering any other part of the question. And didn't volunteer the name of the ship.

Flint and Lavay exchanged a fleeting enigmatic glance.

Gullickson fixed his eyes on the earl now. The red veins mapping his eyes matched the highway of veins hatching his cheeks.

And Violet understood that this was not a pleasant man.

"La Rochelle is about two days up the coast, if the weather is fair," Flint said casually. "Lovely journey, if it is. Thank you for your time and good luck on your voyage . . . Captain."

Gullickson looked longingly for the barmaid, and understood he would not be watered with any more free ale tonight courtesy of the earl.

"On the contrary, thank *you* for the ale and the conversation with a fellow seafarer, Lord Flint, Lord Lavay." Gullickson slid his chair back, got upright, and bowed to them. But he departed at a slight stagger.

"Flint . . ." Lavay's voice was strange. "Drejeck means 'triangle' in German."

"I know." Flint was grim.

"Why is 'triangle' significant?" Violet demanded.

Lavay glanced at the earl. The earl nodded, giving Lavay permission to answer her question.

"Have you heard of the Triangle Trade, Miss Redmond?"

"I have, in fact. I read about it in one of those pamphlets Olivia Eversea left in the Pig & Thistle." *I must have been truly bored that evening to read the pamphlet*, she thought. "It has to do with slavery, doesn't it?"

The two men said nothing. Sipped at their ales.

When she began to understand, a cold knot of horror settled in her stomach.

Slavery.

The Drejeck Group. They were treading the edges of something sinister here.

"But what does it mean?"

"I don't know yet." The earl's voice was clipped. He was clearly tired of *not* knowing things.

He looked at his ale, realized he'd drained it, fussed with the tankard instead.

The sun was lowering into the sea. The sunset was of the gaudy citrus colored variety. The sky looked incongruously cheerful, like a circus tent.

"Miss Redmond?" the earl asked suddenly.

She looked up at him expectantly.

"What did the barmaid say to you when she took you away?"

Bloody hell.

Lavay rotated his head slowly toward the earl in surprise. Then toward her. She was confronted with two pairs of suspicious, unsympathetic, unyielding eyes.

"Apart from *'mon dieu'* and *'je regrette'*?" she said lightly.

But he knew. He must have known. *So happy*, he'd said to her in the garden. Almost wistfully. *Anyone could see it.* And likely he'd seen her face light up again when Polly spoke to her of Lyon.

What use am I to Lyon if I can't remain inscrutable?

She remained tight-lipped. She could do *that* much for Lyon.

"Your brother no longer fears you're my doxie, does he, Miss Redmond?" He sounded almost ironically amused. But there wasn't a shred of warmth in his voice.

She didn't answer. Lavay looked from one to the other. Clearly disappointed there would be no grand pantomime or ambush this evening.

"No," she admitted weakly.

"But perhaps we ought to go to La Rochelle," she added, when it was clear Flint and Lavay were only going to stare at her with cold and faintly surprised eyes. They were remembering that, despite her plethora of charms, she was essentially the enemy.

And still she couldn't resist making a point.

"You may be forced to consider, Lord Flint, that it's not just robbing and sinking. That maybe he has a *plan* that isn't *entirely* sinister."

They stared at her.

"And . . . *how* would that matter to *our* mission, Miss Redmond?" Lavay asked politely, finally.

She saw the earl's mouth twitch at the corner in appreciation.

She fell silent again.

Something shifted in the earl's expression. She suspected he was forcibly recalibrating his own sanity. Perhaps he wondered how on earth he could lose sleep over desiring a woman who was *determined* to free a murderous pirate. The straightening of his spine was a way to impose a subtle distance.

And then we are agreed on the distance, Captain, she thought. Relieved.

Odd that relief should feel so bleak, however.

"Of course we shall go to La Rochelle." He ironically lifted his empty tankard to her.

He sounded like a man determined to win no matter the cost.

Chapter 19

In solidarity with Violet's mood, the weather was fitful and uneasy the moment they sailed from Brest. A blue sky was streaked in strange shreds of clouds on the first day; on the next, alarmingly dense fog gave way to glassy clear skies in the afternoon. It was still a sharp, breathless pleasure to emerge from the galley to the deck to absolute uncertainty of the weather, to the changeable vastness of the sea and sky.

Unsurprisingly, there were no serendipitous meetings with the earl on deck. Oh, she *saw* him. Twice. Briefly. Rather like spotting a ghostly galleon sailing on the far horizon. If he saw her, he convincingly pretended he did *not*. He was a man of formidable discipline, after all, and likely he'd managed by now to corral his sanity and categorize her as inconvenient cargo, undesirable, untouchable, given his mission.

Lavay still dutifully promenaded her about deck twice each day. But even *his* charm had become rote and distracted; he was warier of her now, too. But according to Hercules, Captain Flint was spreading tension like a contagion among the crew, pushing all of them to keep *The Fortuna* sailing as swiftly as they safely could. Both Hercules and Violet were silently aware of the steadily eroding stores of grain and potatoes and cabbage, and Hercules, out of loyalty, remained close-lipped about it.

In La Rochelle, the captain would likely need to do some more of his nimble maneuvering to keep his crew paid and fed for another week.

A week beyond that and things would become a little dire.

All eyes were on La Rochelle.

On the third day Violet emerged from the galley to find the sky gray and leaden, sagging beneath the weight of ominous clouds. Below the sea was flat and lightless; it simmered and foamed like a cauldron.

She was a country girl. She recognized the makings of a storm when she saw one.

She took a deep breath of the crackling air as a hot wind whipped at her dress and threatened to yank her hair from its pins. She put her hands up to rescue it. She didn't dislike the impending wildness.

Suddenly, as though she'd never disturbed a moment of his sleep, as though she'd sat across from *him* in the mess for the past two nights while he forked her labored-over potatoes into his mouth rather than avoiding her entirely, the earl was next to her within three emphatic strides.

If he'd been ready to speak, the sight of her stopped him.

The wind whipped his hair into absurd spikes and turned his shirt soufflé.

She stared at him.

He stared at her.

How foolish I am, she thought, with sudden frightening clarity. He was so much more *real* than everything else around him. *I* only feel real when I'm *near* him. In that odd moment, everything that had come before him seemed like a dim dream.

She suspected everything that came after him would seem that way, too. She was already ruined.

And with the realization came the strange sense of falling

and falling, exhilaration and despair. *Unfair.* A word he would have mocked.

Her heart instantly hammered away at her.

He still looked weary; the hollows beneath his eyes had deepened. Her impulse was to reach up and smooth them out. She wondered if he would nip off her fingers if she tried it. His demeanor certainly suggested something of the sort.

She wondered what he saw in her face. When he spoke, she sensed the effort that went into keeping his tone neutral. "We've a storm coming on fast. Go below, Miss Redmond, and stay below until I tell you it's safe to emerge."

It was a moment before she recovered from simply hearing his voice; she savored it. His meaning registered belatedly. "But I've seen storms before, Captain. Perhaps I can be of some—"

"Do not argue with me. Go. *Below.* Miss Redmond." Urgency crackled from him. His patience was clearly stretched so taut the breeze would pluck a note from it any second.

She recoiled. She knew she had no right to feel wounded, but his lashing words made her breathless. She took a few steps toward the ladder. Then stubbornly turned to him.

"But how long will it be dangerous to—"

He pivoted and shouted across the deck, making her jump. "Mr. Corcoran! Will you please escort Miss Redmond below to her cabin and ensure she *stays there*, and return to the deck immediately? We'll need all hands on deck for this one."

"Aye, Captain!" Corcoran's big boots thumped hurriedly across the deck.

And the earl took one last long unreadable look at her. He drew in a breath, visibly squared his shoulders.

Then whirled and stalked off muttering, "Bloody Bay of Biscay. Bloody *pirates*. Bloody, bloody, *bloody*—"

She couldn't hear the last word. She suspected it was *woman*.

But Corcoran got her by the elbow so quickly she gasped. He summarily steered her to the ladder as she looked over her shoulder and all but clucked her down it, like a hen with a chick.

She protested and questioned the whole way. "But what is the trouble with the Bay of Biscay, Mr. Corcoran? Is it always dangerous? It was so calm when we set out."

Will Flint be in danger?

"Well, the Bay of Biscay, she's a temperamental bit o' water, ain't she, Miss Redmond?" he said soothingly. "Nivver fear. We've sailed in all manner of weather, aye? 'Tis a storm coming on, 'tis all. The captain, 'e knows 'is ship. Just do as 'e says and ye'll be all right."

But he was clearly already distracted, too, and his grim expression made lies of his soothing words.

"But how do you know this storm will be so very terrible? I've seen storms before, Mr. Corcoran. "What should I—"

"You should stay in 'ere, as the captain says." As if this was all anyone ever needed to know.

He opened the door to the cabin, guided her in, and released her elbow.

"Dinna leave the cabin now, Miss Redmond, until ye've been told that ye can. Captain's orders. And dinna worry."

And with a quick insincere smile and one final tip of the cap he closed the door hard, and she heard his boots slam, hurrying for the deck.

She stared at the closed door. The feeling was all too familiar: she was being collected, herded like a pet.

Funny how there was nothing like being ordered not to worry to *inspire* worry.

Through the window she could see the sky was just a shade lighter than charcoal and the light peculiarly, eerily flat. It was just past noon, but the clouds purely united against allowing daylight through.

It was certainly threatening. It was not officially a storm. Yet.

Very well, then. If she were to be *imprisoned* for the duration, perhaps she would read.

The first real swell began so gradually as she crossed the room to fetch a novel she'd borrowed from the captain that she almost mistook it for her own breathing. She settled on the bed, and within moments realized the bed—the ship—was rising and rising and rising and still rising. Vertigo set in.

Suddenly the heavy bed slid forward, nearly bucking her off.

She leaped from it and stared at it as if it had suddenly become mammalian. Staggered backward warily.

And that's when thunder exploded the ship.

That's how it felt. The sound was apocalyptic. She gasped and flung her arms up over her head, crouching in terror while *The Fortuna* heaved and shuddered like a whipped dog. The sound echoed and echoed intolerably, dwindling to a growl.

Lightning seared the flat slate sky white. It left her cabin night black by contrast. Burnt shadows of her furnishings floated before her eyes. Wind howled in the corridor now, and her door rattled, as though some great creature fleeing the storm longed to join her inside. The ship lurched sickeningly again, and she wrapped arms around her stomach, before it rose and rose and rose at the mercy of a monstrous swell.

Before she could grasp onto something, anything, for balance, she was sent wheeling like a drunk backward against the bed. When the ship dropped hard into the trough of the wave she toppled backward on the mattress.

Lightning scorched the room white again.

And then, like fistful after fistful of nails hurled at the window, came the rain. Relentless.

How could the window withstand it?

How could anyone stay upright on deck?

A very pure almost cleansing fear took her out of her body for an instant:

The earl had talked about clinging to a shred of exploded ship in the aftermath of a storm. She squeezed her eyes closed.

She clung to the counterpane with clammy hands. The air was dense, but fear chilled her; her teeth chattered. Her trunk shifted and slid at an angle to her, tipped, as an angry wave lifted them; she watched it warily.

And to think she had always found the unknown and the uncertain *exhilarating.*

Beneath her the belly of the sea heaved and then lifted the ship higher and higher . . . and then dropped it. For a bizarre moment she was a little airborne. Her stomach seemed to land hard before she did. She tried not to retch. The chamber pot had slid clean across the room. Clanking to a halt against the far wall.

She thought of Flint tumbling and tumbling across the deck of a ship—

Later she couldn't remember going out of the door. She could recall fighting through the passage, hands against the wall for balance in the bucking ship, wind howling in gusts, finding every available cranny. She seized the ladder up the foc'sle, but even that was woozily snatched from of her grip as the ship tossed at the mercy of a wave.

She got herself up with some effort. On deck, she kept a ferocious grip upon the ladders as a violent wind lashed her. Waves were monstrous black walls all around them. Sideways rain soaked her to the bone in gasping seconds, stinging her skin.

Sweet Jesus.

Where *was* he? Dear God, *where*?

"Violet! What the bloody hell are you doing?"

She could just see him through the wall of rain and the tangle of hair suddenly in her eyes. Alive. Roaring.

Furious.

The ship dipped sickeningly. She scrabbled for balance, her feet skidding uselessly. Through the slanting bars of rain she saw him, soaked to the skin, hair plastered against his skull, as they struggled to keep the sails up, the yardarms from snapping.

"Go *BELOW*!" he bellowed. "I told you to *stay*—"

She screamed her reply, and yet she could scarcely hear her own voice over the elements. The wind caught her voice, turned it into a shredded, faint thing. "I was *afrai*—"

The wave came from everywhere and nowhere. A dark monster arcing over the deck, she was helpless to do anything but watch it come inexorably down. With an effortless brute power it slammed her legs out from beneath her and tore her grip loose from the ladder rail.

Her scream was lost to the wind and roar of the sea, as she tumbled over and over and over again and again.

She landed hard. Breath was knocked from her. Her head spun; she wasn't certain she was upright and flat against the deck or even alive. It was everywhere dark. She pushed her hair away from her eyes, which solved the darkness a little. She was on a firm surface; she struggled to stand. Was she still on deck? Her lungs still wouldn't fill with air; and her wet gown trapped her legs.

"Violet!"

Flint was screaming. She heard terror in it, and even in the midst of her own suffering his ripped at her. And yet his voice was scarce more than a ringing in her ear.

Maybe she was dead already.

She pushed her hair away from her eyes and the deck came into view. A mast. How had she wound up near the wheel? She coughed.

"Flint!"

She couldn't get the word out; her lungs were still struggling to refill with air.

The ship tipped and heaved like a toy, and she slid again, her hands futilely scrabbling for purchase, for anything, anything near to hold fast to.

Her stomach heaved; she wretched and wretched and water poured from her. She moaned softly.

She looked up just as another great curl of water reared toward her.

"Flint!" This time sound emerged. But it was too late. She sobbed out her terror as her arm went up to cover her face; the other flailed out for a hold and found nothing.

And then something firm, something pliant and human seized her just as something crashed hard, rattling the deck. She screamed, or thought she did, but it was a poor shred of sound. Flint seized her by the waist, jerked her hard upright, swept her legs out from under her and took her in his arms.

Rain battered them. He was rooted as a tree.

"Hold on," he roared in her ear.

Weakly she was able to latch her arms around his neck and she did indeed hold on for dear life, burying her head into his hard chest. Shivers of terror and cold wracked her. The ship was tossed hard forward again, a sickening tip she felt in her gut, and Flint slid before balancing himself, nearly taking both of them down. He righted himself, cursing. It was then she realized he'd tied a rope to his waist, and he was tied to a mast.

Dear God.

"Is she all right?" It was Lavay. Four screamed words, measured out heavily, though the wind would have batted them right back into her mouth.

"If she's still alive," Flint shouted, "I'll kill her."

This sobered Violet rather quickly. He must have known damn well she was alive.

"I have the wheel, sir!" Lavay shouted. "See to her."

Somehow Flint freed himself from the rope. She closed her eyes. *He'll do everything else*, she thought drowsily. Surrendering.

She was carried below in Flint's wet arms, and he held her as carefully, as tightly, as though he held his own life in his hands.

She felt his breathing like bellows as he held her, as he took his seven-league strides through the corridors to his cabin. She wasn't a feather to begin with and now she was soaked to twice her weight, and she was beginning to feel alert and alive enough to pity Flint his burden. Why had she done it?

And where her hands gripped him she thought she could feel his heart pounding like the waves themselves. She pressed her cheek against his chest to feel the hard labor of his lungs swaying his chest, to feel the thump of life beneath his skin. She heard her own heart sending blood ringing through her ears.

He pushed open his cabin door and deposited her on the floor as though she were as breakable as an egg.

She unlocked stiff fingers from his neck.

And they parted slowly, as if each were afraid she would topple.

She didn't.

"Are you injured? Can you stand on your own?" His voice was low, terse, commanding, even as it was almost breathless. He roughly shoved his hair away from his face.

Violet's body heaved with great wracking coughs, and she struggled for clear breaths and took handfuls of her hair and shoved them away from her face.

She managed to nod: *I can stand on my own.*

His usually golden complexion was ashen with fear and chill, the skin stretched taut; in it his eyes glittered like obsidian. His hair and clothes streamed water onto the floor, onto that beautiful red and cream carpet. He was a fountain.

"Truly?" he demanded.

"Truly," she tried to say. Surprised when her voice emerged a mere croak.

There was a streak of blood on his cheek. He was injured! She made a sound, and began to reach for him.

Suddenly he was in front of her, his hands were running quickly, efficiently, over her limbs, her ribs, her face, her throat. His hands were cold, too.

"I'm sound enough." She was still breathing in gasps, but now the words were recognizable as words. "The wind was knocked from me. I've bruised knees. I think I'm otherwise quite fine. Just a tumble. Just a shock."

He whirled and lunged rummaging under his bed, fishing for something.

He came up with a flask, uncorked it, and pushed it into her hand.

"Take a long, fast drink."

She did as commanded. It was like swallowing fire. It coursed instantly through her veins, and she coughed.

He took it from her and took two gulps. Wiped the back of his mouth. Then corked it and almost slammed it down on the little table holding the chessboard, which had slid across the room.

The ship heaved sickeningly, rising the crest of a wave, and sent the bed sliding a few inches toward them. Like a shy pet. Unsure of its welcome.

"Thank you," she gasped. She wiped her mouth. "You saved my life."

"Yes," he said tersely.

She couldn't read his mood.

They regarded each other silently.

"Asher . . ." His first name had just slipped from her. "You've *blood* . . ." She reached a hand out.

He jerked his face away from her touch as though it might scald him.

She was abashed. Her hand dropped.

And this was her first clue that something was terribly amiss with him.

Chapter 20

"I'm sound. I swear to you," she soothed, stammering. "I've never known anything like it." She reached out two placating hands to touch his chest. "I was tumbling and tumb—"

He seized both her wrists in one hand before she could touch him and raised them roughly high over her head, walking her backward, pinning her to the wall. He studied her ferociously, as if picturing her manacled to a dungeon wall and liking the image.

"How could you be so bloody *stupid*? If you were a man, I would have you flogged for disobeying orders. Tied to the rigging. Thrown in a dungeon. I still might order it."

She'd never seen such scorching fury. Every word seemed to have been plucked with tongs fresh off a blacksmith's forge. He held her fast for a second longer. He released her hands abruptly.

She brought them slowly back down to her waist, lest a sudden move inspire him to snap them off. She rubbed at her wrists, and blue glare met blue glare, and their angry breathing mocked the storm outside. He pushed his hair out of his eyes. Breathing roughly.

She stared at him in silence, shivering.

"Take off your dress," he said flatly.

She froze.

"I *beg* your pardon?" Her teeth chattered out the words.

"Take off your dress."

"I—"

Like lightning striking, his hand darted behind her and snatched loose the laces that bound it up.

She was stunned breathless. She tried to speak; her voice seemed to have congealed.

"Finish," he ordered calmly. "Otherwise I will finish the job for you."

His tone left her no doubt that she didn't want to choose the latter option.

He stood back from her, giving her enough room to follow his orders. And then waited, the bloody arrogant man, as though he had all the faith in the world that she would. But the furious heat of his body cloaked her, began to warm her, and his knee shifted slightly to press against the join of her legs, a wicked, dangerous pressure she would shy from if she could. That she *should* shy from.

But now it was all she could think about: that knee, his body heat, her fear, his command.

I can take you whenever I please.

"I don't wa—"

"Do. It. Now," he said far too calmly. Making it abundantly clear his patience was frayed to breaking.

Her hands flew behind her neck. Her heartbeat sped, nearly choking her. Clumsily she managed to finish what he'd begun, loosening the laces enough to spread them, so that the bodice of her dress began to sag. He watched like a sentry. She reached up and dragged down one sleeve, exposing a bare shoulder, the top of one breast.

She stopped, realizing what she was doing.

"The other sleeve."

She hesitated. "If you would just turn ar—"

"The *other*—" And then he swore a quiet oath and yanked the other sleeve down.

And the dress, loose to begin with, sagged as if suddenly shot and slid down the length of her, catching at her hips. It was wet; it needed an extra push, so she gave it a push until it crumpled and pooled at her ankles. She stepped out of it, and her groin moved against his knee, and again, that delicious catch of danger-laced pleasure. He watched her, his eyes black, inscrutable.

Cruelly, he kicked the dress out of the way, no doubt knowing he might as well as be kicking her, given how she felt about her clothes.

She stood now in front-lacing stays and stockings and a chemise.

"The stays."

"My lord . . ."

"The *stays*," he repeated. Sounding incredulous she'd deign to speak after he'd issued an order.

She obeyed. Her hands reached up to between her breasts, to the laces of her stays. He watched her like a gaoler as her fingers unthreaded them. Spread them loose. Peeled them from her arms. Her breasts, lately caged and lifted up, were loosed now behind the fine, near-transparency of her chemise.

He stared unabashedly as she was slowly revealed to him, dark erect nipples pushing against the dampened fabric.

"The chemise."

"I can't . . ." she whispered.

"Lest you want it torn from you, you'll remove the chemise," he explained, each word measured with terrifying precision.

She clutched at the fine, wet fabric of her chemise, heart slamming. Searching for a way in past that white-hot fury, for a sign that he was bluffing, for anything, anything that would give her a foothold on his mood, a way to regain control.

He gave her back nothing but searing, black, carnal intent. His anger had a momentum, an objective.

And she understood now what a child she'd been, and what a formidable enemy he could be.

He drew in a sharp impatient breath and shifted warningly toward her.

She yanked the chemise up and away from her body, released it from her fingers; it floated to the floor like a ghost.

He gave it a kick.

She stood in stocking and garters, and covered her nudity, arms crossed like bandoliers across her breasts.

"Hands down, Miss Redmond."

Swallowing in anticipation, she slowly lowered her hands, so her breasts were entirely bare to his view.

And then suddenly he reached behind him, seized the blanket from his bed and dropped it over her head like a shroud, pushed it back from her face, and then proceeded to gently, briskly rub dry her chilled flesh, dragging it testingly down her arms, beneath her sodden hair, over her torso, her breasts, gently along her ribs, her hands and fingers, dropping to his knees, rubbing each of her legs, along the way his skillful hands pressing muscles, tendons, ascertaining for himself that she was indeed unharmed. He would have elicited squeaks if she'd been injured.

Hardly a seduction. She'd seen her brother dry off a wet dog in just that way.

"Does anything hurt?" he said kneeling from the floor, where he had a view of her pale thighs and two very wet satin garters. The blanket in hand, he peeled each stocking down from her cold thighs, then from her clammy feet, and tossed them aside.

"No," she said, subdued and now thoroughly embarrassed.

Finally he was satisfied the roses were back in her skin and her lips weren't blue and that nothing was broken. She tingled everywhere from the ministrations, shy, shocked, ashamed, and woefully, woefully aroused.

And then he stood back from her, stripped off his own shirt, and scrubbed his own beautiful torso hard with the blanket, rubbed it through his hair. And watching this was warming, too. And then losing patience, he flung both blanket and shirt aside with an oath.

They stood inches from each other, each breathing hard from a tangle of emotions. The storm, losing its fury, gently seesawed the ship now. She heard the poor chess pieces rattling around on the floor, taking cover beneath the bed.

Violet pushed a lank strand of damp hair from her face, tucked it behind her ear. She wrapped one arm across her chest to cover her nudity.

"You're *bleeding*," she insisted softly. She tried again, touching her cheek to show him where.

This time he allowed it.

But his voice was slow and hard and cold. "It's *your* blood, you bloody . . . little . . . fool."

To prove it to her, his thumb swiftly, lightly touched her cheek; it stung. He held his hand up to show her: blood.

She stared, astounded. Touched her fingers to her cheek. Her fingers came away with blood, too. Odd that it hadn't been washed away.

"It's a scrape. You won't need to be stitched up by the surgeon like a sail or a net. You won't be at all marred." Still curt. And ironic. "You could have been killed, but at least you won't have any scars."

She brought her hand down.

And for long silent seconds they stood, one entirely nude, one semi nude, inches but a universe apart, his knee all but wedged between hers. The force of his desire and his fury and whatever other enigmatic emotion had him in its grip unnerved her. But she'd never wanted anything more in her life than to melt into him. To soothe him, to take and give comfort.

She wanted it as much as she feared it.

He knew. And something shifted when he moved that knee infinitesimally closer, and pleasure burned through her like that whiskey.

"Where do you want me to touch you?" he demanded, voice low and taut.

Everywhere.

"I don't want you to touch me," she whispered.

"Stop *lying* to me."

"I'm not—"

He lifted his hands up abruptly, as a pair. She flinched.

But he held them there, like someone handing off his weapons in surrender. Offering them to her for her own use. His eyes were glitteringly furious, eyebrows sardonically arched. He stared at her white nudity with arrogant confidence, as if it had always been his right to do exactly that. As if she were a banquet and he the sole guest.

She felt beautiful.

And she felt like a whore.

She hated him in that instant. He was punishing her for her rashness with her own nature, the nature he'd uncovered. It was a positively *brilliant* punishment. She wanted to sob out the unfairness of it, to thump him with a fist. Unfair that he should know her so well, so much better than anyone else ever had, should continually strip her of subterfuges until she was without defenses of any kind.

She wanted him.

She knew one swift sharp hike of the knee into his sensitives would really solve this.

For a few minutes, anyway. Until he caught up with her.

The ship tipped gently to the side, and then to the other, groaning softly.

"Show me, Violet," he whispered, coaxing now like the devil himself, his tone so, so . . . *sympathetic*, so infuriatingly knowing. It lulled like a mesmerist. And his knee shifted just the slightest between her legs again, and her breath caught as hot shards of pleasure pierced. She swallowed. "Show me. Or tell me again to go to the devil, and I will go."

He knew, he knew, what she would sell her soul for in this moment. He could surely see the heart beating in her throat, the flush in her skin, and feel her breath, rough as his, against his skin. All of these things gave her away.

She turned her head away from him with some effort. Knowing his eyes still followed her every move.

But even as her head turned, her hands came up, as though they could now do precisely as they wished now that she was no longer watching them.

And they rose until her palms lightly touched his.

When she turned slowly back to look at him, his expression had changed. For a moment they both seemed mesmerized by the contrast of her white fingers against his long brown hands, the relative smoothness of hers against the roughness of his. She avoided his eyes, watched her own hand carefully, as she drew her fingertips slowly down from the tops of his, a caress that felt stolen, an attempt to sooth him, that revealed a deeper, more complicated truth beneath the fury of the moment.

And as though he couldn't help it, he gently laced the fingers of one of his hands through hers. Reassuring her. Then unlaced them slowly, but kept his palms against hers. He would not release her from her punishment.

Or from her reward.

Their eyes met. The moment stretched. She gathered courage. She inhaled shakily, and breathed out shakily. And she felt his breath hot against her skin, as though he were helping her breathe.

She closed her eyes, and gripped his hands, and drew him slowly toward her, and his body all but melted against her, covering her protectively, warming her, almost an apology for exposing her.

And she settled his hands over her breasts.

Here.

She was certain she would see triumph in his eyes. But he sighed, a shuddering sound. Her ducked his head into her throat, as though all along he'd believed her decision was in question, and that if she'd done otherwise he might have died.

"Here?" His voice was a hoarse whisper into her ear, and his voice too was a caress. The very air around them was sensually charged, erotic against her skin. His palms shifted to reverently to savor the weight of her breasts.

"And shall I do this?" His thumbs ran over her nipples, already ruched to painful tightness.

Pleasure howled through her, jerking her head back.

"Yes." She could hardly choke out the word. "Please, yes."

She shifted restlessly to accommodate the rush of sensation, encountered that knee, and ground her body against it. Bliss again spiked. Her head tipped back against the wall, her eyes half-closed, exposing her throat to him, and he kissed her there. Not a tentative kiss. The hot, tender brand of his mouth, the scrape of whiskers, the delicate touch of tongue against her pulse. Thorough, carnal, possessive. A kiss he'd likely thought about, planned for days. His hands kneaded, skillfully stroked her breasts until she writhed beneath his hands, rippling with the waves of pleasure sent everywhere through her.

His bare flesh against hers was glorious. He was, as usual, radiating heat like a human sun.

"*Violet,*" he whispered against her mouth, just before he kissed her there.

She met his mouth with nearly a sob of relief, as though years and not days had separated their lips. His tongue dove greedily, tangling with hers, and her hands slid down, down over his chest, found his trousers, found and cupped his hard cock, and she slid her hands over his slim hips and pulled him against her.

Please.

He arced back, dodging her touch, denying her that pleasure now. Denying himself that pleasure.

He took his mouth away from hers and slid his hard body down, and arced her backward in his arms to take a nipple into his mouth.

He bit gently.

Sweet Mother of . . .

He sucked.

Shocking and exquisite, the sensation too much and not enough, and filaments of hot pleasure lit her veins. She was aflame. Her hands tangled in his wet hair, guiding him, encouraging him.

But still she wanted more, thought she couldn't say what that might be. She felt doomed to want like this. Her knees began to give way; she clung to him, her hands gripping his shoulders.

"*Flint . . .*" It was a plea.

"I know," he soothed hoarsely, and there was promise and torment and triumph in the tone, for she'd just revealed to him he could torture her for as long as he pleased, because he alone was the means of her deliverance.

His hands slid from her breasts and following a trail dictated by the curves of her body, cupped her arse, squeezed.

"Shall I show you?"

"I don't know . . ." She choked on the words. Her entire body seemed dedicated to enjoying the progress of his hands.

"Shall I show you what you want?" he whispered insistently.

"No," she whispered.

And yet his hands never stopped moving over her body, never stopped lightly stroking, never stopped lighting fires everywhere in her until she burned, burned for him, and she would have protested had he stopped for even a moment.

They paused to cover the curls between her legs. She pressed her body up against his big palm.

Yes, yes, yes.

"No," is what she whispered aloud. But the word emerged sounding like its enthusiastic opposite.

"No?" he disputed softly. And then his finger slid lightly along the crease between her wet curls.

"Dear God," she managed hoarsely. "I meant . . ."

"You meant 'again'? Go right ahead and nod if this is true."

Bastard sounded *amused*. Even as his voice shook with his own suppressed need.

She nodded. Pride be damned.

Only his touch and what he could do for her mattered now.

She didn't want to wonder how he knew where and how to touch her. She only cared now that he did and that he didn't stop.

And his fingers slid between her legs, and she parted them for him.

"Oh God." Could bliss be unbearable? This nearly was.

She sensed still there was more to be had. Instinctively, she slipped her hands into his trousers, covering his hard cock, stroking, and then greedily pushed them down, down away from his hips. She wanted him.

He hissed out shocked pleasure. His voice was a raw groan.

"Violet . . . you'd best not . . ."

I can take you whenever I please. Oh, he likely could. He was likely capable of it. He wanted to.

But he wouldn't. She realized then he was protecting her from himself. And from herself.

Or he was trying to. She was making it difficult for him.

And still, his body rigid with desire, he suddenly, his body shaking, dragged his cock along her wet crease, tormenting both of them. She pressed against him, and yet she felt how hard and implacable he was, how enormous. She was afraid, and somehow she knew she wouldn't stop him if he chose to take her.

How could she want something she should *never* want? She wanted to scream from the injustice of it.

He lifted up her thigh with one hand and thrust forward again, to lightly, lightly drag his cock against her. So close, but never really breaching her.

She pulsed, and arced toward him.

This time a groan was torn from him.

"Please," she choked out.

But he stopped. His breathing wracked him. "*Enough.* Violet, I beg you, have a care." It was a warning and threat.

She was coated in sweat now, and so was he.

Flint was *begging*. It was sobering. She was greedy for pleasure, for whatever it meant, but it was hell for him, because he was withholding his own.

For her sake. She should have known he would.

"Trust me," he whispered. And he stood back from her, but he still supported her thigh so he could slip a finger deep into her.

She gasped at the invasion, tensing around him. But then his finger slipped out again, and expertly stroked her until an exquisite wash of sparks began to rain over her skin, then slipped in again.

"Yes . . ."

She tried to watch his face, fixed her eyes on his blue eyes, but her head thrashed back, and her breathing was ragged as she moved her body in time with his hand, asking for more, showing him how to touch her. He knew.

"Flint . . ." It was a question. She heard the trepidation in her voice. The need for reassurance.

The need for more.

"I'm here," he murmured.

She wanted him to stop, because everything in her was hurtling toward something glorious, terrifying and inexorable, but something she needed. She wanted to know.

"God, Flint . . ."

"I have you." His voice was a gasp in her ear. "I have you. Just let go."

"Don't stop."

The most important command she had ever in her life uttered.

"Wouldn't dream of it," he murmured.

He didn't stop. And now her breath was sawing, and need banking and banking until at last she bucked fiercely, shamelessly, beneath his swift, knowing fingers, her nails digging into the hard muscles of his arms. Surely she was hurting him. She didn't care.

And he was there, he was there, as he'd been on the deck just minutes earlier, to save her, to give her what he needed.

Her release came at her like that wave, as total and shocking merciless, nearly blacking her consciousness, shattering her into a million glittering fragments. At last free her to float on an indescribable, longed-for bliss.

The storm had abated.

The ship rocked only slightly now; it had entirely ceased sliding the furniture about. The chess pieces still rattled around the floor of the cabin. A book skidded from the place it had lodged when thrown from the bookcase.

Motion. Everything always in motion.

He held her loosely. She buried her face in his furred chest. Humbled and amazed, limp and sated.

Embarrassed and very pleased.

"It's . . ." she murmured.

Again, like the sea, like her first sight there were no words for what had just happened. Unless they were, *"I should very much like to do more of that."*

"Isn't it?" he agreed ironically.

And therein contained a warning.

Damn.

At last she truly understood what he'd wanted her to understand. This was in part why he'd done this for her. So she would know why men would kill each other over women, why men and women upended lives for each other.

She understood fully why. And she understood how dangerous it truly was to toy with it. As she had been toying with it. He'd *tried* to warn her.

She felt abashed now.

She knew what she needed to say. Or what he would likely next say.

But she didn't want to say it just yet.

"You ought to take your wet trousers off," she murmured.

She felt his smile curve against the top of her head. And then just as quickly it vanished, and she felt him go rigid as anger revisited him.

He stood back from her. "Why, Violet?"

She looked up. "Why? What do you mean?"

He shook his head. "I gave you a command. I *know* you heard it. I know you understood it. And yet you went up on the deck *anyway.* I know what's best for everyone in these circumstances. Why did you do it? Do you respect me so very little?"

"No!" She was stunned "How can you *think* that?"

"I *told* you what to do. How can I *not* think that? You test me at every turn. I know how to *keep you safe*. I've been a commander of a ship for nearly twenty years. I gave you a command because I knew it would keep you *alive*. And if you were in danger I would come for you. Will you promise to obey my commands for as long as you're on board my ship? Will stay below decks if you've *any reason* to believe there's danger above?"

"I'll obey your commands on board the ship. I'll stay below decks if you feel it's dangerous to be above." She repeated as if taking an oath. To soothe him. "I trust you."

He stood even farther back from her. She regretted the loss of his heat.

But his coat was hanging over the back of a chair, and he reached for it and settled it over her shoulders. It was huge and dry and smelled of him. She slid her arms into it. Proving yet again he knew how to keep her safe, how to protect her.

"Then why did you do it, Violet?" he pressed quietly. Relentlessly. A strange tension in his voice.

As though he knew the answer and waited breathlessly to hear it from her.

She faltered. She only knew the answer as she spoke it. "I . . . couldn't stop myself. I couldn't stand knowing—I needed to know if *you* were—I needed to know that you would be . . ."

He was absolutely motionless. Eyes hot. Almost a warning not to say it.

". . . safe."

The word was already on its way out of her mouth. It dropped softly into an absolute silence.

Some other compelling force had driven her out on deck to look for him. It hadn't been her mind.

She thought of her scrupulously genteel brother Miles punching Lord Argosy in the face over Cynthia Brightly.

The gently heaving ship sent that book sliding toward them from where she'd hidden it under the bed.

The earl stared at it. He went absolutely motionless. As though it were a poisonous spider. He glanced furtively up at her.

She understood immediately that her expression told him she knew precisely what was pressed in Miles's book on Lacao.

Resigned, he slowly bent to pick it up. He held it, looking down.

And a long quiet ensued.

"Violet . . ." he began. She watched that beautiful chest fill and sink with a long breath. Gathering courage.

It was a moment before he had the courage to meet her eyes.

And then he did, and his face was subdued.

"Violet . . ." he said carefully, dryly. "I would have known much more than a twinge of regret if you had been washed overboard."

She closed her eyes briefly. He'd quoted her again, from the very first real conversation.

She thought of the jasmine blossom. And now she knew he likely collected images of her the way he did that blossom.

The way she hoarded impressions of him.

He gave a short rueful laugh at his own expense. It sounded very like pain.

Their words seemed to hang and echo in the cabin. Seemingly innocuous. Impossibly fraught.

And when she said nothing, he seized the now damp blanket and wrapped it around his waist. And then he sat down on the bed, and disappointingly, with alacrity, got his trousers off from beneath it without a rampant display of nudity then strode over in all his gorgeous, battered glory to his wardrobe press to choose another shirt and a pair of trousers. But he did nothing so bold as to dress in front of her.

He turned instead, holding his clothes in his arms. He seemed to be waiting for her to do or say something.

She was still unnerved. She buttoned up his coat around her and gathered up her sodden, ruined clothing. She glanced down at her feet.

"My slippers have gone to sea," she said ridiculously.

He still wasn't ready to smile about her nearly being washed overboard.

She buried her hands deep in the pockets of the coat that smelled so like him she might as well have been wrapped in his arms. She thought her heart may very well burst from her chest.

"Violet . . . this . . ." He paused, though they both knew precisely what he meant by "this." Their tempestuous carnal contest, in other words. ". . . must end."

She heard herself make a sound. As though he'd swiftly drawn a splinter from her skin.

"You know it as well as I do," he insisted softly.

She breathed into the silence. Another sort of wave came crashing down on her then, and she knew a moment of dark endless disorientation, which in a way was a peculiar rescue.

She might have accused him of being afraid again if a peculiar relief hadn't lurked within her devastation.

He was right, of course. They both knew that "this" could only end in betrayal—for one of them would need to unforgivably betray the other when it came to Lyon Redmond. And then there was the little matter of her almost certain ruin and *his* plans that had naught to do with her.

What point was there in continuing anything that could

only end badly? And she really couldn't envision any other kind of ending.

So much for adventure.

Still, she could not find her voice.

He didn't look any livelier, either, really.

"Of course," she said finally after a moment. Her own voice surprised her. It was faint but steady. She heard it as if it were coming from underwater, appropriately enough. "Of course it must. We shall . . . keep our distance."

She looked up at him for confirmation.

He nodded, bleakly, agreeing to the wisdom of that plan. "Distance," he repeated.

And so the pot and the kettle parted ways, Violet to the vole hole. And something dully occurred to her as she marched for her quarters:

Lyon had likely been sailing in the very same storm.

But she hadn't thought about *his* safety until now.

Chapter 21

In the days that followed, they kept their distance. And the weather improved, but only in comparison to the violent storm. It could be said that the weather *sulked*. The sky remained a ghastly, heavy iron gray, matted with rain-bloated clouds. The sea was a restless matching sludge.

As usual, miraculously, it matched Violet's mood to the point of mockery. The only way to avoid sinking into emotional sludge was to look ahead: to finding Lyon. To uncovering truth in La Rochelle.

At least there was a wind.

It carried them swiftly and truly toward La Rochelle.

They sailed through the Pertuis d'Antioche on a day when sun was determinedly burning through the cover of clouds, and dropped anchor in the harbor. As usual she and the earl and Lavay were lowered into the launches and rowed to shore.

Past, unsurprisingly, *The Olivia*. Sleek, swift, beautiful, tethered. Mocking them with their ignorance and her enigma.

Once the launch reached shore, Lavay and two of the crew were dispatched to discover which ships were currently in port and what cargo they carried, and to haggle for some additional supplies.

A hack took the earl and Violet through La Rochelle's

ancient cobblestoned streets, trod by Huguenots and Knights Templar, to the profoundly English offices of Hayman, Hayman and Littlemont in the Rue d'Eglise.

The hack ride was short, the conversation between the earl and Violet absurdly polite, stilted, innocuous.

A harried, bespectacled, and skeletal Englishman dressed only slightly more impressively than a clerk—blue coat, brass buttons—introduced himself as Mr. Littlemont and ushered them into a parlor decorated in sturdy old English furniture. He rang for tea. It arrived in a delicate blossom-painted English teapot pot born by a maid.

Violet stared, disoriented, at the pink blossoms and porcelain. It seemed an artifact from a distant world, *her* world. She'd only been away just shy of a fortnight allegedly attending a house party hosted by Lord and Lady Peregrine.

Nothing had ever been *less* like a house party than her time with the earl.

She lumped in four sugars, just because they were there and because she could.

They all sipped genteelly. Very English.

But Violet realized that the earl hadn't introduced himself with his new title. Strategically, no doubt. He'd simply introduced himself as Captain Flint. Likely thinking that Mr. Littlemont would speak more freely to a sea captain than to someone acquainted with the English king.

"You're a trader, I understand. Are you perhaps a potential investor then, too, Captain Flint?" Littlemont was hopeful. "If this is true, you must desire an element of risk then, and I will be quite honest and say our fund was doing quite well up until a year ago. Since then we've been besieged by the most atrocious luck. Pirates have rather decimated our resources. Captains will no longer work for us. Perhaps your show of courage will inspire others to come forth."

The earl cleared his throat "Yes, but Mr. Musgrove in

Brest and Monsieur Fontaine in Le Havre suggested that I speak with you about possible employment and investment opportunities, and I trust their word implicitly."

". . . as did Captain Moreheart." Violet said innocently, quite conversationally. "Didn't he, Captain Flint?"

The sudden rigidity of his spine, the twitch of the earl's fingers on his teacup: oh, she'd made him angry. The cup looked absurdly delicate in his hand. He could crush it with a squeeze.

She'd *had* to say it. She refused to dance around the possibility that his precious Captain Moreheart was among a group of investors they were beginning to suspect of despicable deeds. Of trafficking in human cargo. And she needed, for her own sake as well as Lyon's, to believe her brother had a purpose to piracy beyond greed and destruction.

Littlemont, oblivious of the subtler byplay, beamed. "Of course. And Captain Moreheart, too. Moreheart was a good man."

The blood slowly left the earl's face.

He glanced down at his knees, held himself utterly still. Absorbing the blow.

Oh God. I'm so sorry, Flint.

But she'd been *right.*

And hope she had no right to entertain, hope that had very little to do with Lyon, and everything to do with the earl, began to stir.

The earl looked up at an oblivious Littlemont again, recovering with a speed Violet admired almost painfully. He was accustomed to blows.

"I was also warned of the risks of investing," the earl continued smoothly, "but I'm persuaded of the potential for the profits seem immense. And there's very little I wouldn't do for immense profits."

The two men laughed chummily together. Violet shot him

a sidelong look of amazement. *He's a better actor than I am.* But then, he'd acted the part of gentleman for years, while never really feeling like one.

Violet raised her cup for another bracing sip.

"And of course, I'm no stranger to risk," the earl continued with an air of pleased-with-himself arrogance. "Still, quite a number of your ships have gone down. I believe he said they were *The Caridad*, *The Steadfast* . . ." He held out his hand, ticking them on his fingers, and paused.

It was a test. A prime for Mr. Littlemont's informational pump.

Violet's cup froze midair. She held her breath.

"The Maria Louisa, *The Temperance*, and *The Oceanus*," Mr. Littlemont confirmed glumly. "Those are the ships. *All* ours. We shall be bankrupt soon, I fear. And it began as such a *profitable* endeavor. We've only two ships left at his point. *The Prosperar* sets sail for Cádiz this week, and *The Grey Gull* will head for Calais."

"Which was why Captain Moreheart, rest his soul, thought I might be a likely captain," the earl said somberly. "If anyone can protect a ship from pirates and discourage them from future attempts, it's me and my crew."

"Did you hope of captaining one of the coastal trade ships or one of the large cargo ships, sir? The large cargo ships seem the sort of challenge you'd be equal to, and the pay is *considerably* higher. As is the share of profits, from what I understand."

Violet saw the earl hesitate. "Well, you pose an interesting question, Mr. Littlemont. I'm not certain. It may depend on the nature of the journey. The large cargo were headed for . . ."

Violet's heart accelerated. She didn't dare look at Littlemont. She examined the little flowers on the teapot.

"Well, the large cargo ships return *from* America, sir, but I'm uncertain about every stop on their routes. I believe the

West Indies is part of the route. The purpose of the coastal route cargos are to purchase cargo for the larger ships, but I'm not privy to the nature of the cargo either, sir. The moneys from the sale of it are funneled through Mr. Musgrove and then to our firm, where we simply disburse and invest as advised. You'll need to speak to Mr. Musgrove regarding this. But we've only the one ship now, and it's at sea. It's as though Le Chat has methodically cut off all of our limbs."

Violet drew in a deep audible breath and settled her teacup gently, gently down on its saucer, overcome with a surge of emotion.

Lyon was trying to stop the slavers.

He was doing it for Olivia.

She'd been right! It *wasn't* just robbing and sinking!

It was unbearable not to at least elbow the earl at that moment.

Littlemont was still speaking. "So an influx of capital would be *very* welcome. You might wish to honor Captain Moreheart's memory by following in his footsteps. For I know it's what Captain Moreheart did—he captained ships and invested his own money at the same time, and he prospered until recently—so it's not without precedent."

Mr. Littlemont looked almost touchingly eager. He folded his thin long hands on his knees, almost in an attitude of prayer.

"Perhaps I ought to speak again with Mr. Musgrove and other members of your group before I commit funds," the earl suggested.

"Please do let us know as soon as possible, sir."

"Lyon is targeting those particular ships because they're using the money to purchase *slave ships*?" Violet was stunned. "The Drejeck Group is running *slaves*."

If she expected the earl to rejoice, she was wrong.

"It would very much appear that the Drejeck Group is running slaves," he said calmly. His face was thunderous and abstracted. He tapped his hat rhythmically against his hand as the hack took them back to his ship.

"He's doing it for Olivia Eversea, Flint. To prove himself to her! He *must* be. It's *her* cause, after all. Good heavens, it's—it's—"

"Don't you dare say romantic," the earl snarled.

It was precisely what she'd been about to say.

She blinked. And fell abruptly silent. Belatedly she realized her joy and triumph and giddy sense of revelation was thoughtless: the earl had been dealt a blow.

He'd need time to become accustomed to his hero being a scoundrel.

But please care, she begged him silently. *Surely you can forgive Lyon this.*

Hope was a thing with teeth for her then. Barbed, breathless. She'd spent two days ruthlessly tamping it down. Accepting things as they were. And here it was again.

"Violet, don't forget that Le Chat is rumored to have robbed and sunk other ships, too. Not just ships financed by the Drejeck Group. Recall the conversation in Le Havre at the Viscomte Hebert's dinner table."

She wanted to shake him. She wanted him to seize upon this hope the way she was seizing upon it.

"But why would he track these particular ships—*slave* ships, from the sound of it—all the way to their ports? He said—he *said*—only five. Two more. He has two more to sink, and The Drejeck Group has only two more ships. Surely you can see—"

"Stop it." He said it low, vehement. "Stop it now."

She was shocked.

He closed his eyes slowly against some wave of emotion, and then opened them again.

"Violet. I don't care *why* he's doing it. Whatever justice you or I may think Le Chat is meting out is a matter for the British Navy. Not the misguided quest of one man."

"That one man is my *brother*." *Care, Flint. Please care.* For *me*.

He groaned a laugh. "I am reminded incessantly of that."

"But Flint . . . he's doing it for her. *And* he's deterring other slavers."

"It's still *wrong*."

He was implacable.

Hope vaporized. Leaving her hollow.

"Of course." The words so bitter they tasted acrid on her tongue. "I forgot that what matters is the *bounty*. And your *plans*. Lyon, my brother, the person I love, ought to hang. How would you know what it's like, Flint, when you've never had a family? Even if your venerable Captain Moreheart was involved in all the nefariousness and deserved his fate."

The earl's head turned toward her very, very slowly. The force of his blackly furious amazement nearly pinned her back against her seat, and for an instant she knew real fear.

He visibly collected himself.

"I will forgive you for that." It sounded like a warning.

She was silent. She knew she'd gone too far. She'd wanted to hurt him. She'd succeeded.

She gave a curt nod, an apology.

"Violet . . ." He gave a short, incredulous laugh. And shook his head a little. He was astounded he couldn't make her see sense. "If Captain Moreheart was involved in running slaves, it's nothing less than despicable. The notion *sickens* me. And I don't know why he did it. It is indeed out of character for the man I knew but the need for money makes men do mad and desperate things—chase pirates up the coast of Europe, for instance—and that *may* have been the reason. I may never know. But in the same way it never mattered to you whether

Lyon was indeed a criminal or on some noble quest, it simply doesn't matter to me why Moreheart did it. It should. But you *preferred* to believe Lyon was on a noble quest. And you can call it now what you will. But you still would have tried to save him from me, and the gallows, had he been a criminal. Tell me you disagree."

She didn't. So she was quiet.

"If Moreheart perished in the launch after Le Chat sank *The Steadfast*, he was murdered as surely as if Le Chat ran him through with a sword. I have been charged with a duty that will reward *me* and avenge him. We both deserve that. Damn it, Captain Moreheart *mattered* to me."

He filled his chest with air, and exhaled, bringing his hand up to shade his eyes. To steady his temper.

Then brought his hand down. His face was pale with fatigue and whatever other emotions he battled. He quieted his voice with obvious effort.

"And I am sorry. I am truly sorry if you ever thought this would be otherwise. The circumstances are what they *are*, Violet. I thought I made that clear to you. Forgive me if *anything* I did led you to believe otherwise. But I honestly don't believe I did."

She stared blankly, numbly at him.

Moreheart mattered to you.

And Olivia matters to Lyon.

The way I wish I mattered to you.

She understood now that, jasmine blossoms notwithstanding, she simply never would matter enough to him. After all, he'd had no real experience of love.

Just loyalty. Just steadfastness.

He saw her face. He sighed and sank back against the seat of the hack. And gave a short bitter laugh.

"Oh, I've survived worse than hatred, Violet. And I'll survive yours. I've known for some time that yours would be the cost of my success, and believe me, I took no pleasure in that. I truly thought you understood. And this is the only thing I regret: that you ever thought otherwise. So hate me if you must. Nothing changes."

He waited for her to speak.

But there was nothing else to say.

Chapter 22

The dark, relentless, infamous Bay of Biscay fog had set in the moment he'd irrevocably killed whatever regard Violet Redmond held for him. Flint felt mocked. It rather mimicked his internal state.

It had been inevitable. He would endure.

He was less certain that she would. He'd seen more promising expressions on men who'd just been shot. But he'd never *lied* to her about anything.

But almost as a punishment, as a way to mock him for being the rudderless man he'd been before he met Violet, for two days out of La Rochelle they'd sailed in this fog. Flint was far too seasoned to find it romantic or mysterious. It was nature's way of colluding with attackers and hiders and smugglers, when it wasn't causing shipwrecks. And though he could navigate this part of the coast easily enough—it had been thoroughly explored by sailors before him, every undersea rock formation upon which a schooner could founder painstakingly mapped—Flint always listened harder in the fog. Sound was deceptive; it bounced about in the mist, deceiving listeners.

And because he was listening harder, faintly, starboard, he heard a series of sounds in quick succession:

A grunt. A thump. Another thump.

"To the *guns*!" he screamed.

Because he knew even before he saw men spidering up the side of the ship. Knives held in teeth, pistols in waistbands, swords swinging at hips. He knew those sounds as he knew his own breathing: the grunt was likely Greeber taking a gunstock to the forehead if not a knife to the gullet, the thump was his body falling hard, and the third was the pirate landing with both feet on the deck of *The Fortuna*.

Where was Violet?

He hoped to God she was below.

It was the last thought he had before his men swarmed the deck from everywhere on the ship, and the sound of pistols unlocking, swords unsheathing, feet slamming wood planks as they ran for positions of attack and defense. Flint leaped from the foredeck and shoved a boot into the chest of a pirate who had a leg over the side of *The Fortuna*; his body sent up a spray of water when the sea swallowed him.

His men, bless their sweet black hearts, were nasty, vicious, accomplished fighters and were hacking at any hands that dared cling to the sides of the ship as though they were vines in the jungle, hacking at the ropes they'd used to scale *The Fortuna*. Screams and oaths, splashes as bodies hit the water followed. The ring of steel against steel, and the brute thud of bodies striking other bodies in combat.

"*Guns,* Corcoran!" he screamed. "Man them!"

"Aye, sir!" Corcoran swiftly took up his position there.

For where there were pirates there was a ship, and once they fought back these men, it was only a matter of time before the pirates fired on *The Fortuna*.

Violet and Hercules, below in the heat of the galley, were arguing over how he should prepare the meat for dinner when what sounded like a herd of cattle thundered over their heads.

Violet went still, puzzled, tipping her head back.

But Hercules's face blanked. His cleaver hovered midair.

And when slowly, slowly his lips curled into a snarl, she understood what hackles were, because hers certainly rose.

"What is it?" she asked faintly.

And then they heard screams, muffled through the layers of the ship.

He dropped the cleaver with a clatter, and dove beneath the table, emerging with something she'd never seen before: a scimitar, longer than his arm, with an edge sharpened for death. The blade flirted arrogantly with the dim lantern light. Winking.

The knife slipped from her hand. Her palms were clammy with terror.

"Hercules—tell me what is *wrong*!"

"Pirates. Stay *here*."

Anyone *else* might have said that with less glee.

Quick as a vicious terrier he scrambled out of the galley and clambered up to the deck.

Dear God. She thought quickly through the rush of terror. Could it be Le Chat? But how *could* it be? They weren't carrying cargo. Did he know she was aboard?

What the bloody hell was *happening*?

Flint would kill her if she went up on deck. Perhaps even *literally*.

But if Lyon were indeed among the pirates, he would never harm Flint if he saw her.

She fingered the knife, and eyed the cleaver, and opted for the second one.

When a blood-congealing scream cut through the battle din, Flint grinned, knowing he would see Hercules flying up the stairs from the galley swinging his scimitar. Howling his inimitable battle cry, he leaped toward a bug-eyed pirate in a moustache and ludicrously festive striped shirt aiming a pistol straight for him, and whipped his sword up beneath the man's hand. The pistol flew in a spiraling upward arc and came down, crashing to the deck, skittering across it.

And came to a halt at Violet's feet.

She reflexively seized it and slunk to crouch behind the long boat, her heart clogging her throat. Thumps and roars of pain and shouts of "Duck, Greeber!" and "Look out, Captain!" ricocheted around her. She tucked up her knees and bent her head between to make herself as small and invisible as possible, but not knowing whether Flint was unharmed or whether Lyon was on board was unbearable, so she peeked.

She ducked when she could have sworn the glittery amber stare of a pirate met hers from across the deck. It was only the flat lozenge of the sun, burning through the fog at last, glancing off pirate jewelry.

The second thing she saw was a disarmed pirate holding a sliced and bleeding wrist in one hand while Corcoran and Hercules hooked their hands beneath his armpits. He kicked and swore in a language she'd never before heard as they heaved him overboard. His screams ended when the water engulfed him.

Sweet Mother of God.

If she survived, she vowed she would *never* long for novelty again.

She rose to her knees again, her eyes just above the edge of the longboat. She watched in a special kind of hell, a heart-swelling awe, as Flint threw his beautiful body ruthlessly into the battle, *wading* into it, taking and giving blows, bringing up that great sword and hammering it down again against other blades coming at him with murderous intent. He seized any pirates pummeling his men and hurled them to the deck, ruthlessly stomping them breathless; he nimbly, almost happily, ducked swords and fists swung at him. The blood of other men spattered his shirt.

She didn't see Lyon.

Saw instead scattered amongst the pirates Lavay's golden head, Corcoran's stocky body, Greeber's shining ginger hair. She couldn't bear it if any of them were harmed.

She turned her back on all of it for an instant, leaning against the boat, eyes squeezed closed, her lungs bellows in her chest. She rallied her wits; her breath came in short terrified gusts as she inspected the pistol; it was unlocked. A miracle it hadn't discharged when it had been kicked across the deck. She didn't have time to fumble it open to see whether it was loaded. If it had already been fired, it was now useless.

She could always use it as a club or a projectile.

She peeked up again, and in that instant saw Lavay's golden head flash like a guinea as he fought to disarm a man raining sword blows at him.

And she saw what he couldn't see: a pirate running toward his back with a sword.

She clapped a hand over screams that would have torn her throat ragged.

But with Flint's finely honed instincts, his knack for seeing everything at once meant he was there in a bound. The point was inches from Lavay's back when Flint ran the pirate through.

He pulled his sword free; the body flopped sickening to the deck as though it had never been animate.

Lavay acknowledged his rescue with a salute of a single bob of his head to Flint, his own sword still a graceful, whipping blur in deadly play for perhaps a second or two longer before he disarmed the pirate and ran him through, too.

It was all so *savage* and hideous and glorious and obscenely . . . *proficient.*

She trembled. She couldn't bear to stay there and she couldn't bear to leave, and she prayed in a way she'd never prayed before, with a wordless passionate sincerity and desperation.

She hunched when a deafening roar sent acrid smoke mingling with fog. A great fountain of foam sprayed up over the port side of the ship: The pirate ship was firing upon them.

"FIRE!" Flint roared, even as his sword swiftly parried two men coming at him. *"Corcoran!"*

The men on the guns obeyed. Flame hissed the length of the fuse and *The Fortuna* shuddered with the force of the cannon shot. The next sound was the triumphant sickening crack of splintering wood.

The main mast of the pirate ship was cleaved in two, the top still dangling like a man strung on the end of a rope.

And all at once the edge of Violet's terror was strangely blunted by thrill and the unfamiliar beginnings of bloodlust. She wanted them to win.

They *could* win.

Even though she knew *The Fortuna*'s crew was outnumbered.

Bodies were now strewn haphazardly as rag piles on the deck. She saw Hercules's bald head shining like the butt of a pistol as he swung his cutlass and mercilessly fended off then slaughtered two more pirates who were doing their best to slaughter him. But two more were upon him nearly instantly. He was terrifying indeed. But he was small.

Oh, Hercules.

But Flint was there in time—how did he move so quickly? And together he and Hercules neatly and gorily dispatched the pirates.

But when Flint turned again a pirate stood right behind him, pistol aimed at his chest.

He froze instantly.

Oh, God, oh God, oh God.

And somehow it took only seconds for awareness of the captive captain to ripple throughout the deck

"Hold your fighting," the pirate roared.

"Hold!" Flint shouted to his own men.

The commands were unnecessary. Apart from the writhes and moans of men beaten to the deck, all was now stillness. Men stared at the standoff; a few muttered.

Flint's sword was stilled, gripped in his hand at his flank. His own pistol was tucked into the band of his trousers.

Reaching for it would mean instant death.

"Surrender, Captain Flint. Lay down your arms now, and you will be our hostage. We will not kill you. But if any of your men so much as twitch a muscle, I will shoot you now. Does anyone care to twitch?"

The pirate captain's accent was mysterious but featured extravagantly rolled *L*'s. He was tall, bony and rectangular; his coat flapped from his shoulders like a flag strung from a line. A red scarf was tied over oily black hair roped back in a queue. His eyes were flat and black. She suspected this was a man who had long ago learned to kill remorselessly, and perhaps had even grown to enjoy it.

Violet remembered a description of another pirate at the viscomtesse's dinner party: Ugly, they called him. This must be him. He certainly fit the description.

This wasn't the work of Le Chat, then.

Flint coolly assessed his circumstances. His chest heaved from the exertion of battle; Violet breathed along with him, as though she hoped to breathe *for* him. His shirt clung to him with sweat and blood, his and the blood of other men.

She'd never before seen him at the mercy of anyone or anything.

It was unnatural, like watching the sun sink permanently into the sea. It should not be allowed.

"Come now, Captain Flint. Hand your sword to me, and my men will cease fighting. You know you are outnumbered."

"We *were* outnumbered. Count the bodies on the deck, sir. You were *outmanned*. Our numbers are even."

"And yet I'm the one pointing the pistol at *The Fortuna*'s captain, which means I'm the one who holds the life of her captain in his hands, which means *we* have won. Come now, Captain Flint, lower your weapons and we will lower your men in the launch and take your ship. Since you were so unkind as to disable ours."

"How do you know my name?" Flint was so conversational they might have been sharing a pint in a pub.

"Your legend precedes you, Captain. We know you sail *The Fortuna*, and that she carries a rich cargo, for we learned of this from Captain Gullickson. We want it. Surely I needn't explain this to you. You're not new to the notion of *pirates*."

But Violet knew they carried no rich cargo. *Gullickson* had tried to lure pirates to them! He must have wanted them dead.

"And to whom do I have the pleasure of speaking?" Flint made the word *pleasure* a masterpiece of irony.

"You speak to Le Chat himself, monsieur."

Astounded silence followed by a splintering crack as another piece of the pirate ship's mast crashed to its deck. Which clearly did nothing for the pirate's temper.

"What bloody nonsense." Flint sounded amused.

Oh God, Flint. Don't anger *that creature.*

"Why do you insult me in such a manner, Captain Flint?" he hissed with apparent nonchalance. Violet saw that his mouth possessed teeth and gaps in equal measure, and felt certain when he spoke his words sprayed over Flint like sea foam.

"From what I understand, Le Chat and his crew do not fight like frightened vermin," he said easily. "In other words, they do not fight sloppily and without regard to honor. You are not Le Chat."

Don't goad him, don't goad him, don't goad him.

The captain stiffened. "Very fine words from a man who

has everything to lose in this moment, Captain Le Snot."

Juvenile chuckles around the deck, even from the pirates.

Was he *trying* to get killed? Violet was sweating with terror. Her hands were damp; an ice floe sat in the pit of her stomach.

The pirate captain's black eyes narrowed viciously, assessing the earl, and he shifted restlessly on his feet. He made a great show of adjusting the pistol in his grip so that the barrel of it aimed directly at Flint's heart. That heart she'd felt hammering beneath her fingers when he'd carried her down the steps safely to his cabin after she'd nearly drowned. That she'd felt beating against her own when he'd kissed her.

The ice floe migrated to her throat.

This can't be happening.

The pirate's matted beard hiked up when his fleshy lips curled in a contemptuous snarl. "Captain Flint. The time for questions is over. Lay down your arms. If you do not do so now I regret that I will need to shoot you."

"Flint," Lavay said quietly. A warning.

A pirate poked the tip of a blade into Lavay's throat. A bead of red, brilliant in the foggy light, appeared there.

Violet touched her own throat. The bile of rage filled it.

"Oh, I would surrender to a *man*," Flint said easily. "But I feel rather silly surrendering to a rat, sir. So I fear my surrender is impossible."

Oh, Flint.

He stood, solid as his own ship. Hand on the hilt of his sword. Like a gorgeous cornered savage, seemingly relaxed, at ease, at the mercy of this man. In truth, ready to spring like a beast for the kill, even if it meant he would die in the process.

Violet bit down hard on her lip to keep from screaming out his name.

She wanted to look into his eyes just one more time before he died.

Because she knew what Flint likely knew: He was going to die anyway at the hands of this filthy man, who wasn't burdened by anything like his sense of honor. She knew his own men were likely doomed no matter what he did, or what this pirate said. So he would not allow this fiend to use his honor as a weapon against him, and wouldn't give him the satisfaction of even the pretense of respect. The pirate was vermin. He'd been lucky, and that was all.

And then Flint's men would die at the hands of pirates after watching their captain die with honor.

And *then* they would find her of a certainty. She had no illusions about what pirates would do to her when they did.

"Very well, then," the pirate captain snarled. "I will give you to the count of five to lay down your arms."

Violet also knew instinctively that the pirate was the sort who would fire on four. And then laugh about how clever he'd been afterward over Flint's body.

"One . . ."

Everything about the day suddenly seemed frozen, delineated sharply. *The Fortuna*'s crew stood perfectly still, helpless, breathless. Above, fog and gunsmoke inexorably drifted away, the work of the sun and a freshening breeze. Encroaching sunlight glanced oddly, picking out things that shone: stilled swords and pistol stocks, earrings glinting in filthy nests of hair.

". . . two . . ."

Sounds were painfully crystalline, distinct. The lap of water at the side of the ship. The sudden flap of a seagull wing. A bird mocking them with its freedom to fly away from all of this. All sounds, all sights, were blows against Violet's nerves.

Violet stood slowly. She didn't know how she managed it. Her limbs were numb.

". . . three—"

BOOM!

The silence was smithereens.

And the pistol shot echoed endlessly.

Roars of rage, bloodcurdling battle cries split the air. But the groans of misery and protest settled into confused murmuring, then eerie silence, when the impossible seemed true:

Flint remained upright.

But his face was expressionless. He held his body utterly still. Hand frozen on the hilt of his sword.

A moment of surprise before the agony sets in, Violet recalled.

And that's when understanding collectively took hold of the men on deck.

And every head swiveled to look at the pirate captain.

His face beneath that beard was almost comically stunned.

When realization dawned, his features contorted into surprise, and then horror, and then slackened. The pirate captain's fingers loosened, splayed, the pistol spilled from it to the deck. Before the stunned eyes of everyone on deck, as red bloomed brilliantly over his heart, and then spread rapidly on his shirt, burbled from the corners of his mouth.

And like a sail abandoned by the wind, his body sank, and then he toppled to the deck.

Quite dead.

Instantly that primal rustle and clank, the sound of warfare, muscle and weaponry shifting into immediate action to hold captive every pirate who *wasn't* dead.

And every single man capable of moving spun about to see who'd fired the shot.

Violet lowered the pistol in shaking hands.

Flint's beautiful blue eyes—the word *alive, alive, alive* sang a hosanna in her heart—bored into her. She nearly sank to her knees. She felt weightless with fierce gratitude he simply *existed.*

She would think later about what she'd done to ensure that he lived.

His face was pale, his skin drawn tight over his face. The fierce emotion in it held her upright.

He was the kind of man who could hold up the world, she thought.

"I apologize for disobeying orders, sir," she said softly.

She turned, her skirts whipping about her ankles, and disappeared briskly down the ladder.

Chapter 23

Flint knew from long experience that the blood-buzz and fury-haze of battle receded only gradually, like a red tide, unless he walked it off, paced the deck to point of physical exhaustion.

Violet. Violet. Violet. Her name thumped like a war drum in his mind, calling to him. He saw in his mind's eye again and again her precious, singular face, cold and terrified and brilliant with fury and purpose.

But he was a captain, and he had a duty, and he did it.

Briskly, officially, he sent Corcoran to see to whether she was safe below decks; he reported back quickly that she was. He supervised the throwing of two more of the pirate dead over the side of the ship into the sea. Wounded men were sent to the ship's surgeon to be salved and stitched. He'd lost no men to death in battle, but several were seriously wounded, and Mcevoy had taken a bullet to the thigh, and would be in the sick bay for at least a week, likely, though he'd have the use of his leg.

With cold, swift efficiency, he issued orders for weapons to be collected and inventoried, the deck to be scrubbed, the sails and rigging inspected; he issued compliments for bravery, words of comfort and gratitude for the wounded. There was no room on his ship to house prisoners and he had no interest in keeping pirates alive. The fog had receded enough to reveal a listing pirate ship, its main mast snapped, its hull filling with water from the hole made by the cannon shot. It would sink unless the pirate crew repaired it—if they could repair it.

He didn't care.

Two living pirates remained on board *The Fortuna*: a surly, startlingly hairy brute who spoke not a single word of English, and after much experimentation with a smattering of words in every language Flint knew, was revealed to be Portuguese; and a boy who couldn't be more than twelve years old, and who was scrawny, filthy, English, and terrified.

"Shall I drop them over the side, sir?" This was Greeber, nursing a great throbbing blue lump from where he'd taken a sword hilt to the forehead.

"Sir, please, sir . . . I s-s-served the real Le Chat. I can help ye find 'im!"

The boy stuttered and twitched like a trapped insect. Enormous brown eyes, a pink, pinched nose. His collarbone formed a sharp ridge beneath the filthy shirt. His wrists were bony, attached by knobs, from the looks of it. Potentially a tolerable looking, even handsome lad if he were fattened up a bit.

"Are you lying, boy? You'll go right o'er the edge, if so, and I will know."

To illustrate his point, Greeber seized him by the scruff and hiked him up onto his toes and passed him to Lavay as though he were a sack of potatoes, and Lavay got him by the trousers waist and collar and made as if to hurl him overboard.

"Nay, sir! Please, sir!"

"Oh, very well." Lavay settled him down again, sounding peeved.

"What, then, are you doing with this scoundrel?" Flint gestured with his chin to the dead pirate captain. Who was being hoisted by two of his men in preparation for being hurled over the side. Any men who served and died in his care received respectful burials, with the proper words of God read over them.

The pirates would not. Flint would lose no sleep over it.

"Cap'n Abrega there, 'e stole me from the La Rochelle dock, sir. Needed another 'and, 'e did, an 'e jus' took me and what could I do? Le Chat, *'e* paid me wages."

"Oh? What is the name of Le Chat's ship?"

"*The Olivia*," the boy said promptly.

The men absorbed this for a moment. It was a stunning moment of absolute confirmation. Then again, the *rumor* of Le Chat's vessel wasn't entirely a mystery.

"She's a bonnie craft," the boy added unnecessarily.

"How long 'ad you served?"

"Three ports, sir."

"And where were the last two ports?"

"To Le Havre and Brest."

More silence as this was absorbed.

"Where was *The Olivia* bound when you were taken?" Flint tried.

"Cádiz," the boy said promptly.

Flint went still. He narrowed his eyes. The boy squirmed again. Doubtless Flint seemed terrifying, covered as he was in blood of pirates and sweat and fury.

How would the boy know this of a certainty? But how likely was it that he would produce a destination like Cádiz from thin air?

"D'yer believe this little bastard, Captain?" Greeber gave the boy another nudge.

"You'd betray your former captain, boy, by telling us where he's going?" he said coldly. "How can *I* trust you?"

A tricky question for a boy who wanted to live, and had likely been buffeted by life since he'd been born. The life he led now would either make a hard honest man or a criminal of him. Flint still could not have predicted which of those he would become if he hadn't served Captain Moreheart.

The boy's Adam's apple worked in his skinny throat. "I wants to work, sir. I'll work 'ard fer me keep, only. No pay."

"But were you not on deck moments before attempting to kill my men by orders of that captain?"

"Aye, sir. But 'e would've killed me if I dinna obey 'im. An' 'e's dead now, ain't 'e, sir?"

"Aye, he is dead. You ought to learn the meaning of loyalty."

"Canna learn it from a dead man. Mayhap ye'll teach it to me." Almost cheekily said.

Lavay cuffed him lightly. "You will not speak to Captain Flint with anything but groveling respect, you wee turd. He's the Earl of Ardmay. You'll bow and do it now."

He boy blanched, rubbed his ear where he'd been struck. Agog, he stared at Flint as though he'd sprouted a halo or horns or some combination thereof.

He bowed awkwardly. "Beggin' yer pardon m'lord." Diffident now, if fascinated.

"Have you yet been to Cádiz with Le Chat?"

"Aye, sir. Please sir, ye'll find 'im a' the El Cisne Blanco Inn."

"If you're lying to us, boy, I shouldn't like to be you." The casual tone was uniquely menacing, and it worked on the boy. "And we'll know quickly, won't we?"

That Adam's apple bobbed again. Brown eyes flared defiantly for an instant, then flickered and dropped in fear and submission.

"What will he be doing in Cádiz?"

Silence.

Greeber gave the boy a shake.

" 'e'll sell silks, won't 'e? Merchant name o' Rodriguez

meets wi' 'im in the Plaza de Mina. Dinna ken the time."

"Greeber, take the boy—your name, boy?"

"Mathias, sir."

"—Mathias below and lock him up. Get Corcoran and the two of you can lower this . . . hairy bugger . . . over the side and see if he can get to one of their boats and then to that ship. I'm not terribly interested in his destiny. And I'll talk to the boy later."

The hairy bugger muttered some no doubt filthy sentiment in Portuguese as Greeber shouted for Corcoran's help to carry out his orders.

Flint, who had done his duty, turned at last.

"Lavay, the ship is yours while I go below. And . . ." He considered this for but a moment. "Make sure Miss Redmond doesn't hear about the boy."

Because the Fates had sent him pirates today. And thanks to that boy, the Fates could very well deliver Le Chat to him, too, after weeks of chasing an apparition.

They'd known it would come to this eventually. Regardless of whatever mad noble motive drove Lyon Redmond, Flint would do his duty.

He would win.

And the courts would decide Lyon Redmond's fate. *May the better player win.*

Lavay understood. He hesitated only a moment, and then nodded crisply. Resignedly. Gave an ironic twitch of the brow.

"Aye, aye, Captain. Have I mentioned that I'm glad you're not dead?"

"Your sentiment warms me to the core, Lavay. May I return the compliment?"

Lavay nodded again, as though nearly being killed was all in a day's work for either of them. "Are we changing course, then?"

The need to make split-second decisions and accept accountability for them if they were wrong had been part of his life since he was eighteen years old.

"Aye. We're going to Cádiz."

He was already striding off.

"We'll be closer to Morocco, too," Lavay commented casually as he left.

Flint shot a startled look over his shoulder and kept striding.

He hadn't thought of Fatima in days.

He'd looked death in the eye more than once before. Much was made about what a man saw flash before his eyes when he died. But not until today had Flint seen anyone in particular, and today she was all he saw, and now she was all he wanted to see.

"Captain?"

Lavay again. He stopped and spun about. "Yes?" He was curt now.

"She was lucky again, eh?"

Flint scowled, Lavay's smile became a laugh, and then Flint all but flung his body down the ladder.

He almost ran through the passage to the guest cabin door. He tried the doorknob of the Distinguished Guest Cabin.

"Violet!" He knocked, then flung the door open. It was empty.

Ah. So she'd gone to his cabin, perhaps out of instinct now, perhaps because it was farther away from the scene of violent death. He bound up again, ran for the captain's cabin, strode down the passage and paused before his own door, knocked tentatively, then realized knocking was ridiculous and tried the knob.

The door opened.

He paused in the doorway. Violet was sitting perched on

the foot of the bed, eyes huge and startled. She composed her face when she saw him and turned away without a word. He could see her expression reflected in the rectangle of mirror: pale and tense and contemplative.

He didn't wait for an invitation into his own chambers; he closed the door behind him, locked it, and quietly sat down next to her on the bed.

He couldn't recall the first man he'd ever killed; it had been in battle, his weapon had been a musket, and the man's face had been so distant as to be anonymous; he'd had only one name: the enemy. But he did recall the aftermath. Waking from nightmares. Shaking.

Violet had seen the man's face as he'd been ready to shoot Asher dead. She would probably never forget that face for as long as she lived.

"I killed a man," she said finally. Sounding bemused.

"Yes," he agreed softly.

He wasn't quite sure what to say, or what manner of comfort, if any, was needed. Experimentally, hesitantly, he took one of her hands in his. He hadn't touched her in days, and yet it seemed far too long, and just this touch was a strange relief. As if not touching her was unnatural. Her hand lay in his as impersonally as a glove; her fingers were cool, but not *too* cold: she wasn't in shock. He kept it in his anyway: proof she was alive and unharmed. Gratitude swamped him, momentarily made him weak.

She didn't take her hand back.

"Where is he now?" Her voice was remote, taut. Like someone taking great pains to contain an enormous emotion. He wasn't certain which one yet. "The man I killed?"

"Shark food."

"Ah."

She wouldn't look at him. He studied her profile, that graceful line he'd once himself traced with a finger on the railing of the ship the other night. He studied her for signs of shock or hysteria; he knew he would recognize it in her. In so short a time the twitch of her brows, the set of her mouth, the way her eyes did or didn't light in response to something she saw or something he said had become another of the languages in which he was fluent.

"My brother's wife, Cynthia, once accidentally shot the penis from a statue," she offered.

"Did she?" He was startled.

"But I've never fired any weapons. First time."

"Is that so?" he said gently. "Good aim. Shocking, really."

The corner of her mouth twitched.

"Thank you, by the way. For my life," he added.

The smile fully took hold of her mouth for an instant. Then faded. "Cynthia was trying to impress a man."

This made more sense.

A *little*.

Silence.

"He would have killed you," she mused, and now he heard for certain, understood that tension had been gathering in her voice. "That . . ." She reached for a particular word. Settled on one she clearly found inadequate. ". . . *man* would have killed you."

Never had that word *man* sounded so repugnant.

"That was his objective, yes," he said evenly. "But he didn't. Thanks to you."

He didn't add that it was only one of occasions too numerous to recount he could have lost his life. In a dazzling variety of ways, at the hands of cannonballs, scimitars, fists, starvation, or shipwrecks. It was all part of being a man, really, specifically part of being Captain Asher Flint, the newly minted Earl of Ardmay, and he was fairly certain this wasn't something she wanted to hear now.

She suddenly looked quickly, directly, hard into his face and he watched, astonished, as a flush of pink flooded her skin. She turned quickly away again, as if she couldn't bear to look at him.

Then she sucked in an enormous breath from the air, pressed her palms against her eyes and dragged in a few more breaths from the air. Her shoulders heaved with the breathing.

Alarming.

"Violet?" he said softly, and surreptitiously hooked the heel of his boot over the edge of the chamber pot lurking under his bed and dragged it forth, in case she needed to cast her accounts from shock.

She pulled her palms away from her eyes and stared out across the room.

"I could not have *born* it," she said, her voice cracked. She sounded dazed and astounded and . . . *furious*. Not at all pleased with whatever realization she was having. She turned her face up to him again, and her eyes were fiercer than any warrior's with a sort of accusation and something penetrating and raw and unnerving, as though she was seeing him for the first time and wasn't happy with what she saw. She looked down at his hand holding hers and gave a soft rueful laugh, and her hand finally came to life. She seized his hand and turned it over, traced the lines in his palms almost fitfully, put it down again carefully on his thigh, as though it were a breakable thing he'd loaned her momentarily.

He wished he could read her mood. But he was lost. So competent as a warrior moments ago, nearly helpless now.

"Such a *horrible* thing, killing a man." Her voice was trembling like something in her was about to break.

He understood now. It was eating at her, the fact that she had taken a life. Even if it was to save his. She was just a young woman, not a warrior, and could not expect to rebound so quickly.

"Violet . . . killing is never easy even for a hardened warrior. I can only imagine how you must feel. I'm so sorry—I wish you hadn't needed to—"

Her head whipped toward him. *"Hush,* you *fool,"* she said furiously, her voice hoarse. *"Hush."* And now tears were welling in her eyes, swelling and spilling. She knocked at one with a knuckle as though it were yet another man aiming a pistol at Asher. "I could not have born it if he killed *you. You.* I could not have lived. I simply would have . . . stopped breathing. I would have killed him a *dozen* more times. *Happily.* For you."

And her voice cracked on the last word.

He stopped breathing.

She seemed to curl in on herself. She folded her hands in her lap, straightened her spine, tensed her jaw, attempting to impose her innate orderliness on the chaos of her emotions and the aftermath of bloody chaos. But she couldn't control her tears. They welled, clung to her lashes, plummeted like suicides.

He tried to speak. She'd stolen his breath.

"Violet . . ." The word an awestruck whisper.

He touched her cheek. Her skin was hot with emotion, and soft like the woman who was furious to find herself helpless against it. He knew so many words, in so many languages, scattered and profane though many of them were, yet none came. And maybe her fury and despair had to do with something she seemed to understand so much better than he did: how *terrifying* a thing it is to love. For it owes its sweetness in large part to the razor-edged fact that it could be lost in the blink of an eye, if, for instance, a loaded pistol isn't in hand when one is needed. And this is what the love had done to her, revealed to her: she was someone who could kill. She was capable of enormous love, but she'd lost once before, and she'd kill before she let it happen again. And yet they both knew it was bound to end in heartbreak when he caught Lyon. And he would.

But love—for her brother Lyon—the man he needed to vanquish—was the reason she was here at all.

"Violet," he repeated, his voice brusquer than he preferred. He feared gentleness suddenly. He smoothed her hair out of her face, efficiently, because he thought tenderness might undo her. He cradled her nape with his hand, his fingers playing in the hair there, which was a wild tangle, free of its pins. "Violet."

She looked up at him then, and the fierce tenderness, the uncertainty there, undid him.

He brought his mouth down to hers. It was all he knew to do.

His lips floated near, then brushed hers; his tongue touched the corner of her mouth; tasting salt, the taste of her fear and fury and love. But her lips took brutal command of his. She nipped at them, her mouth parted, and she sought his tongue. And her mouth was so hot and so giving he was ferociously aroused and immediately as frightened as she was, for he knew the greater danger was his.

Because she *knew* how to love. He was a neophyte.

And what began as an attempt to soothe became volcanic as violence withstood and desire held back surged free.

Her tongue sought out his tongue, and this time something at the very core of him, something never before stirred, was found and blissfully incinerated. He groaned. Need wracked him; he shook with it, with the force of desire for this woman, only *this* woman, everything about her, and his hands grappled blindly for breasts, stopping to thumb roughly at her nipples through the muslin until she gasped an oath of pleasure, then sliding along the nip of her waist to furl up her dress. He pushed her down onto the bed, pinned her.

"Shhhh," she murmured against his mouth as they dove into savage kisses again, as though he was the one needing comfort, as he ducked his head into her throat, kissed the thud of her heart there, kissed her eyelids again to taste the salt. He propped himself over her on shaking arms, bridging her, trapping her, his view her brilliant eyes and pale fierce face and wild tangle of hair, and she dragged his shirt up and out of his trousers, shoving it gracelessly up beneath his armpits to rake her fingers down his chest. He shifted to hook his fingers into the edge of her bodice to drag it down. She pushed her breasts against him, the contact of skin to skin maddening and precisely what they'd been seeking.

Her hands were already busy on his trouser buttons, and she'd sprung his cock with shocking efficiency, her hands stroking the length of him. He was swollen, almost leaping in her hands.

"Violet . . ."

His voice was hoarse; he heard it as though it were coming from somewhere outside his body. It was both a hosanna and a warning to her, but he wasn't going to stop. Nothing would make him stop. No word from her, no action could make him stop. Now he needed to take her as much as she seemed to need to give, and the consequences could wait. Excuses or recriminations or whatever that would follow meant nothing now.

She pushed his trousers away, her hands sliding, cupping over the hard flat planes of his arse, gripping his cock, fully, achingly swollen, arcing up toward his belly now, sliding her fingers over its slick dome.

He hissed in through his teeth. "Sweet mother of *God . . .*"

She was taking *him.*

"Please," she said.

The disarray they'd made was astounding. He roughly shoved her dress up entirely out of the way, until it was wadded in rumpled folds at her waist now; mercifully there were no drawers to grapple with. He noted a flash—her eyes swiftly widening as with almost absurd efficiency he swiftly pushed her knees up so he could fit his body between them, one at a time, noting the neat satin garters tying up the stockings, each still free of snags. He dragged fingers down along the unthinkably tender insides of her white thighs, pressing them wider apart, and groaned with pleasure when his seeking fingers brushed between her legs and found her dark curls soaked. Violet arced upward at his touch, gasping, and his fingers slipped between the velvet folds, teasing, testing, and she writhed against them, seeking more pleasure.

He positioned his body above her and took his cock in hand, and at first eased into the tightness of her, as her eyes widened, and then thrust home with unintelligible oath of bliss.

Violet sank her fingers into his arms and sucked in a breath at the bite of pain, her belly leaping with harsh breaths, but the pain seemed right, an initiation, a cost, and it was gone quickly. She wanted to sacrifice, to bleed for him. He hovered above her, allowing her to accommodate the shocking, glorious feel of him filling her. So right, she groaned a nearly animal sound of pleasure.

"God . . . I want . . . you must . . ."

Their eyes locked. He held himself above her, trembling, and his eyes burned her.

His breath gusted against the damp of her throat, raising gooseflesh. She saw the sweat beading his upper lip, his teeth sunk into his lower lip. Felt the force of his desire for her, for *her*, in the hard muscles quivering beneath her fingers, in the fevered heat of skin, in the rapid rise and fall of his vast shoulders. She dragged a finger down the seam between his ribs, stopped a bead of sweat, transferred it to her tongue.

Then slid her hands over his hips where their bodies joined, triumphant, marveling.

His pupils flared; his eyes were midnight.

He drew his hips back slowly, his eyes fixed on her face, watching for her reaction, his eyes flaring in triumph when she threw her head back, and her mouth parted on gasping breaths of pleasure. The hot slide of him inside her was extraordinary, glorious, terrifying; she gripped his arms, not knowing what else to do. He thrust again, and she groaned the wonder of it, and it spurred him on. He plunged again. She locked her feet around his back, and wanted to growl, to scream that it wasn't deep enough. She wanted to *be* him, to be *fused*. She arched her body to take him, and her response fed his need and shredded his control until he abandoned it altogether and let desire set the pace, drumming his cock into her in a primal rhythm, the force of his big body rocking her. She arched to meet him, the sound of his flesh against hers unbearably erotic, his face rapt, focused inwardly now, now as he drove himself toward his release.

She held him when he went motionless above her and hoarsely, joyously called her name.

Not even the most outlandish of the bets inscribed in the betting books at White's would have dared predict that Violet Redmond would kill a man . . . and lose her virginity . . . to a savage *earl* . . . on the high seas . . .

All in one day.

They lay alongside each other, together and apart. A circle of sunlight through the window landed on his belly, like a target.

Who am I now?

Not Violet Redmond, daughter of Isaiah and Fanchette, pristine, wealthy, untouchable, a coveted prize on the marriage mart, a delicious source of speculation in light of her tendency to wildness. Not the Violet Redmond who'd from sheer boredom threatened to cast herself down a well over a petty argument with a suitor and had been pulled back by the elbows. Not the Violet Redmond who'd been cosseted her entire life, rescued and petted by her brothers and parents.

She was in utter disarray. She didn't care. She didn't care about wrinkles or her hair. She was a woman who could kill, who could eat bread rocks, who could survive being pounded by a monster wave and living in a vole hole. She'd been undone completely by this man, turned inside out. She wanted only him, and suddenly life was simply and unbearably beautiful and sad. She'd given everything. She was glad. But Violet felt as anchorless and alone, suddenly, as Asher Flint must have felt his entire life.

To whom or what did she really belong now? She'd just unmoored herself with no guarantee of a future, for she knew how this would end, for it must end.

Still, she would not undo what was done.

He leaned over, propped on his elbow, his smile lazy, his eyes guarded and achingly blue in the sun, and lifted a strand of her hair, which was simply everywhere—fanned on the pillows, stuck to her lips, glued to his body with perspiration.

He drew it slowly out through his fingers, the long, long length of it, peered through it as though it were a net he'd been caught in.

She smiled at him. He began to speak. Hesitated.

"It can be better for you," he finally said gruffly.

"I wanted it," she said quickly. Lest he feel any guilt or remorse. Something to do with her pride.

I wanted you.

I wanted it? Good God. How very proud her mother would have been to hear those words.

"I never would have guessed," he murmured smugly.

So ungentlemanly.

Still, she smiled at that, transformed by one wild bout of lovemaking into a wanton, and rolled over on her back, stretching her arms out behind her head, her breasts arcing upward.

His eyes darkened interestedly, and he feasted them brazenly.

"It can be *much* better," he whispered. He leaned over and drew her nipple into his mouth and sucked gently, traced a lazy figure eight over it with his tongue.

Little rivers of fire fanned out in her blood.

"Oh," she sighed, and she threaded her fingers through his hair.

Her legs shifted restlessly, already wanting to wrap around him again, a heavy desire simmering low in her belly, a now familiar ache of want. Surely they'd spent their lust. Surely, she thought with some despair, it couldn't be an endless, insatiable thing.

She thought of opium addicts, and wine sots, and how more and more was never enough.

"Turn over on your side." A whispered command.

She was disappointed he didn't intend to linger with her breasts, but she obeyed, and tipped.

He gathered the miles of her wild hair into a neat fistful to get it out of his way and dropped it over her shoulder like Rapunzel's rope. Her back thus turned to him, he unlaced the dress they'd so roughly treated and loosened the laces with his fingers.

"Raise your arms."

She obeyed. He slid the dress up over her head, folded it in a cursory sort of way and set it aside. He placed a single gentle, slow kiss at the nape of her neck.

Her nipples were instantly erect as pen nibs. Gooseflesh raced over her limbs.

"Will the crew be wondering where you are?" she murmured.

"The crew knows where I am. They assume I'm comforting you."

They both smiled at the euphemism.

Next he unlaced her stays and together they eased them away from her body.

And now she lay completely nude apart from her stockings, clothed only in close sultry cabin air and the circular sunbeam that had migrated with a few minutes passage from him to her, and the hands of a man who fanned them over her shoulders as reverently as if she were wearing wings. Dragging soft kisses, trailed by feather-light fingertips, down her spine as though it was the road to his salvation. They didn't speak. She could hear his breath now, quiet but uneven, the sound of ramping arousal, and she loved knowing what simply touching her did to him. Her body hummed with wild want but she tamped it, because she was hungry for the detailed knowledge of her body, of seduction, that he possessed. She suspected it was a frontier, limitless as the sea.

Does he love me? Does he even know?

She thought of his face on the deck this afternoon after she'd fired that shot. Unguarded in that moment. Everything he felt was in that gaze.

But what if he does? And it simply didn't matter. She loved him. And love was bigger than she was.

And Violet, the rebel, surrendered to it.

As he'd said the other day, *it changes nothing.* He wanted Le Chat captured and she wanted Le Chat free. In the end, one of them would need to betray the other.

So there is only now, she told herself. She told herself it was enough.

His hand planed along her waist to the rise of her hip, slipped down over her belly, and a tiny involuntary sound of anticipation caught in her throat. Her legs shifted, hoping his hand would slide down between.

"Soon." There was hint of wicked laughter in his whisper.

But that hardly made it better, because now she was nearly trembling with anticipation of whatever he planned to do . . . "soon." He gave a gentle tug on her hip to roll her over onto her back and feasted his eyes somberly on her nude self for a moment, and only later, as she reflected, would she recall that she hadn't known a twinge of modesty as he studied her.

"I think I like you best on your back," he told her earnestly after a moment. Knowing it would earn him a scowl.

Which it did.

He grinned like a wicked little boy, and it was so charming it pierced her through.

"Are you certain *you* don't like *you* best on your back?" he continued relentlessly, with mock concern, and his fingers trailed along her thighs, coaxing them apart. Too easily, almost greedily, they went.

"H-h-uush," she gasped. The need to express outrage seemed so unfair when what he was doing was so delicious and she needed him to continue.

"Because if we're *agreed* on the matter . . . I can think of ways to keep you right . . . there . . . for hours . . . and hours . . . and *hours* . . ."

His voice became softer and softer and softer with every "hour," and the last one was a whisper, a blown breath, between her navel and the triangle of curls.

She throbbed, aching, and when his tongue touched her slick soft center she jerked from the sharp bliss of it.

And his hands pressed her thighs apart and again he stroked her with his tongue, and this time she moaned, the astounding newness of it, the wickedness of it, bowing her upward.

The velvet heat of his tongue against her hot, swollen

cleft was exquisite, and he demonstrated a remarkable genius for knowing just how to lick, and stroke, until she rippled beneath him.

He knelt between her legs and guided himself in, a leisurely lovemaking, looking down on sated, dream-clouded eyes, her arms flung back over her head, her hair a tangled fan, and so slow he took her this time, each thrust searching and precise, the rhythm of his hips nearly languid, until he knew she was coming again, shouting his name in a hosanna he thought he'd never tire of hearing.

And then he slipped out, and lay down next to her, and pulled her into his arms.

He wasn't sure when she began to weep. Just that she *was* weeping. He had the usual male horror of female tears, and she seemed to know it.

"It's just emotion." She sniffed, and brushed her hand across her eyes. "I'm not upset."

Just emotion. Love and fear and loss and longing and the prospect of yet more loss. She was extraordinary, this girl. A warrior's heart beat in her, but she was young, and everything that had happened to her in a short amount of time would have been too much for most stalwart men, let alone a woman.

He murmured soothing nonsense syllables with an instinct for tenderness he hadn't known he possessed. He stroked her hair. And he wrapped her in his arms, held her until she slept.

Chapter 24

The boy Mathias had been right. After two days of mercifully charitable seas, *The Fortuna* sailed into Cádiz. And among the ships in the harbor were *The Prosperar.*

And, naturally, *The Olivia.*

Flint stood on deck and watched that shining jewel of a warm harbor grow closer. He called for the anchor to be dropped. He waited to feel a surge of battle anticipation: At last he had the advantage over Le Chat, and all Flint had ever needed were his wits and a hair of advantage.

Instead, he thought of two nights of Violet Redmond rippling in pleasure beneath his hands. Her soft body asleep in his arms.

And feeling like a traitor, he went below to wake her up precisely as he'd awakened her for the past two wanton days.

Four things told Violet something was very different about this particular trip to shore.

The first was that Flint awoke before she did, bathed and dressed, strapped on every weapon he owned, and quietly left the cabin. *Without* kissing her good morning.

And for the past two magical, thoroughly carnal nights, it seemed he could scarcely stop kissing her when they were alone.

The second was that he returned in a hurry to see her, and they managed to make love without removing anything but the necessary clothes, and there was an urgency, too, that spoke to her uneasily of finality.

The third thing was that *two* launches were lowered. Not just one. For some reason Flint was taking most of the crew, rather than a small contingent, leaving only a small number of men behind on *The Fortuna*.

The fourth was that among the crew was a boy she'd never seen.

A scrawny, somber boy, teetering on the brink of his teens.

Her suspicions were confirmed when she was told by Flint she was to stay behind on the ship.

"No," she said firmly.

"It could get dangerous today," he said absently.

His back was to her. His front was rather focused on Cádiz.

"Asher . . . who is the boy?"

He glanced back at her. Eyes wide in a warning about using his given name. And she felt it begin to open up at her feet: the abyss that life would be without him. It was coming sooner than she hoped.

"May the best player win, Violet," he said softly, finally. "Isn't that what we agreed all along?"

A cold realization charged at her.

"He knows something about Le Chat. That boy! He's leading you to him!"

"He came aboard with the pirates," was all he said after a moment. "We captured him."

"And he knows something!"

"He may indeed." He gave her nothing but cool, distracted command. Watching his men at work.

She wanted to thump him. She refused to act like a child,

or stomp her feet, though she was sorely tempted. "Then bring me with you."

"I'm afraid that won't be possible." He began to turn away to some other business on the deck.

She put her hand on his hard, warm arm. She didn't care who saw. "He's my *brother.* Are you afraid that if I'm there I'll find some way to stop you? Or that you might be less willing to shoot him?"

"You'll see him once we arrest him," was all he said.

"Damn it, Flint"—the salty language and raised voice at least got his eyebrows up—"you know it isn't fair. Do you want to win this way? I told you what I knew. *I* got you as close as you did. I *demand* you treat me fairly."

He looked down at her, and she knew, despite it all, he couldn't resist.

"Make room for Miss Redmond in the launch," he shouted.

A few inquiries at the dock was all it took to learn that the El Cisne Blanco was near the Plaza de Mina, a ten-minute walk through ancient streets thronged with merchants and shoppers and bathed in soft Spanish sunshine.

A wiry, sleepy-eyed clerk hunched over a desk.

"Will you show us up to Mr. Hardesty's room, *por favor*?"

The innkeeper looked up at the whole lot of them. "Ah, Señor Hardesty. He is gone." His dark eyes were nearly bugging with alarm and suspicion. Which could have something to do with all the weapons they were wearing.

"Gone?" Flint fixed the innkeeper with a stare designed to quail him into truth.

"I cross my heart to you, señor." He showed ten fingers twice. "Twenty minutes now. Perhaps longer."

How? Hardesty's men could have watched the sea with

spyglasses for *The Fortuna* and warned him she was sailing into port.

But how would he know they would head straight for this inn?

Unless they'd been watching for that, too. Unless they'd seen the boy with them.

"We'd like to take the room he's lately occupied."

"We have not cleaned it, sir."

Flint scowled his contempt for that excuse and threw a handful of shillings down on the counter. "We don't care," he growled.

The man's eyes widened at the profligate display of money and at all the swords and pistols gleaming on the crowd of disreputable-looking men.

"You will see for yourself, señor, I swear to you. Third room on the right, and here is the key," he said hurriedly, sweeping the shillings into his apron.

Flint snatched the key from him.

He made a quick decision. If anything that belonged to Lyon Redmond was still in the room, if there were any sign of him, Violet was certain to know.

"Miss Redmond and I will go into the room. Half of you guard the entrance to the stairs," he ordered the men. "The rest of you make sure you know the lay of Plaza de Mina before tomorrow."

They found the room in question. The door was ajar by inches. Pistol drawn, Flint nudged it all the way open and peered around the corner.

The room could have been occupied by anyone; nothing seemed particularly piratical about it.

The only possible sign of swift abandonment was a bureau drawer left partially ajar, and that's where the earl went immediately. There was a small bed, sagging a bit in the middle, tightly made up, the wood frame dust-free but scratched and pocked in places from years of users. A large window was hung with rickety shutters, flung open so that the room was ironically illuminated, bright as day, inviting inspection. A stub of candle was pressed into a dish on a tiny table next to the bed.

Next the earl bent to peer beneath the bed, and that's why Violet saw the rosewood box before the earl did.

And all the tiny hairs on the back of her neck went erect.

It was a utilitarian, unadorned, uncarved rectangle about the length of one bound book and about the height of two, and nearly the same color as—and thus nearly camouflaged by—the table it sat upon. It had a hinged lid, currently closed.

It also had a lock that could be easily picked with a hairpin and a false bottom that could be sprung if one only knew where to press. Violet knew this, because she'd been an exceptionally nosy and deft younger sister, and she'd seen Lyon do it once, and she'd done it out of curiosity when he'd left his room.

It was all she could do not to throw her body over it. As though Lyon himself stood there, smirking at her. And as she grew accustomed to the terror of the moment and it ebbed, that familiar, glorious, sun-bright burst of affection and an equal fury yanked her between them.

Lyon had left his family behind without a word.

But he'd brought the bloody box with him, out of sentiment.

And she suspected he'd left it here for her to find. Because she would know something was hidden in it. But *what*?

Her stillness alerted the earl as surely as if she'd gasped.

He straightened abruptly from where he was peering under the bed.

"Violet? Is aught amiss?"

"Nothing's amiss." Her lips seemed strangely disconnected from her body; she *sensed* them go up. She hoped the smile didn't look as ghastly as it felt.

"You're pale."

"I was born pale. It's a family trait."

She could have predicted the tilt of his lips. *You're everywhere pale*, he was thinking, she could tell. *Your throat, your breasts, your long, long legs.* But his smile faded the longer he watched her. To be replaced by a tiny vertical dent between his brows, the precursor of a genuine frown.

Every bit of Violet's strength was required to not only meet that gaze evenly, but to also get a piquant eyebrow up. As if she were playfully *basking* in his scrutiny.

A woozy light shivered on the wall, bounced from the water below through the window.

Asher turned away to look out over the sea, magnetized as always to it.

And then he sighed, and stretched his arms extravagantly, which nearly brought his fingertips in contact with both walls of the small room. He pulled out his watch and reviewed the time, glanced toward the door as if contemplating leaving, sighed and tucked his watch back into place . . . then wandered a little too nonchalantly to the little table next to the bed.

Well, why wouldn't he? She'd bloody been *staring* at it.

She took a page from his book of nonchalance and sauntered to the window and peered out, saw endless water, feigned meditative contemplation. As though that rosewood box hadn't sent up a veritable screech of awareness in her mind. She watched from the corner of her eye.

Asher almost whimsically lifted the candle. Hefted it, placed it down again. Right next to that box.

Violet tensed.

"Cold," he said wryly. "Scarcely burnt. So he didn't snuff a candle an instant before our arrival and bolt."

She produced another weak smile and gave a half turn, to watch.

He dragged a thoughtful finger over the top of the rosewood box.

Her stomach turned to ice. Her limbs followed suit.

"Do you recognize this box?" he asked absently.

"No," she managed. It was only one syllable, after all.

When he tried the lid, she bit her lip hard to send the blood back into her head. A little preventative against fainting.

The lid resisted his tugging.

She knew him well enough to know it was too soon to be relieved.

"Is it locked?" She sounded admirably, calmly curious. But in her ears, her voice had a peculiar echo, as though it had traveled from a long way away to exit her mouth.

He didn't look at her. "Seems to be. Doubtless I can get it open with a hairpin, however. Can I prevail upon you to loan one to me?"

"Violet?" He turned to her swiftly when she didn't answer. Whatever expression he saw fleeing her face caused him to go strangely still and very stiff. As though a sudden movement might jar some old injury.

"Of course," she said finally. She thought her face might crack from the effort of nonchalance. "Just . . . just allow me to find one for you . . ."

It seemed to take an inordinate amount of time for her brain to communicate the message "find a pin" to her hand, and her hand seemed peculiarly ungainly and ineffectual, once she got it up into her hair. As if it didn't belong to her at all. As if she'd borrowed it for the search.

He moved to her. Two tentative steps. When he stopped near she decided then the scent of him, so uniquely masculine and intoxicating, would bring her to the point of swooning until the very day she died. She'd recognize it, find it blindfolded in a room of thousands of men. And as he stood there in all casualness she breathed him in as if it were the last time, because for all she knew it was.

She gave up and dropped her hand from her hair.

His face betrayed nothing of his thoughts, but his eyes were as usual searching her face. She was suddenly violently resentful of his cleverness; it was as invasive as it had seemed liberating. But if he drew any conclusions or magically deciphered the run of her thoughts, his expression never betrayed it. His hand just came quickly up.

She blinked, but managed not to flinch. He stroked it into her hair, and his expression subtly moved as he braced himself against whatever rushed his surface when he touched her. Feelings he would always beat back, never give voice to.

He found a pin, naturally.

And then drew it from her hair gently and too slowly, watching her face the way he'd watch for threats on a distant horizon.

Oh God. He *knew* something was amiss.

"Thank you," he said ironically. "Didn't muss a hair, either. But don't sneeze or it might all come down."

And then she was forced to stand and casually wait while he turned his back on her and inserted the hairpin into the keyhole of that box.

The next few moments were a hell of anticipation accented by the *scritch scritch scritching* sound of Captain Flint, the Earl of Ardmay, attempting to pry into the secrets of yet another Redmond. Though he didn't know yet this was what he was doing.

Until at last the earl removed the hairpin, stood back, and stared at the box.

Hallelujah! He'd failed! And *she* most certainly didn't intend to volunteer to pick the lock while he stood there.

But Flint cast a look at the line of lengthening shadow

between them drawn by the lowering sun. "It's growing late. I think perhaps we ought to just take the box with us and I'll try again later."

He didn't wait for her reply. He tucked the box beneath his arm, turned and said politely, "Thank you for the loan of your pin," held it out to her, and she reached for it.

He seized her hand between his.

A trap! *Damn him.*

She was certain he could feel her pulse rabbiting away inside her wrist.

"Your hand is ice cold, Violet."

The intelligence behind those blue eyes probed away at her. *Has he memorized my face the way I've memorized his? Does a twitch of a lash tell him something about my thoughts, the way the slightest change in light in the sky over the Sussex Downs hints at the coming weather?*

She was fairly certain her face gave him nothing. Because Violet had lately learned what she capable of doing in order to protect the people she loved, and if this meant shooting a man to death to save her lover's life or cultivating a gaming table face in order to save her brother's life, so be it.

"Fatigue," she said lightly. With a one-shouldered shrug that curiously caused him to frown faintly.

He held her hand a moment longer, tightly, as though she were a skip that would bob out to sea if he released her. Tension gathered in his face; she thought he would speak. Then his eyes flicked away from her. And perhaps the shadows were painting everything in the room with more drama and shade than they could rightfully lay claim to. But for the span of a breath she thought she saw something lost, something resigned in his face. There and then gone as if it had never been.

He dropped her hand.

They stared at each other a moment.

"Flint?" she asked tentatively.

"Yes?"

"Why did you tell the crew to make sure they were familiar with Plaza de Mina before tomorrow?"

"Why do you think, Violet?"

She watched him. Then gave a short nod.

He arched a brow, and motioned gracefully for her to precede him out of the room.

Chapter 25

Torture for Violet resumed that evening after a meal taken in a suite of rooms the earl took for himself at a similar, though more comfortable inn, farther along the Plaza. The crew, led by Lavay, were exploring all the pleasures Cádiz had to offer by night, and getting the lay of Plaza de Mina, while Violet confronted a dinner of chicken and peas and rice all swimming in a dark spiced sauce and washed down with what she was told was a good Spanish wine. She could barely swallow any of it. The earl devoured his.

After he'd pushed his polished-clean plate away, Flint set to work avidly on the box with a hairpin, like a man with a whittling project, whistling.

Whistling! The bloody man *whistled* while he worked.

And thus, it a state of suppressed hysterical hilarity and terror she was forced to listen to a medley of sea chanteys while she waited to learn whether the box would yield up proof of Lyon's perfidy.

To a man, her brothers would have said she deserved every bit of torment she was experiencing now. That she had brought it all upon herself entirely.

When the box lid finally gave way with a *POP*, she could have sworn it was the sound of the top of her head flying off.

Asher peered into the box. Then upended it and gave it a hard shake.

A few sad flakes of tobacco rained out. The stale tobacco scent trapped inside soared out and quickly mingled with the lingering aroma of devoured chicken.

"It's empty," he said.

So you think.

Though perhaps it was indeed. But knowing Lyon, she doubted it sincerely.

Absurdly, for a moment, she was disappointed on Flint's behalf. And then exhausted again to feel like a wishbone between her brother and her lover.

He was unnervingly gentlemanly about turning his back and allowing her to slip into her night rail. He was then unnervingly matter-of-fact about stripping down to nothing as per usual and climbing into bed as though that first eyeful of his nude rugged beauty didn't club the breath from her entirely and prevent her from moving for a few solid seconds. He pulled the blankets up to his chest, crossing his arms behind his head, and after she unpinned and brushed her hair smooth, wordlessly she did the same, wondering if this was how wives or mistresses behaved: climbing into bed with men as if it were the natural conclusion to brushing one's hair or cleaning one's teeth. If she'd somehow entered the territory of "kept" or "fallen" and whether there was a protocol she ought to be aware of.

She punched a pillow to soften it, and let her head sink into it, knowing there would be no sleep for her at all tonight as long as the rosewood box sat in the next room. It seemed to swell, that box, taking on grail significance.

It was only after he doused the lamp that she wondered why he hadn't bothered to seduce her. On what could very well be their very last night together.

And five minutes after the lamp was doused, she learned she'd wondered too soon.

He rolled over onto his side and looked down at her. Touched a finger to her lips, drew it softly along them to the line of her jaw. His eyes glinted in the shadows.

For the past two days, he'd reached for her like a man certain of his welcome, or a man who didn't care whether she welcomed him at all because he had a world of faith in the powers of his persuasion.

But his touch was strangely tentative.

He touched her now as though she'd become a stranger.

He suspects something.

She caught his hand as he was tracing her ear. She held it fast for a second or two. Both to tease him with indecisiveness, and to remind herself of his strength. But even as that rosewood box consumed her thoughts, her body knew what it wanted. She dragged her fingernails down his sinewy furred forearm, to flatten against the hot hard planes his chest, halting when she found the hard thump of his heartbeat. His lips impatiently found hers which welcomed him, as his hands impatiently pushed up her nightdress, waited while it snagged on her chin, pulled it off with an oath and flung it to the ground as though it had attacked him first. How she didn't recognize herself: She wanted to unfold like a bloody *flower* when he touched her, wrapping her arms and legs around him, glorying in the opportunity to give, to take.

Good God, what a poor thing she'd been before, a half person. She didn't know what this made her now.

At the very least, it was definitely wanton to want him even as she might need to betray him.

Suddenly he covered her so swiftly, so nearly angrily she stifled a gasp.

He held the heat and weight of his body just above her like

a threat: *I can possess you however I please*. She slid her arms up his chest, clung to him, arched up to brush teasingly against his swollen cock, to tell him she would surrender willingly, to let him know he could take her how he pleased, hard or quickly. Appeasement. She wanted quickly; she wanted him, but she also wanted him asleep.

He knew it.

He wasn't to be appeased.

He sat up again abruptly instead, straddling her thighs with his full weight, peeling her hands abruptly from him. And then with another swift move that made her gasp he knelt between her legs, lifting her calves over his shoulders. Then he laced his fingers through hers and pressed her hands flat above her head, pinning them. Imprisoning her. Forbidding her to touch him.

He seemed to have a plan.

He positioned himself between her legs, teased her where she was damp and aching. She swallowed a gasp; her flesh pulsed its protest, its yearning.

Damn him.

And then he did it again, until she arched for him, urging him on, and the need surged and ebbed, then surged again, a thing with claws.

He denied her.

"*Asher* . . ." she begged.

It was what he wanted to hear. And this time he breeched her, but slowly, so achingly slowly she had no choice but to experience as if for the first time the thick heat and power of him, to recognize how tightly they joined, how right it felt. So slowly want and anticipation rippling outward everywhere in her body, pressing against the very seams of her being, a dam in danger of dangerously breaking.

See me. *Feel* me. *Only* me.

This was his intent.

He pulled back, and slowly moved again.

"God . . ." she whimpered. "*Please.* Faster." She choked the words shamelessly.

And he shifted slightly. A strategic shift to be sure, because his next swift precise thrust sent pleasure arcing through her like a lightning strike, so total and shocking it nearly blacked her consciousness.

So this was a sensual attack, a conquering. She struggled silently with her thoughts: *This is just pleasure, and pleasure is temporal, and needs are met, and I can live without him.*

But he moved again, in just the same way, against the same place inside her. And again. And then again. So slowly, until a long primal groan tore from her, half pleasure, all agony of want.

She was lost; he'd won. There was only Flint and what she needed from him.

She begged, with his name, with threats, to give her release. He gave a short dark laugh. She thrashed her head back, fought with him for her hands so she could claw him into doing her bidding, pummel him, urge him on.

He kept her trapped. He wanted her to feel only where they were joined.

He gave her no mercy.

He knew how intense the pleasure could be. He would allow her no less.

He moved again, and now she moved with him, taking him deeper than she knew possible. And again.

And again.

She heard him fighting against his own need to drive himself home, his breath shuddering now, his palms hot and slick with sweat with the effort of his restraint. His body shaking.

And still it built and built in her, a crisis of pleasure.

"*Asher . . . God . . . I'm going to . . . I . . .*" She was frantic, careening toward an edge from a height she'd never dreamed existed.

He growled then, and unleashed himself and plunged, all but slamming into her like a man outracing death, fighting for his life or for hers, and her release at last crashed through her. She screamed the white-hot bliss of it as though she was being murdered. As though she were being born.

Quiet, perspiring, nude, dark.

Impressions flicked on like fireflies around her. She was sated. Limp. Killed and possessed and humbled in the most pleasant of ways. She'd actually *screamed.*

Asher.

Rosewood box.

Oh damn.

"Violet."

"Mmm?"

"You would tell me if aught were amiss?"

Her heart stuttered. She was fully alert now.

"Aught? The weather, the food, the accommodations, your attentions to my body, things of that nature?"

"Yes. Or your health. Things of that nature."

His delivery was light. But the question was not.

And at first she doubted it was the question he truly wanted to ask. Perhaps he hoped he'd made love to her until she was his senseless slave, and thus helpless not to answer his questions. She considered it likely the beginning of the interrogation she'd feared all night; that he would ceaselessly pelt her with little questions until he jarred loose the big secret throbbing in her conscience.

He was concerned for her health? Touching.

But . . .

Ohhhh. Her *health.*

She was a woman, a pampered one but less sheltered than

her mother would have preferred to believe, and she knew precisely what indiscriminate lovemaking could lead do. And so did he.

Bastard children.

In an instant she was grateful for the dark, because she was certain she was scarlet everywhere. Her skin glowed with the heat of self-consciousness. From wanton lovemaking . . . to motherhood? Inadvertently she inched a little away from him. Space in which to think of what this might mean.

The price of recklessness. Of slipping her family tether. Of learning who she truly was.

But she wanted a family.

And he wanted a dynasty.

But between them it was impossible, because tomorrow likely meant the end of *this.*

"I would tell you if aught was amiss."

Which was tantamount to a lie, because she wasn't certain this was true. Even if she were with child, she might or might not tell him, for his sake as well as her own.

But it was what he wanted to hear.

Conversation ceased.

A moment later he drew his finger slowly, lightly down her spine, tracing each pearl of it. Tentatively. Almost whimsically. It was affection. Possession. Entreaty.

It changes nothing, she thought, and she knew he knew it, too.

He will undo me, she thought. Her felt heart swollen in her chest.

He was asleep soon after.

When he was sleeping soundly, snoring with an abandon and respiratory variety impossible to fake, she slid out of the bed and crept into the next room, where the fire still burned with some life.

The box sat on the small writing table, splayed open, exhaling tobacco. As soon as she touched it guilt poured through her, for heaven's sake, as surely as if she were a little girl again, sneaking into Lyon's bedchamber to root out her brother's secrets.

Ha, Lyon. I may save your life this time.

She snatched it crouched swiftly near the fire.

Which is when one of her knees cracked like a pistol shot.

Holy—!

She squeezed her eyes closed. Went very still. Seconds later the fire, like a co-conspirator, obligingly popped just as loudly, and threw up a shower of sparks to boot.

Mercifully, the man in the next room continued snoring.

She settled the box into the hammock made by her crossed legs and night rail and ran her fingers over the bottom of it, pressing precisely, searchingly, firmly, like a physician seeking the source of an ailment. The passing minutes stretched her nerves tight as pianoforte strings, until she feared any stray breeze would pluck a minuet from them. Finally, her thumbs worried, pressed, a place near the bottom right corner. And the bottom of the box rotated completely, and the contents thumped into her lap.

She fished the first thing out, as it was a book, and the corner of it dug into her thigh. She plucked it up; the must of age fluttered up from its pages. A quick fan through it revealed they were covered in a sprawling, arrogant hand. It was a journal of some kind. She quickly turned it over to read the cover, leaned nearer the fire.

The ground dropped out from beneath her.

And she kept falling, and falling, but each time she read the words they were precisely the same.

Property of Captain Moreheart, commander of The Steadfast.

Bloody *hell.*

Proof. Proof that the person who possessed this had indeed sunk *The Steadfast.*

She quickly fished the second thing out of her lap. But she already knew what it was. She'd found it in this box the first and last day she'd pried into it. And here was the definitive proof that Lyon was Le Chat.

It was Violet who'd discovered what he'd kept in that false bottom when he was a boy. It was the first secret she'd ever bothered to keep, too, because it made her oldest brother seem that much more romantic and heroic, and even at a young age she knew what their father would have done to Lyon had he learned it. She wondered now about how different the lives of so many would be if she hadn't kept that secret.

She held the miniature of Olivia Eversea, the woman who had sent Lyon away, the woman who, indirectly, was the reason Violet was sitting here in the dark while a sated earl she loved more than her next breath snored in the next room. It was like every miniature portrait in that it didn't capture the essence of its subject. A person Violet had known since she could remember, whom she'd seen in church every Sunday apart from the few times a fever had kept her away, a person inextricable now from Redmond family history. Olivia Eversea's face was faintly heart-shaped; there was a wicked innocence, something of the imp, in her chin and the cant of her eyes, which here had been rendered whatever blue the artist had to hand. The color, Violet knew, was not quite right. Her soft dark hair was piled a little too haphazardly for Violet's elegant tastes, but then everything about the Everseas had always been a bit too haphazard for her tastes. Her neck was long and fair, and around it was a locket; she'd been painted in a green, low-necked dress.

The Everseas admittedly weren't an ugly clan.

Violet was tempted to hurl Olivia's miniature into the fire along with the book and that box.

But now that she knew about love, and how unlikely and inappropriate and inconvenient and consuming and cripplingly serious and operatically ridiculous it could be, she couldn't bring herself to do it. Olivia was Lyon's folly and downfall. Just as the earl was hers. As much as she hated to admit it, throwing Olivia into the fire would be like throwing Lyon's heart into the fire.

She knew a quick righteous fury, imagining her brother Lyon Redmond, the family *heir*, forced to flee so quickly he'd jettisoned the thing she knew was most precious to him.

Unless it no longer was.

Or unless he'd purposely left it.

But why, and why?

And suddenly she was almost certain he'd left it for her to find. She gave the book a little shake, and a sheet of foolscap slipped out of it.

Somehow I'm not surprised it's you who found me, even though Miles is the family explorer. Father will kill you, of course, when you go home. For you will go home. And when you begin reading Captain Moreheart's journal, you'll understand why I'm doing what I'm doing, and for whom I'm doing it. You'll also, when you reach the end of it, know why I can't go home—not yet—and why I suspect you'll go home and won't tell anyone you've seen me, or what you've read here. But I will leave that up to you. I leave the fate of the journal up to you, too.

Do you know what she said to me? You haven't any real courage, Lyon. You'd never stand for anything. You're your father's invention, and you'll have your father's money. How can I love you when you don't know who you are?

I know a little bit more about who I am now. But it's not whom I expected to be. I entrust her image to you.

Much love to you.

So she quickly began to read through the journal. A few pages confirmed her darkest fear: The Drejeck Group was indeed participating in the lucrative, illegal, horrific Triangle Trade—trafficking in human beings.

And Captain Moreheart had more than once captained one of the ships. There were logs of slaves bought and sold.

But it wasn't until she saw a name on the last page of that journal, a single name in a list of investors, that she understood why Lyon, who had likely set out to do something heroic, now needed to protect the reasons he was doing what he was doing until he'd finished off the Drejeck group altogether.

And why he couldn't just leave what he'd discovered up to the authorities.

Oh God.

She felt jittery from the incompatible combination of exhaustion and nervous excitement and the fitful firings of her brain as it tried to assemble facts. She needed to think, but emotions slammed her in waves, one after the other, fury and love and fear, and there never seemed enough space between them to clear her head. She dropped her face into her palms hard, an almost-slap, and breathed in hard. *Think like a man,* she told herself.

She remembered again what Asher said about being shot, about how there was a moment of blessed numbness, of surprise, really, before the agony set in.

Steady breathing came from the room next to her. For a disorienting moment her breathing swayed in time with his, and it was as though she breathed for him and he breathed for her.

She huddled next to the fire with her arms wrapped around her knees, surprised, to realize how strong she really was. She could thank the earl for it. She remained that way until her stiff, cold toes and fingers told her the fire had burned low enough to cease giving off heat. She straightened her spine, and took a deep breath, and pushed her hair away from her eyes.

She felt a surge of fury with herself when her fingers came away damp. *Damn, damn, damn.* She could think like a man, she could act like a man, but she was a woman after all, and women wept.

And then got on with what they needed to do.

She quietly opened up the writing desk, found the quill and a pot of ink that hadn't clotted, and wrote two notes.

One said:

Forgive me. But I know you understand why I did it.

The other said:

He knows you'll be in the Plaza de Mina tomorrow.

P.S. I love him, Lyon. Did you ever think such a thing would happen?

Love, your sister Violet

She sprinkled sand over both.

The first she left where it was, on the writing desk.

The second she folded in half and kept gripped in her hand as she quickly slipped into her day dress, leaving the laces undone. Speed was of the essence. She seized her shoes and her portmanteau. She knew she couldn't linger, couldn't silently kiss him or gaze one last longing time at his sleeping form, because he had that knack for knowing when she was watching him. She had no doubts she'd wake him up with a yearning gaze, despite the fact that their lovemaking had clubbed him into a stupor.

And so she hardened her heart in the hopes she could prevent it from breaking before she could accomplish what she needed to do, and she tiptoed out the door to the sound of the man she loved sleeping peacefully.

Chapter 26

Flint awoke before dawn, and even before his eyes opened he knew she was gone.

Gone, gone.

He didn't hear breathing. He couldn't feel her presence. He quickly sliced a hand over to her side of the bed; it was too cool for her to have rolled out simply because she'd wakened early.

He shot out of bed and strode, nude, into the next room. The fire was dead, the room lit by the gray light of dawn, and the plundered rosewood box lay splayed on the floor.

He knelt, gingerly, as if over a body. Then gently lifted it up.

So it had a false bottom. Why hadn't *he* thought of that?

And she'd *watched* him surgically go at the thing last night with a hairpin. She must have known the entire time about the bottom.

What had she found inside?

He held that box, and suddenly knew his entire plan was farcical.

He'd thought to assemble a life from pieces. He thought of the things he'd kept in his cabin on the ship. A painting. A chessboard. Trophies of the regard of other people. And all of it seemed foolish to him now, mere paste imitations when held up to the light of real love, like Violet's love for her brother. And his love for her.

His whole life would now be a paste imitation of life without her.

Violet was the only person with whom he'd ever truly belonged.

Devastation held him motionless.

Next he found the foolscap message.

Forgive her? He was temped to crunch it in his fist and hurl it across the room.

He smoothed it tenderly over and over, irrationally. It may have been the last thing she touched.

He'd all but handed her the opportunity to betray him: He'd told her about the crew searching in the Plaza de Mina. She was no fool. She'd found something in that box, and the ever-startlingly resourceful Violet would have found a way to warn her brother that Flint and crew would be coming for him. In a sense, he suspected he wanted to see what she would do with the opportunity to betray him.

He had no right to use the word *betrayed.*

He wandered like one punched in the head into the bedroom, the battered box in one hand. He sat down hard for a moment on the edge of the bed. Distantly, among the emotions that swamped him, he found one he wanted to court: fury.

He held it focused in the beam of his mind, coaxing it into full flame, until it drove him to his feet and got him into his clothes. Still stuffing his shirt into his trousers, pushing hair back with one hand, he strode furiously down the halls hammering on the inn doors to wake his men.

She might have chosen to do what she thought was right.

But it didn't mean she'd succeeded yet.

Flint's crew had been thorough in both their pleasure seeking and in their questioning in and around the Plaza de

Mina, and they learned that when in Cádiz Mr. Hardesty could often be found in Los Tres Pescaderos, a pub of sorts on the Plaza de Mina.

The Three Fish was a graceless, shadowy, low-ceilinged room built of brick and propped up on thick splintering wood pillars he needed to dodge as he entered. Smoke—cigar, cooking, pipe—commingled, obscuring faces. Everywhere men were slumped over drinks or sprawling in easy conversation. It was a splendid place for sub rosa meetings.

But when he saw, even through the smoke, deep in the shadows near the bar, the line of a particular spine, the elegant curves of a profile. Flint's heart leaped into his throat. In seconds he was almost airborne with joy.

And then the smoke migrated away, clearing like clouds.

He'd been wrong.

He turned to Lavay. "Wait for me outside. I'll call if I need you."

Lavay hesitated, then gave a curt nod.

He'd unlocked his pistol before he'd arrived. Heart a dull hammer in his ears, he casually wended through the crowd of unsuspecting strangers to the straight-backed man sitting at the shadowy table.

His Redmond profile turned away from him.

He stood until Lyon Redmond, not the least surprised, looked up at him and lifted eyebrows in welcome. He'd been expected.

Handsome devil, indeed, as Musgrove had accused. He had his sister's blue eyes, vivid even in the dark. The aristocratic angles in the face were an echo of hers, too, only his were hard and masculine and stubbled.

"Good day, Captain Flint. Are you going to attempt to arrest me? Or shoot me? Something more dramatic?" He sounded as though he were proffering a menu of options.

Flint stared down at his grail.

And Lyon languidly stretched out a leg and pushed the chair across from him away from the table. Inviting him to sit.

Flint sat. He pulled the chair close into the table, close enough to hide the pistol he slid from his coat to lie in his lap. He swept a hand in the air to signal the barmaid over. She'd perhaps adapted to her environment like the creatures who live in caves, for she saw him straight away. She sauntered over, skirt swinging like a bell over her hips that might as well have been on hinges. She had flare.

"Dark, *por favor*."

Lyon was motionless. He didn't even his drum his fingers. He didn't appear particularly tense.

The two men said nothing at all until she brought the ale to him and he'd taken his first long sip.

"I thought Violet would try to warn you I was coming," Flint began.

This amused Lyon. "Try? You ought to know her better by now. She *succeeded* in warning me. I had a note from her this morning. Succinct and revealing. She's resourceful, my sister. She paid someone on the docks to row the message out to *The Olivia*, and one of my men made sure I received it. They always know where to find me."

Flint wasn't surprised. She'd talked her way aboard his ship, after all.

"But . . . then why are—"

"—am I here? I'm here because of the postscript she wrote on her message, Captain Flint. I decided I needed to see you for myself. And as for Violet, she is even now on a packet back to England. I arranged for her passage. She'll be home in two days, lest she take it into her head to foment more mischief."

Flint nearly reflexively stood. She was gone, and he knew where!

Then stopped himself when he realized what he was doing.

He saw Redmond tense, almost infinitesimally, and knew the man was likely every bit as armed as he was. That he likely cradled an unlocked gun in the hand resting in his lap.

He forced himself to remain seated. He was here to collect Lyon.

"You ought to know that ten armed sailors are waiting outside to take you the moment I say the word, Redmond."

"Hardesty," he corrected with cool politeness. "If you would. In this place, anyhow. You *do* have Mathias? The boy? Is he safe?"

"He's with us. He was impressed by the Portuguese pirate who boarded my ship. We kept him on. He proved useful."

"Abrega. I hear he's been claiming to be me." Ironic curve of a smile.

Flint could hardly bear to look at Lyon, and yet it was impossible to tear his eyes away. He looked so bloody much like his sister it was a torment.

"Abrega won't make that claim anymore."

"Ah." Lyon's brows twitched up appreciatively. He understood it was an oblique way of saying Abrega was dead.

They were quiet again.

Flint regarded his quarry curiously. "Why did you do it?"

Lyon stared at him for a long time with a half smile. And then he jerked to attention.

"Oh! My apologies. You expected I'd actually *answer* that question. To confess all. And yet I'd heard you were clever."

He toasted his stalker, lifted his tankard of ale to his lips and sipped, turning casually in his chair.

"Here is the thing, Captain Flint," he began almost apologetically. "I waited for you, rather than racing ahead of you yet again. For a reason. But if you choose to attempt to take me,

I will not go without a fight. And I assure you that one of us, if not both of us, will be dead thereafter. No matter what."

The two men sat across from each other in silence. On the surface of things, they appeared to be two friends, two acquaintances, two exceptionally well-made gentlemen sharing a conversation.

Beneath the table, two pistols were unlocked, balanced on knees, gripped in white-knuckled hands.

"So be it," Flint said easily.

"So do you love my sister?"

Flint made a small sound. Shock or pain; he couldn't control it.

And at this Lyon Redmond swiveled in his chair and sat bolt upright. "You *do* love her."

He sounded startled at the realization. And so much like a sibling for an instant Asher was both amused and envious of the long, deep history, the taken-for-granted love between Redmonds.

He heard Lyon Redmond inhale; he heard a creak as he leaned back in his chair. He glanced up, and his profile—that stubborn chin, the straight nose—was so reminiscent of Violet that Asher felt stabbed clean through. He breathed in deeply, took in only old and new smoke. Tried to find anger and resolve. To buoy himself against the sensation that he'd been shot in the hull and would sink and sink.

Flint remained stubbornly quiet on the topic.

"May I ask you something, Captain Flint?"

Flint nodded warily.

"*Why* do you love her?" He sounded again so much like a sibling that Flint almost laughed, even as he bristled.

"What do you mean?"

"I love her. I *have* to love her. She's my sister. And I do. But I love her in *spite* of herself, bless her heart. I know she's willful, capricious, and I fear far too spoiled to be a proper wife to any man, and like as not it's the fault of my parents and my brothers. She's funny and insightful and desperately clever, though God knows she's never applied her intelligence to anything in particular. I would kill for her, and I would kill any man who hurts her. I have had, shall we say, reason to question her judgment in the past, if not her tenacity. She's my blood. I want to know why *you* love her."

Flint still couldn't bring himself to say it aloud. Whether or not he *loved* Violet was a matter between him and Violet, and perhaps it was moot now. And still . . . this was a man who shared her blood. Who'd had the privilege of knowing her his entire life. When he spoke, he spoke for Violet's sake.

"I've very little experience of what they like to call the finer emotions, Mr. Redmond. I haven't your talent for grander expression . . . I can only tell you . . ."

How in God's name to describe Violet? It was like trying to describe his own heart, which naturally he'd never actually *seen*. It was an *idea*, his heart; he felt it beat inside him, sending life coursing through his veins. He needed it. It was everything.

"You don't know her, Mr. Redmond, any more than you can say you know your viscera. She's part of you. I had to . . . *learn* her. She had to learn *herself*. And Violet . . . she has a . . . magnificent heart. A fierce warrior's heart. Nothing . . . *small* . . . would ever do for her. Not a life in Sussex, not the usual domesticated English aristocratic husband, not a life of needlework and managing the servants, though this could very well be what awaits her anyway. She came across the sea to find you, and by God she did what no one in your family, and no one else who has diligently hunted you, could accomplish. She persuaded *me* to allow her to do it. This, I assure you, is very nearly impossible."

"Violet is persuasive," Lyon said ruefully.

"And *I* am impossible," Flint said grimly. "It's why the

King chose me for this mission. She loves her family, but none of you know her *heart*. She, I believe, found everything she needed in me, on this journey. She was *afraid* to love in part . . . because of you. But for love of you, she gave me up. She did it for you." He heard weariness in his voice. He stopped a moment. "That's Violet. That's who she is. And that's the choice you forced her to make. You ought to be proud." The words were so sharp, so bitter, he could nearly taste them.

"May I point out an irony?" Lyon said.

"I doubt I can stop you."

"You likely wouldn't know her at all if not for me."

Flint took this in slowly. Inhaled at length. Exhaled. But said nothing.

"You're welcome," Lyon said ironically.

"It doesn't change what I came here to do."

Lyon ignored this. "I can almost see it," he said reflectively, after a moment of studying Flint. "I can almost see why the two of you could love each other without . . . *incinerating* each other. You're *certain* she loves you?" He sounded unflatteringly skeptical.

"She killed a man to save my life. She was the one who killed Abrega."

Lyon's expression didn't change at all. But he did go strikingly still. His fingertips pressed so hard into his tankard of ale they went bloodless. "Did she?"

He didn't sound as surprised as he ought to. His voice was steady enough, but it had gone soft. His eyebrows winged up then; he drummed his fingers against his tankard. And stopped. After a moment he smiled a smile so bleak, so full of loss and ache that Flint all at once understood the cost to him of his exile.

"Violet," Lyon finally said. That single soft word rang with love and exasperation and memories and regret.

Flint suddenly recognized something critical, and possibly

deadly: Here he faced a man possessed of control equal to his own. But Lyon Redmond had come by his strength in ways unique to his journey and his history. That elegance, those manners, the demeanor, the spirit—all were fashioned of finely wrought steel, and honed like a blade.

Lyon Redmond was either a man on a pilgrimage in search of salvation, or a man out to burn on the pyre of his own love for a woman.

Regardless, he still suffered.

Flint wasn't unaffected.

And yet when another silence fell, Flint shifted his pistol in his lap, preparing for the inevitable.

But Redmond was thoughtful. He seemed to be contemplating how to begin a story. He shifted slightly.

"Tell me—what wouldn't you do for Violet, Captain Flint?"

Flint didn't yet know the answer to this. Though he was perhaps closer to knowing.

"I haven't yet been tested."

Lyon smiled slowly at this, and shook his head. "Ah. Clearly you haven't a soul of a poet, then, sir. You cannot be lured into hyperbole: 'There's *nothing* I wouldn't do! Nothing!' And etcetera. *I* can. I like hyperbole. Don't fear it, Flint! Believe me, there's some truth to all the purple words that surround love, you know. When you love someone more than life—and it is indeed possible to love someone more than life, or otherwise poets wouldn't have gone on and on about it over the centuries—and you know, you *know*, you were born for only one person . . . imagine you cannot have them without tearing everything else you know asunder. Without hurting and disappointing all the other people you love. What then would you do?"

"Well, naturally, I'd go out and sink ships."

"Witty, Captain. Would you settle for less than what you want?"

"I have never settled for less than what I want."

Implicit in that statement was the fact that they both knew what Flint wanted: to bring Lyon Redmond, Le Chat, to justice.

"Very well. Let's say then you've made the decision to tear the life you know asunder in order to be with this person you love. A difficult decision to be sure. Putting it lightly. Because you cannot imagine a life without her, and the alternative left to you is a lifetime of desolation, as you don't intend to don a hair shirt or join a monastery or fling yourself into the ocean and drown. And so you go ahead and do the unthinkable and tear your life asunder . . . only to discover the person you love won't have you after all, and she actually has a *reason*."

Flint, despite himself, was drawn into this narrative, and his mind crept toward imagining what it must have been like for Lyon. Then shied back from that dark place: how he'd wanted Violet untenably in those long nights, knowing they were doomed for the very reasons they loved each other: the unshakeable loyalty, the courage, the determination and passion.

And how the first time he'd known he'd been loved, he'd been given wings. And they'd been snatched back before he'd ever properly learned how to use them.

And suddenly Lyon's desolation seemed indistinguishable from his own.

"For you see, Captain Flint, I, too, never settle for less than what I want. Or never thought I possibly *could*. I'm a Redmond. If only you truly understood what this means. So I set out to reorder the world in a way I thought would make me worthy of her love. But my quest has changed me in ways I never anticipated, and I'm not the man who once loved that girl. There's much more to my journey yet. And here's a bitter irony: I've found in becoming heroic, in becoming *worthy* of her, I've painted myself into an untenable corner. I've more work to do to prove someone's innocence or guilt. And you, Captain Flint, though an admirable man, understand far, far less about what I've done, and why I've done it, than you think you do."

He paused. Took a long draught of his pint. Drank it down almost to the bottom, but left a half inch or so sloshing there. As though he knew when he reached the bottom his time would be up.

Flint watched Lyon Redmond, he understood that beneath that cool Redmond elegance, that control, the measured irony of his words, was a man whose passions were likely twice as volcanic as Violet's. Darker, more committed, more rooted in suffering, even more arrogant and less forgiving. Fascinating. Was he like this when he'd left Sussex? How this man must have chafed beneath his father's rule. The golden Redmond son, the hope of his father and family. How extraordinary his control must have been even then, for no one had known he'd done anything but bask in the glory of being Lyon Redmond.

"So tell me . . . what do you want above all, Captain Flint?"

"What I want is justice for *The Steadfast* and for Captain Moreheart. A man to whom I owe everything. My entire future fortune, depends upon bringing you to justice. And it's what I want. So . . ."

He began to stand, and saw Lyon stiffen, poised to do whatever he needed to do.

He, like Lyon, could throw himself on a pyre, too. Because fire cleansed. She'd won, and he'd lost.

It had stopped mattering. Her happiness was indistinguishable from his own.

No matter what became of him, he wanted her to know he loved her.

"You'd best get out of here, Redmond. Your secret is safe with me."

Lyon's eyes flared in wary surprise. He froze. And his smile, when it came, was slow, and crooked, and he looked very like Lavay when Lavay was being insufferably *knowing.*

"Ah. You *do* love her more than life. Splendid. And that, my dear Lord Flint, is what I came here today to discover."

Whatever he felt was between him and Violet. "Go before I change my mind, Redmond."

And Lyon stood. All tall, lean, indolently lethal grace. And with a fluid motion, the way another man might tuck away his watch, he locked and tucked his pistol away.

"Try Sussex, Flint. I paid for her passage on a ship sailing out to Calais, and from there she'll board one that will take her to England again. She's already on her way. Godspeed, Flint. Until we meet again."

With astonishing speed and grace, he slipped deeper into the pub, until smoke closed over Flint's vision, and when it had cleared again, Lyon was gone.

Chapter 27

Violet had been away for nearly three weeks, during which everyone assumed she was enjoying a house party at Lady Peregrine's. The message inquiring after Violet would reach Lady Peregrine's only today, which would confuse the lady and prompt gossip.

But nothing like the gossip Violet was about to cause.

She was contemplating the results of her adventure and what now might become of her, when Jonathan peered around the corner.

"Miss Redmond . . . you've a guest."

She heard the fruitless clacking of Morton's footsteps following Jonathan. His legs were shorter.

"Mr. Jonathan, I should have preferred to announce it more formally."

"My apologies, Morton," Jonathan said, wide-eyed in mock contrition. "It isn't every day you get to announce an earl. I say, Vi, are you going to faint?" He sounded less concerned than astonished. "You've gone white. Should I send the big bugger away?"

"No. Go away, Jonathan," she said faintly, rudely.

All the announcements were moot anyway, because Flint, who had no patience or use for the social niceties when he was on a mission, stood in the doorway, listening to all of this.

The footman's arms jutted out and Flint absently dropped his coat and hat upon them. Morton bore them away.

"The big bugger begs a private word with your sister," Flint said politely.

"When you put it so nicely, I can't see how I can deny you that pleasure, my Lord." Jonathan had extraordinarily fine manners when he chose to use them, too.

And Jonathan wagged up his eyebrows and backed away, and closed the door, mouthing a word she thought might be *Lavay.*

She scowled quickly at him out of habit, then turned.

Oh God.

It was so very, very clear that Flint was the only man for her. That he belonged to her, and she to him. Without him, she knew she'd become thin and glittery-eyed and take up causes like Olivia Eversea, which she was tempted to do anyway. Or become an eccentric burden to her parents, a secret shameful relative hidden away somewhere, destined to become part of the Redmond family lore.

Because she had a rather large secret of her own.

"Why are you here?" she began cautiously.

"I've come for you," he said simply.

"*Come* for me? How like an order that sounds. And yet we're not on your ship anymore, Captain Flint. I haven't peeled a potato in weeks, and you cannot make me do it now."

It seemed he'd exhausted his words.

And she was abashed, suddenly, because he was pale, too. She couldn't bear to see this man look uncertain.

"I'm sorry I left you as I did," she offered tentatively. She was surprised when her voice emerged a mere whisper.

"I know you are," he said gently. "I wouldn't have done anything differently. You did the right thing."

"I . . . did?" Wondering which of the things he meant: leaving, or taking the rosewood box, or warning Lyon, or—

He smiled faintly at her wariness. "All of it was right. You did it for someone you love. You never pretended you might do otherwise. We both knew it."

Why was he standing on the edge of the carpet, as though it were lava, and she was an island he could merely aspire to reaching?

She couldn't bear not knowing. She had to ask. "Flint . . . *why* are you here? Where is Lyon?"

"I'm here because I wanted you to know that I did what *I* did . . . for someone I love."

Her hands were damp. She, who'd once thought she'd *expire* from lack of novelty, wasn't enjoying this particular game of suspense. She drew them down the front of her skirt nervously. Something she wouldn't have dreamed of doing just a fortnight ago. She'd become more amenable to mussing things when circumstances required it.

"And *what* did you think was right?" Her nerves were drawing tight as bowstrings. Her voice was faint and nearly shrill.

He paused. "I saw Lyon."

There was a beat of silence.

And then he smiled a slow crooked smile. So pleased with himself. With her.

She thought she might just swoon. She thought she would draw that smile around her like a shawl, let it cradle her like a hammock. Her hand nearly went out to touch the back of a settee. Then she refrained and collected herself.

"You *saw* Lyon?" she repeated. Coaxing it out of him was torture. "You . . . spoke to Lyon?"

"Yes. And then I left Lyon."

She was stunned. "But . . ."

"Violet . . . he looks so like you." He gave a short, wondering laugh. His hands pushed his hair back nervously.

"*Where* is he?" She looked about wildly. "*What* was right?"

"*Loving* you is right, Violet," he said easily. "I left him in Cádiz. He has more work to do. He says. He looks quite fit."

Fit.

"Flint . . . I found Captain Moreheart's journal in Lyon's box and . . . all the investors were listed. I know what Lyon is doing and why he's doing it—I so didn't want to tell you about Captain Moreheart—"

"I know. Of a certainty he was captaining and investing in slave ships. They all were." He sounded grim. "I cannot begin to guess why. I can't condone it. But I can't grieve him any less. I suspect justice was meted to him, though it wasn't Lyon's justice to give."

"There's one thing you don't know, Asher." An expression, inexpressibly tender and fierce, flickered over his face when she said his name and she felt shy. *I do love you.* "One of the investors listed on the last page of Moreheart's diary is . . . Jacob Eversea."

Flint frowned, puzzled. Then his face cleared. "Olivia's father?"

Violet nodded. "It would kill her. And ruin the Everseas if anyone discovered. I've been left with a loaded gun, so to speak. Bloody Lyon is leaving me to decide what to do about it."

"Poor bastard." He meant Lyon. "And I thought *we* had a dilemma for a fortnight." He sounded almost amused. "He said he had more work to do regarding proving someone's innocence or guilt."

Silence fell. She watched her father's clock pendulum swing out the time. It was time for a very careful and specific question.

"But Flint . . . so that means . . . you don't want to capture

Lyon anymore? That you'll tell the King you failed?"

"Well, I'm not partial to the word *failed*." Oh, good. He sounded amused. "But Violet . . . when I saw Lyon, I knew I was sunk. I live only to make you happy, Violet. You're *necessary* to me. I belong with you. And please, for the love of God, may I touch you now?"

It was only now that his composure was crumbling that she saw how powerfully he'd tried to keep it intact.

She all but bolted across the carpet for him, and she reached out her hand, and he reached out his hand, and their hands clung there, joining and separating their bodies from a distance of about two feet. Hers was cold, and his was warm, and he gripped hers as though she were anchoring him to the earth, or the means by which he would launch, like a kite.

She needed to know more. "But that means . . ."

"It means I love you, Violet. I have never said that aloud to another human being."

He said it quickly and tonelessly. As if he was afraid of the words.

Violet stood basking in those words the way she might a sunbeam after a long, gray day. She closed her eyes. And she knew she was lit from within.

"Do not let me just *stand* here having said those words," he said stiffly. "It's undignified."

"I love you, too," she said softly, hurriedly. Feeling abashed. Eyes still closed.

Egads. So this was what it was like to be in love. Awkward and foolish, indeed.

And he furled her abruptly into his body and sighed his relief when they were folded together, because their bodies knew what to do when words made them feel human and awkward. She melted into him without reserve. She pressed her ear against his chest to hear his heartbeat, to feel his breathing, wrapped her arms around him to reassure him she was here and would never leave him.

He would never again be alone.

"It also means," he said over the top of her head, "I've land, but no money to support it. Just the grand title. You could always marry Lavay instead. I think even he has more money than I do at the moment."

"I have a dowry," she said absently. "My father will be pleased enough to marry me off to an earl. I think. Even one such as you."

She stood back abruptly to find him looking amused at the "such as you," and as he was unwilling to relinquish her, she leaned back into the cradle of his arms.

"But wait . . . we are to be married?" she asked, forgetting to consider whether she ought to have waited for him to ask.

"I should think so. Don't you? Should I have issued a more romantic proposal?"

"No. We're not romantic," she breathed.

"Not romantic at *all*," Flint murmured about an inch from her lips. "But I may *die* if I don't kiss you right this—"

His lips just took hers, and their kiss was, quite frankly, savage.

She reveled in it. It was new, because it was a promise, and precious and humbling, and bogglingly erotic. He kissed her like a man starved, like a man intent on taking her in just a few minutes, and she gave like she thought she'd never give to anyone, her hands tangling in his hair, his hands and arms wrapping her tightly.

"But your home in America . . ." she said against his lips when they decided they needed to breathe. "All the things you wanted . . ."

"You're my home. I'll go wherever you like. Whether it's by land or sea." He moved in for more kissing.

"Truly?" She stood back for a moment. Bit her lip.

He looked worried. "You're *thinking*, aren't you? Don't." He leaned in again.

She remained just out of reach of his lips. "But I might like to live in America. Or perhaps you'll like Sussex. And you have your own properties in England, too. I suppose it depends on whether you want your baby to be born an English or American citizen."

His expression went as blank as though she'd clubbed him in the head. His arms loosened.

She hadn't meant it to happen quite like that.

"You're . . . we're . . ." He stopped.

She would never forget his expression for the rest of her life.

This is what joy looks like. She nearly wept. She could feel the tears burning at the back of her eyes.

"Going to be a family." And now she was shy again. "Are you going to faint?" She held onto him. "You're very pale."

"It's the color of bliss."

She smiled a small smile. She was, in truth, afraid. The future dizzied her. But *someone* needed to look after the Earl of Ardmay, and she would have the privilege of it for the rest of her life. She had no doubt he was equal to the task of looking after her.

He saw something in her face. "Are *you* going to faint, Violet? Do we need to move over to the settee?"

Before she could answer he'd swept her up in his arms. Taking command.

"Yes, we *do* need to move over to the settee if you want to kiss me and . . . otherwise . . . properly. The door is locked. See if you can kiss me until I at least see stars."

And Captain Flint, always equal to a challenge, complied.

They both saw stars, of course. The sort by which they would navigate the course of forever.

978-0-06-198662-8

978-0-06-168930-7

978-0-06-118953-1

978-0-06-143439-6

978-0-06-189447-3

978-0-06-187812-1

Visit www.AuthorTracker.com for exclusive information on your favorite HarperCollins authors.

Available wherever books are sold, or call 1-800-331-3761 to order.

ATP 0710

At Avon Books, we know your passion for romance—once you finish one of our novels, you find yourself wanting more.

May we tempt you with . . .

- **Excerpts** from our upcoming releases.
- Entertaining **extras**, including authors' personal photo albums and book lists.
- Behind-the-scenes **scoop** on your favorite characters and series.
- **Sweepstakes** for the chance to win free books, romantic getaways, and other fun prizes.
- Writing **tips** from our authors and editors.
- **Blog** with our authors and find out why they love to write romance.
- **Exclusive content** that's not contained within the pages of our novels.

Join us at
www.avonbooks.com